So Damn Lucky

DEBORAH COONTS

A Tom Doherty Associates Book
New York

SO DAMN LUCKY

Copyright © 2012 by Deborah Coonts

All rights reserved.

A Forge Book
Published by Tom Doherty Associates, LLC
175 Fifth Avenue
New York, NY 10010

www.tor-forge.com

Forge® is a registered trademark of Tom Doherty Associates, LLC.

ISBN 978-0-7653-6795-2

Forge books may be purchased for educational, business, or promotional use. For information on bulk purchases, please contact Macmillan Corporate and Premium Sales Department at 1-800-221-7945 extension 5442 or write specialmarkets@macmillan.com.

First Edition: February 2012
First Mass Market Edition: March 2013

Printed in the United States of America

0 9 8 7 6 5 4 3 2 1

Forge Books by Deborah Coonts

Wanna Get Lucky?
Lucky Stiff
So Damn Lucky

To Barb Nickless and Maria Faulconer

ACKNOWLEDGMENTS

My son, Tyler, and his wonderful new wife, Lisa, who fill every corner of my life with sunshine.

Barb Nickless and Maria Faulconer, great writers who make this writer better and who grace me with the wonder of true friendship.

The dream makers at Tor/Forge: Tom Doherty, Linda Quinton, Bob Gleason, Patty Garcia, Cassie Ammerman, Whitney Ross, and Katharine Critchlow. Thank you for your continuing amazing support.

Susan Gleason, agent extraordinaire.

The city of Las Vegas, for adopting me as your own.

So Damn Lucky

So Damn Luck

Chapter

ONE

Some things in life are best savored alone—
sex is not one of them.

This happy thought occurred to me while pi-
loting a borrowed Ferrari and staring at the smiling couples filling the sidewalks along the Las Vegas
Strip. Walking hand in hand, they were living,
breathing reminders of the sorry state of my own
love life.

"Lady! Watch out!"

I heard the shout in the nick of time. Slamming
on the brakes, I narrowly avoided sliding the front
end of the Ferrari under a tour bus. A sea of Japa-
nese faces appeared like moons in the back window, peering down at me. Then cameras blocked
the faces, flashbulbs popping as I shrugged and
waved while trying to appear unruffled.

The young man who had shouted stepped over
to the car and peered through the open roof, like a
judge eyeing the accused. "Are you okay?" he asked.

His face flushed, his eyes glassy, he looked like he was still recovering from last night's party or getting a head start on the next one.

"Thanks to you," I said as I restarted the car, which had stalled. "I know better than to think about sex while doing something potentially life-threatening. What was I thinking?" I cringed as the words popped out of my mouth. Even I couldn't believe I'd said that. Clearly, I needed to get a grip: First I couldn't stop thinking about sex; now I was talking about it to strangers. This was *so* not good.

"What *were* you thinking?" The kid smirked at me as he took another gulp from the glass clutched tightly in his hand. "Care to . . . enlighten me?" he asked after wiping his mouth on the sleeve of his sweatshirt, which had NYU printed in bold blue on the front.

The sweatshirt looked new. He looked twelve. I felt old.

"Another time, perhaps," I lied. I didn't really intend to flirt with the kid. However, with Teddie, my former live-in, gallivanting around the globe playing rock star for the last six weeks—and the foreseeable future—my prospects looked pretty dim. Teddie and I had been really good for a while. Now, I didn't know what we were.

Sexual self-preservation clearly had kicked in.

"Go easy on those walktails," I said. "They're deadly and the night is still young." It was a blatant attempt to steer the conversation away from the current topic.

"Walktail?"

"That drink in your hand, small enough to take with you, but potent enough to leave you puking in the gutter."

The kid's face grew serious as he held up the brew for inspection, looking at it with a newfound respect. "Yes, ma'am," he said, his voice filled with awe.

My smile vanished. Despite careful study, I was still unable to figure out at precisely what moment in time I had gone from being a Miss to a Ma'am. What changed? Whatever it was, I wanted it back like it used to be—along with a few other things, but they would all take minor miracles. While I believe in magic, miracles were pushing the envelope, even for me.

I squeezed the paddle shifter and put the car in gear. Easing around the still stationary bus, I hit the gas. The night held an October chill—refreshing as the wind teased my hair. A full moon fought a losing battle as it competed valiantly with the lights of the Strip. I knew stars filled the sky, but they weren't visible in the false half-night of Las Vegas at full wattage.

My name is Lucky O'Toole and, as I mentioned, the Ferrari isn't mine. It belongs to the dealership at The Babylon, my employer and the newest addition to the Las Vegas Strip megaresort explosion. By title, I am the Head of Customer Relations. In reality, I'm the chief problem solver. If a guest at the Babylon has a "situation"—which could be anything from an unplanned marriage, an unfamiliar bed partner, a roaring headache, or an unexplained rash, to a wife and kids given a room on the same floor as the mistress's suite—I'm the go-to girl.

Lucky me.

Actually, I love my job. And I miss Teddie. As the two appear mutually exclusive, therein lies the rub.

But, enough of that—I had wallowed in self-pity for my allotted ten minutes today. No more private pity party for me; I was on my way to the real thing.

The invitation read:

> *Inviting all family, friends, and former dancers to a farewell party in honor of the forty-year run of the Calliope Burlesque Cabaret. October 24, eight o'clock sharp, backstage at the Calliope Theatre, the Athena Resort and Casino. Present this invitation for admittance.*

To someone in my position, being invited to parties was part of the exercise, but this was one guest list on which I never expected to find my name. I wasn't family, nor was I a former dancer—although with my six-foot frame, I guess dancing might have been a career path had I not been averse to prancing in front of strangers wearing nothing but stilettos and a thong, with twenty pounds of feathers on my head.

That left friend. As the sole individual responsible for shutting down the show, I doubted I qualified under that category either. Perhaps they invited me because of my unparalleled ability to smooth ruffled feathers, or maybe for my irritating inability to overlook a pun no matter how tortured. Who knew? However, I never could resist a good mystery, so despite the niggling feeling I'd received an invitation to my own execution, I accepted.

After having to go back to the office for the invitation, and after the near miss on the Strip, I pulled the Ferrari up to the front of the Athena. Careful to extricate myself from the low-slung car without giving the valet an eyeful up my short skirt, I then tossed the keys to him. Wrapping myself in a warm hug of cashmere pashmina to ward off the night chill, I straightened my skirt, threw back my shoulders, found a tentative balance on four-inch heels, and headed inside.

An aging Grand Dame, the Athena had seen better days. Like a ship marooned on the shoals, torn and tattered by the elements, the Athena had been savaged by time and inattention. Moored at the wrong end of the Strip, surrounded by lesser properties, she now boasted only faded glory. Her carpets stained, her walls dingy, and her décor dated, she reeked of quiet desperation. While she still boasted "The Best Seafood Buffet in Vegas" for less than twenty dollars—which brought in some of the locals—her gaming rooms were rarely more than a third full. In Vegas, folks are quick to abandon a sinking ship—even if the slots are loose and the staff friendly.

My boss, Albert Rothstein (also known as The Big Boss), recently acquired the Athena from the previous owner, who had decided the best way to beat The Big Boss was to frame him for murder. In a high-stakes game of cat and mouse, The Big Boss had eaten the canary—with my help, I'm happy to say.

The fact that The Big Boss is also my father is a closely guarded secret—so close that even I was in the dark until recently when, facing the prospect of imminent death at the hands of a heart surgeon, The Big Boss decided to come clean. I still wasn't sure how I felt about the whole thing, so I ignored it whenever possible. I was pretty happy with the way things were before the big bombshell, so I didn't see any reason to rock the boat. The Big Boss saw it differently; now that he'd claimed me—and made his relationship with my mother public—he wanted the whole world to know. Not a hooker's chance in Heaven, thank you very much. Don't get me wrong; I loved him like a father . . . always had.

But who the heck wants to be the boss's daughter?

Expecting the usual sparse crowd, I was surprised to see a throng milling about the Athena's dismal lobby and spilling into the casino. Having spent my formative years in and out of Vegas hotels and my adult life working in them, I rarely noticed the fashion choices of the river of humanity that flowed through. However, tonight their choices were hard to ignore.

Space creatures of all shapes and sizes mingled, giving each other the Vulcan sign of greeting. It was like the Star Trek Experience at the Hilton used to be, but better. While I'm not that well versed in aliens, I thought I recognized a couple of Klingons, a Romulan or two, multiple Ferengi, and a collective of Borg. As the Borg passed, their faces impassive, I thought about saying "Resistance is futile" but I stifled myself. The whole thing made me realize how much I missed the Hilton's hokey institution. When they shuttered Quark's, the Hilton had closed a whole chapter of my youth. Strange new worlds must be explored, I guess.

Scattered among the Trekkers—they'd been Trekkies when I was young, but one vehement Klingon had corrected me and I was not one to argue with an angry Klingon—were little green men, bubble-headed aliens of 1950s movie fantasy, a Wookie or two, other wild *Star Wars* imaginings, and several truly original creations. Some of the aliens were even disguised as humans—one of whom I recognized.

Junior Arbogast, hoax exposer, fraud buster, and legend in his own mind, made his living debunking UFO sightings, alien abductions, and paranormal phenomena in general. Junior and I had bonded over an interesting outing to Area 51—

the local Air Force spook palace north of town, and the epicenter of UFO lore. He had spent an hour facedown in the dirt, a gun pointed at his head, while I endeavored to talk the Lincoln County sheriff out of arresting him, and the Cammo Guys, as the security service hired to protect and defend the perimeter were so lovingly referred to, out of perforating him. Now, each year when the spookies held their annual convention in town, Junior and I usually found time to have a drink together, which I enjoyed. Yes, he could be arrogant and a pain in the ass, but he was bright and knew BS when he saw it. I liked that about him.

Built like a fire hydrant, with a shock of wiry dishwater-blond hair, pale eyes under heavy, bushy brows, and a nose that had been broken more than once, Junior loved a good fight—the product of a childhood in the mountains of West Virginia. He didn't tolerate fools well, so he had few friends, a fact that didn't seem to bother him. How I managed to stay off his blithering idiot list was an enduring mystery.

"Are you merely observing the mating rituals of alien life-forms, or are you looking for the next Mrs. Arbogast?" I whispered as I sidled in next to him.

"Ah, the great quipster, Lucky O'Toole. I was wondering when you'd turn up," Junior mumbled through a mouthful of hot dog. He swallowed, then took a healthy swig from his gallon-size Bucket-o-Beer. "You jest, but I'll have you know," he continued, "a renowned professor at one of this country's most storied institutions of higher learning postulated that all alien abductions around the world could be explained as a simple cross-species breeding project."

"So everything really is about sex?"

"Especially in Vegas. If sex doesn't happen here, why come?" Junior stuffed in the last of his hot dog and washed it down with more beer.

Why indeed, I thought as I watched the UFO aficionados—some true believers, but mostly half-baked hangers-on who liked a good party with a weird group of folks. I could identify—I lived there.

People and aliens packed in around us, their energy infectious. A television crew trailed one of the local talking heads apparently on the prowl for content for a "wacky and wonderful" segment for the nightly news. Everyone seemed to be waiting for something.

"What's going on?" I asked Junior, since he appeared to be waiting as well.

"We're all about to witness a spectacular example of professional suicide."

"Really? Whose?" I felt the inner flicker of some primal calling—probably the same unsavory instinct that draws us all to the scene of disaster. I didn't like it.

"Dr. Zewicki."

"Ah," I said, not needing any more explanation.

"Zoom-Zoom" Zewicki had been a train wreck waiting to happen for years. A former astronaut and the twentieth-something man launched into space, with a PhD in some obscure science from one of the world's foremost universities, Zoom-Zoom had one major affliction: He used to be somebody. In recent years, he had resorted to quirkier and more outlandish stunts to make sure we all remembered that.

"This must be my lucky day. First I get to witness professional suicide, then I get to preside at a funeral."

"My, you're a glutton for punishment." Junior wadded up the paper wrapper from his hot dog and stuffed it in his pocket.

"That will be my epitaph," I said, only half joking. "I'm sure 'taking punishment' is part of my job description but, fool that I am, I didn't read the fine print. So, what treat does Zoom-Zoom have in store for us?" I glanced at my watch—eight-fifteen. Fashionably late to the party, I still had a few more minutes before my tardiness would be considered another salvo in my one-man war on the Calliope Girls. The war was a figment of their imaginations, of course, but I didn't want to toss any unnecessary grenades.

Before Junior had time to answer, a hush fell over the crowd. Heads turned as Zoom-Zoom stepped to a podium on a dais at the far end of the lobby.

A short man who kept himself fighting trim, Dr. Zewicki wore his hair military short, his shirts pressed, his slacks creased, and a look of encroaching madness in his dark eyes. He leaned in to the microphone, got too close, then drew back with a jerk as if the resulting squeal was from a snake coiled to strike.

"Thank you all for coming." This time he got the distance to the mike just right. His unexpectedly deep voice echoed around the marble lobby and rippled over the crowd. He waited until the last reverberation died before continuing. "My statement will be brief and I won't accept any questions at this time. For those of you who wish to know more, I will be holding a formal presentation Thursday night, in Rachel, as part of Viewing Night."

Expectant murmurs rolled like waves through the crowd.

Dr. Zewicki fed on the attention of the crowd like an alien spacecraft sucking electromagnetic energy from a thunderstorm. Pausing, he milked it, then waited a few beats more until every head turned his direction, every voice quieted. Staring at the crowd, a serious expression on his face, he pulled himself to his full height and announced, "I have recently experienced an alien abduction."

The murmurs of the crowd rose on a cresting wave of expectation.

"My abductor's message is simple and twofold: When we die, they come and take our spirits. Some spirits pass through to the next life, but those of us with unresolved issues—those who were murdered, perhaps—live on with the aliens. And now they wish to open a channel."

The wave of expectation broke into a cascade of excited voices, flooding the lobby with a rushing torrent of questions. . . . Questions that would remain unanswered: Zoom-Zoom Zewicki had left the stage.

Stunned, I needed a few moments to find my voice. "Did he just say what I thought he said?"

"Tortured souls live on with the aliens and Dr. Zewicki can talk to them."

"I'm sure the homicide division at Metro will be thrilled to have alien assistance." I shrugged off a chill that shivered down my spine. Talk of murder messed with the Vegas magic—magic that was part of my job to deliver.

Junior looked at me, his face inscrutable. "Talk about a meteor hitting the atmosphere! A lifetime of achievement incinerated, just like that." He snapped his fingers in front of my face.

"The death of a star," I whispered.

"And the birth of a pop-culture icon," announced Junior, his voice as hard as flint.

Zoom-Zoom Zewicki had just pegged the fraud buster's bullshit meter.

I left Junior plotting the pulverization of the last remaining pebbles of Dr. Zewicki's reputation, and headed toward the Calliope Burlesque Theatre on the far side of the casino. Working my way

through the throng took me longer than I antici-
pated. I had just reached the edge of the crowd
when I felt a hand on my arm.

"Ms. O'Toole?" Young and soft, the voice was
unfamiliar.

"Yes." I turned and found myself staring down
at a blue-eyed Ferengi.

The alien thrust an upside-down top hat at me.
"Would you be so kind as to deliver this to Mr.
Fortunoff? He left it in the bar. Normally, I would
take it to him myself, but Security is not allowing
anyone backstage except those invited to the party."

"Sure." I grabbed the hat, surprised by its weight,
as the Ferengi melted back into the crowd. That a
magician would need a top hat to pull something
out of seemed logical to me, so I didn't think the
request odd. I peered inside the hat . . . empty.
Turning it right-side up and shaking—nothing fell
out. Whatever.

A lesser luminary in the world of the Dark Arts,
Dimitri Fortunoff specialized in sleights of hand,
mind reading, and other parlor tricks. He performed nightly as the entertainment between the
first and second acts of the burlesque show.

I tucked the hat under my arm and strode
through the casino. Flashing my invite to the security guard, I pushed through the double doors into
another world. While decorations and scenery
adorned the audience side of the curtain, creating
the illusion of a bright and exciting world, a different, workman-like world existed behind the

curtain. The stage was empty, illuminated by bare bulbs that would be extinguished during the show. Scenery hung in the rafters on counterweighted pulleys. Other accoutrements, including Dimitri's magic tricks, were stuffed unceremoniously into every nook and cranny, creating an obstacle course for the unwary. At the appropriate time during the show, each piece would be moved into position; after its use it would be removed in a well-choreographed, painstakingly rehearsed dance.

Forty years of dust and grime, forty years of pain and sweat, forty years of hopes and dreams, forty years of Vegas history—and I had swept it all away with the stroke of a pen. A matter of dollars and cents, the decision had been easy to make. Living with it, however, was a different matter.

Extraordinarily tall, beautiful women in heavy makeup and little else dotted the backstage area, each encircled by friends, family, and adoring fans clever enough to talk their way in. I noticed Zoom-Zoom Zewicki orbiting GiGi Vascheron, the star of the show. No wonder he had disappeared from the stage so quickly.

Shorter women in costume also hosted clusters of partiers. The show photographer darted in and out, memorializing the event for posterity. Everyone talked in hushed voices. If anyone smiled, I missed it.

The few men who danced in the show weren't visible. Neither was Dimitri Fortunoff.

Nobody's eyes met mine as I gently pushed my

way through the crowd. However, I felt the daggers hurled at my back, and I didn't really blame them. In their shoes, I'd hate me, too.

I found my conjurer in his dressing room hiding from reality.

"Well, if it isn't the grim reaper," he growled when he noticed me filling his doorway. "Did you come to gloat, or are you just slumming?"

A tall man with a barrel chest, droopy features, hangdog eyes, and a down-turned mouth, dressed in a poorly fitting tux, Fortunoff looked more like an undertaker than an entertainer. Slumped in a chair, one leg crossed over the other, a plate balanced in his lap, he eyed me as he forked in a bite of chocolate cake with one hand. The fingers of his free hand worked a coin over and under, from thumb to pinkie, then back again.

A number of plastic glasses dotted the desk and shelves. Plates with partially eaten cake stuffed the small trashcan in the corner.

"Looks like you've had a party."

"A wake."

"The world moves on, Dimitri." Mesmerized, I watched the coin dance between his fingers. "The Big Boss is spending millions refurbishing this place, turning it into Las Vegas's first eco-friendly, totally green hotel."

"Eco-friendly in a town known for depleting all the available local natural resources . . . an interesting concept."

"We like to appear to do our part."

"An illusion."

"You should know," I fired back. "Besides, I've heard you've moved on."

"Yeah? How so?"

"Rumor has it you're the Masked Houdini."

A magician who hid his identity while exposing famous illusions for a national television audience, the Masked Houdini had aroused the ire of illusionists far and wide. In fact, when we announced he would be doing the Houdini Séance on Halloween, several death threats had appeared in my office—some for me, some for the Houdini. The police were unable to trace the notes, but we'd heightened security as a precaution.

"The rumor is just that, a rumor. No truth to it," Dimitri intoned. His eyes held mine briefly, then skittered away.

"Right. Truth or not, somebody obviously believes it. I wouldn't take the threats lightly." This was old ground for us, but I felt the need to cover it once more.

"I'm touched by your concern."

I might have imagined it, but I thought I caught a glimpse of a grin lift one corner of his mouth, then vanish.

"Don't let it go to your head," I said. "I'm just covering my ass. If the Masked Houdini doesn't show up on Halloween, I'm toast."

This time I was sure I saw a smile.

"Did you bring me a present?" Dimitri tilted his head toward the hat under my arm.

"Not me," I said as I thrust it at him. "A Ferengi."

Dimitri raised an eyebrow.

"Don't ask. The UFO folks . . ." I trailed off, figuring that was enough of an explanation.

He took the hat. His brows creased into a frown when he felt the weight. Reaching in, he pulled out, of all things, a rabbit, surprising us both. "Cute, but trite, don't you think?" he scoffed.

Snow white, his black nose flaring excitedly, the poor creature looked terrified. Reaching to pet it, I noticed something tied to its dainty, jeweled collar.

A note.

I unfurled it and my blood ran cold.

In red lipstick, someone had scrawled "DIMITRI FORTUNOFF MUST DIE."

Dimitri paled. He dropped the rabbit as he fell back in his chair, grabbing at the bow tie knotted around his neck.

I snagged the bunny just before it hit the floor.

"Water. I need water." Dimitri's face was now turning crimson. "I can't breathe."

"Molly," I screamed, shouting for Dimitri's assistant, as I put down the bunny. She hadn't been in her cubicle when I'd walked by earlier, but she had to be close by. "Molly!" I knelt by Dimitri and managed to get his tie unknotted and his collar loosened. I was opening my mouth to shout again when the girl materialized in the doorway.

"What happened?" Molly asked, looking flustered and out of breath. Trim and sturdy, she had an athlete's body and an efficient manner. Her dark hair was cut in layers and styled to look unkempt. Concern clouded her brilliantly blue eyes as she looked first at Dimitri, then to me, then back again.

"He's just had a shock. Get some water, would you?"

Dimitri gulped air. When Molly returned with water, he gulped that, too. His normal coloring slowly returned, and his breathing settled back to a steady pace until a sheen of sweat was the sole remaining evidence of his panic attack.

"Are you okay?" I asked, when I thought he could answer.

"Fine." He pushed himself upright in the chair and set about retying his tie. "Well, as fine as anyone could be after having their life threatened."

I sat back on my heels, my knees pressed together. "I found using Thumper as a delivery vehicle particularly menacing, didn't you?"

He gave me a sneer. Molly hid her smile behind a dainty hand.

I pushed myself to my feet, then realized the bunny was nowhere to be found—he had escaped in the commotion. "Molly, you better go find that rabbit. He'd certainly liven up the show, but I'm in enough trouble with the girls already."

She glanced at the magician, then bolted.

"Do you want to cancel tonight's show?" I asked, turning my attention to Dimitri. "We really should call the police."

"And then what?" Dimitri mopped his brow with a multicolored scarf, then tucked it back up his sleeve. "All the other threats have been false alarms and the police have found nothing."

"You have a point. They haven't been successful with the notes delivered to my office addressed to the fool who hired the Masked Houdini—which, by the way, would be me. I've increased security. I don't know what else to do."

"You're getting notes, too?"

"Just lucky, I guess." Hands on my hips, I tried to look stern. "Seriously, I think you should cancel the show."

"No." Dimitri looked adamant. "The show must go on."

He didn't smile, so I don't think he meant that as a joke.

"Well then, come on." Grabbing Dimitri's hand, I gave him a tug—neither of us was particularly eager to cancel the final performance in a forty-year run. "This is your swan song. Make the most of it."

"I wish you hadn't put it quite like that."

"You'll be in front of a packed house," I said as I brushed myself off, then straightened his tie. "What could possibly happen?"

. . .

THE mood in the front of the house was even more somber than backstage, if that was possible. Patrons filed into the theatre—the most important among them following the ushers to long, communal tables placed perpendicular to the stage that sat six per side. Guests of lesser importance were left to fend for themselves. If any of them wanted a beverage of choice, they had to get it themselves at the bar window on the left side of the theatre, the queue for which already snaked halfway across the large room.

Statuesque women greeted each other with hugs and air-kisses. Some cried while their escorts shifted uncomfortably from foot to foot. Nobody smiled when they looked in my direction.

I felt like a creep.

Unaccustomed to being in the midst of so much hostility, for a moment I was flummoxed. Casting my eyes around the room, I finally spied a safe haven—a small gaggle of elite magicians. Purportedly the members of the Magic Ring—a secret ruling society within the mystical arts community—I had checked them into the Babylon yesterday and taken charge of their VIP stay.

"Mr. Mortimer." I greeted the man who had made all the arrangements for the group. "How are you enjoying Vegas so far?"

"It's been lovely, thank you," Mr. Mortimer said, his eyes lighting up when he saw me. "And this show is a particular treat."

A short man, almost as big around as he was

tall, Mr. Mortimer had dancing eyes and a quick smile. A ring of snow-white hair circled his otherwise bald head. The buttons of the silk vest stretching across his blossoming midsection looked ready to burst, but he appeared unconcerned.

"We were so sorry to hear the show is closing," he continued, clearly unaware he was talking to the harbinger of death. "It's one of our favorites—a Vegas institution."

"Where are you sitting?" I asked.

He consulted his ticket. "Table Seven."

"Me, as well. May I show you the way?"

We worked our way down to the front and took our seats as the lights dimmed and the orchestra played the first chords of a lilting tune. The curtain parted and the company of clothed dancers, male and female, took the stage in a rousing cabaret number. The audience, many of whom were former dancers, whistled and clapped for their compatriots. When the topless ladies, or the nudes as they are referred to in the business, sashayed onto the stage, the admiration of the audience grew louder. Some of the women smiled, but most stayed in character.

Despite having seen my share, topless shows remained a mystery to me. First, the women weren't even buxom. With the shortest of them measured at five foot ten and none of them weighing more than a hundred and thirty pounds, how much bust could they be expected to have? Of course, my initial expectation had been they would all have been enhanced like most of the strippers in town, but that was not the case. A sort of weird reverse discrimination prevailed in Vegas: The very best showgirls had to be *au naturel*. I bet those women's boobs were the only natural things left in town. Heck, even the grass outside the Wynn was plastic.

Wishing I had taken time to wait in line for a drink, but worried I might not have lived through it, I sat back, tried to relax, and watched the show. At the completion of several rousing dance numbers, each punctuated by the appearance of the nudes, the curtain fell on the first act.

After a brief moment, the curtain again parted. The scenery had disappeared. A large rectangular wooden crate resembling a phone booth with a glass front and sides stood vertically in the center of the stage. Shiny brass angles, attached along the edges with neat rows of rivets, held the box together. Although it was hard to tell, I thought the crate was full of water.

Mr. Mortimer and his friends gasped in unison. Leaning over, he whispered in my ear, "That's Houdini's Chinese Water Torture Cell."

"Houdini? Like Harry Houdini?"

Mr. Mortimer nodded. "I can't imagine where Dimitri got it."

Our eyes shot back to the stage as Dimitri Fortunoff appeared, clad only in old-fashioned swimming attire. Molly and several of the dancers accompanied him. The magician waved to someone off stage, then glanced up as a block and tackle descended from the rafters. It bore a wooden plank, cut with two round holes.

"Is this part of his normal act?" one of Mr. Mortimer's compatriots asked.

"Not as of a month ago," I replied, a ball of dread growing in my stomach.

"Ladies and gentleman," Dimitri began. "As you all know, tonight is our last show, and I've been perfecting a special escape for you."

When he paused, you could hear a pin drop.

"Harry Houdini, widely considered the best of all time, developed the escape I am about to do for you. First, my ankles will be placed in this stock." Dimitri held up the wooden board and removed an open padlock, which released the two halves, allowing it to be positioned around his legs.

An assistant then bent, threaded the padlock through two D rings, one on each half of the stock, and snapped the padlock closed.

"Thank you," Dimitri said to the girl, then continued. "After volunteers from the crowd have checked all the apparatus thoroughly, I will be handcuffed then lifted and lowered headfirst into the chest you see here, which is filled with water. My beautiful assistants will then padlock the top in place."

A nervous murmur rippled through the room.

"You must be convinced the chest is nothing more than it seems, that I have not tampered with it in any way. Now for the volunteers." With one hand shielding his eyes from the lights, he looked over the crowd. His eyes came to rest on our table. Pointing at us, he said, "You. All of you. Would you be so kind?"

Catching my eye, he shook his head at me, so I remained behind as the magicians at my table filed onto the stage. Zoom-Zoom appeared from backstage and joined them, even though he hadn't been called.

Dimitri didn't seem to mind. As he watched, the men examined every pane of glass, every nook, every cranny of the chest. When they had apparently satisfied themselves, Dimitri asked them, "Could you see any alterations in the chest that might explain an easy escape?"

Each of them shook his head. "We could not," announced Mr. Mortimer in his stage voice—apparently he'd been voted the group's spokesman, as the others remained silent, merely nodding their agreement.

"What about you?" Dimitri pointed to one of the magicians, who looked most unhappy at being singled out.

A hawkish man with angry eyes, he glared at Dimitri. "If this box has a trick, I do not know it."

"Why don't you ask Mr. Houdini?" Before the man could answer, Dimitri turned to address the crowd. "Some of you may be too young to remember the acclaimed mentalist, but may I present The Great Danilov."

The crowd clapped politely as Danilov took a bow, and shook Dimitri's hand. After a whispered exchange with the magician, Danilov hurried offstage.

"Or you?" Dimitri pointed to Dr. Zewicki. "You claim to talk to the dead. Maybe Mr. Houdini will speak to you."

"Doubtful. No one ever said he was murdered," Zoom-Zoom hissed as he ducked backstage.

The other magicians filed after Danilov and retook their seats as Dimitri announced, "Ladies and gentlemen, these men are part of an august group of magicians. If they can't see how I perform this escape, then it must be a very good trick indeed."

"I have a really bad feeling about this," Mr. Mortimer again whispered in my ear as he settled himself in his seat. "It's long been believed the secrets of the chest died with Mr. Houdini."

"Could Mr. Fortunoff have a new trick up his sleeve?" I asked.

"There are only so many ways to get out of a chest filled with water that's locked from the outside."

I didn't like the hint of impending doom in his voice. I fought with myself. I wanted to stop the whole thing. But what if he really could get out of that contraption? He wasn't suicidal, as far as I knew, and I was in enough trouble already. Against my better judgment, I decided to let the show go on.

We watched as the assistants first checked the shackles and tested the block and tackle. Then they helped the magician as he was lifted, then lowered into the tank. Quickly the women lowered the lid and snapped several padlocks in place around its edge, effectively securing it to the chest—with Dimitri clearly visible inside.

I held my breath as the assistants drew a curtain around the chest and left the stage. Apparently the rest of the audience felt as I did—they didn't move. Not even a whisper broke the silence.

An eternity passed. Then another.

The audience grew restless. Nervous whispering buzzed.

Finally someone shouted, "It's been too long. Somebody get him out of that thing."

Other voices joined in agreement.

"Come." Mr. Mortimer ordered as he rose to his feet and grabbed my hand, pulling me with him. His friends fell in step behind us as we started for the stage.

We had made it to the first step when Molly ran out from stage left. Her face was stricken, streaked with tears.

"Oh my God! He's dead!"

Chapter

TWO

♡

"Keep everybody back!" I shouted to the security guards who rushed from their post by the entrance as I yanked the curtain aside. I didn't wait to see if they could follow orders. Photographers rushed in, flashbulbs popping. On the stage, people formed a ring around the Houdini water box, paralyzed, frozen with horror. Dimitri floated in the water. He didn't move.

With one quick glance, I located a sledgehammer resting against the side wall just off the stage, probably put there by the magician as a backup plan.

"People, stand back," Mr. Mortimer shouted.

Adrenaline spiking, I swung the hammer at the glass. A spiderweb of tiny cracks formed, but the glass held. I raised the hammer to swing again, when the weight of the water broke the weakened glass.

The rag-doll body of Dimitri Fortunoff washed out at my feet. Apparently he'd made it as far as extricating his hands and feet.

Molly immediately dropped to her knees and began CPR. Kneeling beside her I reached to find a pulse. His skin was cold, clammy. My fingers had yet to find the trace of a beat when paramedics shouldered through the crowd and took charge. Within minutes, they had Dimitri strapped to a gurney, a breathing device over his face.

"Where are you taking him?" I asked.

"UMC," one said over his shoulder, as they rushed Dimitri out and the crowd closed around us.

For a moment, no one said anything as we all stared at each other, completely stunned at what had happened.

"Does anyone know if Dimitri has any family?" I asked, feeling sick to my stomach.

"He had a wife. She . . . died," Molly said, her voice choked with emotion.

"Anyone else?"

"He didn't speak of anyone."

That left me to go to the hospital, sign the papers. I'd do it anyway—I felt responsible. He'd died in my hotel, on my watch, and I'd even been warned it was coming. Guilt settled over me, constricting my heart. While Dimitri's day was worse than mine, it wasn't considerably worse. I'd almost rather trade places with him.

Grabbing two security guards from out front, I posted them around the water torture box. "Don't let anyone near this thing. Not until the police arrive. You got it?"

If someone had tampered with it, there would be hell to pay.

"I always thought this thing was cursed," remarked Detective Romeo as he paced around the contraption, his hands behind his back, his eyes wide with delight. He looked like a kid at Christmas.

"Cursed?" Tired of standing while I waited for the police, I had roosted on the steps to one of the set pieces. Everyone else had either scattered to the dressing rooms or milled in the hallways. I wouldn't let anyone leave until the police arrived. Now that they had, I thankfully transferred the mantle of responsibility to the young detective.

With his rumpled suit, poorly knotted tie, and raincoat, Romeo was channeling Columbo. Perhaps he was compensating for looking all of twelve years old with his messy sandy-brown hair and guileless face. Or perhaps he didn't know how to dress. Either way, I was glad to see him—he was my contact with the Metropolitan Police Department (Metro to all of us Las Vegans), and he owed me.

"Houdini insisted on absolute loyalty from all those around him," Romeo explained. "There's a quote attributed to Houdini. Something about wanting his show to be the best in the world while he was alive, and after he was dead, wanting none other to be like it."

"So if all his secrets were buried with him, how is this here?"

"Theodore, the brother, defied Harry. He gave the original torture cell to a friend."

My heart momentarily leapt at the name. My

Theodore was in Helsinki, or Moscow, or Prague—some faraway place I hadn't been to and couldn't picture. Right now I sure could use one of his hugs—but that, of course, wasn't going to happen—a fact that amazingly made my day even worse. "So you think Harry Houdini cursed this thing from beyond because his brother didn't do as he asked?"

"Not really." Romeo looked a bit sheepish. "But it makes a good story."

"How do you know all of this?"

Romeo reached up as if pulling something from behind my ear, then showed me the quarter in his previously empty hand. "I'm a bit of an amateur magician, using the term loosely."

"I never knew that about you," I said, truly surprised. "Why haven't you told me before?"

"It never came up. And besides, I didn't think being a prestidigitator would add *gravitas* to my whole detective gig."

"Perhaps not, but that word is impressive."

Accustomed to my sarcasm, Romeo ignored me.

"So, if this water torture thing was on public display or whatever," I said when I couldn't get a smile out of him, "its secrets must be well known."

"Actually, no. None of those close to Houdini ever breathed a word, and the original torture cell was destroyed by fire."

"Yet here it is," I said, not understanding any of this.

"Perhaps a replica. There was one, but no one

knows where it is. And rumor has it another one was made without permission by the woodworker hired to fashion the original. Or it could be something thrown together from old pictures of the exterior." Romeo reached out to touch the box, then thought better of it. "I wonder if this is the original replica or the fake?"

"Can you have a fake replica?" I mused out loud. "And who would care as long as it works?"

"The person who owns it," Romeo said, chosing to ignore my musings. "The real replica would be worth close to two million dollars."

"Two million! I guess it's safe to assume a lesser magician toiling in a show long past its prime probably didn't have that kind of money. So, if Dimitri doesn't own it, who does?"

I left Romeo examining the torture cell and looking for clues, or whatever it was detectives do. His men were busy questioning everyone who had been backstage, out front, or who had access to the torture cell—a process that would probably take most of the night. The young detective was humoring me, I could tell. It's not as if I knew a crime had been committed. Was this a trick gone horribly wrong, or had someone tampered with the water box? How would we know if no one knew its secrets?

Lost in thought, I charged through the casino and ran smack into a chest I recognized. "Dane! What are you doing here?"

He grabbed my shoulders to steady me. "Looking for you."

A long, tall drink of Texas charm, Paxton Dane was a watchdog for the Gaming Control Board; the Babylon was part of his territory. At six foot four, with wavy brown hair that begged for fingers to be run through it, emerald green eyes that seemed to give half of the female population an urge to strip on the spot, and an aw-shucks manner, Dane was a walking, talking, living, breathing sexual tractor beam. Tonight he looked especially hunk-a-liscious, in creased jeans, crocodile kickers, a tweed blazer in browns and greens, and a shirt that matched his eyes and accented broad shoulders that tapered nicely to his narrow waist.

And wouldn't you know it, in addition to being the stuff of female fantasies, he was also a nice guy with the whole Southern chivalry thing going on. Add the fact that he didn't try to hide his attraction to me, and I found resisting him darn near impossible, even with my considerable talents.

"Why are you looking for me?" I asked, unwilling to resist him holding on to my elbow as he escorted me to the door and the waiting valet. The heat of his hand radiated through the thin cashmere of my sweater. A jolt of attraction arced through me. My brain said no, but my body didn't speak the same language. Clearly, fighting with myself was a losing battle. . . . Briefly I wondered if that was even a battle that could be won. If so, between me and myself, who would win and who would lose?

"I heard about your interesting evening," Dane said, his mouth close to my ear, spreading the warmth. Like liquid chocolate, his voice was smooth, delicious. "I thought maybe I could help." He whistled in appreciation as the valet eased the Ferrari to the curb. "That car still makes my pulse pound."

"And here I thought it was me," I shot back, then cringed. Sometimes my mouth works before my brain engages—another example of that body/brain disconnect. Flirting with Dane didn't seem like the smartest thing to do, especially given my libido situation.

"That goes without saying." He gave me a wry smile.

"Did you bring a ride?" I asked.

"No, Paolo dropped me off." Paolo was the Babylon's head chauffeur and he normally worked the night shift.

"Well, then, Cowboy, put your ass in some class." I handed the valet a twenty, then folded myself into the car, making a mental note that next time I drove the thing I would not wear such a short skirt. "I'll give you a ride, but I doubt you're going to like where I'm headed."

THE cool night air streamed in through the open top as I followed traffic up the Strip. There were shorter routes to UMC, the University Medical Center, but with a handsome man in the car and an unsavory task awaiting me, I was in no hurry. Ignoring Dane's presence, men called out to me from the sidewalks. "Nice car, lady!" one guy shouted. "Want to take me for a ride?" another added. "I'd like to rev your engine," a young man shouted.

Safe in the car, and with a chaperone, I rewarded that one with a wave.

Dane looked over at me and raised an eyebrow. "Do you always attract this sort of attention?"

"If I had known what a man-magnet this car was, I would've sold my soul a decade ago to get my hands on one."

"I wouldn't think you'd need the car," Dane said as he put a hand over mine.

I didn't have to look at him to see the warmth in his eyes—I'd seen it before—and I could feel it in his touch. "Dane—"

"I know." He removed his hand.

Where his fingers had lingered on mine, my skin now felt cold.

"Where are we going that I won't like?" he asked, kindly letting me off the hook.

"UMC." I shivered as I said the letters. Nothing good ever brought me to a hospital—at least not since I was born in one, but I don't remember that. The last time I'd been there The Big Boss had died, once, been shocked back to life, then had emergency heart surgery. "I need to check on the magician and see if they can give me a preliminary cause of death."

"Wasn't it an accident?"

I gave Dane the whole story, as it existed so far—the rumors that Dimitri Fortunoff was the Masked Houdini, the death threats, the Chinese Water Torture Cell.

"If you don't know how he was supposed to get out in the first place, how will you know if someone rigged the water thing so Mr. Fortunoff couldn't escape?"

"I've asked myself the same question and I still have no idea. But if we can start ruling things out, like drugs or a heart attack, maybe we can close in on what really happened."

"That's gonna be like trying to scratch your ear with your elbow."

I had a sinking feeling he was right.

THE emergency room at UMC was a hive of activity when Dane and I pushed through the doors, adding our bodies to the bustle. After waiting in front of the check-in desk for several minutes, I finally managed to get the attention of one of the nurses.

With hollow eyes and the pallor of the walking dead, she pushed a strand of hair out of her face and hooked it behind an ear as she gave me the once-over. "What can I do for you?" she asked. Even her voice sounded exhausted.

"A magician from the Athena was brought in a

little while ago," I said. "Tall guy, dressed in vintage swim trunks. He drowned. I'd like to talk to the doctor who signed his death certificate."

The nurse again brushed at the strand of hair that refused to remain moored behind her ear and out of her face. She consulted a clipboard. "Hon, we've had two ODs, a gunshot wound, three stab wounds, several heart attacks, and one guy with a lightbulb broken off in his . . . well, never mind." She glanced up at us and gave a weak smile. "But no drowned magicians."

"Really? You sure?" I leaned across the counter and looked at her list. "The paramedics said they were bringing him here."

The nurse snatched away her list. "No drowned magician."

"If they didn't bring him here, where did they take him?"

THE night was still relatively young when, with Dane dogging my heels, I pushed through the doors into the lobby of the Babylon Resort and Casino—my home away from home. Which, come to think of it, due to the hours I worked, felt more like home than home did. Not good.

The Big Boss's pride and joy, the Babylon was an architectural work of art with its soaring ceilings covered with blown-glass hummingbirds and butterflies in flight, polished marble floors, and intricate inlaid mosaics. Bright swags of multicolored cloth were tented above the reception area, reminiscent of an Arabian market. Adjacent to Reception was the entrance to The Bazaar, an avenue of high-end shops where the top luxury brands beckoned conspicuous consumers with a dazzling show of bling and wildly expensive designer threads, shoes, and accessories. People came from far and wide to gaze in awe, even if they couldn't spring for any of the treasures.

A river of water, our very own version of the Euphrates, meandered through the lobby and into the casino beyond. Lined with flowering plants and filled with goldfish and carp, the stream hosted several pairs of swans and numerous families of ducks—one of The Big Boss's touches that necessitated a vet on retainer for bird birth control. Swans are foul-tempered beasts and too many ducks can get messy—and they breed like rabbits; we learned that the hard way. Railed footbridges arcing over the Euphrates provided easy access to the other side as well as picturesque spots for photos.

Directly across from the reception area, separated behind a wall of floor-to-ceiling glass, loomed an indoor ski hill of man-made snow. The runs were closing for the night. A few people still stood at the window, watching the skiers making their last dash down the hill. While a ski slope wasn't particularly consistent with our Ancient Persia theme, it got people in the doors, which was the whole point. The Big Boss was a genius when it came to pulling people inside—the critical Vegas success skill.

Dane and I dodged a cluster of folks, their faces turned skyward as they admired the ceiling and its splash of colorful creatures in flight. We headed for the stairs that would take us to the Mezzanine and my office.

Once out of the lobby, with our footfalls echoing off the metal stairs and reverberating in the stairwell, Dane asked, "What next?"

Pressing the bar on the exit door and pushing it open, I threw over my shoulder, "I hit the phones. I'm going to find where they took that magician if we have to call every hospital in town." For-profit hospitals had been sprouting like weeds in the suburbs, so I had my work cut out for me.

"Let's split the city. You take the west half, I'll take the east," Dane offered.

"Deal." The light in my outer office still glowed, so I didn't bother rooting in my bag for my keys.

Miss Patterson, my stalwart first assistant, manned her desk like a captain at the helm of her ship. A fabulous almost-fifty with spiky golden hair, warm eyes, and the best bullshit meter of anyone I'd ever met, Miss P was the compass that kept my office on course. I'd be totally at sea without her.

Tonight, she wore a trim gunmetal gray suit with a hint of lace at her décolletage, a stunning David Yurman necklace of turquoise and gold, matching earrings, and a hint of wicked in her eyes, placed there, no doubt, by her much younger lover, The Beautiful Jeremy Whitlock.

She greeted me with a fleeting smile and a raised eyebrow when she saw Dane behind me. If she had an opinion about his presence, I couldn't tell. Her manner was efficient, her tone clipped when she said, "Good timing. Your mother is holding on line one."

And this night had been going so well . . .

My mother, Mona, gave a whole new meaning to the term "high-risk pregnancy"—her meteoric mood swings put anyone who crossed her path in mortal danger.

At an age where she should have been looking forward to grandchildren, she found herself inexplicably with child. She had been sixteen when she had me—an inconvenience that could have been due to hormonal overload and its resulting stupidity. But now, being of a certain age and having had some prior experience, Mona should have known better.

To compound matters, she hadn't worked up the courage to tell The Big Boss he was going to be a parent . . . again. I was the sole keeper of her secret—lucky me.

"Mother," I said, keeping my voice passive until I could gauge her mood.

"Lucky, darling, could you stop by when you have a moment? I need your help."

Sweetness and light. So unexpected. I smelled a

rat. "What with? I'm working a pretty big problem of my own."

"Oh, it won't take long," she said breezily.

I heard my father's voice in the background, a scuffling noise, then his irritated growl boomed over the line. "Could you get up here? Your mother is plotting the annihilation of the Pussy Palace and I need your help."

STILL clutching the receiver after the line went dead, I must have looked stricken as Miss P and Dane stared at me owl-eyed from the doorway.

"Is everything okay?" Miss P asked, clearly alarmed.

"Do either of you know what the Pussy Palace is?" I slowly recradled the phone.

"I do," Dane announced, looking a little sheepish. "It's a new whorehouse in Pahrump. I believe it opened in that abandoned hotel just down the street from your mother's place."

"I don't think I'm going to ask how you know that," I said, narrowing my eyes at him.

"I don't think I would answer if you did." He gave me a look of pure innocence.

My mother owned Mona's Place, the self-styled "Best Whorehouse in Nevada," and she would consider competition moving in an act of war. Giving weight to her delicate condition, I made a mental note to lock up all the firearms.

"At least that explains why Mother is on the warpath and The Big Boss is at the end of his rope.

I've been summoned to referee. Could the two of you start on the call list?"

I saw the question in Miss P's eyes. Raising my hand, I stopped her. "Dane can explain it to you. I shouldn't be too long unless The Big Boss strangles the woman before I get there. And frankly, if he does, he'd be doing us all a huge favor."

MOTHER had moved into The Big Boss's apartment on the top floor, the fifty-second, of the west wing of the hotel. For some odd reason, I liked the fact that my parents were living in sin, thumbing their noses at the world—there was a cosmic symmetry to it. They'd met at a party when Mona was a teenager turning tricks and lying about her age. The Big Boss, twenty years her senior, was a golden boy in the casino business. They'd fallen madly in love. The resulting pregnancy—me—had been an inconvenience and an embarrassment to my father's employers.

Too late he discovered Mother's true age. Threatened with a felony prosecution, the choice was simple—he denied everything and she refused to name the father—*my* father. Unbeknownst to anyone, they had spoken every night since. Neither ever married. When The Big Boss faced death, he called for Mother, and she'd been front and center in his life—and apparently, his bed—ever since. Talk about history repeating itself!

At least, if I hurried, this time around there wouldn't be any felonies involved.

THE sound of happy people playing hit me before I reached the casino. The come-on songs of the slots competed with the buzz of voices and the piped-in background music, creating a symphony that was music to my ears. A full casino was essential to my job security.

Tonight the large room was packed—all shapes and sizes ringed the table games, three deep around some. The slots were fully occupied. Patrons waiting for a machine circled lazily like sharks timing the kill. Delilah's Bar, the main watering hole, sat on a raised platform in the middle of the casino. Colored cloth tented above it, carrying the theme from the lobby into the large room where it was repeated over and over to give the feeling of a comforting Persian marketplace. Torches flamed under glass. Cascades of flowering plants draped from pillars and latticework, defining the cozy space of the bar. Water features burbled in the corners; a wall of water cascading behind the bar was the centerpiece. I heard someone playing the piano, but I didn't stop to listen. Teddie used to play the piano in Delilah's while he waited for me to end my day. Too many memories . . .

As I strode through the casino, dodging patrons, I tried to read the crowd—it was a game I played. Where were they from? What did they do? What were they looking for in Vegas? Were they finding it? The aliens still in costume were easy, so I eliminated them. The two guys in plaid shirts and creased jeans leaning against a pillar, sipping drinks and eyeing the ladies, looked like two lawyers from Dallas. Their look was too studied—a purchased casualness . . . lawyers for sure. The three guys in suits with open collars and loafers with no socks shouted European. I didn't know any red-blooded American male who would be caught dead wearing nice shoes with no socks. And everyone on this continent knew suits in Vegas screamed "over the hill."

My eyes came to rest on a lady nursing a yard of daiquiris. I'd pegged her age to be somewhere mid-fifties. She wore tight pink spandex pants, and a tee shirt stretched to its limit across her very ample chest. Emblazoned across her front was the slogan "If these were brains I'd be a genius."

I smiled. I couldn't help myself. Glancing down at my own inadequate chest I figured if hers were genius material, mine were double-digit IQ at best. Ah me, just one of my many inadequacies. If I weren't rushing to the scene of a future crime, I'd stop and talk to her. Anyone who would wear that shirt in public was worth knowing.

On the far side of the casino, I pressed the button, summoning an elevator, and stared at my reflection in the polished brass doors. Tall, and after enduring the last six weeks of enforced loneliness, I'd finally made it to trim. My skirt was loose and the front kept chasing away around to the back. I'd never had that problem before—I assumed some fashion trick I didn't know would solve the issue, but for now a safety pin was in order.

My hair, recently returned to its natural light brown, brushed my shoulders in soft waves. A thin fringe tickled my eyes, drawing attention to their size and their . . . blueness. With a deft touch and some blush, my recalcitrant cheekbones could sometimes be encouraged to show themselves— tonight wasn't one of those times. And if eyes really are a reflection of your soul, then mine was an old, tired soul.

As the bell dinged and the elevator doors eased open, I gave my appearance a "C," chalking up my deficiencies to too many hours at work, too many days without rest, and no sex. All were related, but I was too tired to make the connections. I wondered how long the flight was to Helsinki, or whatever faraway place Teddie played next, and how much a first-class ticket and some sleep would cost. Whatever the price, I was close to the point that I'd pay it no matter what . . . if only Teddie asked me to come.

But he hadn't. He'd been distancing himself more and more—I couldn't remember our last conversation—had it been four days? Five? Even though I didn't want to acknowledge it, Teddie had not only put distance between us, he was truly gone—he just hadn't told me so. Our time together a distant, exquisite fantasy . . . a memory, nothing more. The thought cracked my heart. Something needed to be done; I just didn't seem to have the proper knife to sever the tie that binds. I so enjoyed being one of a pair. . . . So now I dangled, like the condemned at the end of a rope, unable and unwilling to free myself.

Stepping into the elevator, I stuck my magic card into the slot and pressed PH, then leaned against the side and shut my eyes. Fifty-two floors, forty winks, that ought to at least help.

It didn't.

"There you are." My father stopped his pacing as I stepped from the elevator. He'd been lurking by the doors, apparently waiting for me. "It's about time. I can't do anything with the woman. She's lost her mind!"

A short man, his dark hair now turning a distinguished salt-and-pepper, his features still chiseled, his body the envy of men twenty years his junior, he came to a stop in front of me. Dressed in a white polo shirt and casual slacks, he looked . . . sexy. I shivered. Now that was a creepy thought to have about my father. Of course, the father thing was still pretty new . . . but still, I needed to get a grip.

I must've been staring because my father said, "What?"

"I don't think I've seen you out of your suit before, except in the gym, but that's different."

For a moment, he stared at me, his eyes blinking furiously. There was anger there, and a hint of amusement. All was not lost.

"There must be some weird affliction affecting the women in my life—neither you nor your mother is making any sense whatsoever," he finally announced.

"That's our job—keep you men off kilter so you don't think you're running the world."

"Running the world?" He rolled his eyes, another first. "I can't even run my life. I've been chasing my tail ever since your mother moved in." He made a sweeping gesture with one hand, as he grabbed my elbow with the other, urging me inside. "You have to talk some sense into her."

"She is sort of an unguided missile in the battle of life, isn't she?" I would've added he's obviously been chasing Mother's tail as well, but I stifled myself—he looked on the brink of homicide as it was.

"She'd charge Hell with a bucket of ice water." He shot me a half-smile that looked a bit forced. "I love that about her."

"Me, too. I'll see what I can do."

Our steps echoed off the burnished mahogany floors as he escorted me through the vast main room of his apartment—past lesser works of the Great Masters (small pieces from his impressive collection on display downstairs) hanging on the leather upholstered walls and appropriately lit with brass fixtures, and past tasteful arrangements of furniture constructed of woods from various continents and hides from various beasts, all sitting on perfectly knotted, exquisitely hued silk carpets. He didn't even let me linger at his wall of floor-to-ceiling windows to drink in the incredible view of the Strip.

He stopped at the entrance to the hallway leading to the private areas. "She's in the master bedroom."

"And that would be . . . ?"

"Through the double doors at the end of the hall. You can't miss it. Good luck." He turned on his heel and headed for the bar.

As I stared down the long corridor in front of me, I felt like Indiana Jones entering a cave to face life-threatening challenges. Except, for me, there was no treasure at the end of the test. The soft carpet cushioned my steps as I advanced on the double doors.

"Mother?"

"In here, dear," she cheerily replied.

This was not good. Mona always used honey to lure the bear to the trap.

Mother sat in the middle of a huge four-poster, her long legs crossed, her brow furrowed. She'd pulled her dark hair into a hasty knot at the nape of her neck. A few tendrils had escaped and curled softly around her face, hiding any hint of her penchant for plastic surgery. Her skin flawless, her blue eyes luminous, she looked younger than me—not something I took pride in, but I refused to engage in a war of the scalpel with her.

She chewed on the end of a pencil as she stared at a notepad, which she held at arm's length, too vain to admit she needed reading glasses. Without glancing up, she motioned me over.

I paused awkwardly at the edge of the bed, taking a moment to drink in my surroundings. A very masculine room, blues and browns dominated the color scheme, with hints of gold in the damask headboard and bedspread. Another wall of windows captured the Strip at a jaw-dropping angle. A few animal heads hung on the far wall over the fireplace, glaring accusatorily. I never understood the whole dead zoo thing, and I didn't think I would want to sleep in one. Mother, on the other hand, looked right at home.

"Sit." My mother patted a spot on the bed next to her.

Instead, I grabbed the desk chair and pulled it around so I could face her. Sitting on the bed my mother shared with The Big Boss didn't seem right. In fact, the thought made me queasy. I'm very visual, and having right in front of me the prop where in all likelihood my future sibling was conceived didn't help at all.

Never one to wade into the shallow end, I decided to leap headfirst into the fray. "Want to tell me about the Pussy Palace?"

Mother's smile snapped down into a frown as she glared at me. "They moved in right down the street! Can you believe it? Trying to steal my thunder. Imagine!"

I didn't think that's what they were trying to

steal but, valuing my life, I didn't say so. "What are you going to do?"

"Compete!" she announced proudly. "First, I'm developing a list of specials I thought we might offer."

"Specials?" That queasy feeling hit me again.

She consulted her notes. "We could do golf packages with the championship course that opened recently in Pahrump—I know they're trying to attract new business."

"Your slogan could be 'Come, play a round, then play around with us,' " I suggested. "There's got to be something about a short stick . . . or maybe something about not feeling up to par . . . or maybe 'We can polish your balls.' "

Mona narrowed her eyes at me. "What about a flat-rate program on our slow days—all the sex and liquor you can stand between the hours of four and seven in the afternoon, for one low price?"

"You've been doing some thinking," I said, biting back my smile.

"Oh, I'm just getting started. We could have a loyalty club—"

"Twelve punches and the thirteenth is free?" I suggested, warming to the game.

"I knew you weren't taking this seriously," she huffed. "Sweetheart, this could really work—orgy parties like the sex clubs here in town, daily specials, which we already do, discount coupons."

"What about a movie night? You could show

some of the porn I get for the girls at Smokin' Joes."
I was teasing, but she took me seriously, scribbling
the idea on her pad.

"And a senior night?" she asked.

"No, you'd have to charge them more," I remarked, trying to keep a straight face. "The old
men take too long."

"Now you're being snarky." She put down her
pad and gave me that all-knowing-mother look.
"Not getting any, are you?"

"I *have* hit a dry spell with Teddie being gone
and all."

"Being a good girl and keeping the home fires
burning?"

"You make me sound like Tom Bodette in those
silly Motel Six commercials . . . 'We'll keep the light
on for ya.' Whatever happened to those anyway?"

"They went the way of the dodo."

"Cute. Are you trying to tell me I'm being stupid?"

"Teddie's chasing his dream; you need to find
yours."

My dream was a man at home; Teddie's dreams
took him on the road—I didn't see an easy solution, so I did what I always do with an impossible
personal problem—I shelved it—and changed the
subject. "Mother, you can't keep doing this."

"Doing what?"

"Pretending life is going to go on as it always
has." I reached over and took her hand. "You cannot have it all."

"Why not? Why do we have to play by other people's rules? Why do we always have to give up something, a part of ourselves, to get something . . . someone . . . we want?"

"Maybe it's the price the universe charges for dreams. The Big Boss is a very important businessman. He has a certain reputation to uphold. With prostitution illegal in Clark County, you two in bed together puts him in a very awkward position—not only with his corporate investors, but with the Gaming Commission as well."

"What should I do?"

"Give Mona's Place to Trudi, tell The Big Boss he is going to be a father, and live your life at his side."

My mother seemed to shrink within herself. "I've been thinking about it—I know you're right. But give up Mona's Place? I can't bring myself to do it," she whispered.

"Why not? Trudi would do a great job—she's been with you forever."

"I'm afraid I would lose myself."

"Mother, that business doesn't define you. The Big Boss doesn't define you. You would never tolerate that—you're not one to hide in anyone's shadow."

"I know. If I want a new life, I have to let the old one go." She gave me a piercing look that was pretty easy to interpret—the relationship doctor should focus on healing herself.

Head in the sand, my heart as delicate as paper-thin Victorian china, I chose to ignore her.

Mona straightened her back a little—her confidence growing. "This is such a different world here. I don't know the rules. You and Albert handle it all so seamlessly, with such ease."

"You'll get used to it. Actually, it's not that different than running a bordello in Pahrump. We're still in the service business; we just deal with more money and larger egos here in Sin City." I could see her starting to believe me. "Life with The Big Boss is your dream come true. Don't lose courage now. Seize it before it's too late."

"But Mona's Place is my legacy—it's the only thing I have to leave to you."

"It's okay." I patted her hand. "You've given me a lifetime of wonderful memories and that's even better." Personally, I would be appalled to wake up one morning to find myself the owner of a whorehouse in Pahrump, but it would hurt her to tell her so.

She swiped at a tear. "Now you're just being nice."

"It happens occasionally." I pulled her toward the edge of the bed. "Come. We need to rescue Father from a bottle of Wild Turkey."

THE Big Boss sat on one of the large leather couches facing the brilliant lights of the Strip. As he stared out the window, his fingers worked a small scrap of paper, which I knew to be a one-hundred-dollar bill—folding it, creasing the fold, then making another. Without thinking, he would turn the bill into a small origami animal. Lately he'd been on an elephant kick—he made them with their trunks raised—an ancient sign of good luck, he'd said. I wondered if he'd been unwittingly creating fertility talismans as well.

Mother curled in next to him. Looping an arm around her shoulders, he pulled her tight as he stuffed the tiny paper creature into his pocket. Turning my back to my parents, I stood looking out at my city.

"Lucky has helped me make a few decisions," my mother announced, breaking the comfortable silence. "I'm giving my business to Trudi."

Glancing at my father, I saw him visibly relax. His eyes telegraphed his thanks. "I know that will be hard for you," he said to my mother.

"Yes, I fought long and hard for that business. It's a part of me. I will have to find another way to help the girls." She glanced at my father, who gave her a nod. "So, yes it will be hard, but perhaps not quite as hard as what I have to tell you."

"My cue to leave," I said. It hadn't been a rat I smelled—it'd been a setup.

My mother grabbed my hand and held tight. "Don't leave. I need your support."

I tried in vain to extricate my hand. "Mother, this isn't my place."

"What is this about?" My father looked alarmed.

"It's a family matter and we're family. Please

stay. I need you here," my mother implored. Gripping my hand like a lifeline, she shrugged herself off The Big Boss's shoulder and turned to look at him. With her free hand, she clutched his. "Albert, I have something to tell you."

Chapter

THREE

♡

I braced for impact.

"Albert. Sweetheart . . ." Mona trailed off, clearly losing her nerve.

She let go of my hand and I moved back to the window, out of the danger zone.

"Lucky, would you tell him? I can't seem to find the words." The skin drawn tight across her face, she looked stricken—or she needed to change surgeons.

"No, I won't tell him! You know what happens to the messenger."

"Well, one of you damn well better tell me before I shoot you both," my father said. His voice, tinged with anger, rode on an undercurrent of frustration.

Mona took a deep breath. Let it out. Drew herself up. Then sagged once again. She threw a pleading look at me, but I didn't cave.

"Okay . . . Albert . . ." She started once again, this time looking more determined. She looked him in the eye. "I'm carrying our child."

I heard the Fates laughing in the silence that followed.

My father stared at Mona, his face blank, the muscles slack. "What?" he finally managed to choke.

"I'm pregnant."

Another long silence as my father stared at my mother. I thought I felt the planets shift in their orbits—or maybe I was imagining it.

"Are you . . . okay?" my father asked my mother. The color leaked from his face, his eyes mirrored his confusion as he struggled with Mona's blindside.

Having been the first lucky recipient of this little tidbit, I knew how he felt.

"And the baby?" he asked.

"We're both fine, darling." Her eyes saucers of fear, Mona brushed her fingers across his cheek. "And past the danger point."

The Big Boss extricated his hand from hers and came to stand by me, leaving her marooned with her fear. Passing a hand wearily over his eyes, he looked out at the lights.

I doubt he saw them.

I hooked my arm through his, but said nothing,

leaving him with his thoughts. Mother's bomb-shell had hit him hard—I could feel him shaking.

The minutes ticked by as we stood like that, father and daughter, together facing the world. I could hear my mother fidgeting nervously behind us, but for once she kept her mouth shut.

Finally, The Big Boss broke the silence. "You and your mother were the best things to ever happen to me. No matter what happened, I always knew I had you. I love you, you know."

I'd waited a lifetime to hear my father say that to me. And now that he had, it didn't change anything—the earth didn't move, my world wasn't rocked, bright lights didn't flash, and bells and whistles didn't go off. In that moment I realized I'd been standing on the bedrock of The Big Boss's love for years. The words merely repeated what I already knew. "I know."

He nervously swiped at a tear. I did the same.

Then he patted my hand and, pulling his arm from mine, he returned to his spot on the couch next to Mother. She looked terrified.

Gently, he stroked her face. "How?" he asked.

"The usual way. You were there." Mona's cheeks reddened. Well, if this wasn't a night of firsts all the way around!

A grin spit his face. "That much I know, but I thought you were too—"

"Old?" Mona huffed, but she still looked like a deer caught in headlights. "Thank you for point-ing that out."

"You must admit, this child is pushing the envelope," my father teased.

"The final treason of my shriveled-up ovaries." Mona deflated. "I know you're angry."

"Angry? Why would you ever think that? I admit, I am a bit stunned, but angry? No."

Mother and I stared at him, mouths agape.

"Really?" I said. "So this is okay with you?" I'd be lying if I said I wasn't relieved. Mother deserved her shot at true love. So did The Big Boss, for that matter.

"A child is a gift," my father explained to me. "With your mother and me, the gifts seem to come at the oddest times, but that doesn't make them any less special. It took me a lifetime of suffering, watching you grow up from afar, not sharing the joy or the responsibility. When you were fifteen and couldn't live in Mona's Place anymore and your mother sent you to me . . . that was the happiest day of my life."

My mother gripped his hand until her knuckles turned white. Tears leaked down her face.

"I made a choice years ago," my father said, his face sobering. "I took the easy way out. I didn't do right by either of you—I cheated all of us—and I've carried that burden ever since."

Mother and I both started to argue, but he held up his hand, silencing us.

"Now, amazingly, life has offered us a second chance, and me, a chance at redemption. I don't know what I did to deserve it, but I couldn't be happier." He turned his attention to me as he pulled my mother back to his shoulder. "I want you to know how sorry I am, Lucky. I wish I could make it up to you—all the lost years—but your childhood is a thing of the past."

"Oh, I wouldn't be too sure," I said, trying to lighten the mood. Drama makes me nervous, and this evening had served up more than I could handle. "Take care of Mother. That will be more than enough for me."

I left them like that, cocooned together on the couch, savoring their togetherness.

I'd never felt so alone. Everyone else's happiness painted my loneliness in stark relief.

While thrilled for them, my heart ached for that kind of joy for me—not the pregnant kind, but the together kind. My parents had carried their torches for a lifetime. I don't know how they'd stood it. Six weeks and I was ready to chuck everything and race to Teddie's side. Totally pathetic. And futile. It wouldn't work—the price was too high. Vegas was my town—a square peg, I fit here. This hotel was my home; my co-workers, my chosen family. If I turned my back on my life here, I'd be like the girl in *Lost Horizon* who attempted to leave Shangri-La—I'd shrivel and die before I made it past the city limits.

Sometimes life sucks.

The lights still burned in my office as I pushed through the door. "Any luck?" I asked Miss P, who looked like she was making preparations to call it a night.

"Your cowboy is calling the last of them." Clearly she wanted more info on how Dane happened to be corralled into the evening's excitement, but she didn't ask. "He's in your office. And I'm going home to a warm bed."

"And a hot guy," I said, wanting to see her blush.

She didn't disappoint. Waving, she disappeared through the door.

Dane, his feet on the desk, nodded at me, the phone pressed to his ear as he listened to someone on the other end of the line.

Plopping myself on my couch and kicking off my shoes, I leaned back, closed my eyes, and tried not to think about the last time I'd been on that couch. Teddie had been angry. I'd been hurt. Who knew office make-up sex could be so delicious?

"Thank you," Dane said, then slammed the receiver back in the cradle. "What are you grinning at?" he asked.

"A memory."

"It must've been good."

"The best." I raised my head and opened my eyes. He had a weird look on his incredible face. For a moment I thought he could read my mind. Now *that* would be really awkward. "Any luck?" I asked.

"Are you sure the paramedics came and got your magician friend?"

"Absolutely. Two guys, bodybuilder types, little red shields on their sleeves, their shirts a couple of sizes too small."

"You would notice that," Dane said with a smile.

"I'm human; sue me," I countered. "They even had the gurney and the breathing thing. Why do you ask?"

"I struck out with the hospitals, so I called the ambulance companies. No one answered a call at the Athena."

"What are you saying?"

"I don't know who picked him up, or where they took him. Quite simply, your Mr. Fortunoff has disappeared."

AFTER he gave me all the details—whom he called and what they told him—Dane went off in search of liquid fortification. I don't know why I agreed to stay and have a drink with him—weakness, perhaps, or not wanting to be alone. But whatever it was, I felt like I'd started down a path toward perdition. Either that or I was a glutton for punishment. Hanging around Dane right now was like working in a candy store after having sworn off chocolate.

As I moved from the couch to the neutral ground of my desk chair, I pulled my cell phone out of my pocket and checked it. Yep, still on, but eerily quiet. Usually the thing was as irritating as an itch I couldn't scratch. No missed calls either. I tried to calculate what time it was on the other side of the world, but I couldn't get my mind around the math. Was Teddie awake, asleep, eating a meal? I hadn't a clue. The only thing I was sure of was that he hadn't called . . . in several days.

I flipped open the thing and dialed Romeo, trying not to be troubled by the fact I had a police detective's number on speed-dial.

"What did you find out about the magician?" he asked without preliminaries.

"He's been abducted by aliens."

"Is that fact or speculation?"

Oh, I liked this kid. I liked him a lot. "How do you prove a theory?"

"How would I know?" Romeo said—his way of conceding defeat. "I flunked geometry."

"That makes two of us."

"Then, back to my original question: Where's the magician and what killed him?"

"I have no idea and I don't know." I proceeded to give the detective the details.

"Let me get this straight," he said when I'd finished. "We have Houdini's Water Torture Cell. Nobody knows where it came from, who owns it, or how it works. Practically the entire universe had access to the thing before the show. And, Dimitri Fortunoff appeared dead when two guys claiming to be paramedics came and whisked him away, leaving us with no body."

"Did anyone see anything unusual?" I asked, ever hopeful.

"Exactly how would you define *unusual* in a case like this?"

"Good point." I heard the outer door open—Dane back with a much-needed elixir.

"Your magician has disappeared," Romeo said, restating the obvious.

I refused to be amused by the irony. "I'll try to get a line on the owner of the Houdini thing. I'll keep you posted," I said, then closed my phone, ending the call.

Dane set a tall glass filled with pink liquid and capped by a tiny umbrella on the desk in front of me, as I redeposited my phone in my pocket.

"What is that?" I asked, eyeing the cutsey drink. "I know you don't do umbrellas."

Dane grinned as he lowered himself into one of the chairs on the far side of my desk. "Don't worry, I have a backup." He set a tumbler filled with two fingers of amber liquid in front of him, next to his Bud longneck.

"Unadulterated liquor is more my style." I held up the glass and gave it a jaundiced eye. "What is this?"

"It's called a Bacardi Party. There's a professional mixologist at the bar, Ron something. Sean insisted you try it—he wouldn't take no for an answer."

Sean, our head bartender, was always trying something new. I gave the brew a sip. "Not bad."

"He said to warn you, it packs a punch."

"Now you're speaking my language."

AFTER the Bacardi Party, I stashed the tumbler of Wild Turkey 101 Dane had brought as a backup in the fridge as emergency rations. This night had packed a wallop already. Still reeling, I didn't need to add too much alcohol to my already overloaded system.

Dane had polished off two beers while regaling me with stories of his west Texas childhood, with two brothers and a mother perpetually at sea as to how to handle all that testosterone. He'd joined the military to get the heck out of the dust bowl of Lubbock, learned to fly, then landed in Atlantic City when his military commitment ended. The Gaming Control Board there had loaned him to its Nevada counterpart, and he'd stayed.

As I listened, I wished I didn't find so much comfort in Dane's nearness. He was a wonderful storyteller—each of us found humor in the same quirks of life. Warm and gentle, yet strong, I felt drawn to him, and I didn't like myself for it. Loneliness has a way of creeping under one's skin and festering like an infection.

Teddie was so far away—the distance diluting the immediacy of our relationship. No longer could we share the details of our days, or ride the waves of our attraction, or simply find comfort and connection in each other's touch. I needed that . . . we needed that . . . if there was a "we" anymore. . . .

"Thanks," I said when Dane finished. From the

look in his eye, I saw he knew what I was thanking him for. Unable to avoid the siren call of sleep, I added, "I better head for the barn."

"Let me walk with you," Dane offered. "It's late."

Rubbing my swollen feet, I eyed my stilettos. There was no way my screaming dogs were going back in those things, so I opted for a pair of Ferragamo flats I kept in the closet. Stuffing my heels in my Hermès Birkin bag, an insanely expensive gift from The Big Boss, I shouldered it and began flipping off lights.

"Thanks for the offer, but I don't think that would be a good idea," I said as I motioned Dane through the door, took one last glance around, then pulled it shut behind me.

"Why not? I promise I'll keep my hands off."

"It's not that." His shoulder touched mine as he walked toward the elevator—I liked it. Which made the developing ease between us all the more uncomfortable. "We have an insurmountable problem, you and I. Apart from the obvious, we work opposite sides of the fence. A Gaming Control Inspector and an executive with a major hotel cannot be seen to be . . . too chummy." I'd almost said "in bed together"—for once my mouth listened to my brain. "A friendship between us would create a huge conflict of interest."

"I've taken care of that. I put in my notice."

"What?" I whirled on him.

He calmly reached for the handle on the stair-well door, then held it open for me.

"You quit your job? Don't tell me I had anything to do with that." I matched his stride down the stairs.

He repeated the door thing at the bottom, then we headed across the lobby. "No, you didn't . . . well, not really. I quit my job to take a better one. But I'd be lying if I said I didn't consider the added bonus of eliminating the conflict between us."

I didn't know whether to be flattered or appalled. "Where will you be working?" We pushed out into the night air—the evening's coolness had given way to cold.

Distracted when I'd closed up the office, I had left my wrap on the couch.

Dane shrugged out of his blazer and settled it over my shoulders.

I started to argue, but found myself fresh out of backbone.

"Jeremy has asked me to join his agency."

"Private detective? That's an interesting choice." Dane and The Beautiful Jeremy Whitlock. Two more gorgeous men would be hard to find—women would pay just to have an hour of their undivided attention.

I crossed my arms, hugging myself as Dane fell into step beside me, heading down the driveway toward the Strip. I thought about asking him what part of "no" he hadn't understood, but didn't. The truth of it was, I liked having him around, and I didn't want to be alone. But letting him get close was like playing with fire.

"I've been handling investigations for the Control Board, so it shouldn't be too big a leap. And I like the idea of working for myself—I have a bit of an authority issue."

"I noticed."

A comfortable silence settled between us as we made the turn around the hotel, leaving the Strip behind. Like a handful of diamonds tossed on velvet, the stars twinkled overhead, just out of reach. To our south, the landing lights of planes on approach to McCarran hung in the sky like a string of lanterns lighting a path to the party. As we moved farther from the bright lights, the inky black of the night enveloped us. I felt the world fall away.

For some odd reason, a childhood memory hit me. I remembered covering myself with a blanket, creating a void to block out the real world. In that darkness, I imagined my own fantasy world—one with handsome princes, a real father, and a mother whose spirit wasn't bent beneath a burden of a sadness I saw but didn't understand.

And it struck me: That's exactly what I was doing right now—I was pretending. Pretending I could have it all—a father without accepting the burden of being his daughter, true love without surrendering completely, the life I wanted without making the hard choices, joy without pain, happiness while avoiding anger.

Anger. That was it. Anger.

Hit with an unfamiliar urge for introspection, I dug deeper.

No, I wasn't angry . . . I was pissed.

Years of bottled-up frustration, of burying emotion, of going along, of not saying how I really felt and of never being asked bubbled up through the cracks in my self-delusion.

I was mad at Teddie for leaving, for turning his back on us so easily. I was mad at my father for waiting a lifetime to tell me. I was mad at Dane for being so damned good-looking and for not taking no for an answer. I was mad at my mother for teaching me my problems came second to everyone else's.

But most of all, I was mad at myself for believing her, for lacking the courage to fight for me, to fight for what *I* wanted . . . without feeling guilty or selfish. This was my life, damn it, and I'd better start fighting for it.

"Dane."

"Hmmm."

"Where do you find courage?" The need for human contact overriding good sense and propriety, I looped my arm through his.

"I've found courage shows up when you need it." If he thought the question odd, I couldn't tell.

He didn't ask me why I asked.

He was making it impossible not to like him.

. . .

FLASHING lights atop a horde of police cruisers greeted us as we turned up the drive to the Presidio—my home away from work. A tall column of glass and steel, the Presidio was considered to be the toniest near-Strip address in Vegas. On Teddie's suggestion, I had bought the next-to-the-top floor at preconstruction, prehype prices. I would have sprung for the top floor, but Teddie had already laid claim to it.

Out of habit and a penchant for self-flagellation, I glanced toward the penthouse—it was dark; I couldn't see Teddie's balcony, or my own, both of which were on the west side of the building, facing the Strip.

I didn't see any fire trucks amid the cruisers, no flames licking the side of the building, no plume of smoke rising from the roof, so I didn't panic.

A throng had gathered at the entrance. Clustered in small knots, people nervously whispered as Dane and I walked up.

I spied a familiar face. Tugging Dane's hand, I said, "Over here. I see somebody who can tell us what's going on."

A former NFL lineman, Forrest was the bulk of our security force—both figuratively and literally. Tall, black, and menacing when he wanted to be, he gave the residents, including me, a comfort we otherwise wouldn't have.

His face brightened when he saw me, but his eyes still looked troubled. "Miss Lucky, you can't go inside yet."

"What's happened?" I asked, quite conscious of Dane's quiet comforting presence at my side.

"Someone broke into Mr. and Mrs. Daniels' apartment on the twenty-fifth floor."

"That should be simple enough. The cameras in the elevator and on the floors should tell you who it was," I said.

But Forrest shook his head. "No, the burglar came in through the window."

Dane and I both looked skyward—with no balconies below the top two floors, using the window as an entrance seemed impossible.

"The window? Are you sure?" Dane asked.

Forrest nodded. "I heard the cops talking. Apparently the guy had a glass cutter—he made himself a nice, neat hole."

"Took jewelry and money, left all the rest?" Dane continued.

"They haven't said what the guy took, but he was slick, alright. He knew right where the safe was and didn't seem to have any trouble busting into it." Forrest looked at me and I saw the question in his eyes.

"This is Mr. Dane," I said, taking Forrest's cue. "He has a background in security work. Dane, this is Forrest, our safety net."

The two men shook hands.

"I didn't do you all no good tonight," Forrest said, hanging his head.

"Some things are impossible to stop," Dane said, his words a salve for Forrest's wounded pride.

"You be careful, Miss Lucky." Forrest's face was a mask of concern. "If he got into the Danielses' place, getting into yours would be a piece of cake—what with the balcony and being so close to the top of the building and all."

On that happy note, Dane and I took our leave. The police were letting the residents back into the building, so we joined the queue, leaving Forrest to find out what he could.

"He's right, you know. You could be next," Dane whispered, as he grabbed my elbow. I wondered if the whole elbow bit was a chivalry thing or a good excuse to try to knock me off-kilter. Knowing Dane, it was probably both.

"He'd be sorely disappointed in the slim pickings at my place." I tried to sound brave, but even though the thief hadn't been in my home, I felt a vicarious violation. And, in keeping with my recent theme of admitting my shortcomings, I felt a bit afraid.

At the elevators, I put my hand on Dane's chest. "This is the end of the trail, Cowboy."

"What if the burglar is hiding in your place? Fighting bad guys is one of my best things."

"You're milking this for all it's worth, but if the guy looks like Cary Grant, I'm good with that, okay?" I stalled for time while I debated with myself.

"*To Catch a Thief*. Good flick. Grace Kelly, man she was one fine filly."

I narrowed my eyes at him and he gave me a

lopsided grin. "Perhaps not the best night to poke this rattlesnake," I said as I tried to make sense of my whirling emotions. But fear finally prevailed over good sense. "Okay, you can come up. But only to check under the bed and in the closets. Deal?"

"Scout's honor." He made a crossing motion over his chest.

The elevator deposited us in the center of my great room.

"Nice digs," Dane said as he drank it all in. "Sort of minimalist though, don't you think?"

A large space with white walls, an occasional splash of art (pastels depicting the many moods of the Mojave), bright furniture dotting the hardwood floor, and little else, I could see why he would call it minimalist. To me it was uncluttered, and I liked it that way—a huge space in which to breathe.

"Where you been, bitch?" A familiar voice rang out, startling Dane.

"Who's here?"

"Just Newton." I grabbed his arm, pulling him toward the kitchen. "Come, let me introduce you."

"You didn't tell me anyone would be here."

"You didn't ask."

When Newton caught sight of me he shouted, "Asshole!" An expression of true love if ever there was one.

Newton is my one foray into pet ownership—a foulmouthed, vividly hued macaw. The service that came in twice a day to feed him had apparently forgotten to cover his cage. The bird danced in delight, muttering, "Bitch, bitch, I'm gonna smack you."

"As you can tell, Newton had a very sketchy upbringing. I'm trying to teach him better manners, but parrots are like old dogs and elephants."

Dane picked up a piece of browned apple from the dish beside the cage and stuffed it through the bars.

"Watch your fingers."

Newton eyed him warily. "Asshole!" shouted the bird, then, like a snake snagging a mouse, he grabbed the apple, and retreated to the far side of the cage with his prize.

"I never took you to be a pet owner," Dane said as he watched the bird.

"Newton picked me. After hearing his vocabulary, I had to keep him." I threw the cover over the cage. "You're supposed to be checking all the dark corners for bad men, remember? The bedrooms are that way."

I let Dane explore by himself. Tonight had been filled with awkward moments and I couldn't stomach one more—the one where I stood there introducing him to my bedroom and boudoir.

He returned shortly, shaking his head. "No bad guys." If he noticed Teddie's sax in the corner, his clothes in the closet, or his shaving stuff on the bathroom counter, he was too polite to mention them. "I guess you're safe for now."

"Darn."

We stood there awkwardly for a moment, then he said, "I better shove off."

"Right."

I handed him back his blazer and walked him to the elevator.

While we waited, he turned to me. Putting a hand on each of my shoulders, he looked me in the eye, a serious expression on his face. "Don't you ever wonder . . . ?"

I touched my lips with two fingers, then pressed them to his. His skin felt hot to my touch. "All the time."

DANE left me alone with my wonderings. Pummeled by the day, I was too exhausted to think, yet too juiced to sleep, so I dragged my sorry carcass to the shower. After a session in front of massaging jets, the water set on scald, my muscles started to relax, the day drifting away with the steam.

I had barely slipped between the sheets, luxuriating in the sensual feel of 1400-count Egyptian cotton and the downy embrace of a feather mattress, when the telephone rang. Thankfully I had tossed the thing on my nightstand, because I wasn't getting out of bed even if the High Priestess and Keeper of the Secrets of the Cult of Multiple Orgasms was calling. Clearly, I needed to work on my priorities.

"O'Toole." I pressed the thing to my ear, but didn't open my eyes.

"Are you naked?"

The familiar voice sent warmth shooting to my core. Who needed the secrets of the cult when they had someone like Teddie? "Completely," I purred, trying my best to sound sexy. "Are you?"

"No. And, since I'm eating brunch at a wonderful brasserie on the Left Bank, that is probably a good thing—I'd be arrested."

"Not on the Left Bank. What are you eating?" Most couples in the throes of new love had phone sex when apart. Teddie and I had food sex.

"I started with onion soup . . . real French onion soup. Made from scratch with just a whiff of tarragon, the cheese so fresh I could almost hear the cows."

I groaned. "You're killing me. What next?" I couldn't remember my last meal.

"Then a croissant with fresh strawberry preserves and an omelet, the eggs whipped to perfection with a hint of basil and rosemary, accompanied by a nice Pinot Blanc from Alsace."

"Don't they shoot you for drinking anything other than Chardonnay in Paris?"

"Kindly, they've let me live." I heard the distance between us in the hollow echo on the line. "I miss holding you," he said.

"Me, too." I gripped the phone and closed my eyes tight, squeezing back the tears. "I hope to hell you're having a great time, because sleeping in this bed, with nothing but the memories of your touch to keep me warm, is no fun at all. It's like trying to sleep in a haunted house."

"Oh man, Lucky, you wouldn't believe all the stuff that's happening," Teddie said, deftly sidestepping my implicit begging for some morsel, some hint that somehow we were going to work out this tortured thing between us. His voice brightened, burbling with happiness. Why did that hurt my heart so bad? "The audiences have been amazing. They actually listen to my stuff now. The energy is intoxicating."

"That's great," I said only half meaning it, then felt guilty for not wanting the world for him. Well, actually I did want the world for him—I just wanted the world to be me.

"Yeah, they've extended the tour a bit, given me more exposure, a larger part to play. Reza and I are even putting together a duet." Teddie opened for Reza Pashiri, the current flavor-of-the-month in Popville. She had a rabid following worldwide, so Teddie couldn't have found a better team to hitch his wagon to.

"And your music . . . are you writing any songs?" That had been Teddie's original dream, our original dream, and the one I had helped him with—until he'd been seduced by the Dark Side.

"I don't have time."

"That's a real shame. You're brilliant."

"If I sent you a ticket, do you think you could meet me in Paris? It's the romance capital of the world—and the food isn't too bad either."

I couldn't think of anything I'd like more than to share the City of Lights with Teddie. "When?"

"Today."

"Today for you is tomorrow for me, right?"

"Right . . . I think. But I meant as soon as you can."

I thought about the coming weekend. My plate was full. With a sinking heart I realized there was no way. "It's Halloween. I'm in charge of the Bondage Ball and the Houdini Séance. We have the UFO crowd in the hotel, and I'm VIPing a group of magicians. I have to finalize the plans for the restaurant at the new hotel with Jean-Charles—construction starts in a couple of days—and I'm missing a magician."

Teddie chuckled—it wasn't a happy chuckle, but more like a resigned, I-knew-you-would-turn-me-down kind of chuckle. "I figured, but I thought I'd ask. Pretty funny when you think about it."

I didn't share his humor—in fact I thought the whole thing very sad, *très tragique* even. "How so?"

"Not funny, really . . . ironic, if anything."

"I sowed the seeds of my own destruction?"

"A bit melodramatic, but close to the mark."

"Teddie," I started, then paused. Needing time to search for some elusive courage, I pushed myself up in bed and plumped the pillows behind me. Dane had been wrong—I sure as hell needed a strong dose, and courage wasn't cooperating. I took a deep breath. "Is there an us anymore?"

"Of course," he said with a snort, as if my IQ had plummeted.

"But it's not the same," I pressed, surprising myself with a hint of backbone—or maybe it was desperation—who knew? Clutching at straws, I went with it. "We need to talk."

"Not over the phone." His voice held defeat. "Please come."

"I can't."

"Then we'll have to shelve this conversation until later."

The hollowness echoed in the silence between us.

"Lucky, I gotta go," Teddie said, his voice brusque. "We've got rehearsal in an hour."

"Teddie . . ."

"Later."

"Fine." My anger seethed, but probably the only thing I knew about men for a fact was if I tried to make them do something they didn't want to, they would go out of their way to make my life miserable. And, right now, I was miserable enough. "Be safe, Teddie."

And be very, very careful.

Chapter

FOUR

♡

The sun hung high in the sky when I pushed through the front doors into the Babylon. Coming to work late was one of the advantages of being at the top of the totem pole, as was having two assistants—who would cover my butt, no questions asked.

For the first time in eons I had slept soundly, without dreams, without nightmares—without haunting memories of the past. Something had changed. Whatever it was, I felt more at peace with the murkiness of the future, more in control—I liked it. Control was generally an illusion—I knew that—but today seemed as good as any to be delusional, so I went with it.

The lobby teemed with life. Nodding to the valets and bellmen, and with a spring in my step, I joined the crowd. Happy voices swirled around me as I worked my way toward the stairwell. Smiling young men and women greeted each guest as they joined the short line in front of Reception. I waved and nodded when I caught an eye. A cocktail waitress took orders, then darted into the casino. Like a practiced orchestra playing under the direction of a world-class conductor, the Babylon hummed—a lilting tune full of promise and excitement—with nary a strident note.

"Ms. O'Toole!"

I'd spoken too soon.

Sergio Fabiano, our front desk manager, had called to me—I'd recognize his smooth voice, perpetually pitched with panic, anywhere. Dark hair, dark skin, smoldering eyes, and the body of a Greek god, Sergio attracted female attention like misbehaving celebrities attract the paparazzi. However, he was a bit fussy for my tastes.

Out of breath and clearly out of patience, he rushed to my side. "We have an issue on the golf course that needs your attention."

I waited for more, but he just stared at me with those impenetrable eyes. "Are you going to give me a hint, or just toss me to the wolves?" I finally asked.

He threw up his hands. "I do not know what they are saying—something about a gold-plated Scotty."

Gold-plated Scotty? Now that conjured interesting pictures. "I'm on it."

IN keeping with The Big Boss's exacting standards, our golf course had been designed by the best in the business and regularly made the list of top ten courses in the country. Occupying one hundred and forty acres of prime real estate directly behind the hotel, with tall pines, lush vegetation, and numerous water features—including a huge waterfall—the course was an oasis, a seemingly impossible patch of green in the stark browns of the Mojave. Recently we had come under fire for all the water it took to keep it green, but I don't think The Big Boss gave the complaints more than a passing thought.

Did the locals really think people flocked to Vegas to experience the desert? If they did, they were as clueless as the do-gooders trying to "clean up" Sin City. If Vegas became just another buckle on the Bible Belt, then the forty-five million visitors a year would be history and our goose thoroughly cooked.

A young man drove me out to the twelfth tee, where I found two angry knots of people hurling verbal spears at each other. A crowd gathered around them, effectively bringing the day's golf to a grinding halt.

Our head pro, Jay Mc "G," stood bravely between the warring factions; two security guys provided reinforcement. One group clustered behind a gentleman in bright green and yellow plaid pants, a yellow shirt, bright green golf shoes, and a crimson face—proof that golf isn't so much a sport as an excuse to dress badly. The second group consisted of one of our caddies, soaking wet and clad in only a pair of rather thin boxer briefs—made all the more transparent by the soaking—backed by several of his mates. At an impasse, the two sides glared at each other.

Everybody started talking at once when they saw me.

"One at a time," I barked. "Jay, give me the short version."

Before Jay could open his mouth, Mr. Green-and-Yellow pointed to our almost naked caddie and shouted, "I want this worthless piece of crap fired!"

My eyes went all slitty—nobody calls a Babylon employee a worthless piece of crap. I held up my hand and gave him my best scowl. It must've been good—the guy backed down. Of course, I had that whole height-weight advantage thing going for me.

"Mr. Jenkins," Jay said, gesturing toward our potty-mouthed shouter, "lost his temper and threw his putter in the lake."

"You mean all of this is about a putter?"

"Not just any putter. A gold-plated Scotty Cameron," said the caddie. "He threw it in the lake. I swam for it, so it's mine."

I glanced at the lake. "You went swimming in *that*?" The water's unnatural blue-green color reminded me of toilet bowl cleaner. All the water in Vegas looked like that—the result of algaecide, or so I'd been told.

"Yes, ma'am."

I might not always be swift on the uptake, but even I was beginning to understand this was no ordinary putter. "Give me some perspective here, Jay."

"Six grand."

"It's a limited edition autographed by Tiger Woods and the rest of the last Ryder Cup team," shouted Mr. Jenkins. "And it's *Dr.* Jenkins."

A doctor! Terrific. If I lost my cool and stuffed the thing up his ass, maybe he could extricate it with minimal blood loss.

I raised an eyebrow at Jay.

"Perhaps nine grand," he admitted.

Squinting my eyes against the sun, I looked out over the golf course. This was an interesting problem, without an easy solution. If I gave the putter back to the jerk, I'd be letting our people down. If I gave it to the caddie, I'd be a hero in the employee locker room, but I'd alienate a valued guest and run the risk of generating some negative press, and perhaps a lawsuit, in the process. I wondered just how valued a guest Dr. Jenkins was. With everyone watching me like dogs eyeing leftovers, I couldn't exactly call my office and ask how much money the guy kept in play.

"Dr. Jenkins, is this your first visit to the Babylon?" I asked.

"And quite likely my last," he growled.

"Oh, you haven't given us a chance yet." I gave him my best smile—sucking up is a major part of my job description. "What kind of doctor are you?"

"I'm actually a college professor with a PhD in archeology."

"Really? What's your specialty?" I doubted a

pile-it-higher-and-deeper doctor would have much money to wager, but I'd been surprised before . . . and apparently he *did* have an incredible putter. . . .

"I'm considered an authority on the ancient astronaut theory and monolithic structures."

"You mean like Tiahuanaco, Teotihuacan, Baalbek, Rapa Nui?" What can I say? Sleepless nights and a History Channel addiction . . .

He looked at me with a glimmer of respect. "Exactly."

"And now researchers are noting similarities between some of these structures and ancient landforms found on Mars, which raises some interesting questions," I said, as if everyone was discussing this stuff.

"Precisely," Jenkins said warmly. "My life's work is to prove these structures are connected." Dr. Jenkins's face lost its mask of anger as he warmed to the subject. The man was mine. "The Mars finding adds a level of proof to what I have known for years: We've been visited by ancient astronauts before, and in all likelihood, will be again."

For the past several years, the spookies had been praying for an academic with stellar credentials to lend credibility to their cause. Apparently Jenkins was the chosen one—their messiah to lead them out of the murky realm of fringe science.

"So, Dr. Jenkins, you're here with the UFO conference?" I asked innocently.

"I'm the keynote speaker on Saturday."

"I would love to sit and talk with you, perhaps at the cocktail party tomorrow," I said with sincerity—getting a glimpse into what made him tick would be fascinating. "But right now we have a putter problem to solve."

Dr. Jenkins nodded; he no longer looked homicidal.

I turned to the caddie, who had stepped back into his jumpsuit while I talked to Jenkins. "What's your name?"

"Brady, ma'am."

"Well, Brady, what plans do you have for that putter?"

"You mean I can keep it?"

Dr. Jenkins spluttered, but didn't erupt.

"I didn't say that. I just want to know what you plan to do with the thing."

"It'd bring a pile on eBay."

Ah, money . . . the measure of every desire. "Dr. Jenkins, how much is that putter worth to you?"

"Why are you asking?" A smart man, he could see where I was heading.

"You threw the putter away. Brady risked life, limb, and the possibility of a nasty infection to retrieve it. Seems to me that's worth something. Of course, we could just throw the thing back in the lake and you can dive for it."

The rest of the fight leaked out of him as he eyed the water. "I see your point." He even gave me the hint of a grin, now that we were practically colleagues and all. "You have an amount in mind?"

"That's between you and Brady. You two figure it out."

Jenkins grabbed the putter from Jay and motioned for the caddie to follow him out of earshot.

They conferred for a moment, then seemed to reach an agreement.

"Jay, get our good doctor another caddie." I crooked a finger at Brady when he came back to the group. "You, come with me."

By the time I had stalked back to the hotel, the caddie trailing me like a recalcitrant puppy, I had calmed down enough to use words longer than four letters. Stopping in a corner, hidden from curious stares and eavesdroppers, I turned and braced my young charge. "Son, I should fire you on the spot. You put me in an impossible position with one of our guests, who is not only paying a princely sum to stay in our hotel, but who also forked over serious green to play this course."

"But, the guy is a—"

I waggled a finger in his face, just like my mother used to do to me. *God, was I turning into Mona? Just shoot me now . . .*

I tucked away my finger. "I'm not finished. And I don't care what he was. The world is full of jerks. You make serious money here. The list of guys willing to sacrifice body parts for a shot at your job would stretch from Mandalay Bay to the Wynn—

and back again. One more screwup, and they'll get the chance. You got it?"

"Yes, Ms. O'Toole." Brady concentrated on the concrete between his feet. "I'm real sorry."

"Be smart, kid. That guy wasn't going in the lake. You could have finished the round, wormed a good tip out of him, then gone back and gotten the putter later. Everybody would've been happy."

At the softening of my tone, Brady cocked a wary eye at me.

"Remember, you represent this hotel, and the guest—"

"—is always right?" he said, finishing my sentence.

"Heck no. But it's our job to make him think he is."

"IF it isn't our fearless leader," Miss P teased when I pushed through the office door. "It's about time you showed up."

Today she sported a peach sweater that draped provocatively off one shoulder and pencil-leg brown pants. Since gold and turquoise go with everything, she hadn't changed her jewelry. Afterglow had replaced the hint of wicked in her eyes. I never had to ask her about her sex life—she wore it on her face.

"You're the one who told me I needed to delegate more," I quipped. "And I might add you look positively dewy today." I took the stack of phone messages she extended toward me. "Anything important?"

"Chef Tastycakes called to confirm your dinner. He said he would provide the wine and, I quote, 'something special to eat' if you would bring the pictures." Miss P gave me a questioning look over the top of her reading glasses—her lascivious grin was overkill. "What kind of dinner *are* you planning?"

"I call it seduction over blueprints—sort of my own twist on the whole 'come up and see my etchings' scenario," I said, which of course was patently false, but she dangled the bait knowing I would take it—I couldn't disappoint. "And you needn't give me that grin. I know you are quite familiar with Jean-Charles's penchant for misusing words to achieve the desired effect. We both know he speaks the King's English better than we do." Flipping through the messages I handed several back to her and pocketed one from Romeo.

"Wine at seven, dinner at eight. He said you knew where."

"I do." I saw the question in her eyes, but I was not going there. For some reason lately, I seemed to be a glutton for punishment—handsome men, private meetings. Clearly my unsatisfied libido was running the show and putting me squarely in the line of fire. "Chef Tastycakes? Who's the wiseacre who came up with that?"

Miss P tilted her head toward my second

assistant, Brandy, who looked sheepish. "Are you angry?" Brandy asked.

"Heck no. I wish I'd thought of it—it's perfect."

Young, brilliant, and beautiful, with long brown hair, eyes I'd heard nauseatingly described as "bottomless pools of azure as deep and as mysterious as the ever-changing moods of the Aegean," a body like a brick shithouse, hands that should be registered as lethal weapons, *and* questionable taste in men, Brandy was the newest addition to my staff.

"But I would caution you against using Chef Tastycakes in Jean-Charles's presence—you might get more than you bargained for," I counseled.

A world-renowned chef, Jean-Charles Bouclet was The Big Boss's latest coup. Hired to design and supervise the flagship restaurant at the redesigned Athena, Chef Bouclet was . . . French. Enough said.

"Anything else?" I asked Miss P.

"A call came for you a while ago, but there was no follow-up. Something about a gold Scotty?"

"A fracas on the golf course. Already taken care of." At Miss P's raised eyebrow I said, "And here you thought I'd been loafing the day away."

"Oh, and Flash is waiting in your office. She's been on the phone since she took up residence an hour ago. I sincerely hope she's not calling Mumbai or Bhutan."

"With that woman, you never know."

FEDERIKA "Flash" Gordon was Las Vegas's most tenacious investigative reporter and a longtime friend. We'd met while students at UNLV—I kept her out of jail, she kept us both out of the newspapers. A night with too much tequila and a busload of NBA players branded her Flash, but that's all I can say—I've been sworn to secrecy.

Flash occupied Dane's spot from last night—butt in my chair, feet on the desk, a phone pressed to her ear. Balancing a pad on one leg, she scribbled notes in her own unique Sanskrit.

She grinned a greeting as I stashed my Birkin in the closet. Not wanting to even pretend I owned the mountain of paper on my desk, I took the chair opposite her as she finished her call.

If voluptuous ever made a comeback, Flash would be the pinup. Short and buxom, with a riotous mane of red hair, breasts large enough to make a plastic surgeon cringe, and carrying twenty pounds too many according to today's cadaverous standards, Flash regularly poured herself into clothes that resembled rejects from the children's department. Today she threatened to explode out of a tie-dyed Grateful Dead tee shirt that looked like it had been thrown away in the late 1970s, and a pair of True Religion jeans that gave new meaning to the term "muffin top." A pair of pink Christian Louboutin stilettos on her feet and a white Chanel J12 encrusted with diamonds on her wrist completed her carefully crafted costume. Behind the bimbo façade, Flash camouflaged a brilliant mind, a nose for the news, and a killer instinct that would make a pit bull proud.

"That Romeo, he's a little sweetheart," Flash cooed, as she cradled the phone and looked at me benignly—the look she always used before she planted a dagger. "He's my new BFF. You've been demoted."

"Today's my lucky day."

"With all I do for you, I can't believe you're holding out on me." My friend turned on her all-business mode. "Give it up, girlfriend. I want to know all there is to know about the vanishing magician."

"I got the feeling there's more than meets the eye, but a feeling is all I've got." I picked up a paperweight from the corner of my desk—a cockroach, spray-painted gold and embedded in plastic. It had been a gift from the employees after my battle with a guest who had tried to blackmail the hotel with thousands of bugs. For some reason, I liked the thing—it made me smile. "I'm sure Romeo brought you up to speed."

"If that's all you got, you're right—you got zilch." Flash's feet hit the floor with a thud of displeasure. "Look, I've got a deadline every day. This story is huge—it's captured the city. See for yourself." She tossed a copy of this morning's *Review-Journal* in front of me.

A one-inch headline topped a half-page article with Flash's byline. I replaced the cockroach trophy as I scanned the page—a recitation of known facts, nothing more. When I pushed the paper back to her, the top of a photo caught my eye. I flipped the newspaper over to see the whole thing—a picture taken last night in front of the Presidio.

Something hit me. I squinted at the grainy photo.

"Mr. Daniels, the owner of the apartment . . . he looks familiar."

"I'm dying here and you want to talk about a break-in?" Flash said. "Of course he looks familiar, he lives in your building."

"I've seen him." I tapped the paper as I tried to remember. "Recently. And not at home, which I rarely get to visit anyway."

Flash knew me well enough to sit still and let me work it through.

The tick of the clock measured the seconds, then it hit me. "The Great Danilov! Mr. Daniels *is* the Great Danilov," I announced.

"That mind-reading guy who could bend spoons and give people posthypnotic suggestions so they would jump around and bark like dogs?" Flash didn't sound impressed.

I nodded.

"Are you sure?"

"He was at the Calliope party. Dimitri even called him onstage with some other magicians to inspect the water contraption. He singled him out, introduced him to the crowd."

"Introduced him? As a colleague?"

"No." I shook my head as I tried to remember. "At the time I thought Dimitri was rude, almost condescending, but I dismissed it because it was so unlike him. But now, thinking back, I was right—

there was something between the two of them, something personal."

"I'd sure like to know what," Flash said, baring her reporter's fangs. "And don't you find it rather coincidental that on the night the magician disappears, the Great Danilov's apartment is robbed?"

"Don't go jumping to conclusions," I cautioned.

Leaning back in my desk chair, Flash toyed with a pencil. "I sure would like to know what was taken out of the Danilov's apartment," she muttered as she cocked an eyebrow at me.

"No way," I said, knowing where she was going.

"Come on. Romeo clams up when he sees me, but he owes you. I mean, you practically made his career."

"That is way overstating. He's a good cop, and if he doesn't want that information leaked, I would abide by his wishes . . . assuming he would even tell me in the first place, which he probably wouldn't."

"What about a connection between Danilov and Mr. Fortunoff? Could you hit up some of your sources?" Flash cajoled. Apparently I was now one of her minions.

"Let's meet in the middle," I countered. "You do the legwork. Narrow the scope, find something we can go with, and I'll find someone who can shed some light on it. Deal?" I pushed myself to my feet. She didn't say anything, which I took as an indication of her tacit agreement. "Now beat it, I've got to tackle this desk before someone declares my office a Superfund site. Then I have to get a very difficult chef to sign off on the drawings for his restaurant, shepherd a group of VIP magicians through the rest of the week, keep the UFO folks in check, finalize the Houdini Séance and the Bondage Ball, and live to tell about it."

"No wonder you always look ragged."

"I'm *so* glad you stopped by. You do wonders for my ego." I shooed her out of my chair and settled in.

"Is Teddie taking you to the ball?"

"He's in Paris, last I heard."

Flash squeezed my shoulder. "You okay?"

"Sure," I said through a fake smile. I knew she could tell I was lying.

"You *are* going to the ball?" she pressed.

"It's part of my job."

"Do you have a costume figured out?"

"I thought I'd go as the hotel executive in charge. Besides, I draw the line at parading around in public sheathed only in Saran Wrap." Halloween was one of the few weekends in Vegas where nudity was not only tolerated, it was encouraged.

"I'm with you there," Flash said as she grabbed her bag, stuffing the newspaper inside. "I've got mine all figured out—Little Bo Peep with a twist."

"I can hardly wait."

RETRIEVING Romeo's phone message from my pocket, I pushed aside some papers, then smoothed it out on my desk. I waited until Flash said her good-byes to the girls and closed the outer door behind her before picking up the phone.

Romeo answered on the first ring. "This is the screwiest case," he said, diving right in. "I hope you got more than I got."

"What do you got?" I asked, not wanting to show my cards until I saw his.

"An abandoned ambulance twenty miles south of Jean. The guys are long gone. We're running trace on it now, but I doubt we'll find anything meaningful."

"Who owns the ambulance?"

"An outfit here in town. They reported it stolen yesterday afternoon. Nobody saw who took it."

"We already have a description of the guys who showed up at the Calliope Theatre masquerading as paramedics," I said, showing my flair for the obvious.

"I've showed you mine. Now show me yours," said Romeo, the student playing the master.

I felt like a momma bird that had pushed a fledgling out of the nest and now watched it fly, so I told him about the Daniels-Danilov connection.

"That raises some interesting questions, doesn't it?" Romeo remarked when I finished.

I was smart enough to know a rhetorical question when I heard one. "You wouldn't happen to know what the thief was after, would you?"

"It's not my case, but I know the gal working it.

She owes me. I'll let you know if I come up with anything."

"Great. If we could just start making a connection or two . . ." I mused out loud. "What about Molly Rain, Mr. Fortunoff's assistant? Did she have anything useful to say?"

"Molly Rain? I didn't know she worked for Dimitri."

"You know her?"

"Yeah, we took some magic classes together and we're both members of the Houdini Club."

"She's a magician also?"

"Strictly small-time, like me," Romeo said, sounding modest.

"Tell me about the Houdini Club."

"We're just a group of amateurs who like to practice the stuff Houdini made famous. Sometimes big names drop by to show us something cool, but mostly it's folks like Dimitri who help us with tricks and refining our presentations. Marik Kovalenko got the whole thing started years ago. When he shows up, it's a really big deal."

Marik Kovalenko. Now there's a name I hadn't heard in a while. We'd both hit Vegas at about the same time. Our paths had crossed when The Big Boss had put me in charge of booking a show for an event with national exposure. Marik had auditioned, but I had thought his act wasn't polished enough, so I picked someone else. Now an international superstar specializing in escapes and making pachyderms disappear, he'd never forgiven me.

"Has Mr. Kovalenko been by recently?" I asked.

"Last week. Why?"

So he was in town. Interesting. "You never know when we might need a Houdini expert," I said in reply.

"Good point," my young detective remarked.

"Back to Molly," I said, redirecting the conversation. "What did she have to say?"

"Nothing. We didn't talk to her."

"Why not?" I asked. "Molly, of all people, should know something."

"She wasn't there."

"What do you mean she wasn't there? Of course she was there. I saw her before the show, then she ran out on stage crying about Dimitri. Heck, she even gave the poor guy CPR until the paramedics arrived."

"She didn't leave with them?" Romeo asked in his detective voice.

"No, I talked to her after the paramedics had taken away the body."

"Terrific," Romeo said. "Now we have two disappearing magicians."

Chapter

FIVE

♡

"Do you own a gun?" Dane's voice sounded from the doorway.

"It depends. Who do you want to shoot?" I didn't look up from the pile of paper I was still working on, despite another hour invested.

"I'm serious."

"What would I need a gun for?"

"It might come in handy—you never know. That guy last night didn't seem to have too much trouble breaking into your building." Dane sat on the couch and stretched his long legs in my direction.

I tried not to stare.

"Your place would be even easier." Dane gave me that look, as if he knew what I was thinking.

It made me a little hot and bothered, which, lately, wasn't at all unusual.

"We established *that* fact already, thank you." I'd never thought of gun ownership before. Always a Pollyanna, I'd had a sense of security in my apartment—a false sense, apparently.

"You should really think about protecting yourself."

"A gun seems like overkill, don't you think?"

"Sarcasm, the defense of last resort."

Dane really was too clever for my own good.

"I know this guy," he continued, eyeing me with those unsettling green eyes. "I could hook you up."

"Whenever someone has told me 'I can hook you up,' it has always turned out badly."

"If you're trying to sidetrack me, it won't work—I have a one-track mind," Dane said, his face a mask.

"The Curse of the Y Chromosome."

Momentarily at a loss for words, he shot me a dirty look.

Two points for the home team. I resisted a victory smirk.

"Seriously, let me take you to the shooting range. You can get the feel for handling a firearm, then we can go from there."

"Shooting at something does sound appealing."

"Great." He slapped his thighs as he rose to go, then threw me a look as my words registered. "I'll pick you up in front of your place. I'll be the one wearing a flak jacket. Is eight o'clock tomorrow too early?"

"In the morning?"

"It's best to get there early. You wouldn't believe the number of folks interested in firing fully automatic weapons."

"It's fun to be naughty." I slapped my hand over my mouth the minute the words escaped.

"I wouldn't know. I'm a good boy," he deadpanned.

"My ass." I threw up my hands. My mouth could get me in more trouble . . .

Dane laughed. I wished he'd quit doing that. At least he was a good sport, letting me hang myself with my own rope.

"I'll meet you out front at eight, although I can't promise I will be even marginally functional," I said. "And for the record, I don't want some wimpy, girly gun."

He narrowed his eyes at me. "Would that be a technical term?"

I felt like sticking my tongue out at him, but didn't. I was in over my head as it was.

He turned to go.

"Oh," I said, stopping him. "A chance to squeeze off a few rounds with an Uzi would be . . . cathartic."

He gave me a long look over his shoulder, but didn't ask for more. I liked that. Damn.

As I watched his perfect backside disappear out the door I wondered exactly when I had lost the ability to say no to Dane.

SIGNS of life in the outer office stilled and the phone stopped ringing by the time I signed the last piece of paper on my desk. Being a people person, I had initially been overwhelmed by the mountain of office work that came with my job. At first, I thought I would use the "Goodwill" method to handle it all—let it accumulate, then get rid of anything I hadn't touched in a year. That worked until the piles of papers began drifting to the floor . . . and until Miss P took to filling my chair with the offending missives.

With far too much glee, I took the whole stack of signed documents and deposited it in my first assistant's chair. Two could play this game.

Giddy with the thrill of victory, I retrieved my Birkin and stepped to the mirror in the tiny bathroom to make necessary repairs. After touching up my lipstick and combing my hair, I stowed the tools of the trade and took stock of my reflection. Not bad, but still nothing any poet would write a sonnet about, if they even did that anymore. Once I had been the inspiration for songs Teddie had written, but now he followed the beat of a different drum—and I hadn't heard that song in a while.

Teddie's call last night had been the first in a long time—okay, it'd been five days, seventeen hours, and thirty-two minutes . . . but who's keeping track? When he first left, I'd tried reaching him, but any attempt rolled to voice mail. After a while I quit—his explanations for being out-of-pocket didn't ring true and I desperately wanted to avoid any hint of desperation. The truth of it was, with time and distance, while I missed him in my bed, I missed talking to him most of all. Once upon a time, we'd been best friends.

Now I didn't know what we were. Why I kept the home fires burning, I don't know. Loyalty? Inertia? The spine of a jellyfish? Who knew? The whole thing clouded my days as if someone painted my vision with broad strokes from a bucket of gloom—which was *so* not me.

Even *I* was getting tired of myself.

Grabbing the plans for the new restaurant and tucking them under my arm, I took a quick look around. Back from dinner, Miss Patterson burst through the outer door just as I clicked off my office light. Her glowing face, her lilting laugh, and an odd distracted look in her eye told me The Beautiful Jeremy Whitlock was in range.

Hot on her heels, he filled the doorway—all six foot two, two hundred and something pounds of delicious Aussie. Golden brown hair that matched his eyes, broad where he should be and not where he shouldn't, with dimples to set a girl's heart aflutter, Jeremy had taken a shine to Miss P and never looked back. Since their first date, they'd been stuck together like two hard candies in the summer sun until they'd almost melted together, impossible to tell where one ended and the other began.

"Hey, Lucky! Maybe you can tell me," Jeremy said when he caught sight of me.

Over his shoulder Miss P shook her head, her eyes wide and scared, her smile vanishing.

"Tell you what?"

"My lady's birthday is coming up, but she won't tell me which one. Do you know?"

"Yes."

He rubbed his hands with glee as he winked at Miss P. "So, which is it?"

"If Miss P doesn't want you to know, do you really think I will tell you?" I brushed past him as I said to Miss P, "Forward the phones to Security, close up, and head home. I'll be off-property, but close by. If anything comes up, I can be reached on my cell."

"Can't you give me a hint?" Jeremy gave me his best hangdog look as he put himself between the door and me.

"Silly man." I put a hand to his chest and moved him aside. "I wouldn't betray a friend if the fate of the free world hung in the balance."

He shot me those dimples. My heart fluttered. God, save me from myself.

I checked my cell—the battery was charged, the power on, no missed phone calls, no voice mail (What else was new?)—then dropped it in my pocket. "I gotta run. If I don't hurry a certain Frenchman will lace my dinner with arsenic, and I won't see tomorrow."

Tardiness offended Chef Bouclet, especially when he was cooking.

AT the stroke of seven, the elevator disgorged me on the top floor of the Athena. I followed an empty hallway covered with threadbare carpet, past walls plastered with grimy wallpaper dotted with lighter squares that marked where artwork had previously hung. At the far end of the hall, the double doors to the former flagship restaurant stood open. The restaurant had been "Closed for Renovation" since the chef walked out almost a year ago.

Now a vast, empty cavern—dingy and worn, the carpet torn, the hardwood floors scratched and bare, the light fixtures old and broken—the space held none of its past glory. However, with high ceilings and 180-degree views of the Strip through its walls of glass, it held promise.

I followed my nose and the sound of whistling— the tune sounded strangely like "La Vie en Rose"— which led me straight to the kitchen. Jean-Charles Bouclet, his back to me, whistled as he jiggled pans and peeked under lids.

"You better be nice to me or I will report you to the French Ministry of Culture," I teased, then delighted at the hand-caught-in-the-cookie-jar look on Jean-Charles's face. "I thought true Frenchmen disdained that silly tune as American-inspired drivel."

"I am whistling it for your benefit," he replied, a smile breaking his face as he wiped his hands on the cloth hanging from his waist and rushed to greet me.

He was most definitely *très magnifique*. Trim and tall enough, a few years older than me by my best guess, Jean-Charles carried himself with regal bearing. His soft brown hair curled over his collar and his blue eyes sparked with his every emotion. His smile, albeit infrequent, could take a girl's breath. Tonight he wore his chef's attire, which covered what I knew to be a godlike physique and a nice ass. And then there was that accent. . . .

He took my hand and lifted it to his lips, surprising me. We'd not crossed the business formality barrier before. My hand pressed to his lips, he raised his eyes to mine, catching them for a moment. Even though I was prepared for his act, my pulse leapt. When his skin touched mine, something shifted inside me. Clearly, my body had lost any discernment whatsoever—starved for attention, now any male would do. Even one who was shallow, and transparent, using his considerable charms to get his way.

Typically French, Jean-Charles elevated seduction to an art form. Like a birthright, he wore the manner of a man accustomed to females dropping at his feet, offering him their souls—and everything else.

That was *so* not me. And he was *so* not my type. I repeated this last phrase over and over in my head in hope that I would actually believe it. Unfortunately, men like Jean-Charles were everybody's type—at least for a weekend.

Culinary wunderkinder are like magicians—all sleight of hand and illusion—their celebrity status hinging on their ability to make us believe we are fools if we can't recognize their genius. Jean-Charles Bouclet had the formula down pat. On a good day, I found the whole prima donna thing silly. On a bad day, I found it irritating. Today had not been a particularly good day.

"You are beautiful," Jean-Charles said, looking as if he actually meant it.

"Thank you." I narrowed my eyes at him. "I don't trust you when you're being nice. If you're trying to butter me up, it won't work."

"Why would I spread you with butter?" His eyes, a delicious shade of robin's-egg blue, widened with innocence.

"You wouldn't, not if you know what's good for you. It's a saying that means you are being nice to get something you want." I couldn't tell if he was playing me or not. I didn't like to be played.

"Ah," he said, but he didn't respond to my implication.

Still holding my hand he led me to a small table next to the gas stove. Patting a stool he said, "Sit." He poured a bloodred wine from a decanter into a pencil-stemmed glass as I took my position on the stool as ordered.

Leaving the plans rolled up for now, I set them on the floor at my feet, next to my Birkin. "Whatever you are cooking, it smells delicious."

"But of course." He turned his attention back to the various pots and pans. Using the towel to protect his hand, he lifted lids and tossed contents of sauté pans. "Did you know they have a farmers' market here? It is open all year," he said in a pleasant, conversational tone as if he were talking about the weather rather than girding for battle.

"Civilization finds Las Vegas, the last outpost?" At his frown, I turned off the sarcasm. If he wanted to be civil before first blood was drawn, I could rise to the occasion. "No, I didn't know. I don't cook."

"Food is one of the pleasures of life," Jean-Charles announced with that approachable arrogance the French mastered and made uniquely their own. "Perhaps I will educate you to its pleasures."

The innuendo irritated me, but I had my answer: He was playing me. I pointed to the stove. "Tell me what you're cooking."

Jean-Charles's mouth formed a thin line. "Cooking is such a common term. Your mother cooks. I create."

He obviously didn't know Mona. Her only experience with a kitchen was to walk through it on the way to the garage. "Sorry," I said, not feeling the least bit remorseful. "What are you . . . preparing?"

His frown indicated he didn't find that word any more appealing, but he let it go. "This new hotel . . . *Cielo, non*?" He paused and gave me that Gallic look, quizzical yet confident.

"*Cielo*, yes. A Spanish word meaning 'Heaven,'" I confirmed unnecessarily—the man spoke five languages. "Cielo, as the refurbished Athena will be known, will be Vegas's first green property, completely environmentally friendly."

"So I thought." The chef nodded, his mouth still

set in a firm line. "I have done many restaurants. All are wonderful, but you give me a problem."

"I've been told I'm good at that."

"I would believe that, yes. But this problem I have is what will be this wonderful restaurant I will make here, in this, how do you say it? This green hotel?" When he said the word *green*, his face contorted as if he'd taken a bite of lemon.

"The idea of eco-friendly may not be palatable, but I assure you it is timely. And don't think our guests will be reduced to rubbing two sticks together to heat their bathwater. A stay at Cielo will be a luxurious, indulgent experience. I'm counting on you for food to match."

"Your Big Boss has much faith in you." Jean-Charles cocked his head as he looked at me. "I do not think it is misplaced. You are a force."

"Remember that," I said in all seriousness.

"I cannot forget." Jean-Charles's eyes snapped with sudden anger. "You disgraced me in front of my staff."

"You disgraced yourself—I merely cleaned up the mess." Our first duel had been over broken crockery and a temper tantrum.

A moment passed, then he gave me that Gallic shrug and a disarming smile, breaking the tension, but he had given me a glimpse behind the mask. "Perhaps you are right, but let's not talk of such things now."

"You were telling me about your idea for the concept of this restaurant?"

"*Oui.* To be consistent with your earth-friendly theme, I want to build this restaurant around locally grown, organic produce and locally raised, natural beef and poultry. The seafood will be flown in fresh, of course."

"You do know we are sitting in the middle of a desert?"

"A trifling matter." He dismissed my comment with a wave of his hand, as if swatting at a pesky gnat.

"If you throw enough money at it," I growled, mostly for my own benefit. The line in the sand had been drawn.

"Try your wine, it has breathed long enough," Jean-Charles suggested, shelving the battle for later.

When it came to wine, I didn't need to be asked twice. Grasping the stem of my glass, I lifted it, peering into its maroon depths, then swirled it and watched the legs of the wine trail into the glass. I took a sniff, then a taste, letting the lush liquid linger on my palate and the elegant bouquet fill my nostrils before finally swallowing.

"There are only two wines in the world," I said in answer to Jean-Charles's raised eyebrow. "A fine wine from Bordeaux and everything else. What is this? I've not tasted it before. It's balanced, subtle yet complex, with a knockout nose—full-bodied with a hint of fruit. Black currant, maybe. Absolutely divine."

"A ten-year-old bottle of Chateau Lafite-Rothschild. And you described it perfectly."

Chateau Lafite-Rothschild! A wine served to royalty. An elixir of the gods! Jean-Charles had broken out the good stuff—the heavy artillery. I didn't know whether to be flattered or to run for cover.

"It exceeds its reputation. You were saying?" I prodded.

He stared at me for a moment, as if his thoughts had flown. "What?" he said.

"The farmers' market? Organic? Natural beef? Fresh seafood?"

"Yes, yes." He refocused. "The farmers' market will be a good resource. I've worked out deals with various vendors already. What they can't get locally, they bring from California."

"Your menu will change with the seasons, then?" I took another sip of wine and groaned in delight, eliciting a delighted grin from my chef.

"Perhaps weekly, even daily, depending on what I can get."

"You're making it very hands-on. How will you handle that when you move back to New York?"

Our contract required he design the restaurant, develop the menu, train the staff, then conduct quarterly inspections once he had everything running smoothly. The assumption had been he would return to New York and his namesake restaurant there.

Bending down, Jean-Charles used the towel to pull open the door of the oven. Incredible aromas billowed out. "I'm not moving back."

"You're not?" My glass halfway to my lips, I stopped. I thought my heart skipped a beat—the ultimate mutiny. Surely I imagined it.

"I find life here interesting." The chef gave me a wry smile and a half shrug. "I am liking the burger restaurant—Americans have curious palates."

While waiting for his space in the Athena, Jean-Charles had opened a gourmet hamburger restaurant, to resounding applause, in the Bazaar at the Babylon.

"You don't find Vegas culturally bereft?"

"Perhaps, but this city has other treasures. We can be . . . friends, *oui*?"

"Let bygones be bygones? Water under the bridge and all of that?"

Clearly not fluent in colonial vernacular, he eyed me. "*Oui*," he said, hesitation in his eyes. "If this means we no longer fight, I happily agree."

He was lying through his teeth. I'd publicly put a huge bruise on his ego. He was a man—at some point he would make me pay. "That's what it means." I raised my glass in toast. "To friends."

He tilted his head in agreement and clinked his glass to mine.

Oh yes, he was very good indeed.

DINNER was superb. Given that it was late fall, and Jean-Charles insisted on cooking with seasonal vegetables, my expectations were limited. After all, what can one do with gourds besides fill them with beads for the kids to shake in music class? And I'd never been a squash fan—until now.

A culinary magician, Jean-Charles showed his skill in preparing lamb chops over a vegetable ragout, herbed artisan bread with freshly churned butter, then, in the finest European tradition, a light salad, and a cheese plate to follow. All complemented by a second bottle of Chateau Lafite-Rothschild. Classy, delicious, just enough, but not too much, elegant . . . The Big Boss had hired a winner.

And he was forcing me to reevaluate my stance that cooking is a universal skill—excepting Mona, of course.

Once he'd served us both, Jean-Charles had also proven himself as adept at small talk as he was in the kitchen—a natural charm emanated from him like excitement shimmered off the Strip. For a brief time we pretended to be friends.

This spirit of détente continued after dinner, when we settled down to business. We tussled a bit over minor changes to the drawings, but no blood was drawn, no body parts sacrificed—until we hit a sticking point over a wood-fired brick oven.

"Let me make sure I understand," I said. "You want a fifty-thousand-dollar oven, one that uses only wood as a heat source, requiring a special staff member who will do nothing but be in charge of

the fire. And this oven will be used only to make
flatbread appetizers?"

"*Oui*," he remarked, his disdain evident, as if
an oven like this was standard equipment in every
tract house.

"That fifty grand is going to put you over
budget."

He waved a hand at me and made that blowing
sound that French people make when they think
someone is being stupid. "The budget. It is only a
best guess, *non*?"

I felt my eyes getting slitty. Negotiating is one
thing, implying I am *un imbécile* is another thing
altogether. "So, the amount we have budgeted for
your salary and bonuses, that can be adjusted at
will also?"

"You are making fun with me," he said, his
voice low, hard. "You may not take my oven."

"I assure you, I am not making fun. And, for the
record, I may do as I wish. Read your contract;
once you sign off on the budget, you are stuck with
it." We glared at each other for a moment.

"You are the most . . . interesting woman. As
irritating as a sand flea, but interesting." Anger in-
fused the chef's face, a muscle working in his jaw.
But another, illusive emotion flashed in his eyes.

Interesting was not an adjective I expected.

"The oven is important." He paused, capturing
me with those incredible eyes that now had gone
all dark and deep. "Things have changed for me

recently—I have made some personal decisions which have allowed me to add depth and complexity to the concept here. If you trust me, I will not disappoint."

Accustomed to being his own boss, the effort to explain himself cost him—I could see it in his face. After what I considered to be an appropriate lapse in time—one that would allow me to capitulate but keep my pride intact—I said, "Okay, I will trust you—you get your oven."

A grin split his face and he banged his hands on the table. "More wine!"

"But you must give me something in return."

His grin vanished. "What?"

"The fresco and we drop down a notch in quality on the chairs." The fresco was a thirty-thousand-dollar line item—a wall painting to be done by a local artist.

"What will replace the fresco? It is an important visual when guests walk in the door. I think it would establish the country French motif."

"Agreed. But it's not worth the cost. The artist has no name recognition, so you get no real bang for the buck."

"Bang for the buck?"

"Value." I leaned forward, covering his hand with mine—crossing every line in the business handbook. I gasped at the effect his touch had—like thrusting my hand into a flame. I yanked back my hand. Even though I knew there was no real burn, I rubbed the imagined one and said, "I'm sorry. Inappropriate." What had prompted me to do such a stupid thing?

His eyes dark and serious, he cocked his head and nodded once . . . slowly.

"Jean-Charles, although you think differently, I'm on your side. If your restaurant is a success, we both win. Help me out here. Can you trust me to find an acceptable replacement for the fresco?"

"I get my oven, the chairs will be sturdy and comfortable, but one price point down, and you will find a replacement for the fresco that meets with my approval." He stuck out his hand. "Deal?"

Warily, waiting for the singe again, I put my hand in his. Even though I was half expecting it, my body's reaction to his still surprised me. A touch . . . then a jolt.

I must be way hornier than I realized.

We toasted our agreement with another splash of that wonderful wine.

His glass in one hand, the other crossed across his chest and tucked under his elbow, the Frenchman eyed me. "So, where do you think you will find this new focal point for the entrance of my restaurant?" he asked, skepticism infusing every word.

"I already have it."

"What?" He leapt to his feet, anger flushing his cheeks. "You tried to fool—"

"No. I needed to see if you trusted me, if you will work with me. I will not be bullied, or manipulated, and if that was how our relationship was going to be, then I needed to make some adjustments."

"A test, then?" He lowered himself to his stool, but he still looked totally torqued.

I didn't blame him—I didn't much like games either, but I had to know what I was dealing with. "We're partners, not combatants, as you seem to think. It is imperative we work together. We must trust each other."

"Agreed." He put his hand on top of mine.

I worked to hide my reaction.

Chewing on his lip, he stared at our hands together on the table. When his eyes lifted to mine they were filled with warmth, his mask of wariness slipping.

I eased my hand from under his. "Jean-Charles, we have to work together . . ."

"Yes." His mask fell back into place. "So tell me what this wonderful thing will be."

"What wonderful thing?" His touch, his eyes had set me adrift—I was totally at sea.

"To replace the fresco."

"Right." I composed myself, or tried to anyway. "My vision was a piece of artwork—exquisite, recognizable, but not overpowering—your food should be the centerpiece, the focal point, if you will."

"Yes, precisely." The last vestiges of his anger evaporated, a look of interest settled across his features.

"I was thinking one of Van Gogh's earlier haystacks. They are intriguing, easily identifiable, and fit with your French country theme. Would that work?"

For once my French chef had nothing to say. He could only stare. When he found his voice he said, "So you wish to save thirty thousand dollars on a painting, yet will spend tens of millions on a piece of art to replace it?"

"No, we already own it. The Van Gogh is a piece in The Big Boss's private collection. Right now it is on display in a small gallery in the Bazaar, but I think I can talk him into loaning it to us."

"I think it is a good thing you are on my side," Jean-Charles said with a grin.

Now he was getting the picture.

I took private delight in my pun. What can I say? Simple girl, simple pleasures.

AFTER helping with the cleanup, over the chef's objections, and with only questionable reasons for staying longer, I said good-bye.

In front of the elevator, Jean-Charles took both my hands in his and gave me a kiss on each cheek, leaving me unexpectedly affected. In an unusual position—I'd never wanted to jump the help before—I found myself clueless as to what rules of engagement applied to our particular battle. Of course, he really wasn't the help—he was a partner, at least as far as the restaurant went. Staring at my reflection as I rode down, I wondered if, in our game of crossing swords, would I have a parry for his every thrust?

For some reason, the thought made me sad. I didn't want to war with the beautiful Frenchman. There was something about him . . . not just the normal hormonally driven leap of lust, although there was that. But somehow being with him left me strangely settled; he was a kindred spirit, a fellow warrior in the battle of life.

Dreading the emptiness of home, I headed for the Babylon and its crush of humanity and merriment.

As expected, the lobby teemed with people—laughter and happy voices echoed off the marble, putting a smile on my face if not on my heart. So strained and distant, my last conversation with Teddie lingered, but I wasn't going to let it suck the juice out of the evening. I sidled onto an empty stool at the bar in Delilah's, which was full of energy and people. Someone pounded out tunes on the piano; I tried to ignore them.

Sean, our head bartender, ended a conversation with a pretty blonde at the end of the bar and moved in my direction. "The usual?" he asked, when he stood in front of me.

A cute kid with spiked hair, a receding hairline, and a ready smile, Sean liked to tell the women his last name was Finnegan and he was Black Irish. In fact, his last name was Pollack and he was from Jersey—in Vegas, we all could be who we wanted to be—even if we couldn't have what we wanted.

"No, just soda and lime. I have a very fine Chateau Lafite-Rothschild sloshing around in my stomach. I refuse to adulterate it with any lesser spirits."

"Been hanging with the highbrows?" Sean filled a tall glass from the gun and knifed a wedge of lime on the rim, then set it in front of me.

"Apparently." I tilted my head toward the blonde. "Friend of yours?"

"Acquaintance. She's an independent contractor."

"Don't tell me any more," I said, as I took a sip of soda and grimaced—tasteless beverages were not my thing. "I don't want to know."

In Vegas vernacular, being a young, beautiful, female independent contractor meant one of two things: She was either a stripper or a hooker. And hooking was illegal in Clark County, the home of Las Vegas. If, in fact, that was her trade it would fall on me to escort her out of the hotel—a less than stellar ending to a near stellar evening.

"No worries there. She's a high-end stripper at one of those fancy gentlemen's clubs."

I didn't think "good" was an appropriate response, so I said nothing.

"Hey, Lucky! How're they hangin'?" Junior Arbogast asked from over my shoulder.

I let my head drop—it was a long way from France to West Virginia—I needed a moment to adjust. "Hangin' high and tight in keeping with the current fashion," I replied. I didn't ask him the same thing because, frankly, I didn't want to know—way too much information—even on a full stomach.

"Me and my friends are throwing back some Buds." He motioned to a rowdy gang in the corner. "Want to join us?"

"Interesting collection," I said as I eyed Junior's party—a group that included Zoom-Zoom Zewicki and Dr. Jenkins, the man with the golden putter. "Have you gotten a bead on the astronaut who talks to dead people?"

"He's a curious guy. I thought I had him figured, but I'm not so sure anymore."

"And Jenkins?" I asked, as I let Junior lead me back to his table.

"A true believer," the fraud-buster whispered in my ear. "Nice guy, but with a big chip on his shoulder."

Ridicule could do that, I thought, as I smiled a greeting to the small group. Dr. Jenkins made a space between himself and Zoom-Zoom, and I pulled up a chair. Several men at the table nodded—the women stared for a moment, unwelcoming looks of competition on their faces. Two men on the far side of the table, their heads bent over a computer, didn't look up.

A foreigner now in their midst, the conversation stalled as they eyed the newcomer—I hate it when that happens. So awkward. I resisted the urge to jump in and say something stupid.

Instead, Dr. Jenkins did it for me. "Do you make a habit of joining strange men in the bar?"

"A hazard of my profession, I'm afraid." Having lost my interest in bubbles that hadn't come out of a bottle with a cork, I pushed my glass away. "Who are the strange men at this table?"

That broke the ice and comfortable conversation again swirled around me. I signaled the waitress and ordered a split of Veuve Clicquot—much better bubbles.

"How is the conference going for you so far?" I asked Dr. Jenkins.

"Far better than I imagined. Surrounded by believers, I don't have to explain myself or justify my theories." Jenkins fell quiet for a moment as he looked over my shoulder to the casino beyond, a faraway look in his eye. When his focus returned, he said in a small voice, "I can't tell you how nice it is to be in a group of people who don't think I'm crazy."

"Some of the greatest scientific thinkers were considered heretics until time proved them right."

His face brightened. "Are you a believer, Lucky?"

I had to think about that for a moment, so I took the time to savor my champagne. Whoever thought of putting bubbles and alcohol together should have a place in Heaven. "When it comes to alien life-forms, I'd have to say I'm an agnostic. I'm not sure I'm convinced, but to think our tiny planet, one of billions, is the only one capable of supporting life, approaches a scientific improbability."

"Well said." Jenkins saluted me with his Bud, then took a long pull.

"Is Dr. Jenkins boring you with his talk of ancient astronauts?" Zoom-Zoom Zewicki asked, leaning in next to me. Coming from such a small man, his deep voice always surprised me.

"Not at all." I shifted my focus to the former astronaut.

His demeanor calm, his face relaxed, he'd lost the wild-eyed look of yesterday. If I didn't know better, I'd say he looked . . . normal.

"Having traveled into space yourself, what do you think of Dr. Jenkins's theories?" I asked.

"Space . . . we know so little."

I wanted to ask him what he had learned from the aliens, but I stifled myself, and let him continue uninterrupted.

"Floating weightless, the earth a blue orb against a backdrop of billions of stars . . . It makes you feel very small, insignificant—overwhelmed with an appreciation for the fragility, the preciousness of life."

"Did you see anything that surprised you?" I asked.

Junior eyed me across the table as he listened. He knew where I was going.

"I did have one interesting personal experience. We had initiated our reentry sequence, but were still outside the Earth's atmosphere, when I noticed bright lights traveling very fast near the Earth's surface."

"UFOs?"

"Yes. We couldn't identify them and they flew.

But whether they were aliens, I don't know." Zoom-Zoom's steely eyes held mine. "The lights altered course, paused, then darted in a new direction as if they were looking for something."

"What?"

"Who knows? But they lingered near thunderstorms as if the energy attracted them."

"They could have been refueling," Junior offered.

Zoom-Zoom pursed his down-turned lips, but refused to take the bait. "You know Dr. Jenkins has hidden talents? If you get him liquored up enough, he just might show you his parlor tricks."

The astronaut ignored Jenkins's frown.

"What talents?" I asked, only marginally interested. Tricks really weren't my thing—they made me feel stupid. God knew I felt that way often enough without outside assistance.

"Yes," Zoom-Zoom continued, "he has quite the mind-reading act—nobody can figure out how he does it. No assistant to help. Nothing planned in advance, he can do it on the fly—quite amazing, really."

There was something in Dr. Zewicki's eyes as he talked, glancing occasionally at Dr. Jenkins, who didn't look at all pleased by the revelations, but I couldn't place it.

"Will you show me?" I asked Dr. Jenkins even though he clearly was less than pleased. "Please?"

"His talents are impressive, but I'm sure he

can't perform here," Dr. Zewicki said, sounding as if he was goading.

With an irritated jerk, Jenkins took my hand as Zoom-Zoom watched. Closing his eyes, he concentrated, his skin turning suddenly warm where it touched mine. When he opened his eyes, they were dark, deep holes—windows to a different place, a bridge to my soul. I didn't like it, but, like a swimmer caught in an undertow, I was powerless to resist.

"You are pining for a lover—someone far away." He paused. "A singer."

"Anyone who asked around could know that," I said. "It's common knowledge—unfortunately."

Jenkins leveled those disconcerting eyes on me. "Do you want me to tell them the secret you hide?"

My blood ran cold. "What secret?"

"Your father?"

Jerking my hand out of his, I said, "That is quite enough."

He stared at me, then gave me a wry smile. "He loves you."

I thought about asking him if the lover I pined for did as well, but I didn't really want to hear his answer. Besides, the whole experience left me a bit shaken—as if Jenkins had done a Vulcan mind-meld on me. My whole life was an open book—I shouldn't have to share my thoughts as well.

One of the two computer guys shouted, "I got it!" breaking the weird spell Jenkins had cast over me.

I felt reality returning. Zoom-Zoom leaned in and whispered, "Pretty creepy, huh?"

"Thanks for the setup." I shot him an irritated glance, but he didn't seem too upset about it.

The computer dude turned his machine around to face the rest of the group, who quieted.

"What are those two doing with the computer?" I whispered out of the side of my mouth.

"They're trying to tap into the radio feed of *The Bart Griffin Show*," Zoom-Zoom said.

"Who?"

"A talk-show host," Dr. Jenkins added. "His nightly show covers unexplained phenomena, from UFOs to alien abductions to ancient astronauts— the whole gamut. He takes call-ins, which can be quite amusing."

"Let me get this straight. You guys are sitting in a bar in the entertainment capital of the universe, and you're going to stop everything to listen to a radio show?"

"It's not as crazy as it sounds," Junior jumped in. "The guy has gone commando."

"He's not wearing any underwear?" I asked, rhetorically. "That's not so interesting—people do it all the time in Vegas."

"Not that kind of commando." Junior gave me a disgusted look.

"This week Bart Griffin is broadcasting from

various hidden locations around Area 51," Zoom-Zoom explained. "He moves every hour to keep the cammo guys off his trail."

"The Air Force will shoot him if he blunders too far inside," I warned, probably unnecessarily. Junior had personal experience with the business end of an M-16 thanks to the cammo guys, a faulty map, and two six-packs of beer.

"Cool, huh?" Junior said, his eyes alight. "But there's more. Rumor has been swirling all day that he's going to make some sort of announcement about your vanishing magician."

"Dimitri Fortunoff?" Now they had my attention. Who knew his disappearance had been classified as an "unexplained phenomenon?" Although it fit.

"That's the one," Dr. Jenkins confirmed.

"Turn up the sound," I instructed. "I'm all ears." The possibility that the commando radio host would have any meaningful insight into the magician's demise was remote, but waiting to hear him out couldn't hurt.

"This is it." The computer guy turned up the volume.

"For all you people in Vegas worrying about Dimitri Fortunoff, I have a word from him to you," said the disembodied voice, a deep masculine rumble. "The word tonight is actually a phrase. It is 'pray be quick.'"

Then he signed off and our group fell silent.

"'Pray be quick'? That's it?" I asked my

tablemates. "And how could it be from Dimitri, when he's dead?"

Blank faces stared back at me.

"People have been known to make contact from the Great Beyond," Zoom-Zoom Zewicki said quietly, his face a mask.

I thought about arguing with him, but trying to change the mind of someone who had already tossed reason out the window was like trying to throw a large loop with a short rope. "If he's trying to tell us something, what is it?"

"It's a clue," computer dude number one said.

Clearly he shared my flair for the obvious. "I *know* it's a clue, but to what?"

Again, blank faces stared at me. For a group big on theories, they were strangely quiet.

I rose to go. "Gentlemen, it's been interesting . . . and confounding. Perhaps a new day will bring enlightenment."

"There's supposed to be another word tomorrow night," Zoom-Zoom added. "Maybe it will add clarity."

I had my doubts.

IN contrast to last night, quiet reigned as I strolled up the drive to the front entrance to the Presidio. Forrest manned his post in the lobby.

"Hey, Ms. Lucky. Long day?"

"Normal day. How about you?"

"Same, except I heard the weirdest thing." Forrest's voice dropped to a conspiratorial whisper. "You know the cat burglar?"

I nodded, my interest piqued. "How much did he get away with?"

"I don't know, my friend didn't see the list the Danielses made." Forrest's eyes were wide with wonder. "The weird thing was, he *left* something."

"You mean like a calling card?"

"Yeah," Forrest said. "Like on TV."

"What was it?"

"Something like a note."

"What did the note say?"

The big man shrugged. "That's all my friend would tell me. He was one of the cops on the scene; he probably shouldn't have opened his big flapper as it was."

"Would you let me know if you hear more?"

"Sure thing. All I can say is, it sure was good nobody was home. The guy's a crackerjack for sure."

Great, not only did we have a cat burglar, we had one who wanted to rub the victim's nose in it. The sick SOB.

And it was a sad day when our security guard's sources were better than mine.

Romeo and I needed to have a chat.

HOME—my former refuge, now my prison—holding me hostage with distant echoes of happiness, fading memories of a love gone missing. Clearly

I needed a change of scenery, another place to lay my head for a while. I tossed my bag and jacket on the couch, kicked off my shoes, and headed for the kitchen to check on Newton. At least I knew where I stood with him—as long as I provided food and a warm place to live, he loved me.

And they say you can't buy love.

Whoever said that had clearly never been to Vegas.

Newton's cage was buttoned up for the night, so I didn't disturb him. Instead, I headed for my bedroom, dropping clothes as I went. A long soak in the tub would do wonders.

In designing the build-out of my condo, I had insisted on two things: walls of glass and a bathroom that would find a place on the list of the top ten best bathrooms of the world—assuming I was inclined to allow a television crew into my boudoir, which I wasn't. A space larger than my first apartment, carpeted with thick pile, with a jetted tub that could fit me and several of my friends comfortably under a wall of glass looking south toward the airport, a shower for two with multiple nozzles, a double vanity, and a water closet with a television and no cell service, my every wish had been fulfilled.

A set of slatted double French doors opened into a walk-in closet so large it had a chaise, enough shoe racks to have delighted Imelda Marcos, and closet space sufficient to hold my lifetime collection of vintage designer clothing—my one major vice—and Teddie's hand-me-downs. If he took a powder, I hoped he wouldn't take back his collection of Oscar de la Renta and Chanel gowns—remnants from his highly successful days as Las Vegas's reigning female impersonator. Of course, if he left, I'm not sure I could wear his clothes.

I opened the tap on the tub to a preset temperature and let the deep basin fill while I removed my makeup and the rest of my clothing. Just before submerging myself, I checked my cell. No missed calls. No text messages. Nothing. Nada. Zilch.

Teddie had gone AWOL.

Chapter

SIX

♡

Today was a perfect day to shoot someone.

I shielded my eyes against the glare of the morning sun. Happy that I had grabbed a jacket as I headed out the door, I zipped it against the morning chill. Breathing in the cool, fresh air, I felt myself relaxing . . . a bit. Sleep had been elusive. Tossing and turning, thoughts and worries steamrolling through my brain, I'd finally taken refuge in a large wingback chair with a steaming mug of java, and watched the sun bring life to the new day.

In the early morning, with the lights of the Strip extinguished, the sidewalks empty of tourists, and commuters populating the streets, Vegas resembled a normal American city.

I nodded to a young woman clutching the hand of a child dressed in a school uniform as they walked by.

After years of going to bed as the hurricane of excess and excitement raged, then waking up to . . . a place suspiciously like Southern California, I no longer thought the two faces of Vegas odd. In fact, I thought each was essential—the normality offset the craziness so we could all live here and not lose ourselves.

Lost in thought, I didn't notice the sleek, midnight blue convertible until it eased to a stop in front of me. Dane stepped out of the driver's door.

"Nice wheels," I said. As greetings go, it was a bit lame, but it was better than "nice ass," which was also true. "Aston Martin?"

Dane nodded as he opened the passenger door for me. "A Vantage."

"So work is a hobby for you?" I had to wait for his answer until he settled himself behind the wheel.

"I know how much you like well-engineered cars," Dane said, as he put the car in gear and pulled into traffic. "A friend of mine works at Gaudin. He let me borrow it."

As he drove east on Tropicana, we fell into easy conversation about the merits and deficiencies of all the toys sold by the Gaudin dealership, including my favorite, Porsche, which has no deficiencies whatsoever. Dane didn't disagree, scoring major points in the process. My life sure would be simpler if I could find something to dislike about him—but it wouldn't be nearly as much fun.

THE Gun Store occupied a long, low-slung building constructed of cinder blocks and topped with tin. In a valiant attempt to combat the assault of the sun and the heat of the desert, someone had painted every surface white. Similar commercial buildings bracketed the store and lined the opposite side of the street as far as I could see. The neighborhood reeked of old East Vegas and hard times.

Dane parked the Aston Martin two spaces from a beat-up Ford F-150 that looked like it had been painted with Krylon. The license plate said SHOOTR, and the bumper stickers would make the NRA blush with pride. Being from Nevada, a live-and-let-live state, I could relate. The pickup and our convertible were the only two cars in the lot.

"Are they open yet?" I always felt like a fool waiting for a man to walk around to let me out of the car—especially since I was fully capable of doing it myself. So I did, and unfolded myself into the day.

"Like I said, I know this guy . . ." Dane grinned at me over the top of the car. "He's opening for us. We'll have the place to ourselves."

The white cinder-block motif continued inside, where someone had painted the floor bright blue. The shooting range consisted of a reception area, where patrons picked their weapon of choice—anything from several fully automatic weapons, sniper rifles, and 50-caliber cannons to tiny semiautomatic handguns. The shooting bays, with a bench rest at one end, a backstop at the other, and an overhead pulley system to move the targets, occupied the remaining area of the building. I could see several of the bays through a wall of glass opposite the front door. The pop-pop-pop of rapid single-shot fire sounded from the range, but I couldn't see the shooter.

Dane and I stood at the counter and surveyed the possibilities. Guns of all shapes and sizes hung from pegs, covering the wall behind the counter. A bipod-supported cannon called The Saw caught my eye, but I dismissed it as too gaudy; not to mention it would probably knock me on my ass.

"I'm thinking an Uzi and maybe an M16," I said. All this firepower made my trigger finger twitchy.

"The perfect solution: Kill the intruder and take out a few neighbors in the process."

The neighbor right above me sprang to mind— not that I really wanted to shoot Teddie. However, making him suffer held some appeal. The guy had been acting like a toad. If he wanted to blow me off, the least he could do was tell it to me straight.

"Okay, no M16, but I've always wanted to

shoot an Uzi—something about the name, the whole Mossad thing—I don't know."

"I think we can handle that," Dane said, his brows creased in concentration. "But I really want to teach you to shoot a handgun, get you comfortable with it."

Without asking my opinion, he settled on a Glock. Had he asked, I would have agreed—constructed of polymer, the Model 19 was light, compact, easy to use, and deadly. And it fit my hand better than the Beretta or the Walther PPK.

The sound of shooting stopped. A tall man, dressed in black and wearing ear protectors and safety goggles, walked into view in the shooting area. He waved at us through the glass, then checked his weapon, leaving the receiver open, hung his ear protectors on a peg on the wall, and let himself out through the locked door into the reception area.

Dane and the man shook hands, then Dane said to me, "Lucky, this is Shooter Moran. We kicked around a bit together in the service."

"Nice to meet you," Shooter said, as he took my hand in his huge paw. "I could tell you stories about this one." He cocked his head toward Dane. "He took a bullet and still saved—"

"That's enough," Dane interrupted. "Don't fill her head full of your exaggerations."

Shooter gave me a wink. "The Captain never liked anyone talking about him."

"Captain?"

At a glare from Dane, Shooter changed the subject. "So what's it going to be, Captain?"

"The Uzi and the Model 19, and enough ammo to assassinate several targets. My lady here has a serious case of red ass she needs to work out."

"Yes, sir." If Shooter thought Dane's pronouncement odd, he was gentleman enough not to quiz me.

I, on the other hand, unfettered by social strictures, shot my shooting partner a glare. Lately people had been reading me like a billboard, and I didn't like it.

With his arms full of trays of ammo, safety goggles, ear protectors, and several targets, Dane motioned for me to grab the weapons and follow him. We set up in a shooting bay at the far end.

"Do you want to throw some serious lead at whoever stuck a burr under your saddle, or do you want to start with the handgun and work your way to virtual homicide?" Dane placed a pair of safety goggles over my eyes, donned a set of his own, then hung a set of ear protectors around my neck. Then he attached one of the targets to the clips and ran it along the pulley system to the far wall.

"Let's do the handgun first."

Only half listening I watched Dane, his face serious, his eyes a deep green, as he carefully explained the proper handling of a handgun. He showed me the various parts of the gun, how to chamber a round by pulling back the slide, how to change the magazine, reiterating twice that the Glock had no external safety so I had to be ready to shoot when I put my finger on the trigger. He had nice hands, strong hands . . . and he looked so cute when he was serious. . . .

"Let me fire it first, then I'll help you," he said. After putting the protectors over his ears and motioning for me to do the same, he took a bent-knee stance, arms extended in front of him, both hands on the gun, and squeezed off a couple of rounds—all of them kill shots to the target's upper torso.

"Impressive," I said after removing my ear thingies.

"Now you try it." Dane took one hand off the gun and motioned me in front of him.

With my back to his chest, his voice warm in my ear, I held the gun as he indicated. His arms on either side of me, he closed his hands over mine. He smelled like soap with a hint of something musky, something masculine—safe, yet with a hint of danger.

"I fired three rounds, so you have twelve left. Just squeeze smoothly. The gun doesn't kick much. Don't be nervous," he whispered. With one hand he eased my ear protectors back into place, then regripped my hands.

I felt his breath on my cheek, his chest pressed to my back, his arms around me. My skin warmed to his touch. Don't be nervous? Who was he kidding?

Closing my eyes, I took a deep breath and settled myself. I hoped shooting was like riding a bicycle.

In my previous experience, I was always instructed to aim for the body, the largest target. I opened my eyes and sighted on the target's head. Taking instruction was not my best thing.

With quick, precise pulls, I squeezed off five rounds. Four hit my mark, one grazed an ear—not bad after all this time.

"Beginner's luck," Dane said, raising his voice to be heard since we both had our ears covered. He dropped his hands but stayed pressed against me. "Now you do it on your own."

I repeated the exercise, this time with better luck—all five shots hit where I aimed.

Dane pulled my ear coverings off as I set the gun on the rest. "You've done this before."

"Once or twice. Growing up in Nevada was like growing up in Texas, just more so. Shooting at cans on the dry lake bed outside of town was a common summer game."

He spun me around to face him. There was a challenge in his eyes and a grin on his face. "Why didn't you tell me?"

"You didn't ask."

"Yes, I did."

"You asked if I owned a gun, not if I knew how to shoot one." For a moment I thought he was going to kiss me. For a moment I wanted him to, but then I realized he deserved better than to play a bit part in a childish game of revenge. Then, out of nowhere, the thought occurred to me that I was better than that—and I deserved better than to be left in limbo. Teddie had some answering to do.

"A full clip, ten points for a head shot, five for a body shot?" I said, tossing down the gauntlet.

"You're on." Dane left, then returned with his own gun, a Walther PPK. He slammed a magazine home, ran his own target to the far wall, donned his protective gear, and said, "Fire when ready."

I don't know how much ammo we burned through. Sometimes he won, sometimes I did, and in the end, it didn't matter. We laughed, we teased, and when we'd finished, I no longer wanted to shoot the Uzi.

EVER the eager beaver, Brandy already manned her desk when I arrived. Her youthful enthusiasm and diligence warmed my heart, but made me feel old. Had I ever been so single-minded? Would I do it all over again, knowing the price? Of course I would, but it's nice to imagine I might have had a choice.

Besides, it wasn't my professional life that was causing me angst. Still no word from Teddie—he had fallen off the face of the earth. What was I supposed to make of that? Okay, I was sorta getting the hint, but I didn't want to believe it. And I'd be damned before I called him.

"Anything interesting?" I asked my young assistant.

"Detective Romeo called."

"Are you sure the call was for me?" I teased. The young detective had been putting a full-court press on Brandy. I didn't know the current status. Brandy had taken off my head the last time I injected myself into her private life, so I didn't ask, but I wasn't above a little gentle probing.

"Maybe for both of us," Brandy said, her face blushing a nice pink. "But he asked if you had any leads on the owner of the Chinese Water Torture Cell. What is that?"

"A new method of retraining recalcitrant employees. Call Romeo back, tell him I'm working on it, and ask him if he has a lead on Molly Rain."

"Okay," she said with a smile. "Mr. Mortimer called. He wants a few minutes of your time."

I glanced at my watch—ten-fifteen and I still hadn't had breakfast. "Ask him to join me in Neb's at eleven, if that's convenient."

Brandy made a note. "That's all so far, but the day is young."

I stashed my purse in the closet, locked my new Glock 19 in my desk drawer, and had just settled behind my desk and a new pile of paper when Miss P burst through the door.

"We need to talk," she announced. After closing my office door, she perched on the edge of one of the chairs across from me. Dressed entirely in black, she fidgeted with the single gold chain around her neck.

"You look positively macabre today. Who died?"

"My youth," she wailed.

"Do you want a large, public funeral, or just family and friends?"

"I'm serious. In a couple of days I'm going to turn . . ." She paused, looking over her shoulder at the door. Satisfied it was closed, she leaned across the desk and said in a ragged whisper, "Fifty."

"It's not a death sentence."

"It might as well be. Life, as I know it, is over." She twisted the gold chain until I thought her face would turn blue. "Jeremy is only thirty-five. I have shoes older than that. What's he going to say when he finds out?"

"Let me get this straight: We're talking about the Jeremy who brings you flowers twice a week, who drives you to work and sees you home safely at night." She started to say something but I silenced her with a raised finger. "The same Jeremy who finds several excuses to stop by each day just to see you—even though he spends every night warming your bed?"

"But—"

"I'm not finished. The Jeremy who hasn't looked at another woman since he first caught sight of you? That Jeremy? Is *that* who we're talking about?"

"But I'm *fifty*!"

"I fail to see the catastrophe," I said, refusing to go to general quarters. If Miss P didn't look so miserable, I would find the whole thing amusing. Not too long ago, Jeremy had been framed for murder; Miss P sailed right through that with

Midwestern aplomb and a stiff upper lip. And now a simple birthday had her on the ragged edge. "He's seen you naked, right?"

"Naked, in the stark light of day," she admitted. "With no makeup and my hair slicked back after washing."

"And he didn't run screaming for the hills?"

She gave me the barest hint of a smile as she shook her head.

"Heck, if that didn't put the fear of God into him, I doubt a silly little thing like a zero birthday is going to rock his world."

"Okay. Maybe you have a point, but do you think I could fudge just a bit?" She stopped worrying with the chain. Smoothing a hand down the sleeve of her shirt, she pecked at an invisible imperfection.

"Eventually someone will let the cat out of the bag. Which do you think will upset him more, your real age, or the fact you didn't trust him with the truth?"

"When you put it that way, it sounds awful." Her eyes held mine.

"It's your call," I equivocated. Far be it from me to tell her what to do; after all, my love life wasn't exactly going swimmingly.

"Why does life have to be so hard?" she sighed.

"If it was easy, everybody would do it."

MR. Mortimer waited at a two-top near the window overlooking the golf course when I arrived at

Nebuchadnezzar's, the Babylon's sumptuous buffet, at 11:10—late, as usual.

"I'm sorry," I said, as I took the chair across from him. "My job keeps me dancing like a cowboy with a six-shooter."

"Not to worry, my dear. Can I offer you something to drink?" A glass of white wine sat in front of him—nothing like an early start.

Today must have been casual day for the magician. He wore a pressed white shirt, a black suit, a waistcoat complete with pocket watch and chain, and a purple bow tie. His white hair neatly combed into a perfect halo, his complexion ruddy, his eyes worried, he looked like a man on a mission—or a banker from the nineteenth century.

"I don't need anything to drink, thank you. Have you had a chance to finalize the arrangements for your dinner?" The annual meeting of the Magic Ring was scheduled for tomorrow evening in our Golden Fleece Room. The group numbered less than twenty, but they wanted strict privacy.

"I made a few changes, nothing major." When he took a sip of wine, his hand shook. "I need a favor."

"Name it."

"I want to examine Houdini's upside-down again."

"His upside-down?"

"That's what he called the Chinese Water Torture Cell, the USD for short."

I went still as I eyed him. "Why do you want to see it?"

"The replica has been hidden for years. I'd like to get a closer look." He twirled the wineglass between his fingers, pretending to be fascinated.

"I see." And I did; he wasn't a very good liar, which struck me as odd given that he's spent his life perfecting the art of fooling people. "Is that the only reason?"

His eyes flicked to mine, then back to his glass. He seemed to be caught between an angel on one shoulder and the devil on the other. Finally, he deflated. With a sigh, he said, "I'm afraid one of our own might have acted on the rumors about Dimitri being the Masked Houdini."

"You mean, taken revenge?"

"Yes." Again, his eyes flicked to mine, then skittered away again. "Magicians are a secretive and jealous lot."

"Do you know the secrets of the Water Torture Cell?"

"No."

"Then how will looking at the thing help?"

"I don't know," he said, honesty flashing across his face.

I eyed him, looking for any hint of prevarication. Not finding any, I caved. "It couldn't hurt to let you have a look. I assume you're coming to me because the police still have the scene cordoned off?"

"You and that young detective seemed to have a rapport the other night."

"I'll call Detective Romeo, if you do something for me."

"And that would be?"

"As you said, the magic community is small and very jealous. Rumors abound. And you and your friends sit atop the food chain. If I get you a look at the USD, as you call it, you have to tell me who owns the darn thing."

MR. Mortimer agreed he would try to discover the owner. We settled on tomorrow afternoon for our next meeting. He left, and I went in search of sustenance. A bountiful feast, Nebuchadnezzar's offered a plethora of the world's cuisines—some of which I could identify. I wasn't sure I wanted clarification as to the others—they looked venomous and deadly—suspiciously like something one would worry about stepping on in a tidal pool. Lacking gastronomic courage, I stuck to the safe stuff—a salad and some fruit to make me feel virtuous, ribs and mashed potatoes to make me feel like I'd actually eaten. I resisted the chocolate cake just to prove I could.

The waiter brought the Diet Coke I ordered, and I dug in, even though I wasn't really hungry. Halfway through the salad and fruit, I lost steam. Flash found me playing with a mound of cold mashed potatoes and staring out the window at the golfers below.

"What're you trying to do, build the Devil's Tower in hope the aliens will return?"

I looked at the pile of starch on my plate—it did sort of resemble a rock formation. "Out of all the weeks of the year, this is the one the aliens should pick—all their followers are here."

Today Flash's tee shirt advertised a Rolling Stones concert from the mid-1980s, but the rest of her attire was unchanged. She had piled her hair on top of her head, leaving a few tendrils trailing provocatively around her face.

With the look of a bear eyeing a salmon, she stared at my plate.

I pushed my food toward her. "You can have it. I've had enough."

Without a word she dropped her ample backside into the chair across from me, grabbed my fork, and tucked in. "You smell like you've been in a shoot-out," she said through a mouthful of meat.

"Really?" Holding my sleeve to my nose, I took a whiff. She was right.

"You haven't shot anybody and not told me, have you?"

"You'd be the person I'd use my one call on." I took a sip of my Diet Coke—*What should I tell her? What should I keep to myself?* "Eau de Gunpowder is a new scent I'm trying. Just a dab behind my ears to add to my aura of mystery and danger—what do you think?"

"I think if Letterman ever needs another smart ass on his writing staff, you're a shoo-in."

"At least we know I have one marketable skill." I marveled at my friend's appetite as she dug into another rib, then forked in a heaping bite of potatoes. She must have a tapeworm. "So to what do I owe the honor of your presence?"

"I've got a bit of background on Danilov, but I've run into a brick wall. Maybe you can help."

"What kind of brick wall?"

"Area 51."

"Interesting. You'd better start at the beginning." I settled myself back with my Diet Coke, my mouth shut, my ears open.

Flash closed her eyes for a moment—I knew she was reviewing her mental note cards. "I don't have much. Born in Ohio, psychic abilities so high they couldn't be measured, involved in multiple projects through the years, earned a PhD from Stanford." Flash paused as she took another mouthful of spuds then chased it down with a slurp of my Diet Coke, ignoring my frown. Drinking from the same glass was one of my pet peeves—right up there with sharing toothbrushes. "He made his money on the entertainment circuit—bending spoons, telekinesis, hypnosis. After a while, his novelty wore off and he went underground."

"Area 51?"

Flash ignored me—she was a stickler for telling a linear tale. "He kept warning the military how easy it would be to hypnotize a whole bunch of folks without them even knowing it, then turn them loose in the country. And on a prearranged signal, they would do whatever they'd been told to do."

"The Air Force finally listened to him?" I asked, trying to get her to jump ahead.

Flash scowled but kept going. "Five years ago, they put him in charge of some secret program at Area 51."

"What kind of program?"

"You just hit the brick wall."

"How did you discover the Area 51 connection?"

"A former employee. He didn't know what Danilov was involved in, but he remembered seeing him on base."

"Could your source's story be corroborated?"

"I found some photos online taken by UFO cover-up conspiracy theorists. They showed employees waiting in line for Janet flights. Danilov was in several and the time frame matches up. That's the best I can do."

Made up of six 737s painted white, with a single red strip down the side and no markings other than tail numbers in small black letters, the Janet Flights operated out of a high-security terminal on the northwest corner of McCarran, shuttling government employees to Area 51 and the Tonopah Test Range.

"I know someone who might be able to help us," I said. "Give me a day or two."

Flash nodded as she polished off the last rib.

She knew better than to ask me who. "I'm going to shake down Mr. Danilov/Daniels regarding the break-in at his home. I'll ask him about the Area 51 thing, but knowing those spooks, I expect he'll put up a fight."

She had that pit bull look in her eyes.

The man didn't stand a chance.

HALFWAY back to the office, my phone vibrated in my pocket. My heartbeat quickened as I retrieved it and looked at the caller ID—the office.

Deflated, I answered. "Whatcha got?"

"There's a problem in the Temple of Love," Miss P said.

"Can you give me any particulars?" In the lobby, I changed directions, heading into the Bazaar.

"Have you met Mrs. Olefson?" Miss P asked.

"Of the Saginaw Olefsons and currently staying in the Sodom and Gomorrah Suite?"

"That's the one."

"I checked her in a couple of days ago. *She's* in the Temple of Love?"

"Yes," Miss P said. Her voice sounded funny. "She wants to get married."

"Really?" I didn't try to hide my surprise. Mrs. Olefson was ninety if she was a day. "Good for her."

"Not really. She wants to marry her Shih-Tzu."

"She wants to marry her dog?" I stopped in my tracks. A man following too closely behind me dodged to avoid knocking me down, then shot me a glare as if to say walking and talking ought to be illegal—or I shouldn't be allowed out without a keeper. "I guess that's better than marrying a potbellied pig," I reasoned aloud. "Women do that all the time."

"Yes, but the two-legged variety, not the four-legged," Miss P shot back. "Mrs. Olefson won't take no for an answer. Delphinia's at a loss."

"Tell her I'm on my way."

BUILT of huge blocks of sandstone, the Temple of Love, the Babylon's wedding chapel, anchored one end of the Bazaar. Twenty-foot double wooden doors with brass fittings guarded the entrance. A large wooden beam stood at the ready to be dropped into place to secure the doors against an invading horde. The beam was just a prop—the doors never closed. Love was a twenty-four-hour business in Las Vegas.

Smaller than expected, the interior of the Temple was sparsely decorated with urns of reeds to soften the corners, a mat woven of papyrus on the floor to dampen any noise, and brass torches on the walls to provide ambiance and subtle lighting—an empty theatre in which a bride could stage her wedding fantasies.

Stopping just inside the doorway, I paused to let my eyes adjust. "Anybody home?"

Delphinia, the Babylon's head wedding planner, rushed to greet me. Everything about Delphina screamed "average" . . . until you looked into her eyes. A deep violet, they were windows to an old soul. "Lucky, thank you. I didn't know what else to do," she whispered, wringing her hands. "I tried to explain to her that under the laws of Nevada. . . ."

"I know. You did your best," I said, squeezing her arm in reassurance. "Let me take a shot."

At the back of the temple, Mrs. Olefson sat in an overstuffed chair that swallowed her tiny frame. Dressed in a slim St. John suit, a string of pearls, and sensible Ferragamos, with perfectly coiffed white hair and a tasteful gold watch, she reeked of old money and upper crust. With a cup of tea perched on her lap and a tiny ball of fur curled at her feet, she stared into space.

"Mrs. Olefson?"

The little dog yelped in surprise, startling its owner—her teacup rattled in its saucer. She turned worried eyes my direction.

"I'm sorry, I didn't mean to scare you." I squatted down, extending a hand toward the dog. "Will he bite?"

"Good heavens, no." Mrs. Olefson gave me a wan smile. Her accent was hard to place—Midwest for sure . . . maybe with a hint of foreign.

"I'm Lucky O'Toole," I said. "I work here at the Babylon." I scratched the pooch behind one ear; he rolled over and presented his tummy. "I checked you in the other day."

"I remember," Mrs. Olefson said. "Milo likes

you. You should be pleased—he has impeccable taste."

"He's just rewarding me for making an exception to our no-pets policy." I stood and relieved her of her empty cup. "Why don't we take a stroll and you can tell me what's going on and what we can do for you?"

She gave me her hand, and I helped her out of the soft cushions. Once on her feet, she brushed down her narrow skirt and hooked her black patent leather purse over a forearm. Heading for the doorway, she looked steady on her feet, but I held her arm just in case—she didn't seem to mind. Nipping at our heels, Milo trailed behind.

Ambling in silence, we joined the flow of shoppers.

"My husband and I had no children," Mrs. Olefson began. "He left me very well off. All our extended family . . ." She shot me a sad look. "All the worthwhile ones, anyway, have been taken care of."

The crowd growing thicker, I knew it was a matter of time before someone stepped on poor Milo, or tripped over him, so I scooped him up and tucked him under one arm.

"Now that they have their money," Mrs. Olefson continued in a tired voice, "no one wants to come see an old woman anymore. Milo is all I have left."

"And you're worried about his future if something happens to you?"

"I can't even imagine the feeding frenzy after

my death. Milo will be left out in the cold and my money will go to the government. Then what's left of it will end up in the hands of people who don't give a whit about me." She looked so sad . . . and lonely. "I heard you could leave all your money to your spouse and not pay any estate tax, so I thought I'd just marry Milo and solve that problem for good."

"I'm afraid that might be a little difficult, and besides, you still would have to find someone to care for him and manage his money."

Her face crinkled into a frown. "I hadn't thought of that. Sometimes I forget Milo isn't a person." She reached for the dog as a child would reach for a comforting blanket or toy. Cradling him in her arms, a look of peace settled on her face.

"Many people feel that way about their pets." I maneuvered her toward the entrance to the Burger Palais. "I think I can steer you toward an acceptable solution to your problem. Let's talk about it over lunch—my treat."

"Is the food good here?" Mrs. Olefson asked, glancing up at the sign.

"The best. And the French chef is to die for."

A spark of interest lit her eyes as I led her to a quiet booth against the wall and helped her scootch in.

Jean-Charles would have a cow over the dog.

AS it turned out, neither one of us was very hungry, so we both settled on extrathick chocolate shakes. We drained them dry over talk of estate planning, family dynamics, and mortality. The lunch crowd had thinned by the time Mrs. Olefson formulated a plan—Milo would be happy with the little girl back home, who lived with her mother down the hall—the young lady practically lived at Mrs. Olefson's apartment as it was. Perhaps she would set up a trust for the girl and her mother—and for Milo, of course. Then what money she didn't use to fund the trust, she would leave to charity—she already had several in mind.

"I won't wait until I get home," Mrs. Olefson announced. "I will call my lawyer when I get back to the room. You've been such a help, dear." She gave my hand a squeeze across the table. "It's hard to be the last one to get to the end of your bean row. The only folks I have left have their hands in the cookie jar—their opinions can't be trusted. I have no one else."

"You have me." I gave her one of my cards.

"So where is the hot French chef you promised me?" she asked, a wicked twinkle in her eye, as she stowed my card in her wallet.

On cue, Jean-Charles stepped out of the kitchen and surveyed his kingdom. Wiping his hands on his ever-present towel, he spied me. With a wave and a grin he launched himself in our direction. I stood as he approached.

He took my hands in his and bussed each cheek. "So wonderful to see you."

There was that zing thing again. "Jean-Charles, may I present Mrs. Genevieve Olefson."

He bowed slightly then took one of her hands and kissed it. "My pleasure, Mrs. Olefson."

"Oh my," she said, a hand fluttering to her chest. "Lucky said you were delicious, but I had no idea."

Jean-Charles shot me an amused glance. "Really?"

I felt my cheeks reddening, which must have been visible because Mrs. Olefson said, "Oh, now I've said something I shouldn't have."

She didn't look too broken up about it, if you ask me. In fact, I'd say she looked pretty proud of herself.

"You two young people would make a nice couple." As I slid back into the booth, I shot her a warning glance, which she blithely ignored. "Well, neither of you are wearing any wedding rings."

"Mrs. Olefson," I said, trying to regain control of the conversation, "this is Chef Jean-Charles Bouclet." I caught myself before I said Chef Tastycakes—maybe I was getting a rein on my mouth, but I doubted it.

"*The* Chef Bouclet? Of J-C Bistro in Manhattan?"

"Madam, you flatter me. You have dined with me?" Jean-Charles scooted in next to me, his thigh pressed to mine, effectively cutting off my escape.

Glancing at my tablemates, it dawned on me

there were far worse ways to spend a portion of the afternoon. So, trapped by the handsome Frenchman, I decided to sit back and enjoy my good fortune.

Chapter

SEVEN

♡

So you think I am—how do you say it? Delicious?" Jean-Charles asked after we returned Mrs. Olefson to her suite. The excitement of the day had left her needing a nap.

"I think the Mona Lisa is exquisite as well, but that doesn't mean I want to take her home, so don't get the wrong idea."

He grabbed my arm, stopping me in the middle of the lobby. People filed by on either side of us, creating a cocoon of disinterest around the gorgeous Frenchman and me. "But you like me, *non?*"

Unsure of the proper response, I stared at Jean-Charles. Did I like him? Unfortunately, yes . . . more than I should. So far, he appeared about as deep as a puddle after a storm . . . and as volatile as a two-year-old. Yet . . . I couldn't shake the feeling it was all an act. And there was that heat thing when our skin touched. . . .

"You *were* very nice not to mention Mrs. Olefson's dog. . . ." I said.

"Lucky! There you are!" The Big Boss called to me across the lobby, turning heads and saving me from sure disaster—I'd never been so happy to see him.

The crowd parted for The Big Boss. When he arrived in front of us he shook the chef's hand. "Jean-Charles, I trust Lucky is taking care of your needs."

Well, I *had* been happy to see him.

Jean-Charles kept his face impassive. "For the most part, *oui*."

"Good." The Big Boss narrowed his eyes and looked at me, then back at the chef. I held my breath, hoping he wouldn't dig the hole I was standing in any deeper. I breathed a sigh of relief when he said, "If you two are finished, Lucky, I'd like a word."

Jean-Charles nodded then, and taking my hand, he raised it to his lips as he gave me a penetrating look, and took his leave. What was that about? And why did my hand fit so well in his? Thinking like that would do nothing but get me in trouble— even I knew falling for a co-worker was an invitation to complete ruination. And then there was Teddie . . . who couldn't seem to put enough distance between us.

My father hooked my hand through his arm. "Let's go for a walk in the Hanging Gardens."

Our garden area surrounded three swimming

pools, one for family, one for adults only, and one
for VIPs, hidden by tall palms, where topless bathing was allowed. A lazy river connected the three
pools, widening into grotto bars at strategic locations. A jungle of flowering vegetation lined the
pathways and trailed from the balconies of rooms
above. A Swiss Family Robinson–inspired tree
house, the open-air Garden Bar, dangled above a
small section of the adult pool, providing much
needed shade—and a wonderful viewing platform
for the bar patrons.

We settled on a bench in a secluded corner of
the gardens. My father cast a jaundiced eye at me.
"What was that back there? There was enough
spark between you and Jean-Charles to jump-start
the space shuttle."

"He's like a pretty woman, using his charms to
get what he wants. I've got a handle on it."

"Mmm." My father didn't look convinced.

"So what did you want to see me about? Mother
isn't plotting the overthrow of a small nation or
something, is she?"

"No, no. Not today, anyway. At least not that
I've been told, but I'm often left out of the loop."
Distracted, my father tore a flower from its stem.

I waited him out. Frankly, I didn't want another
problem, another issue to resolve, but the look on
his face told me that's what I was going to get.

A hummingbird darted from flower to flower in
the warmth of the sun. Bees buzzed, but I couldn't
see them. The murmur of happy voices drifted on

the cool breeze as guests greeted the day and went in search of the perfect lounge by the pool. Glasses clinked, a champagne cork popped—late lunch at the Garden Bar.

My father had plucked every petal from the flower when my patience ran out. "So, does she love you, or love you not?" I asked.

"What?"

I nodded at the pile of petals at his feet.

"She loves me," he said with a smile, but his eyes had that worried look to them. "That's the problem."

My heart sank, but I tried to keep my emotions off my face. "Getting cold feet?"

"Of course not!" he snapped, looking annoyed.

"Well then, would you stop being so darned obtuse and tell me what's going on?"

"You don't need to get angry."

"Sorry. Apparently I have a lot of my father in me."

He glared at me but didn't disagree. I wasn't sure whether that was a good thing or a bad thing. Like a child lost in the forest, he looked nervous, unsure—I'd say terrified even . . . if I didn't know him better.

The fight in him ebbed away and he sighed. "What do women expect from a marriage proposal?"

I don't know what I had been bracing for, but that wasn't it. I didn't try to hide my grin as I leaned back and turned my face to the sun. Love—it brings all of us to our knees—even the mighty. Closing my eyes, I lifted my face to catch the last long angles of sun. What *did* women want from a proposal of marriage? What would I want?

After a moment of thought, I said, "Sincerity."

Openly skeptical, my father asked, "That's all?"

"That's everything," I replied.

HOUSEKEEPING occupied the entire first basement level of the hotel. The amount of machinery, staff, and supplies required to keep a hotel the size of the Babylon operating at its five-star level was overwhelming. Sonja Falco, a force of nature, rode herd over all of it. She used a small, cramped corner near one of the huge steam presses as her office and base of operations. I could usually find her there.

The noise of the machinery, the hiss of steam, made talking impossible, and shouting only modestly effective, so I nodded at the staff members shepherding the laundry through the process as I worked my way toward Sonja's office. She'd made the journey difficult on purpose—she didn't want many visitors.

A trap even for the wary, the laundry area was a maze of knee-knockers and head-bangers. By the time I'd run the gauntlet, I'd hit my head twice on low-hanging pipes and singed my calf when it got too close to a steam relief valve, but I was getting better—the last time I'd visited Sonja I'd needed stitches.

Sonja looked up when I loomed over her. She didn't frown, which for Sonja equaled a smile. A short, round woman, her long black hair captured in a net at the base of her neck, she was known for her sharp tongue, but respected for its judicious use. And if you wanted a favor from Sonja, you'd better ask her in person.

"How's everything going?" I asked, raising my voice to be heard.

"You didn't come all the way down here to ask me that."

"I want about forty or fifty old blankets, if you have them." The Babylon regularly took blankets out of service—if they were a little bit worn, had a hole from someone smoking in bed (even though smoking was not allowed, guests did it anyway, and we charged them for the resulting fumigation), or were otherwise deemed less than five-star quality, they were stockpiled for the Salvation Army, Goodwill, and other charitable organizations.

"We got at least that many. Are you hitting the tunnels again?" At my nod, she continued, "I'll pull some aside for you. When do you want them?"

"Tomorrow, late morning?" At her nod, I continued, "I'll arrange for the truck."

I made it out of the laundry without further bodily harm. Flipping open my phone, I hit the button for Romeo.

"I have a bone to pick with you," I said when he answered on the second ring. "How come you didn't tell me the cat burglar left a note in the Daniels apartment?"

"I didn't know," he replied. "The cop working the case got pulled to work a double homicide in North Vegas. She's up to her ass in alligators and hasn't had time to return my phone calls. It'll be a couple of days until she comes up for air, I suspect. Simple burglaries aren't sexy enough to get much attention anymore. Who told you about the note?"

"Do you know anything else you haven't told me?" I said, ignoring his question. "Like maybe what the thief took?"

"As I said, I haven't been able to corroborate any of this with the detective in charge, but one of our men on the scene told me the thief took cheap jewelry—nothing of any value."

"From the safe?"

"Apparently."

"Who had access?"

"Only Mr. Daniels. The wife claimed she didn't know the combination and had no idea what her husband kept in there."

"What did the note say?"

"Eden."

"That's a word, not a note," I said. "Do you have any idea what it means?"

"Not a clue."

"Have you found Molly Rain?"

"Haven't even picked up a scent."

"I need a favor," I said.

"Only one?" Romeo said with a lilt in his voice.

"No, actually two. First, could you run Dr. Jenkins through your computer?"

"Jenkins? How does he fit in?"

"If I knew, I wouldn't need your help. But he did this weird mind-reading thing on me last night. Really spooked me. I couldn't tell how he did it. Flash has tied Danilov to Area 51; I was just wondering if Jenkins might have a connection as well since they both are into that mind-reading stuff. It's a long shot, but the more info we have. . . ."

"I'll put him through." Romeo paused.

I figured he was taking notes, so I waited.

"What else do you need?" he asked, not sounding at all put out—if anything, he was a good sport.

"If you let Mr. Mortimer look at the Houdini thing, he's going to tell us who owns it," I announced, as if I knew that for a fact.

Romeo paused while he did a mental cost/benefit analysis. "Couldn't hurt to let the guy look at the thing, and maybe we'll get one piece of solid information."

"Great! How about tomorrow afternoon around two?"

"Are you coming with him?"

"Do you really think I would consider ducking out of this show just as it's getting good? Fool that I am, I'm riveted. I wouldn't miss it for the world."

. . .

MISS P and I met at the door to the stairwell—she was on her way out. With her purse over her arm, her sweater around her shoulders, and a silly grin on her face, I'd bet my last dollar she was through working and on her way to play.

"Knocking off early?" I asked.

"No, I'll be around for a while—I thought I might stay close until the UFO folks get their cocktail party underway. I'm just heading to the bar for a quick drink with Jeremy."

"Your job driving you to drink?"

"No, just my boss," she deadpanned. "Want to join us?"

I hesitated, vacillating between duty and dereliction for about three nanoseconds. "Sure, but only if you knock off and leave the UFO people to me." Maybe her job wasn't driving her to drink, but mine was . . . along with a few other things.

"You sure?"

"My evening is free," I said, trying not to pout. "Go have some fun with your Aussie-boy."

Jeremy had snagged a corner table in Delilah's. As I trudged up the steps to the bar, I noticed he wasn't alone—Dane lounged in the second of four chairs. The two men stood as we approached.

"You're late," Jeremy teased Miss P, then gave her an enthusiastic kiss that made her blush to her roots. She looked at the chair next to his, then decided his lap looked better. He didn't seem to mind as he handed her a flute of champagne.

As I took the seat next to him, Dane gave me a

grin, but his eyes skittered away—he looked uncomfortable.

"Hey," he said. "Want something to drink?"

"How about a Diet Coke?" I hadn't had much to eat and the night was still young.

Dane headed toward the bar, leaving me stranded with the lovebirds, who cooed between themselves.

I hazarded a glance at the piano—the bench was empty. Many a night I sat there while Teddie played me a tune and sang me a song—a distant memory . . . not to mention a distant lover, which wasn't working for me at all.

Aware of Dane's presence at my side, I looked up. Clutching his Bud in one hand and my soda in the other, he stared over me—a look of panic in his eyes.

I turned, following his gaze.

Flash advanced upon us. She eyed the Diet Coke. "Cowboy, if that's for me, you've got me all wrong." Then she reached a hand behind his head and pulled him into a long, slow kiss. "I've missed you. Thanks for calling." Then she saw me. "Hey, girlfriend, are you joining us for dinner?"

"No, just holding your place until you got here," I said, launching to my feet. "The Diet Coke's for me, I'm still on the clock."

"Never knew that to stop you before."

"I'm turning over a new leaf." I relieved Dane of my soda. "Thanks. You guys have fun."

I smiled, probably a stiff smile, but it was the

best I could do. Nothing like being the fifth wheel. As I left, I didn't look back. I might be lonely. I might be sad. I might even be jealous. But at least I had my dignity.

On the other hand, dignity never kept anyone warm at night.

Dane and Flash? I wrestled with that picture as I stalked across the casino, into the lobby, and up the stairs to the Mezzanine. She'd never mentioned him before. She missed him? What did that mean? Did he like her? Had he slept with her? And why did I care?

After draining the last of the Diet Coke, I crushed the can in my fist, tossed it into a waste bin, and headed for the Golden Fleece Room. The cocktail party for the UFO crowd was just getting underway.

AT the cash bar, I traded virtue for a double Wild Turkey on the rocks. Two long sips dulled the pain a bit.

"Man, you're suckin' on that like a calf on a tit," Junior Arbogast said, appearing at my elbow. "Havin' a bad day?"

"More than one—I'm stringing them together."

"Corn whiskey won't help."

I looked into the concerned eyes of my friend. "You're right. Thanks." I handed the glass back to the bartender. "Things are sort of piling up on me right now."

"They do that from time to time. Haven't ever heard of anyone dying from it, though."

"Not directly," I said, as I scanned the crowd for familiar faces, ignoring Junior's quizzical look. "Have you heard any more from the commando radio guy?"

"He's holed up in Rachel waiting for dark, then he'll move into place. His show doesn't air until eleven."

"Could you arrange for me to pay him a visit? I'd like to get his story straight from the horse's mouth."

"Would this be about those messages from your vanished magician friend?"

"You got it."

"I'll see what I can do."

"Thanks," I said as I let my eyes wander—without a glass in my hand, I was all fidgety.

A short man, deep in conversation in the far back corner of the room, caught my attention. Zoom-Zoom Zewicki. He looked angry. Clusters of partiers blocked my view of the woman he was talking with—I caught a glimpse, then nothing. Curious, I leaned around until I got a better view.

Zoom-Zoom glanced up and caught me staring. He said something to the woman. She whipped her head around. Molly Rain! Our eyes met and held. When I started toward her, Molly turned and ran through a service door in the back wall. Not caring about the stares, I ran after her.

As I moved to dart around him, Zoom-Zoom stepped in my path. Had he not grabbed my arm, I would have fallen. "Lucky, what's the hurry?"

"I'll be right back, okay?" I jerked my arm out of his grasp and hit the door running.

I was too late. Molly Rain was gone.

"Did you do that on purpose?" I demanded of Zoom-Zoom when I returned to the party.

"The girl is distraught enough. You looked loaded for bear. I didn't think this was the appropriate time or place for you to question her."

"The police are looking for her."

"She's been in touch with Detective Romeo."

I had nothing to say to that. If that was true, Romeo was dead meat. "Do you mind me asking what she wanted from you?"

"She wants me to try to contact Dimitri. They were lovers, you see. She's beside herself. She wants to know if he's okay on the other side."

After all this time in Vegas, I should have mastered the art of talking to crazy people, but "uh huh" was all I could think of to say. Clearly, I was losing my grip, and Junior Arbogast had been wrong—drinking would most definitely help. The whole world had gone nuts—I might as well join in. "And have you managed to make contact with the late Mr. Fortunoff?"

"Thursday night at eleven. We have a séance planned out at Rachel—part of the whole UFO conference entertainment. You are welcome to come." He put a hand on my arm as I turned to go.

"But I warn you, these things can be dangerous, life altering."

"Life altering would be good."

DR. Zewicki was right—I was indeed loaded for bear. Not feeling the least bit sociable, I snuck out the side entrance, leaving the spookies to party on without me. Too antsy to head for home and with all under control, I was at loose ends. An unusual state of affairs—a problem I had no idea how to solve. I needn't have worried. A call from Mother caught me wandering aimlessly through the lobby.

"Lucky, you need to come up to your father's suite right away." Her voice sounded tight, choked.

"Mother, what's wrong? Are you crying?" My mother rarely cried—normally she made other people cry—or, in my case, want to shoot something.

"It's your father . . ."

"He's okay, isn't he?" My heart constricted—the memories of the phone call announcing he'd been rushed to the hospital still fresh in my mind.

"No, he's not okay!" Mona wailed. "He's mad at me. He left here in a rage. I don't know where he's gone."

"People do argue, Mother. Even people in love."

"But I've never seen him like this," she whispered as she choked back a sob.

"What set him off?"

"He asked me to marry him. He got down on his knees and everything."

"That's great!"

"I told him no."

AGAIN, words fled. I was once again at a loss—this was sooo not good. So I took a call from Security instead—perhaps I'd have better luck communicating with them. If not, I was going to need a go-between all my own . . . happy thought. "Mother, hold on a minute," I ordered. Not waiting for her reply, I switched to the other call. "Whatcha got?"

"We're responding to an injury in Room Fourteen Six Seventy," Jerry, our Head of Security said, his voice calm—just another day at the circus. "Thought you might want to be in the loop."

"Is it serious?"

"I didn't get that impression. The man who reported it couldn't stop laughing."

"On my way." I clicked back over to Mona. "Mother—"

"How *dare* you put me on hold! I'm *in extremis* here. Don't you ever—"

"Cork it, Mother. The needs of our guests take precedence over yours. I'll be there as soon as possible. Don't do anything else stupid, okay?" My "okay" was rhetorical, even if she couldn't grasp that. I hung up on her in mid-whine.

WHEN I knocked on the door to Room 14670, Jerry let me in without a word, the look on his face stoic. "This one is more up your alley than mine, I think."

A woman, mid-fifties, forty pounds overweight, and naked as the day she was born—except for a towel draped between her legs—hung suspended from the ceiling in a sex swing. A long rope, strung through a grommet on the ceiling, connected Velcroed belts around each thigh, spreading her legs wide. Her large breasts, lifted and separated by a harness, hung like ripe fruit. First looking at us over one shoulder, then having to switch to the other as she rotated, she managed to choke out between fits of laughter, "Ya'll gotta get me outta here. My legs have gone numb and I'm laughing so hard I'm gonna pee." Laughter would have doubled her over had that been possible.

A man, the same age and looking like he had also spent too much time at the trough, wiped the tears from his face with a handkerchief. He wore a huge grin and a towel around his ample waist, nothing else. An empty bottle of Tattinger lay on its side on the floor, which explained some of the giggling.

"I'm Harry Simpson from Muskogee. That there's my wife, Mavis."

"I'm Lucky O'Toole, Head of Customer Relations. How can we help?"

"Well, me and Mavis came with the bus tour for the UFO conference. We don't cotton to all that woo-woo stuff, but the spookies are a fun bunch—sure a lot more interesting than the folks back home."

"Harry, get to the point, honey," Mavis instructed

from her perch—her voice held the patience of a long marriage.

"Right. Well, in our bag of Vegas stuff we saw this flyer from Smokin' Joe's Sex Emporium—they said they delivered, so we thought when in Vegas . . ." He nudged me with his elbow and gave me a wink. "Everyone could use a boost to their between-the-sheets time, right?"

I treated the question as rhetorical. One actually needs a sex life before they can give it a boost.

"Anyway," Harry continued, fighting laughter as he glanced at his wife. "I strapped her in that thing and hoisted her up there, but I'll be damned if I know what I'm supposed to do with her like that."

Jerry rubbed a hand over his face, hiding his smile. Biting hard on the inside of my mouth, I refused to look him in the eye.

"Maybe we ought to get her down," I suggested. "Then you guys can start with some of the less . . . adventurous . . . stuff. Then maybe once you get the hang of it . . ."

Both Harry and Mavis looked at me wide-eyed, then burst out laughing. Jerry turned away.

"That's the thing," Harry said, when he'd gotten control of himself. "She's stuck."

"Stuck?" I asked, as I eyed Mavis.

"Yup." Harry nodded. "She's hung up tighter than a large calf in a small momma."

I closed my mind to that visual as I surveyed

the problem. "It looks like the rope has one of those safety catches—like window shades."

"Well, I'll be danged," Harry announced, as he looked where I pointed. "No wonder I could only make her go up."

"Come on," I said, grabbing the end of the rope trailing out of the catch near Mavis's left thigh. "Put your weight to it. I'll back you up. Let's get her down, preferably without cracking her like a wishbone after Thanksgiving."

"WHAT took you so long?" Mother turned on me the minute the elevator doors opened to their penthouse apartment.

"You'll be amazed to know I actually have other responsibilities that sometimes take precedence over your problems," I growled, as I advanced on her. "What in God's name were you thinking?"

She retreated to the couch. Crumpling in on herself, she wedged into a corner using several pillows as a shield. "You sound just like your father."

Mother's tear-streaked face took the fight out of me. Settling in next to her, I brushed a strand of hair out of her face as she looked at me with big eyes. "Why don't you tell me what happened?"

"He was so cute, really—so earnest and sincere." Once a mother, always a mother, she brushed at a spot of dirt on my shoulder as if taking care of me would make everything right again in her world.

"He'd even bought a ring—one of those ten-table rings other women wear."

"Ten-table rings?"

"So big you can see them ten tables away."

"Ah." I held her hand—her skin was cold. "I'm at sea here, Mother. Sincerity. A huge ring. Why again did you turn him down?"

"He's only marrying me because I'm knocked up," she wailed.

The laugh, so long contained, now burst free, bubbling out of me despite my best efforts to keep it contained. At my mother's frown, I laughed harder—I couldn't help myself. Tears streaked down my face as I struggled to breathe.

My mother yanked her hand from mine. "I don't find this funny at all," she huffed.

"From where I'm sitting, it's hilarious. I just pray to God that idiocy is *not* an inherited trait." I headed for the bar in search of a drink—clearly I was way behind the rest of the people in my little corner of the universe. I splashed a finger of Wild Turkey into a tumbler, then threw it back. The trail of fire brought tears to my eyes, but I didn't care. Fortified, I returned to loom over my mother. "Pull yourself together, Mother. Go wash your face, put on a fresh outfit, and go find him. Start with the bars—that's where most men I know go to nurse a demolished ego."

"You think I'm being silly, then?"

"No. I think you've lost your friggin' mind. Blame it on hormones and beg his forgiveness."

A few minutes ahead of my mother, I went in search of The Big Boss. As expected, I found him in his favorite spot in the Garden Bar overlooking the pools and the hanging gardens.

When he glanced up at me, his eyes held the glassy stare of more than one double-bourbon. "I guess you heard." It was a statement, not a question. "She doesn't want to marry me."

He looked so sad, I wanted to spank my mother—then strangle her, but that would be too good for her. Somehow, maybe this pregnancy was a bit of the payback the woman deserved—an attention getter—if she only paid heed.

"Of course she does," I said, the conviction of truth ringing in my voice. "Hopefully, she is on her way down here, so I only have a few minutes—I don't want her to see me with you. May I give you a word of advice?"

"Fire away."

"Next time she pulls a stunt like this, do a caveman."

"And risk certain death?" A fleeting grin lifted one corner of his mouth.

"She's all blow and no go. Trust me, I've been handling her for years."

"So I should take matters into my own hands?" he asked.

"Absolutely. For God's sake don't let her think she wears the pants in the family—she'll make your life a living hell." I turned to go, then turned back.

"You know, I'm beginning to doubt your sanity— she's my mother, I *have* to deal with her. You, on the other hand, can cut and run."

This time I got the full wattage of his smile. "If she passed a burning building, she'd rush head-long into it—you gotta love her."

"Brave, but not wise."

"You have a lot of your mother in you."

"I'm not sure this is the best time to tell me that."

LOVE has a way of scraping back the layers of self-protection, leaving us exposed and vulnerable. The joy must be worth the pain, since humans keep fall-ing in love, but you couldn't prove it by me. Oh, I had the pain all right, but the joy was proving a bit elusive.

Right now, all I wanted was the escape of sleep.

After retrieving my Birkin and my Glock— leaving a loaded weapon in my office didn't seem like the best plan—I pounded the pavement to-ward home. My sights set on a hot bath, then cool sheets, I barely nodded at Forrest. "Nothing new on the Daniels robbery?" I asked without pausing to talk.

"Nothing more than the firestorm set off by your friend, that loud woman with the paper?"

That stopped me. "Flash?" I asked, turning to face the big man.

"That's the one!" He nodded. "She hit the eve-ning news with some story about Mr. Daniels having been the head of some secret program at Area 51."

"Really?"

"Yup." Forrest dropped his voice to a conspiratorial whisper, causing me to move closer. "Here's the kicker: apparently those papers stolen from Mr. Daniels were secret documents, smuggled out of Area 51."

That ought to bring some unwanted attention, I thought. "What kind of program was it?"

"They didn't say. The Air Force is pissed and backpedalling fast. Sorta fun to watch, actually—they think we're all so damned dumb, telling us the base doesn't exist. You can see the friggin' thing on Google Earth, for chrissake!"

"There is a divine justice to it, isn't there?"

"Yes, ma'am." Forrest shot me a brilliant grin, then sobered. "This is dangerous stuff, Ms. Lucky. Be careful—you being alone and all. If you need anything, you shout."

Alone. I hated that word. Worse, I hated that reality.

If I hadn't already completely lost my smile thinking about love and the splash Flash had made—talk about poking a stick into a beehive—his comment evaporated any vestiges of good humor.

My apartment was empty, the bird quiet, when I tossed my bag on the couch after retrieving my firearm—next to the bed would be a good place for it—then headed for my bedroom.

I reached to open the nightstand drawer. Then I saw it. On my bed. My blood froze.

A stuffed white rabbit. A glittering collar. A note.

The note read, "DEATH WALKS. BEWARE."

Chapter

EIGHT

♡

W ith my pulse pounding, the Glock gripped in both hands, I first dropped to my knees and checked under the bed. No one there.

Moving from room to room, I checked every corner, every closet, every window—the rooms were empty, the windows intact and locked. Even the balcony doors were secure with no signs of jimmying. Nothing was missing. Nothing had been tampered with, as if the intruder had drifted in like smoke through the cracks.

Satisfied I was alone, I set the Glock on the kitchen counter within easy reach and dialed Forrest.

"Has anyone been in my apartment today?" I asked when he answered.

"Only Miss Tracey to look after the bird. I let

her in and waited while she did her thing, like I always do."

"You've been on duty all day?"

"Yes, ma'am. Why?"

"Someone's been here. They left a note."

THE adrenaline ebbed as I sat on a stool at my kitchen counter waiting for Forrest—he insisted on coming up. I didn't argue. Not only was I alone . . . now I was scared.

Forrest arrived and took a turn through the place as if I wouldn't know an intruder when I saw one. In a few minutes he reappeared in the kitchen, his face flushed, his eyes angry. "No one's here, but somebody's messin' with me and I don't like it."

"Messing with *you*? He's been in *my* place."

"It's *my* building," Forrest growled, eyeing the Glock on the counter. "I'm responsible." The look in his eyes left me with no doubt that, if Forrest got his hands on him, the intruder would be sipping his meals through a straw.

"Would you mind checking Mr. Teddie's apartment? It's the obvious jumping-off point to get to my balcony," I asked, not wanting to go through Teddie's place myself. Seeing his things, smelling the hint of his cologne lingering there, would make his absence too real . . . as if it wasn't real enough already.

"Sure thing."

. . .

FORREST reported back when he had finished reconnoitering. "No sign of any forced entry anywhere. I even checked the roof."

Not what I wanted to hear. "If I had an idea how he got in," I said, "I might be able to keep him out."

"You got someplace else to go tonight?" Forrest asked.

"I'm not scared off that easily." Putting my gun in my pocket, I escorted him back to the elevator. "You go on home. I'm sure your shift is long over. I'll be fine."

"Too bad Mr. Teddie isn't here. I'd sure feel better if you wasn't alone."

"I'm fine," I said, trying to convince myself. Then I realized I didn't have to try—I really was fine. A little bit of adrenaline and a lot of angry were the perfect antidotes to a pity party.

"Shouldn't we call the police?" The big man couldn't hide his worry.

"I'll take care of it."

After the doors closed behind him, I phoned Romeo. "Sorry if I awakened you," I said when I heard his tired voice.

"Sleep? What's that? They could sublet my apartment, and I'd never know."

"I just got home myself. Somebody broke in. They left me a note."

"What kind of note?"

"The same kind Dimitri Fortunoff received, except my rabbit is stuffed—which is a good thing since they left it on my bed."

"Well, what do you know, we actually have a real crime—breaking and entering. Up until now, this whole thing has been smoke and mirrors, and the higher-ups refused to let me spend precious government resources investigating. Now maybe I can sink my teeth into it." He sounded thrilled.

I was less so. "Glad to be of service." I guess he wasn't including the previous break-in as part of Dimitri's disappearance, which was understandable—so far we hadn't been able to connect Danilov to our magician.

"Do you know how they got in?" Romeo asked, warming to his task.

"Magic."

"No signs of forced entry, huh? Any of the windows unlocked?"

"No."

"And the balcony doors? What kind of lock do you have on them?"

"One of those locks where you turn the little thingy in the door knob, why?"

"No deadbolt?"

"I'm thirty floors up, I didn't think a break-in was that likely."

"Lucky, I could pick that lock in under twenty seconds, and I'm not even that good."

"The fact that you have even developed that skill should give me pause," I groused, not the least bit pleased with his revelation.

"Do you want me to come over? I can bunk on a couch or something after I go over the place."

"Thanks, but not necessary. You won't find anything here—whoever this guy is, he's darned clever." As I stared across my great room, I pictured the guy sneaking through. "And if he shows his sorry ass here again, he's going to be looking at the business end of a Glock."

Romeo laughed. "I'd pay good money to see *that*. I've seen what you can do when you're angry." The last time he'd seen me really angry, there had been a broken nose and blood involved—it was a proud moment.

"You haven't talked to Molly Rain, have you?" I asked innocently.

"No, I told you we haven't been able to get a bead on her. Why?"

"Just wondering."

A noise jolted me out of a deep sleep.

I bolted to a sitting position. Heart hammering. Ears straining . . . listening.

Silence.

Did I imagine it?

A scuffling noise. A light thump.

Someone was in the apartment!

Easing from under the duvet, careful not to make a sound, I grabbed the gun. I tiptoed to the doorway and flattened myself against the wall beside the opening. Dane had been right about always having a round in the chamber.

Taking deep, quiet breaths, I steadied myself. Both hands on the grip, the gun at the ready in front of my chest, I waited.

Where was he?

Muffled footfalls. Swishing sounds of movement. Growing almost imperceptibly louder. He was heading this way.

Time froze. Fight or flight? Trapped, I had no choice.

Blood pounded through me. Sweat trickled down my sides. Adrenaline fired every nerve, forced every brain cell to high alert.

I could hear him breathing. He was close. Not more than a few feet away.

Sounds of movement stopped. I held my breath, afraid to make the slightest noise.

Seconds dragged by. Would he leave? Why did he come back? To finish the job? To leave another note? Or to see just how scared I really was?

The moonlight silhouetted a man as he eased through the door. Focused on my bed, he didn't look in my direction.

Leveling the gun at his head, I growled, "That's far enough, you son of a bitch!"

The man's head swiveled toward me as he jumped away. "Lucky? For God's sake don't shoot."

"Teddie?" I didn't dare believe it. I hit the switch, flooding the room in light.

There he was—big as day. Spiked blond hair, beautiful blue eyes . . . that grin . . . and that ass. One look and I tossed the gun on the bed and leapt into his arms, burying my face in his neck. He smelled of exotic places. . . .

Holding me tight, he pressed the length of me against him. "What the hell do you need a gun for?"

"To put the fear of God into people who sneak in on me," I said, not wanting to explain further. "And what's with the surprise? You scared the pee out of me."

He squeezed me tight as he ran one hand down my back, over my hip. His breath caught. "I had to see you," he whispered against my neck.

We were still for a few moments, drinking in the nearness, our bodies remembering . . .

He leaned back, touching my face, a smile tickling his lips. "God how I've missed you," he said before his lips met mine. His kiss sent arcs of heat and desire, frissons of excitement racing through me. He deepened his kiss and the world disappeared.

"Tell me I'm not dreaming," I said, when we came up for air.

"I must be," Teddie said, gasping as my hands found a gap under his shirt—time and distance hadn't diminished the combustion when our skin touched. "I hoped for an enthusiastic welcome, but I didn't imagine a naked woman with a gun."

"Tonight is your Lucky night," I said, as I worked his shirt and sweater over his head and let my hands roam across his bare chest. Looking into his eyes I bit back a seductive grin. "You must be tired."

"Don't play that game with me. I didn't travel halfway around the world, visit every major American city, and arm-wrestle some poor woman in Cleveland for the last seat on the very last flight to Vegas to come here to sleep."

Scooping down, with an arm behind my knees, the other wrapping my shoulders, he picked me up and carried me to bed. With quick movements, he kicked off his shoes and stepped out of his pants, joining me under the covers.

If this was a dream, I never wanted it to end.

Touching his face, tracing the angles and planes, finding tangible proof in the warmth of his skin. "You're really here," I whispered.

He didn't extinguish the light. Instead he pushed back the duvet and let his eyes travel the length of me. A muscle worked in his jaw, but he kept his pace slow, his strokes tender.

I matched his pace—relearning the curve of his shoulders, the breadth of his chest . . . savoring the feel of him, the taste of him.

His hands, his lips, traced a trail of fire across my skin. More insistent, he recaptured my lips, deepening his kiss . . . tongues tangling, ragged gasps.

My hand drifted lower, finding him.

A visceral memory. Heat, and torment . . . a cry against the life that tore us apart . . . and gave us a moment together. When he buried himself inside me, the tumblers to the lock fell into place—my heart opened . . . and I was no longer alone.

DAWN brightened the eastern sky and yet we fought sleep.

Teddie held me in his arms, one leg thrown possessively over me. He stroked my cheek, ran his thumb over my lips, leaned in for a soft, sweet kiss.

"Why didn't you tell me you were coming home?" I said, as I traced the outline of the muscles of his chest, unable to stop touching him.

"It was a spur-of-the-moment thing. I wasn't sure I could pull it off." Teddie lifted my hand to his lips, then pressed it back to his chest before continuing, "Reza got laryngitis—she wasn't improving. You couldn't come to Paris. So I hopped a plane—do you have any idea how hard it is to get a flight into Vegas for Halloween?"

"The higher the price, the better the prize," I teased.

"The price I paid was pretty steep. That woman in Cleveland was ruthless—she took every dollar I had."

I rolled over, straddling him. "Well, then, time for me to give you your prize."

Teddie grinned, anticipation lighting his eyes as he reached for me. "How did I get so damned lucky?"

. . .

COMPLETELY exhausted, blissfully drained, I had one last thing to do before wrapping Teddie around me and surrendering to sleep: I had to officially take the morning off.

Brandy answered on the first ring.

"I won't be in until noon. Is there anything I need to know about?" I said, too tired to wrestle with the niceties.

"All quiet," Brandy said, sounding in control and rather pleased with herself. "I took care of a problem at Reception—a reservation mix-up. I found a room at the Bellagio and negotiated a good rate for the guests who had a reservation here, but no room."

"Very good. Now chase down Vera and ask her how her staff managed to confirm a reservation without a room."

"Already done. She wasn't happy with me—something about taking lessons from my boss."

"Obviously, I'm superfluous. Good job. I have my cell if you need me."

"Is everything okay?" my second assistant asked. Apparently she was taking mothering lessons from Miss P as well.

I looked at Teddie, his head propped on his elbow as he looked at me. "It's way better than okay."

THE alarm clock jangled me out of a dead sleep. Adrenaline spiked, my heart racing at the assault. Daylight streamed through the windows. The duvet pooled at the end of the bed. I was cold. Reaching to pull the covers over me, memories flooded back. Teddie. I rolled over.

The other side of the bed was empty.

Sitting up, I pushed the hair out of my face as I took stock. No sign of Teddie. If that had been a dream . . .

Then I smelled it—coffee.

Teddie appeared in the doorway clad in a pair of sweatpants and a grin, holding a mug in each hand. "I heard the alarm. Thought you might need a jump-start."

"Today, I might need to bypass the usual delivery options and just mainline the stuff." Taking the mug, I savored the wonderful aroma—vanilla-nut, my favorite—then took a tentative sip, testing the temperature.

"You going to tell me about the gun?" Teddie asked as he sat beside me.

"It's a long story and I have a few things I have to take care of this morning, but if you'll move, I'll tell you my sorry tale—which begins with a top hat, a rabbit, a note, and a vanishing magician—while I take a shower."

"I am *so* glad I'm here." Teddie offered me a hand, helping me untangle myself.

"See what you've missed?" I pulled him to me. Skin on skin, I lost myself in his kiss. Before passing the point of no return, I pulled away and led him into my boudoir—I really did need to show my face at work.

Arms crossed, he leaned against the open shower door as I took care of business and brought him up to speed.

"So what do you think is going on?" he asked when I'd finished. "Is the magician pulling some sort of publicity stunt? Or is this whole thing a trick gone bad?"

"Either were possibilities until the B and E, and the threatening note. Now Danilov is all twitchy, Molly Rain is on the lam, and I've stepped on somebody's toes. Seems like more than a harmless stunt."

"Hence the gun," Teddie said with a frown. "I don't like it."

I could've said, "If you were here, your opinion would matter," but I didn't. Instead, I changed the subject. "Now it's your turn," I said, as I wrapped myself in the towel he handed me, then squeezed the water out of my hair.

"Being on the road has its ups and downs, but it's still an unbelievable ride. The energy of tens of thousands of people, screaming, chanting, singing along is intoxicating." He followed me into my closet, where I opened my underwear drawer and peered inside.

"May I?" he asked. At my nod he chose a red lace bra, matching bikini briefs, and garter. With wickedness in his eyes, he watched me don his choices along with a pair of silk stockings. "You take my breath away."

I rewarded him with my best kiss and offered a

silent thank you to Mona, who insisted that, while fast cars and short skirts got a man's attention, sexy underwear sealed the deal. For once, she had been right and I had actually listened.

"So you like the rock star thing?" I asked, praying his answer was no, but knowing in my heart that wasn't the case.

"It's more than I ever imagined." He pulled me into an embrace. "I know it's not what we talked about, what we envisioned, and I'm sorry for that."

"You have to chase your dreams, Teddie, wherever they lead." I tried to smile, but I don't think I pulled it off.

"With six weeks of concerts behind us, Reza and I are finding a rhythm. I'm even getting some fans of my own."

"I had no doubt." One of Teddie's charms had always been that he remained blissfully unaware of his incredible talents. "How long do you think you'll be on the road?" I asked, reaching for an air of casual indifference as I pulled a slim Tory Burch skirt and matching sweater set out of the closet.

"She's booked for several years with a few months off for various holidays. There's talk of keeping me on for the rest of the gig and doing some recording during the downtimes."

"I see." Turning my back on him, I busied myself with face and hair. "Where do I fit into all of this, Teddie?"

If he heard the pain in my voice, he blew right

by it. "Can we talk about that later? This doesn't seem like the right time."

I turned to face him. "I need to know where we stand."

"Later, okay?" His face closed, his voice flattened.

I had my answer.

"What do you have on your plate today?" he asked. "May I ride shotgun?"

"First I need to requisition a van out of the truck pool, then I need to pick up some old blankets from housekeeping."

"Do you have a new job I don't know about?"

"Crazy Carl Colson has gone underground. If I expect to lure him into the light, I need bait for the trap."

SEATED in the passenger seat of the van as I drove, Teddie stuck his hand out the window into the slipstream. He looked tired, and somewhat distracted. Unfortunately, he also looked quite delicious in his ubiquitous jeans that left just enough to the imagination, and his ratty Harvard sweatshirt he had rescued from my closet. Heeding my suggestion, he wore a pair of old Nikes on his feet.

"Are you going to fill me in on this little adventure, or am I just along for the ride?" he asked.

"I got to know Crazy Carl a couple of years ago when Security at another of The Big Boss's properties picked him up—he didn't fit the mold of our usual clientele. They thought he was silver mining and wanted to throw him out."

"Silver mining?"

"A lot of the folks down on their luck troll the casinos looking for credits the slot players forgot to cash out—you'd be surprised how many they find," I explained, as I headed south on the Strip. "He swore all he wanted were some old blankets. I was running several departments at the hotel, Housekeeping was one of them, so the guards brought him to me."

"And he became your friend."

"Hard not to like a guy who was collecting donations for the people who live under Vegas."

Teddie's head snapped around and he stopped playing with the wind. "*Under* Vegas?"

"There's three hundred miles of storm drains under the city—it's possible to enter on the west side of town near the Two-fifteen and end up all the way east past UNLV without ever coming aboveground—and that's just a small stretch."

"People live down there?" Teddie asked, unable to hide his skepticism.

"When you've got nowhere else to go . . ."

"Crazy Carl, tell me about him."

"He's a permanent resident of the storm drains. Although he could live aboveground—he has a small federal pension—he stays underground for protection."

"From what?" Teddie asked, as if he didn't believe a word.

"The Others, at least that's what he calls them."

"So he really is crazy?"

"I don't really know, but I'm pretty sure if he doesn't have a delusional disorder he's flirting with one," I said, as I took a right off the Strip onto Tropicana. "He's convinced there are people who can read minds, put posthypnotic suggestions in your head without you knowing it. He's truly afraid. When the nightmares start and the terrors come, he retreats to the storm drains."

"What do you want from him?"

"A connection. Crazy Carl used to work at Area 51. So did Danilov."

TEDDIE didn't ask any more questions. Just past Decatur, I pulled off the street, nestling the van among the desert shrubs dotting the open field. Laundry put out to dry covered some of the bushes. I smelled the hint of charcoal and something cooking riding on the gentle breeze. Grabbing the few supplies I brought for emergencies, I stepped out of the truck.

As Teddie and I started through the sand toward the entrance to the drains, I caught movement out of the corner of my eye. When I turned to look, no one was visible, but I knew they were there. The homeless found shelter in this field among the scrub.

"I can understand the flashlight, but what do you need the golf club for?" Teddie asked.

"A deterrent." I thrust it at him. "Here, you're in charge of defense."

"This is not sounding like a good idea."

I agreed with him, but I wasn't about to say so.

The mouth to the storm drain was tall enough for me to stand upright and wide enough for Teddie and me to walk abreast. Graffiti art, some of it very good, covered the walls and ceiling. A few feet inside, Teddie stopped me with a hand on my arm. "How far are you planning on going?"

Eyeing the darkness, I flipped on my Maglite. "About fifty feet in there's a tunnel that angles off this main line to the right. It opens into a huge junction room. Carl's camp is in there."

"It can't be safe."

"Hence the golf club and my manly-man escort—that would be you, by the way. But I doubt we'll run into anybody—we're not going far. Besides, everyone is afraid of Crazy Carl."

"Should we be?"

"Probably, but we come bearing gifts."

Teddie stayed at my elbow as the world turned Stygian, our existence reduced to a thin beam of light. Untouched by the warmth of the sun, the dank air held the chill of the night. A half-inch of water sloshed beneath our feet. Smoke hung like a thick cloud above our heads. I tried to ignore the scurrying sounds in the darkness.

"Where's that smoke coming from?" Teddie whispered, as if speaking out loud might stir the ghosts.

"Carl probably has a fire."

"In here?"

We made the turnoff to the right and I stopped. "Carl? Anybody home? It's Lucky."

Backlit by the glow of his fire, Carl loomed in front of us. "What's the word?"

Carl always insisted on a code word—just so he knew it was me and not somebody else controlling me. I didn't know how someone would do that, but sometimes it's best not to quibble with Crazy Carl—I didn't tell Teddie that part. "Engelbert Humperdinck."

He strode forward and wrapped me in a big hug, which I was ambivalent about since his bathing rituals were sketchy at best.

A tall man, Carl had me by several inches and a hundred pounds. His hair was matted and wild, his beard scraggly, his dark eyes the eyes of the hunted. A flash of white as he grinned. "Lucky! How the hell are you?" His voice boomed, echoing around the cavernous space. "Come, come, you're just in time for lunch."

"This is my . . . this is Ted Kowalski," I said by way of introduction, as Teddie and I followed Carl to his camp.

"Good to meet you," Carl tossed over his shoulder. "Any friend of Lucky's is welcome here."

Carl's place reflected his engineering background. Sand fortifications surrounded the main living area, which consisted of a queen-size four-poster bed with matching dresser, a nightstand with washbasin, and a charcoal Hibachi. The coals burned hot as smoke rose into a manhole—Carl had pushed the cover aside to create a flue. A rifle lay across the foot of the bed.

"This place is amazing," Teddie said.

"Almost all the comforts of home," Carl said with a shrug. "I'm cooking hot dogs. Want some?"

"Sure," I said. Carl considered it bad form to turn down an offer of sustenance. "But we can't stay long. We've brought blankets and a few other things. Thought you might need them now the nights are getting colder."

"Mighty nice of you." Carl sat on the ground as he tended the fire and gave me a shrewd look. "Now what can I do for you?"

"What does the word *Eden* mean to you?"

Carl's face went slack, his eyes all buggy. "Why?" His voice was strangled, as if he would choke on the word.

"Do you know a man named Daniels?" I pressed. "He also goes by the *nom de guerre* 'The Great Danilov.'"

Carl grabbed the long fork that had been stuck over the coals—it had two hot dogs on it, puckered and black from the fire. He held it in front of him, pointing it at me like a spear. Wild-eyed, pushing with his heels, he scooted away from me. His back against the bed, he stopped. "Don't come any closer. You're one of them, aren't you?"

"One of who?"

Teddie started to move.

Carl pointed the fork at him. "Stay away." His eyes darted between us, then to the end of the bed . . . and the rifle.

I moved quickly. Pushing the fork aside, I thrust my face close to his. Pressing my hands to his cheeks, I said, "Carl, it's Lucky, your friend. Look at me. I'm not here to hurt you. I help you, remember?"

My touch brought him back, the wildness left his eyes. "Lucky," he said with sigh—the tension leaving his body. "For a moment I was back there . . ."

"Where?"

"Eden . . . with Daniels . . . and the machines." He shook his head as if trying to shake out the memories. "No sleep. Pain . . ." He growled like a feral animal, cornered, fighting for its life.

I touched his face again. "Stay with me, Carl." Clearly, pressing him about the program was out of the question—I couldn't live with myself if I pushed him past the brink of insanity.

"Right," he said, taking a deep breath. "The images are close. Bad things are happening. I didn't hurt you, did I?" Pain etched his face. Fear lit his eyes. "I couldn't live with it if I hurt you."

"No, you didn't—you wouldn't. Come, let's eat." I slowly removed the fork from his hand. "Let me fix you a hot dog."

Lost with his demons, he sat silently while I located a bun and some mustard.

As I handed him his tube-steak, I said, "I'm sorry if I scared you. I didn't know . . ."

When his eyes met mine, he looked as sane as me. "The Devil walks," he said, his voice not sounding like his own.

A chill washed over me. That's what the note had said. I tried to keep my voice calm. "Daniels?"

"I don't know. Nobody does." Carl reached though the open collar of his shirt. He grabbed a chain, breaking it as he ripped it from his neck. "This belongs to him. He is looking for it."

A gold medallion on a silver chain—one side embossed with an angel, the other with a large tree with fruit and a snake coiled around its trunk. I gasped. "Eden," I whispered.

"How do you know he's looking for it?" Teddie asked. He'd been quiet so long I'd almost forgotten he was there.

"I can hear him," Carl answered. "He is angry."

"May I borrow that for a while?" I asked.

Carl jerked his hand back. "No. If you have this, you are in danger. The Devil will find you."

"I'll be all right." I gently took the medallion from him.

"Couldn't save the others," Carl said, as a tear leaked down his face. "Can't save you."

"WHAT did he mean, he couldn't save the others?" Teddie asked, after we had polished off lunch, calmed Carl, delivered the blankets, and were once again motoring toward the Babylon.

"I have no idea, and since it happened at Area

51—the existence of which the government still denies—we're going to have a heck of a time finding out."

"Either someone did a number on that poor guy, or he's a total whack job," Teddie announced, raising my hackles. "Do you believe him?"

"Absolutely. One day one of our internal security guys was running a polygraph. Carl came by and insisted on being tested. He'd been telling me some of his wilder tales and he wanted to convince me he was telling the truth."

"Was he?"

"He passed the test. But that could mean one of two things: He's telling the truth, or he's convinced he's telling the truth. In my eyes, either outcome lent credibility to his story."

Teddie angled himself so he faced me. "Do you really believe all this hocus-pocus?"

"Some of it—the jury's still out on the rest. I do know there was a joint CIA-military program to find and train psychic spies. Some of it was conducted at Area 51."

"You're kidding?"

"Research it yourself—enough of the info has been released under the Freedom of Information Act that you can get the gist." I turned north on the Strip. Las Vegas had yet to come alive; the traffic was light.

"I'll take your word for it. But what's the connection?"

"I don't know. So far, I have Danilov involved

in a psychic spook program called Eden. How Fortunoff plays into this is a mystery. And the words and phrases Bart Griffin is spewing each night . . . what are they clues to?"

"So all you really know is you're making somebody nervous?" Teddie summed up, cutting to the chase.

I wrapped the chain around the rearview mirror and watched the medallion dangle, reflecting diamonds of golden light. "Rattling cages is one of my best things."

A worried young man greeted me when I pulled into the garage to return the van. "Ms. O'Toole, after you left, somebody came down here asking questions about you and where you took the van and stuff, and it's got me worried."

"Do you know who it was?"

"That astronaut dude I've been seeing on TV— the one who talks to dead people. My grandmother recently passed and I sure would like to talk to her."

"What did you tell him?"

"Only that you took some blankets to the folks living in the storm drains."

Only . . . Had Dr. Zewicki been following me? Watching me? The thought chased a chill down my spine and, to be honest, gave me the creeps.

And if he was . . . why?

"I really don't like this at all," Teddie announced, falling into his male "protector" mode as we headed toward my office.

"Dimitri's gone, presumably dead," I countered. For some reason Teddie acting all protective when he couldn't be bothered to stay pissed me off. "Danilov is acting strange—not to mention the astronaut's antics. Carl has gone crazy . . . er. Something is up, and I better stop it before someone else gets hurt."

"Same old Lucky, tilting at windmills. Maybe you might try focusing on those of us in your life rather than perfect strangers." Teddie's smile didn't take the sting out of his words. "Look, I'm going to check on my old theatre, okay? I'll meet up with you in a bit."

With a hand on his arm, I stopped him. "Same old Lucky? Maybe not. Life evolves, Teddie. When you come back, nothing is as you left it—that's the problem with leaving," I said, surprising myself. My heart knew something had changed even if my head didn't want to admit it. I'm sure he could see the hurt on my face, read it in my voice and my eyes. "And what am I supposed to do? Focus on you? Even though the dream you're living wasn't the one I bought in to, I've been supportive. I've not asked one thing from you." It dawned on me that I'd gotten precisely what I'd asked for—a big fat nuthin'.

"You're right," he said, as he folded me into his arms. "I just don't want you to get hurt."

Hurt? I thought. Yes, I could see hurt in my future . . . but it wasn't the Devil who would do the deed. This whole thing between Teddie and me was coming to a head, but now was not the time or the place—besides, right now I didn't have the self-control to resist homicide.

"Go run off down memory lane," I told him, as I pulled his lips down to mine, testing, tasting. A tingle was left but nothing felt the same as it was. I couldn't place my finger on exactly what had changed, but it was as if Teddie was here *and* somewhere else at the same time. When we had made love it was a physical hunger, but not an appetite of the heart. Close, yet distant—pulling away even as we came together. I could touch him, but he was no longer mine.

Somehow, having him here made me feel worse than had he not returned at all.

"Lucky, there you are!" my mother shouted across the lobby, bringing my day—and my life—back into focus. "I was just coming to find you."

I waited for her as Teddie disappeared into the crowd. Dressed in a flowing peach skirt, orange sweater, gold flats, and her South Sea pearls, she looked radiant. She wrinkled her nose as she arrived at my side. "You smell like smoke . . . and hot dogs. Where have you been?"

"You wouldn't believe me if I told you." I hooked my arm through hers and we both continued toward my office. "Since the SWAT team wasn't called last night, and Security didn't go to high alert, I'm assuming you and The Big Boss patched things up?"

She waggled the fingers of her left hand in front of my face. A square-cut diamond the size of Manhattan sparkled on her ring finger.

"Impressive." Eschewing the stairs, I led her to the elevators and punched the button. "What did you want to see me about?"

"I've been planning my wedding, and I have a question," Mona said as the doors opened and we stepped inside.

"The cards have been a bit cold lately. I'm running short on answers, but fire away." I pressed the button for the mezzanine.

"Do you think I'm too old to wear white?"

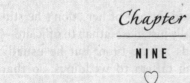

Chapter

NINE

♡

*O*ld wasn't the adjective that sprung immediately to mind.

Mona and I paused at the railing overlooking the teeming lobby below. "White is so . . ."

"Virginal?" Mother asked, narrowing her eyes—focusing the crosshairs.

"There is that. But actually, I was thinking

white is not your best color. This peach is stunning."

She bunched some fabric in her fists and swished her skirt provocatively. "You think so?"

"Absolutely. I'd think about a color theme—strong shades to match your personality. You are going to get married here, aren't you?"

"Oh, no. I was thinking maybe in Pahrump, so all the girls could be there—some of them don't have cars, and that way they wouldn't have to miss work."

"Uh-huh. And do you have someone in mind to officiate?"

Mona pursed her lips and tilted her head, as she looked me in the eye. "I was hoping Nathan Bailey would do it."

"You want Little Diva Eva, the drag queen, to officiate?"

"No," Mona said, in one of her "don't be stupid" tones. "I'd really just like Nathan to officiate—we've been friends a long time. But he usually insists on wearing taffeta to weddings, so that might be a problem."

"Have you cleared this with The Big Boss?"

"He said I could have any kind of wedding I wanted."

Whoo boy, did that man have a lot to learn! "Have you made our reservations for Miss P's girls'-night-out birthday celebration?" I asked, losing courage.

"This Saturday, eight P.M., at the Burger Palais."

"But her birthday is Friday. And since zero birthdays should never go unmourned and I'm paying, I expected her to go five stars."

"Jeremy wants to take her out on her birthday, and she knows you have to stay in the hotel for the Bondage Ball later that night, so she picked the new place. Is that okay?" Mona looked worried.

"It's her day. And it doesn't really matter when or where—all of us together to celebrate is the important thing."

"You look a bit more distracted than I've seen you in a while," Mona said, eyeing me shrewdly. Clearly she had lost none of the clairvoyance that comes with motherhood. "Got a new man?"

"Men aren't everything, Mother."

Her total disbelief evident, she patted my face. "You simply cannot be *my* daughter."

I took comfort in that. "Teddie's home."

"I see." She eyed me shrewdly, her voice cold. "How long is he staying?"

"I don't know. I didn't ask."

"A wise woman recently told me I couldn't keep pretending life would go on as I wanted it to—I couldn't have everything. I think that woman ought to take her own advice."

Mother always could be counted on to deliver the fatal blow.

BRANDY and Miss P doused small fires while I buried myself in paperwork. The pile was small—I whizzed through it—then buzzed for Brandy. When she appeared in my doorway, I asked, "Is now a good time to give me an update on the Bondage Ball?"

"Let me get my notes," she said as she disappeared. Returning with a legal pad in hand, she took a chair opposite my desk. "We're expecting a full house—the Ball has been sold out for over a month. I've coordinated with catering and banquets—we'll have ten cash bars and six buffet-style food stations, which will be replenished as needed through the course of the evening. The sponsors have approved the budget and they will give us a final head count tomorrow."

"The entertainment?"

"Five bands playing rotating sets on three stages. The lead band is The Rats. Their bass player, Patty Garcia, is the boss. Have you heard them?"

I shook my head, feeling hopelessly out of date . . . and old.

"I've confirmed arrivals with all the managers. No glitches so far."

"Security?"

She looked up from her notes, a frown creasing her flawless face. "Something beyond the normal?"

"We are going to have a crowd of near-naked people and free-flowing booze. We need extra security and they need to set up a perimeter to keep gawkers and picketers away. Only people in costume with a receipt for their tickets get in."

Her head down, Brandy scribbled notes as I talked.

"And we need a canvassed chute to hide attendees as they walk through the hotel—apparently nudity offends some of our guests or, at least, some of our dear citizens want us to think so. Better to err on the safe side. Other than that, sounds like you have it covered."

Brandy rose to go.

"Oh," I continued. "Make sure the sponsors send an e-mail to all partiers reminding them they must be covered when they arrive and when they leave the ballrooms. I know that message is on the Web site and on the tickets, but . . ."

"Err on the safe side?"

"Right."

WHEN Teddie hadn't appeared after an hour, I went in search.

Just off the main casino floor, the Babylon's small theatre served as home to Teddie's former show. After surrendering his ball gowns to the siren call of rock 'n' roll, he transferred the mantle of Las Vegas's Foremost Female Impersonator to Christo, his former understudy. Teddie still kept his hand in though, serving as producer.

Stepping around the sign that read DO NOT ENTER, REHEARSAL IN PROGRESS, I grabbed the handle and threw my weight against the heavy door. In contrast to the brightness of the casino, the theatre was dark, the stage the focus of all the lights. Pausing, I let my eyes adjust as I watched Teddie and Christo—apparently they were discussing some nuance of the performance, with Teddie demonstrating, then Christo attempting to mimic. Try as he might, Christo would never be Teddie . . . no one would.

Dane's voice stopped me halfway to the stage. "Lucky! Got a minute?" He trotted after me.

"Sure."

Reaching out, he touched my arm. He looked worried. "About last night . . . me and Flash . . . it's not what it seemed."

"Cowboy, your personal life is none of my business." I was surprised at how badly I wanted to know what was between them, but I didn't ask. I couldn't, I didn't have the right.

"Maybe not, but I wish . . ." He glanced over my shoulder and his eyes hardened, his face closed. "I see Ted is home."

I turned to follow his gaze. Teddie and Christo stared at us. "For now."

"What's the status of all of that?"

"I wish I knew."

He spun on his heels.

"Dane?"

"Yeah." He turned and looked at me. I could see the hard set to his jaw, the emerald of his eyes.

"What do you wish?"

"It doesn't matter." He gave Teddie a glance, then turned and left.

That's where you're wrong, Cowboy.

"**WHAT** was that about?" Teddie asked when I joined him on stage. Christo had disappeared.

"A misunderstanding." Grabbing his hand, I pulled him over to the white baby grand sitting to the side of the stage. "Play one of your songs for me."

He didn't question me further, and with a sinking heart, I knew what that meant.

Seated next to him in front of the piano, I tumbled in a flood of memories—his hands on the keys, his side pressed to mine, his voice filling my heart. I wiped away a tear as he started to sing my song, "Lucky for Me."

When he finished, I rested my head on his shoulder and whispered, "I miss you, Teddie. I miss us, what we used to be."

He looped an arm around my shoulders. "I know," was all he said.

"**ARE** all men compulsively self-absorbed?" I demanded of my father when I cornered him in the gym. "Is there an antidote to gross stupidity, or is it an incurable part of the Curse of the Y Chromosome?"

My father wiped the sweat from his face with a towel. "I think I'm finished here," he said to his trainer, who retreated, leaving us alone. "Do you

want a short answer or an explanation?" he asked
me.

"Both, but make it short and sweet. I have to
meet Teddie out front in a few minutes."

Understanding dawned on his face, but he was
kind enough to hide his pity. "Yes to the first question. No to the second—when it comes to women,
stupidity is genetically imprinted on the male of
the species. And sometimes you have to give up
something before you appreciate what you had."

"You're good," I remarked, impressed with his
ability to be succinct, yet miss nothing. My anger
ebbed as I sat beside him on the bench. "I don't
know what's between Teddie and me anymore—we
started as friends, then it turned all sizzle and
burn—that's a weekend, not a life."

"Maybe so," my father said. "But it's a start."

"What should I do?"

"Do you love him?"

"I think so . . . or at least, I thought so. Although, at the moment, I've forgotten why."

"Honey, when you're in love, when it's the
real deal, you don't think so, you know so. But,
regardless, when you know what you want, in-
sist on it."

TEDDIE waited next to the Ferrari when I pushed
through the front doors and into the day. The sun
felt warm, reassuring, on my skin as I slid behind
the wheel. "How did things finish up with Christo?"
I asked as he slid in next to me. "Is the show doing

well?" I pressed the start button, hit the paddle shifter, and stomped on the accelerator.

Teddie grabbed for the door handle as I wheeled into traffic, tires screeching. "Well enough, but I'll have to reassess when the contract is up for renewal next year."

"Maybe it's time I got a new act, since you've taken yours on the road." I caught Teddie looking at me out of the corner of my eye.

"What's that supposed to mean?" he asked.

"I was agreeing with you. I brought your show to the Babylon and you're not there anymore—perhaps it's time to reassess. Ticket sales are down slightly since you left. However, now is certainly not the time to think about it. We've got to meet Mr. Mortimer and Romeo at the Athena."

Teddie watched me whip the car in and out of traffic. "Somehow, I get the impression we aren't talking about my show anymore."

I hit the button for the CD player and was rewarded with the soothing voice of Luis Miguel. Turning up the volume, I blocked out the world—and the guy sitting next to me, who had somehow decided that our life really was all about him.

ROMEO waited backstage at the Calliope Theatre. With one hand in his pocket, the other on his hip, and his face snapped into a frown, he stared at Houdini's Chinese Water Torture Cell.

"It's too bad problems can't be solved through osmosis," I said, arriving at his side. Teddie hung back, fascinated with a feather contraption hanging from the rafters.

"If they could, I'd be superfluous and life would be pretty boring," Romeo remarked, showing a hint of wisdom beyond his years. He didn't take his eyes off the water box.

"You remember Ted?"

"That man finally get his head out of his ass and come home?" Romeo remarked, his focus still on Houdini's contraption.

"Only until tomorrow morning," Teddie said, his voice flat as he joined us.

Romeo's head snapped up. His face reddened. "Oh, sorry. I didn't know you were here."

Teddie let it go. "Is this where Mr. Fortunoff had his mishap?" he asked, stepping around the trick box.

"I'll be damned if I can figure out how it works," Romeo said, throwing me a dirty look. I guess he thought I'd set him up. How was I supposed to know he felt so protective toward me?

"Can I touch it?" Teddie asked.

"It's been cleared. Forensics has done all they can do."

Silence fell as each walked around the torture cell. I for one was trying to discern how a man locked inside could possibly escape. I assumed the others were as well.

Insight still proved elusive when Mr. Mortimer joined us, the Great Danilov unexpectedly in tow.

Out of breath, his face flushed, Mr. Mortimer didn't look happy.

Danilov, on the other hand, twitched like a skunk on an electrified fence, his eyes darting to the water box and back again. The skin drawn tight over the angles and planes of his face, his lips a thin, taut line, dark half-moons cushioned each eye . . . he looked like a man stretched beyond breaking.

"What are you looking for?" I asked the two men after I had made the introductions.

"Answers," Mr. Mortimer said as he glanced around the group.

Had he come to the wrong place!

"May I?" Mr. Mortimer asked.

Romeo nodded. An odd look settled over his face as he watched the magician run his hands along the bottom of the box, his fingers tracing the metal track for the now absent pane of glass, his toe scuffling through the shards of tempered glass still peppering the stage.

Danilov stood to the side and watched.

Easing over next to him, I said, "What do you hope to find here?"

His eyes darted to me, then away. He jammed his hands in his pockets. "I don't know. I don't remember much about the night Dimitri died. I remember touching the water torture cell. After that, things go fuzzy. I thought perhaps being back here might trigger a memory, something important."

"Are you picking up any vibes?"

He stepped to the water torture cell, touching it with a shaking hand. Closing his eyes for a moment, he shook his head. "Nothing."

Teddie and Romeo watched, neither offering any comments as Mr. Mortimer finished his search and joined Danilov and me. "Find what you came for?" I asked.

"No." Mr. Mortimer grabbed Danilov's arm. "Come, let's go."

"I was wondering something," I said, stopping them. "Two things actually. Who owns this thing?" I made a sweeping gesture toward the torture cell.

"Talk to Marik Kovalenko. He can help you."

Marik Kovelnko; that's the second time I've heard that name recently. I tried to hide my surprise as I pulled the chain and Eden medallion from my pocket and held it up in the light. "Does this have any meaning to either of you?"

Danilov gasped. "The Devil's talisman!" he said, the words strangled. The blood rushed from his face. Then he collapsed in a heap.

Romeo rushed to help him, while Teddie went in search of water.

I kept my eyes on Mr. Mortimer.

The magician stepped closer, his lips next to my ear. "Where did you get that?" he hissed. "That was stolen . . ." He trailed off and his face closed down into a hard, angry mask. "You don't know what you're dealing with."

"Why don't you tell me?"

He gripped my arm and squeezed hard. "If I were you, I'd be looking over my shoulder."

I thrust the medallion at him. He fell back. Then he turned on his heel and bolted, leaving Danilov sitting on the floor with his head between his knees.

Romeo had a steadying hand on Danilov's shoulder when I squatted beside them.

"May I see it?" Danilov whispered.

I poured the chain and medal into his outstretched hand.

"Where did you get it?" He poked at it with his index finger, flipping the medallion over.

"From a friend," I said, watching his face.

"If he gave it you, he was no friend." Danilov's face hardened. "This will bring you nothing but misery. I should know. Several were taken from my safe the other night."

"Is that all the burglar took?" I asked.

"Yes, and some papers. Nothing important."

"What is it?" Romeo asked, nodded at the medallion Danilov still held.

"We used it in some of the . . . experiments."

"In Eden?" I asked.

He nodded, as he took the glass of water from Teddie.

"What kind of experiments?" Romeo prodded.

"Mind games. Nothing sinister, at least not at first. We were testing clairvoyance, remote viewing, telepathic powers, that sort of thing." Danilov pressed a shaky hand to his forehead as he gave a self-deprecating snort. "We were going to be the silent army against the Evil Empire. We were fools."

"What went wrong?"

"They didn't know when to stop. Unbeknownst to those of us in the program, they brought in an expert in posthypnotic suggestion. We were lab rats, and we didn't even know it."

"I don't understand," I said.

"All of us could have some suggestion, either collective or unique, implanted in our minds—a directive we aren't even aware of. A word, or a talisman such as this"—he handed the medallion back to me—"could launch us into action."

"And you wouldn't remember?"

"No."

"Clever," I said, helping him to his feet. "And terrifying. So, you could commit a murder and not remember it?"

"It's a possibility," Danilov admitted. "But there's a huge caveat: We found that only individuals who would consider murder in their conscious state could be programmed to murder in a hypnotic state." Danilov glanced at the water torture cell, then handed his glass of water back to Teddie.

"Now that's a real can of worms, isn't it?" Romeo asked, his voice hard and angry. "How did you make that discovery?"

"We turned him loose."

THE shrill siren of a cell phone cut the tension—and scared me half witless. Teddie rooted in his pocket, glanced at the caller's number, then pressed the thing to his ear and said, "Hey, Mom. Everything all right?" He rose and wandered to the other side of the stage, out of earshot.

"What do you mean, you turned him loose?" I asked Danilov, my blood running cold.

The mentalist looked at me with bloodshot eyes. "He was one of us. He murdered another program member."

"And what happened?"

"We couldn't prove anything. We didn't even know who did it."

"So the murderer walked?" Romeo asked.

"Eden was a clandestine program at a base that didn't exist," Danilov said, as if that explained everything. "Now, those of us who are still in contact refer to the murderer as the Devil."

"That's the name Crazy Carl used," Teddie weighed in as he returned to stand beside me.

I wanted to slap him. Instead I quieted him with a dirty look.

"Carl? Carl Colson?" Danilov asked. "I thought he was dead."

"Why would you think that?" I asked.

Danilov shrugged, but his eyes drifted from mine. "The program was small, most of us keep in touch at least once a year. We haven't heard from Carl in quite a while."

"Who are the others?" I asked.

"I'm not at liberty to say." Danilov's face closed down as he tried to muster himself. "I've said more than I should." With Teddie holding his elbow, he pushed unsteadily to his feet. "May I go?"

Romeo nodded. As Danilov scurried away, the young detective turned to me. "You're holding back. Where and when did you get that medallion?"

I waited until I was sure Danilov was out of earshot. "From Carl Colson, just this morning."

"The guy Ted mentioned?"

"Yes." I glared at Teddie. Threats had been made—and perhaps acted on. Dimitri disappeared, Danilov was clearly scared, Mortimer was angry, and Teddie had to serve Crazy Carl to them on a platter. As if Carl didn't have enough to deal with.

"Can this Carl help us?"

"No. He's given us all he can. He's not . . . stable."

"Drugs?" Romeo asked.

"No, devils." If somehow Danilov was responsible for Carl's demons . . .

"What do you make of this case so far?" Romeo sounded as confused as I felt . . . but not nearly as angry.

"I'm accepting the fact that a group of people with weird abilities have been seriously damaged by their participation in a program we will never be able to learn anything about—not officially anyway. I don't know who all of them are or how they figure into our mystery, but I intend to find out."

"And this Devil person, what about him?"

"A murderer perhaps, but just a man—an evil man, but nothing special. I say bring him on—men I can handle." I glanced at Teddie as he wandered over to the trashcan to throw away Danilov's water cup. "Well, some men, anyway."

Romeo grabbed my arm. "I know you fancy yourself one tough broad, but if Danilov is right, a murderer is on the prowl."

"Or someone sure wants us to think he is."

"Still . . ." Romeo's eyes reflected his concern as he turned to look at me.

"I'm not stupid."

Romeo raised an eyebrow at me.

"I'll watch my back." I gave him a hug because I needed one. "I promise."

"THAT was Mom on the phone," Teddie said to me as the three of us headed back toward the valet. "She and my father are at the airport. They want me to pick them up."

"At McCarran? Like *here*, in Vegas?"

"Yeah, and they want to have dinner with the two of us and your family."

"My *family*? Teddie, you know how your father feels about me. What did he say last time? That I was a bastard child? Wasn't that it?" I asked, knowing full well what he had said. "And you and I weren't even dating then. Now that I've got the scion of the clan in my grubby clutches, blood will be spilt. And I can't even imagine his assessment of my mother!"

"You know what you could do to change his mind," Teddie said.

"No. That is out of the question."

Romeo looked first at one of us, then the other, his eyes growing larger with each verbal volley. Clearly his imagination was working overtime.

"Excuse us for a minute," I said to Romeo, as I grabbed Teddie by the arm and pulled him out of earshot. Lowering my voice, I hissed, "If your father can't like me for who I am, then I'll be damned before I try to earn his respect by trotting out my father. How my parentage makes me more worthy is beyond me." I wanted to say it also made his father look like the shallow ass he was, but I bit my tongue. The man had married money and now felt entitled to look down his nose at us working stiffs.

"Your call," Teddie said, conceding the point. "I'll go get them. They can stay at my place. I'll meet you back at yours after I get them settled."

"I'll make arrangements for dinner," I grudgingly offered—I did not want to officiate at this verbal sparring match, but I didn't see any way to politely recuse myself. "I can't guarantee Tigris, or even one of the lesser restaurants. The hotel is jammed, but I'll do my best."

We agreed on eight o'clock.

Maybe the Devil would find me before then— there was always hope.

MOTHER had been less than pleased when I told her The Big Boss was not invited. Tigris was overbooked. Teddie needed an exorcism. The Devil wanted my soul. And I was going to have dinner with two of his minions from Hell. So far, I was batting a thousand.

After dropping Teddie back at the Babylon, I took my time, meandering through the industrial district west of the Fifteen, heading toward a hastily arranged meeting with Marik Kovalenko. Still amazed he had agreed to see me, I kept glancing in the rearview mirror—no one was there, but I couldn't shake the feeling someone was watching me. I was losing it. All this talk of murder and devils had me spooked.

The magician operated out of a multistory warehouse. From the outside, no one would know the lower floors housed his extensive, multimillion-dollar magic collection and a stage on which he could refine his illusions. The living areas, complete with indoor/outdoor pool, hot tub, and million-dollar view of the Strip, comprised the upper floors.

I was to meet him on his stage.

As instructed, I parked the Ferrari behind the building, punched the number sequence he had given me into the keypad, and let myself in through the back door. Like the white light of a near-death experience, the stage beckoned me through the darkness of the warehouse.

An elephant stood in the middle of the stage, placidly munching hay. With the feral look of a lion eyeing a kill, Marik stalked the perimeter with animal grace, barking instructions at his assistants as they moved panels and pulled curtains. Dramatic music thumped from loudspeakers. Finally, one dramatic flourish . . . and the elephant disappeared. Almost. His tiny tail still swished in full view.

Marik clapped his hands. The music stopped. "Almost," he said. "Myrna, you have to get your panel aligned with the marks on the stage. If you don't, we will all be sent back to the Ukraine and the gulag."

A lithe girl with the requisite Vegas assets—presumably Myrna—gave a nervous half curtsy and rushed back to her spot.

Propping one butt cheek on a crate in the semi-darkness, I watched Marik as he cued the music and they performed the illusion again. Tall and trim, he wore loose-fitting jeans with holes in both knees, and a sweatshirt torn to expose an alluring hint of chest muscles. His long, jet-black hair was pulled severely away from his face and tied back into a tail reaching to his midback. Large dark eyes, tilted at the corners, dominated the flat planes of his face. His slightly oversized nose and thin lips completed the picture, giving him an exotic, feral look.

Even though I could tell Marik was aware of my presence, he worked his staff through the illusion several more times until he was completely satisfied. "Bravo," he said, then dismissed his assistants and the elephant with a wave. "Tomorrow, same time."

Only after drinking his fill from a pitcher of water and draping a white towel around his neck as if the whole magic thing was so terribly trying did he grace me with his attention. "A nightmare from the past, have you come to haunt me again?"

"Get over it, Marik. We were young, doing the best we could. It was a long time ago—too long to spend the psychic energy holding a grudge." Apparently groveling wasn't part of my repertoire today—either that or my give-a-damn had gone on the fritz.

"Perhaps. But I understand you owe me a pane of tempered glass."

"I figured you owned the Houdini thing. I didn't know anyone else who would have the interest and the money. Did you teach Dimitri how to use it?"

"Even I don't know its secrets," he said, as if this fact was a crime against nature—impossible and highly irritating.

"Then explain why Dimitri had it onstage with him. Did you know he was going to try the trick?"

"Of course not. He wanted it for good luck—something of Houdini's. Dimchka was a friend—not the best magician, but a good man. He didn't deserve what he got."

"And what *did* he get?" I had a hard time seeing the great Kovalenko, international superstar, and poor, sad Dimitri hanging with the same crowd.

"Someone killed him, I assume," Marik said with a shrug, but his eyes held a challenge.

What kind of challenge? I had no idea. I sighed and looked around the warehouse. I felt like a puzzlemaster surrounded by pieces, none of them fitting together, as if they were from different puzzles. "Dimitri was my friend as well," I said after a few moments. "Although I only knew him through work, I tried to take care of him."

"He told me that." Marik grabbed my hand, pulling me off the crate. "Come, let's have some wine and, as you Yanks say, bury the hatchet."

"Preferably not in my back." I followed him to the elevators on the far side of the warehouse. "Have you heard about the words Bart Griffin is parsing out each night?" I asked as we rode to the top floor.

The door opened to a vast, unobstructed space with wooden floors that looked original—bearing the marks of time—brick walls and fourteen-foot ceilings. Support columns dotted the expanse with clusters of furniture the only dividers. Light and an incredible view of the Strip streamed through the far glass wall. Marik headed for a half-circle bar extending from a side wall. "Do you still drink Wild Turkey?" he asked.

"My drug of choice," I said, flattered he remembered. "Bart Griffin?"

"Yes." Marik filled a tumbler with two fingers of bourbon and pushed it toward me as I perched on a stool. "First, 'pray be quick,' then last night 'pray tell.'" He poured himself a glass of bloodred wine then motioned me over to the couch.

"Pray tell?" I asked, as I took a seat. Marik settled beside me. We both drank in the fabulous view of the Strip. "Do you have any idea what all that means?"

"No, but it sounds like the sort of code magicians use for mind-reading tricks. Ten words, each word is assigned to a number from one through ten. The magician is blindfolded; an assistant wanders the crowd, and selects an item. As they hold it up, the assistant engages in a running commentary with the audience and the magician. To listen to it, it seems like ordinary conversation."

"But the code words are sprinkled in, and the corresponding numbers indicate a letter in the alphabet—one for A, two for B, etcetera—thus spelling out the item the assistant is holding," I finished. "I saw someone do that on television once—I never knew how it worked."

"That's how." Marik grinned.

While not classically handsome, he was exotic, radiating an animal magnetism. I'm sure it was a finely honed part of his act, and I'd have to say it was effective. But, then again, my opinion couldn't be trusted—my libido was running my life.

"Have you ever seen anyone read minds without resorting to the usual tricks?"

"No, but I understand there are those who

can." Marik gazed at me over the top of his glass, the expression in his eyes unreadable.

"So, how do we interpret the phrases from Bart Griffin's show?"

"Find the key."

DREADING the evening ahead, I'd spent more time than I intended visiting with Marik. We'd made our peace, reminisced, then drank a toast to the two kids from humble beginnings we both had been. Friends who "knew you when" were treasures we both had come to appreciate.

Miss P still manned her desk even though the dinner hour fast approached.

"Are you seeing to the magician's dinner tonight, or am I?" I asked, as I breezed through the outer office. I stashed my bag in the closet and took stock of my desk. The paper fairy must have been on vacation—I could still see black walnut.

"I thought I'd take it," Miss P said from the doorway. "Jeremy's chasing some lead tonight, and I understand Teddie has put in an appearance."

"Only until tomorrow morning, so nothing to throw a party over." With thoughts racing, too nervous to sit, I stepped to my office window overlooking the lobby. "In fact, we are having dinner with his parents tonight."

"Oh," said Miss P, a strict adherent to the if-you-don't-have-something-nice-to-say-don't-say-anything rule.

"In the Burger Palais, the only restaurant with available seating at a reasonable hour."

"Oh."

"Could you try to get GiGi Vascheron on the phone?" I asked. "I'd like to go see her at her office tomorrow afternoon sometime."

"You closed her show—I'm not sure she'll roll out the welcome mat. I understand there's an overabundance of showgirls in the job pool right now."

"Then it's a good thing she has a day job," I snapped.

"I didn't mean to imply—"

"I know. I'm sorry. This has not been a good day, and I'm losing my smile."

The phone rang. Miss P leaned across my desk and answered, "Customer Relations." Her eyes widened. "Yes, sir, she's right here. Yes. Right away, sir." She slowly recradled the phone.

"That wasn't someone calling himself the Devil, was it?" I asked, hope springing eternal.

"Worse. The Big Boss . . . and he's spitting nails. He wants you in his apartment . . . now."

"His timing is impeccable. I could use a good fight."

Chapter

TEN

♡

The Big Boss started in on me the minute the elevator doors opened and disgorged me into the thick of battle. "How dare you invite your mother and not include me? A family dinner with Teddie and his parents? I have every right to be there."

"What makes you think that?" I said, my voice low, my words measured, my eyes narrowing.

"We're family," he bellowed. He still hadn't learned to run for the hills when my eyes got slitty.

His shout brought Mona running into the room.

I motioned her back to where she had come from. "Get out, Mother. This is between me and The Big Boss."

"Lucky, some of this is my fault." Mona wrung her hands, a stricken look on her face, tears in her eyes.

"Not now! Go!"

Mother obviously got the slitty-eye thing—she retreated down the hall, out of sight.

"Lucky, I'm your father." The Big Boss had regained control of his voice, but there was fury in his eyes . . . and hurt.

I *so* got the hurt part.

"My father? Really?" Quivering with barely controlled anger, I clenched my fists at my sides as I stared him down. "All those Christmases, where were you? Not even a card. Do you have any idea what that was like?"

"Lucky, I—" The fury leaked out of him, leaving him deflated.

"Let me finish." Keeping my voice under control took most of the energy in my depleted stores. Not crying took the rest. "I was just a kid," I continued, the hurt a hard, hot ball in my stomach. "I couldn't understand why my father didn't want me. Why he didn't love me enough to even think of me on my birthday. All those years, all those hours, with my nose pressed to the window, waiting, my heart breaking."

I needed a drink, so I did the honors, leaving my father standing there, his face blank. After throwing down a finger of whatever I had poured into the glass—Scotch, I thought—I wiped my mouth with the back of my hand. I didn't like Scotch. Fighting the memories, I took a deep, shaky breath. So long ago, yet so real, so visceral.

"And when I was fifteen and Mother sent me away, I needed you so badly . . . but you didn't tell me, even then." I swiped at a tear as my anger flared. "The two of you—so selfish, thought only of yourselves. And now"—I stalked over to him and jabbed his chest with my finger, as my voice hardened to a knife-edge, as cold and deadly as a steel blade—"now you think you can wipe it all away—pretend it never happened, ignore the devastation you wreaked on a little girl . . . your daughter."

He started to say something, but wisely decided against it.

"Here's a news flash, *Dad*: The little girl is a grown woman now. You waited until it suited you to claim me as yours. Now you can damn well wait until I'm good and ready to claim you as mine."

I turned and ran for the refuge of the elevator. The door closed. I sank down the back wall until I sat on the floor, then the dam burst. Years of pent-up hurt and anger flooded to the surface.

My head in my hands, I surrendered—deep, racking sobs shuddered through me like a tornado through a house—ripping, tearing.

I vaguely remember barking at some guests, telling them to stay out when the elevator stopped at an intermediate floor. After that, I must have stopped the elevator between floors somewhere.

I don't know how long I'd been there, alone with my misery, when the familiar voice of Jerry, our Head of Security, said, "Lucky? You okay?" Tinny and thin, his voice came over the speaker in the ceiling. One of his minions monitoring the eye-in-the-sky cameras must have alerted him to a problem in the elevator.

"Do I look okay?" I growled, as I swiped at my eyes with the sleeve of my sweater.

"You look like you could use a hug from an old friend."

Yes, that was exactly what I needed. "On my way," I said as I released the elevator.

As good as his word, Jerry met me at the elevators and wrapped his arms around me. My head on his shoulder, he held me tight, squeezing the last of the pain until it was only a bad memory. Funny how the touch of a friend could set the world right again.

Out of tears, I was left with the sniffles and the dry, racking gasps that linger after everything else is gone, washed away by the flood of emotion.

Jerry handed me his handkerchief as he led me to his office and shut the door. "The snot rag is only slightly used, shouldn't be a problem."

Ignoring him, I gladly plopped into the chair he held for me. Leaning my head back, I stared at the ceiling. "What a day."

"Mind if I smoke?" Jerry asked.

"Of course I mind. You're killing yourself." My head snapped up as I leveled my best frown—which was probably pretty scary about now—on him.

The smiling eyes of my friend met mine. No cigarettes. His hands were empty.

"You are seriously warped, jerking my chain at a time like this," I said, but couldn't help rewarding him with the smile he was looking for. "You know me way too well."

"I oughta, I've been putting up with your act for over fifteen years now."

Jerry was right, we went way back . . . almost to the very beginning. A tall, thin black man, bald as a billiard ball, and steady as the winter rain in Seattle, Jerry had been my port in a storm more times than I could remember—a surrogate father when my own had shirked his duty.

Leaning back in his chair, he put his feet on his desk. "From the looks of you, I'm guessing The Big Boss got the worst of that round. Between you and me, he had it coming."

A few ticks of the clock passed before the light dawned: Of course Jerry knew. Like I said, he'd been there from the beginning. "Why didn't he tell me?"

"That's a question for your father, not me."

"Who else knows?" I felt control returning—anger simmered under the surface—a productive fire, fueling a sudden, overwhelming urge to set my life right. There were things to be said . . . feelings to be honored . . . dreams to fight for.

"No one who would ever breathe a word." Jerry shot his cuffs, then laced his fingers behind his head—a glint of gold sparkled at his wrist . . . a gold Rolex. "This call is yours, Lucky."

I liked the sound of that. Brushing down my skirt and sweater, I levered myself out of my chair. Surprisingly, I was steady on my feet. "Thanks for the rescue."

Jerry tipped his head.

"Oh, I've got something else I could use your help on . . . and I promise I won't cry."

"Name it."

"I don't want you to break any rules, or invade anyone's privacy, but I want you to tell me when a couple of our guests leave the building and when they return. I wouldn't be averse to knowing who they talk to as well. Can you do that?"

"Piece of cake," Jerry agreed with a smile. "I'm loving this facial-recognition software."

My phone rang as I turned to go. Flipping it open, I pressed it to my ear. "O'Toole."

"Lucky," Miss P said, her voice hollow, shattered. "It's Flash. And it's not good."

WHERE is she," I shouted as I burst into the emergency room at UMC. Heads turned. A nurse glared. I couldn't give a damn. "Federika Gordon?" I grabbed a nurse who tried to scurry out of my reach.

"Are you family?"

Our eyes locked for a moment as I glared at her.

"Okay, I'll take you back," she said with a nervous glance over her shoulder.

FLASH, my sister but for a quirk of biology, reclined in a hospital bed, barking orders. Her face the color of raw meat, her head bandaged, her eyes swollen, she shouted, "I want out of here, now!" Spying me, she brightened. "They won't give me my clothes! I can't go anywhere in this friggin' gown."

I'd never known my friend to be hindered by modesty, but I wasn't going to point that out. "The nurse told me they want to do some kind of scan to check for internal bleeding. If they don't find any, then you can go, so relax, let them do their jobs." Fighting the rage that simmered just under the surface, I pulled a chair next to her bed and took her hand in mine. "What happened?"

Someone, some *thing*, had seriously crossed the line. And they'd pushed me from anger to revenge—a much more dangerous emotion.

Laying her head back, Flash closed her eyes. "I don't really know. I was just leaving work—I'd parked my car on the street—stupid, given the neighborhood and all. I was in a hurry. They snuck up from behind. I never saw them."

"How many?"

"Two, I think." Opening one eye, she gave me a wry smile. "Some reporter I am. I couldn't even give a description to Romeo. In fact, the only thing I could tell him was they both were average height, nothing extraordinary."

"That's a start," I offered.

Flash gave a snort. "Really narrows it down, doesn't it?"

"Do you know what they were after?"

"Not what. Who."

"Really? Who?"

Flash raised her head and looked at me. "You."

"Me?" My blood boiled over.

Flash held out her hand, emptying it into mine. "They told me to give you this as a warning to stay away."

Opening my hand, I stared down at an Eden medallion.

TEDDIE was dressed and ready to go when I made it home. "You're late."

"And you're surprised?" Anger still coursing through me—how dare those assholes come after my friends—I stripped as I strode toward my bedroom, dropping articles of clothing as I went. Halfway there, I stopped and retraced my steps, stopping in front of Teddie. I pulled his lips to mine and drank deeply, enjoying the sensations that shot through me—the sizzle only a simmer, but still there despite my anger and disappointment . . . my hurt, his distance. Apparently simmer was all we had left. Then I shrugged him away. "Nice to see you, too. How was your afternoon? Mine was the pits, thanks for asking."

He followed me into my closet. "Is that your way of telling me I'm being a jerk?"

"Jerk wasn't exactly the word I had in mind." I rolled first one stocking down my leg, then the other. "Let's just say, I'm seeing hints that, in your case, the whole like-father-like-son thing is rearing its ugly head."

Teddie reared back as if I'd slapped him.

"You have left me in limbo far too long," I said

as I poked him in the chest for emphasis. "I don't know where we stand or what to do about it. However, I have a strong impression you quit on us some time ago. When, exactly, were you going to let me in on it?"

Arms at his sides, his shoulders drooping, he stood there looking at me, his face blank. He didn't reach for me.

"I don't know why you came back, but it seems you wanted one last fuck-fest before good-bye. If that's the case, it was pretty low, but we don't have time to talk about it now. As you said, I'm late and your parents are waiting." Placing a hand in the middle of his chest, I pushed him out of my boudoir. "Go. I'll meet you at the Burger Palais in the Bazaar—that was the best I could do at the last minute."

"Lucky, I—"

"Teddie, just go."

TEDDIE and his parents stood at the hostess podium as I arrived. From the angry glares of the people waiting in the long queue snaking out the door, my little trio had shouldered their way to the front.

The hostess shook her head as she ran her finger down the list. "I'm sorry, I don't see your name," she said as I arrived at the head of the line.

Mr. Kowalski caught sight of me first—his face creasing into a look of distaste. Instead of greeting me, he tilted his head in my direction as he nudged his son.

The man whom I had inexplicably thought might be the love of my life gave me a similar nod, then said in greeting, "We're not on the list."

Teddie had inherited his smile from his mother, but everything else from his father: his height, his blond hair and blue eyes, his trim build . . . his arrogant frown—I'd never noticed that part before.

Short and stocky, his mother gave new meaning to the word "plain" with her East Coast don't-call-me-pretty-I-have-a-brain-and-an-MBA-from-Harvard attitude. In her case, both happened to be true. Normally chipper, tonight she looked sad and uncomfortable. I knew how she felt.

Mrs. Kowalski, "Kitty" to her friends and the class act of the bunch, turned and gave me a quick hug and an air kiss. "Lucky, so nice to see you again," she said, trotting out her blue-blood manners, but her words were as cold as a Nor'easter.

"Mrs. Kowalski, I feel the same." I shouldered past Teddie and addressed the hostess. "We're sitting at the chef's table in the kitchen."

"Very good, Ms. O'Toole." The girl looked at me with big eyes. "I apologize for the mix-up. They didn't say they were with you."

It took every ounce of self-control to resist saying "they're not." Instead, I said, "No worries. I'll show them to our table. We're expecting one more, my mother. When she arrives will you show her back?"

"How will I know her?"

"Trust me, you'll know."

A girl popped out of the crowd and grabbed Teddie's arm. "Oh my God! You're that guy! Teddie K! I saw you in London!" Young, blond, and buxom, she bounced with giddiness. I heard a collective intake of breath as every male nearby waited for her melons to bounce right out of her shirt. "May I have your autograph?"

Teddie gave the girl a full-wattage smile as he pulled a Sharpie from somewhere. "What would you like me to sign?"

She gave him a coquettish grin as she pushed up her breasts, which swelled precariously, barely corralled by a last vestige of decency. "How about these?"

With his hand resting on her chest, Teddie complied with a flourish.

"You are so amazing," the woman gushed.

Why did everybody's choice of adjectives seem to be 180 degrees off from mine today?

"I thought you drew the line at signing underwear and body parts? Clearly you've lowered your standards," I said to Teddie, after the gushing groupie melted back into the crowd; then I castigated myself for taking his bait. If I played his game, he got to make the rules. "Shall we?" I asked, motioning Teddie and his parents to precede me. "Follow this wall. You'll see the kitchen on your left. The chef is expecting you . . . us."

Teddie led the group with his mother right behind. As his father passed me he growled, "This is a new low—eating in the kitchen in a burger joint.

Of course, it's pretty much what I expected from you."

Before following them, I gave the hostess a grin and stuck my closed fist toward her. "For luck?"

Her fist met mine in this generation's version of a high five. "I always wanted to be you," she whispered.

"Rethinking that now, aren't you?"

SO much more than a burger joint, the Burger Palais reflected Jean-Charles's refined tastes and European flair. With rough-hewn, burnished wood floors, deep green accents, exposed brick walls with drippy mortar, white tablecloths, and brass sconces, the space beckoned diners, promising a relaxed, leisurely evening of sumptuous comfort food and good wine. The waitstaff, dressed in black with bright white aprons—like Parisian servers but without the disdainful attitude—darted among tables filled with smiling guests. There wasn't an empty seat in the house. Bravo, Jean-Charles.

One of the chef's minions had seated my toxic little group at a round table in a corner of the kitchen separated from the main activity by half-walls of glass—sort of like sitting behind a sneeze shield on a salad bar. From this vantage point, we wouldn't violate any health ordinance or be under foot, but we still had an unhindered view of the choreographed waltz of a master chef and his trained staff.

They had left an empty seat between Teddie

and his mother, presumably for me. Mona would be sitting next to the elder asshole. For some reason that didn't bother me . . . if anyone could handle Milt Kowalski, it would be Mother. Of course, with Mona, I never knew which version I was going to get: the Wicked Witch of the West or the Matriarch of the South with her Junior League manners. Either way she played it, I had a feeling she and the Kowalskis would mix like saints and sinners.

Taking a deep breath and painting on a smile, I breezed into the kitchen.

Turning over his duties to his sous chef, Jean-Charles left the grill and rushed to greet me. Taking both my hands in his, he kissed first one cheek, lingering, then repeated the process on the other cheek—I was beginning to get used to the immediate reaction to his touch. A handsome Frenchman who smelled like charcoal grilled hamburgers, who looked thrilled to see me, and whose touch . . . Could Heaven be any better?

Still holding my hands, he stepped back and looked me over, obviously admiring the pains I had taken with my appearance. "You look stunning," he said, his voice low and warm. Something flashed in his eyes.

"Thank you." My cheeks warmed, my hand felt good in his—this was so not good. "And thank you for fitting us in. I'm sorry for the last minute."

"I am at your service."

A simple "you're welcome" would have sufficed, but whatever game he was playing, I liked it. "May I introduce you to my friends?" He let go of one hand, but still held the other as I worked my way around the table. "Kitty and Milt Kowalski and their son, Ted, this is Chef Jean-Charles Bouclet, our most kind and gracious host."

"Don't forget me!" Mona said, as she sashayed into the kitchen, a vison in a white tunic and cocktail pants, ropes of gold, her new sparkler, and an air of confidence. Turning to Jean-Charles, she said, "*Who* is *this*?"

"Mother, this is Chef Bouclet." She looked him up and down like a tiger eyeing a lamb. "My God, handsome, French, and he can cook, too."

I thought Mother was going to press the back of a hand to her forehead and swoon. Relief flooded through me when she took the chair Jean-Charles held for her. "Honey, he is totally delish!" she said in a stage whisper that fooled no one. She had the look of a mother bear protecting her cub as she eyed Teddie and his parents, while I continued the introductions.

"I can see why Lucky is so beautiful," Jean-Charles said, as he eased Mother's chair in and gave me one of his breathtaking smiles.

Teddie's mother leaned into me. "That man looks at you like he knows what you look like naked."

Thankfully I had only raised my water glass to my lips and had not taken a sip, or water would have spewed from my nose.

"He doesn't know that, does he?" Teddie asked, leaning into my other shoulder.

I glanced up at Jean-Charles, who still grinned at me, his face a mask of innocence, his eyes holding a spark. Was this my payback? Of course, I played right into his hands . . .

"What would make you think that?" I asked Teddie.

"*He* would make me think that."

"He is a wicked little boy. Ignore him." I smiled at the chef. When he smiled back somehow none of this tortured farce mattered. Man, I was sinking fast . . .

"There's a famous Chef Bouclet with an eatery in Manhattan, and one in Paris, I believe," announced Milt. "You wouldn't happen to be any relation?"

"The original location is in Avignon, my home." Jean-Charles pressed a hand to his chest and bowed slightly. "I am the man you speak of."

"No. No." Milt shook his head as he eyed my chef. "The man *I* speak of is brilliant, a culinary genius, he would never be caught dead in a place like this with these sorts of people." He nodded slightly at me when he said that last part.

I was really glad I'd left the Glock at home.

Jean-Charles's easy manner disappeared. "Sir, Lucky is my friend. When you insult her, you insult us both."

With that, I sat up a little straighter. Jean-Charles

gave me a wink as he excused himself and returned to his duties.

Kitty raised her glass of water in a toast. "Well, Milt, ol' boy, once again you've made a hash out of it." She seemed pleased, and half-shellacked. "Would it be possible to get some wine?"

"Kitty, you've had quite enough," Milt announced. "You're finished for the evening."

"Oh no, Milty, I'm just getting started."

Mother waded into the awkward silence that followed. Putting a hand on Milt's arm, she graced him with her best smile and asked, "So, Milton, what business are you in?"

At least I wouldn't have to worry about Mother . . . much.

As Mother and Milt put their heads together in conversation, I turned to Mrs. Kowalski. "Are you still manning the helm of the family business?"

Her eyes lost their sadness when she talked about her work. As she rambled on, I realized I was looking at a kindred soul—competent and appreciated in her career, out of control and demeaned in her personal life. A real unhappy camper. After draining the first glass of wine, she held out her glass while the waiter poured another.

Teddie sat sullenly at my side as the conversation swirled around us. Soon, Mother had both of the elder Kowalskis enraptured by her tales of life in Vegas—half of which were completely fabricated.

His voice modulated so the others wouldn't hear, Teddie asked, "Why didn't you tell me your 'pain in the ass' chef was so . . ."

"Delish?" I gave him an innocent smile. "I didn't think he was your type."

Before he could answer, Milt's voice caught my attention. "Mona, where's your husband this evening?"

"I've never married," she said, giving him the opening he wanted.

"Oh, that's right," Milt said, pretending to have forgotten. "Lucky's your bastard child."

I slammed my hands on the table, making the plates and glasses, not to mention my tablemates, jump. "That is enough," I growled at Teddie's role model. "I have had it with your misplaced arrogance. You will be civil to my mother or you will leave."

Milt matched me glare for glare. Wisely, he shut his trap.

I reached for my glass of wine and took a sip.

The Fates were punishing me . . . but for what? I'd been loyal, kept the home fires burning, been a good daughter . . . well, a so-so daughter, but my heart was in the right place.

I'd been diligent and a good friend.

I'd also been a huge patsy . . . did they punish you for that? Who knew?

Of course, I had also pulled a Jimmy Carter and lusted in my heart . . . probably a capital crime where the Fates were concerned. However, Former President Carter was still walking and talking, but still . . .

And I'd kept my hands to myself! That ought to count for something.

"Milt, she's my *daughter*." Like daughter, like mother. Mona had lost her smile.

I shut my eyes. This was not going to be good. And I had no one to blame but myself—I'd opened the door. And far be it from Mona to resist throwing herself headlong into the fray.

"In fact," Mona purred as she batted her eyes at him, "I've been a working girl all my life."

"Great!" Teddie said, and rolled his eyes.

Conceding defeat, I caught Mother's eye and gave her a smile and a wink. United we stand.

"A working girl? Don't you know that means something altogether naughty here in this town?" Milt poked Mother with his elbow and gave her an evil grin.

"I know what it means." Mother leveled her best stern frown on him. "I own Mona's Place, a bordello in Pahrump. Perhaps I've seen you there?"

For the first time this evening, and perhaps in his life, Milt Kowalski was struck dumb.

"You're a hooker?" he said when he found his voice, the words strangled, his face the color of a ripe tomato.

"*Former* hooker," Mother said as she primly straightened her silverware, then looked at him coquettishly through her lashes. "Now I'm just a madam. Once a girl passes a certain age, being a hooker becomes . . . unseemly, don't you think?"

"Son," Milt said, turning his attention to Teddie, his voice mean, condescending. "Wearing a dress was bad enough, but now you've taken up with a couple of whores? I am so disappointed in you!"

Out of the corner of my eye, I saw Jean-Charles grab a knife.

With a growl, Teddie launched himself across the table at his father. The two men tumbled to the floor, fists flying.

I rescued my glass of wine as the tablecloth and all the place settings disappeared after the two overgrown adolescents. Kitty still clutched her glass with the white-knuckled grip of a drowning man hanging on to flotsam in an angry sea. Mona shot me a look of supreme self-satisfaction across the table. I rewarded her with a smile and a silent toast.

Locked in fury's embrace, Teddie and his father grappled on the floor, grunting and groaning as each took a pounding from the other. Teddie bloodied his father's nose. But Milt got in licks of his own—one of his son's eyes was already beginning to swell.

Sipping our beverages like toffee-noses betting on the races at Ascot, we women sat and watched. Jean-Charles shot me an amused look as he resheathed his knife. None of his staff moved a muscle.

"Shouldn't somebody do something?" Mona asked, not sounding the least bit concerned.

"This has been building for years," said Kitty as she held her glass out for a refill. "Let them have their go. Maybe they'll beat some sense into each other." She patted my arm. "Honey, don't you put up with Teddie's garbage. Sometimes he can be so much like his father."

Now there's a sobering thought. "Is he redeemable?"

"You could do the job. He loves you—I've never seen him like this over a woman before."

If this was his version of love, I wanted no part of it.

"His big heart is his saving grace, something his father lacks," Kitty continued. "But don't make it easy on him. God knows the world has enough asshole Kowalskis as it is."

THE kitchen staff had all placed wagers on the outcome, at least half the patrons of the restaurant stood at the window watching the show, and blood splattered the floor in interesting patterns reminiscent of a Jackson Pollock painting when, finally, I grudgingly called Security.

"Jerry?" I said into my push-to-talk.

"Yo," he answered. "I just got a call about a fight in the new burger joint. They said you were there, so I didn't go to battle stations, although a couple of my guys are headed your way."

"Tell them to hold off a few minutes. I have a front-row seat, and things are getting interesting."

"Wilco," Jerry said. I heard the question in his voice, but didn't feel the need to elaborate.

A few minutes passed as the battle raged, the combatants rolling on the floor like two children engulfed in the fire of rage. With the wall on one side and the table on the other, they couldn't roll far, or do too much damage to anything other than each other. Frankly, the two of them deserved what they were getting and, swine that I am, I enjoyed watching the show.

Too soon, two beefy security guys pushed through the crowd and managed to pry our two "gentlemen" apart. Fire still in their bellies, our two combatants struggled against their restraint, swinging in futility at the other. The guards held them back, but not before Milt got one of them in the jaw.

Milt had a broken nose and the beginnings of two black eyes. Teddie didn't look much better— although his nose bled, it still looked straight, but his eyes were going to be swollen shut soon, and his lip was split. Painted in blood, which now dripped onto their shirts, their faces looked like raw meat, their knuckles bruised from impact with bone. Heads bowed, panting, anger unabated, they both glared at me.

I held out my glass for a refill. Crossing my

legs, I leaned back and assessed the situation. If I didn't know these people, if I'd been called in cold to solve the problem, what would I do?

"Take the old guy with the mouth to the infirmary. After the doc signs off, put him in the holding cell."

"You can't be serious!" Milt growled at me.

"You assaulted a security guard, not to mention the mess you've made in here. One more word out of you and I'll let the police handle it—photos of you bloodied, in cuffs, being dragged away by the local authorities, a drunk and disorderly charge to enhance your résumé. What do you say?"

He glared at me as blood oozed down his chin.

"A night in the drunk tank here or notoriety in the morning paper?" I saw his fight ebb, and motioned for the security guy to lead him away. "Tell Jerry to handle this as he sees fit," I called to the retreating guard, who waved in response.

"And this one?" the remaining guard asked.

I shook my head. "Unfortunately, he's mine. You, come with me," I said to Teddie as I took his arm. "Mother, can I count on you to entertain Kitty?"

"Of course, dear."

"Jean-Charles, I'm sorry for the disruption," I said, as I pulled Teddie toward the door. "Please accept my apologies."

"This evening has been most entertaining . . . and enlightening," Jean-Charles said. "Do you need my help?"

"Not now, thank you. I can handle it."

"That was never in doubt."

TEDDIE sat on my desk as I stood between his legs and dabbed at his face with a damp cloth. Holding a Baggie filled with ice, first to one eye then to the other, he looked as miserable as I felt.

"Are you going to tell me what that was all about?" I handed him a cloth to hold to his nose—it still bled.

"My father is an asshole."

"And you're just now coming to that conclusion?" I wanted to say "takes one to know one," but that sounded childish and I knew in my heart the Teddie who had arrived from Paris was an imposter—he'd been possessed, or something. "You're going to have to stop living your life for him."

"What does that mean?" Teddie's voice took on a hard edge.

"I think you're waiting for him to tell you he's proud of you, and that *so* ain't gonna happen."

"Now you've added pop psychologist to your résumé?"

"Let's just say I'm the poster child for living life for someone else, okay? I know the signs." I checked the rag on his nose—the bleeding had stopped. "We both have made a life's calling out of avoiding ourselves, Teddie. You picked the female impersonator gig because your father would be horrified. Now, you're chasing something else . . .

adulation, I guess. If the world bows at your feet, if *People* magazine anoints you the next big thing, maybe your father will notice. "

Teddie shot daggers at me, but didn't deny it.

"You need to discover what it is you want out of life, but be careful. You've lost your dream, you've lost me, you'll lose yourself if you let others define you."

"I've found a better dream. The singing is for me, Lucky. Nobody else."

"So why did you come back here?" I asked him.

He sucked air between his teeth as I hit a tender spot. "I had to see you."

"Why?"

"To say I'm sorry, okay?" His voice held anger, resentment.

Why he was mad at me, I hadn't a clue. "Sorry for what?"

"For promising you the world, then chasing a different dream. For not being here. For not being a shoulder for you to lean on."

"You were doing great until that last part." I rinsed the bloody rag in a bowl of water, then continued wiping his face. Even though I knew each plane, each curve, each angle by heart, I memorized them anew as I gently washed the blood away. "I wanted to share life with you, Teddie. I don't need you to help me through it."

"Oh, that's right. I forgot. You don't need anybody."

"You're intentionally missing the point, Harvard boy." Finished, I stepped away, taking the bowl and rag to the kitchenette, then returned with more ice. "I loved you, Teddie. A part of me will love you forever, but you're chasing a different dream now, one that I think you're trying to tell me doesn't include me. You didn't come home to say you're sorry. You came home to say good-bye."

"Maybe so, but I didn't come back here to have one last fuck-fest, as you so delicately put it. When you're not with me, it's easy to forget the attraction between us."

Maybe for him.

"But when I saw you again, you were there in the flesh, I had to hold you, to have you. I'm sorry."

Sex under false pretenses was never okay, so I didn't tell him it was.

"Why don't you come with me?" he asked, knowing the answer.

"First, if you really wanted me too, you would've offered that option much sooner. Second, if you'd settle for a woman content to wash your underwear and make sure you're fed and laid at regular intervals, then you're not half the man I think you are."

"I've got to chase it, Lucky." When Teddie looked up at me through the puffy slits of his eyes, I could see the truth, and the hurt, there. "This is a dream come true."

I wanted to tell him he had been my dream come true, but I had banished groveling from my bag of tricks. Besides, even though it's one of the seven deadly sins, I'd take pride over pathetic any day.

He added, "As you said, I need to start living life for me."

In my opinion, he'd already gotten a jump on that, but I didn't tell him so.

Chapter

ELEVEN

♡

I sent Teddie home in the limo.

With his parents at his place, and him at my place, I had no place to run and hide, so I stayed where I was most comfortable . . . at work, among friends. Surrounded by happy people, a lilting tune emanating from the piano at Delilah's, shouts echoing through the casino, I ran face-first into the difference between being alone and being lonely. The fact that a cure for the first wasn't necessarily a cure for the latter was one of life's cruelest ironies.

Mr. Mortimer sat at the end of the bar nursing

a cocktail and a frown. Taking the seat next to
him, I motioned to Sean. "How about one of those
mixed berry infusion things you make?"

"You got it."

"How was your dinner, Mr. Mortimer?" I
asked my fellow barfly.

He glanced up, startled. "Fine. The food was
superb."

"And the conversation? You didn't happen to
address the ruckus over the Masked Houdini, did
you? I've hired him for the Houdini Séance this
Saturday, Halloween."

"He was practically the entire topic of conversation. Imagine, one of our own, breaking the Magician's Code! Our members are calling for blood."

"Maybe they already got it," I said casually, as
I took a sip of the pink-colored martini concoction Sean set in front of me—a berry blast that had
one heck of a kick—perfect. "I know we touched
on it before, but I'm sure you've heard all the rumors about Dimitri Fortunoff being the Masked
Houdini. Did you know my office received threats
and Dimitri received one the night he died?" On
the theory that if I didn't say it out loud, then it
wouldn't be true, I left out the part about me being on that list as well.

"I didn't know that. " Mr. Mortimer's face
snapped into a frown.

"Was he the Masked Houdini?"

"I really couldn't say." Mr. Mortimer shrugged
as if he didn't care. His face told me otherwise.

"*Did* one of your magicians take matters into his own hands?"

"What would make you think that?" His hand was unsteady as he took a sip of his drink.

"Letting out your secrets couldn't be good for business," I pressed. "Sounds like a motive to me."

"Magic is about illusion," Mr. Mortimer explained. "Knowing the trick and still being fooled can enhance the experience even more." His eyes met mine. "People like to be fooled."

My eyes held his, my voice held a threat. "Not me."

The magician was the first to break eye contact as he cleared his throat. "Yes, well, magic appeals to some and not to others."

"You wouldn't happen to have any insight on the words Bart Griffin is spouting, would you?"

Mortimer fixated on the waterfall behind the bar. "Fairly obscure, aren't they? I really haven't a clue."

I didn't expect he would, or that if he did, that he would tell me, but I felt like asking, taking comfort in at least being right about *something*. Small comfort, but I'd take it.

"How did you come to know of the Eden medallion?"

He glanced at me, then looked away. "Danilov. We've been friends a long time. We started in the business together."

"Really? Are you into mentalism as well?"

"No, I find it a curiosity, nothing more. My

specialty was sleights of hand, parlor tricks, that sort of thing. In fact, I was the first to wander the streets with a camera filming tricks in front of casual bystanders. Now it seems every magician starts as a street performer."

"You know what they say about imitation . . ."

Mr. Mortimer stared into his drink. "I suppose, but I've found I'm a better organizer than magician. I run our professional organization now."

I didn't know whether to believe him or not. Other than a healthy distrust of everyone right now, I had no reason not to. And, to be honest, I was too tired to work up more than a hint of energy on the subject. Thoughts pinged randomly in my empty head. Reaching for one was like trying to kill a swarm of gnats with a fly swatter, and about as effective. I stared into the pink liquid in front of me as if trying to divine some hint of truth. Finally a realization dawned.

"Where is Mr. Danilov? You guys are usually attached at the hip. Wasn't he at the dinner?"

"Yes, but something came up—he had to leave early."

MR. Mortimer bid me adieu and I switched to nursing a soda and killing time, still avoiding the unavoidable at home. No matter how hard I tried, I couldn't get my mind around the fact that Teddie was bugging out, once again proving there is no sure thing in the game of love. When had he fallen out of love with me? And why hadn't I noticed?

Pressing the heels of my hands to my eyes, I forced back tears. For a brief time, life had been perfect. How do you get over that? Let it go? I had no idea. A song sprung to mind—"I'll Never Get Over You Getting Over Me." Teddie was usually the one with a song for every occasion.

Taking a deep breath despite the ache in my chest, I pulled myself together. My heart would heal. Like a scar over a deep cut, time would mask the pain. Life would go on. Maybe one day, it would be perfect again.

Miss Patterson's call caught me working up the courage to go home—to face the thing I feared the most.

"Lucky, I'm sorry to bother you, but can you break away for a moment?" She didn't sound panicked.

"Why haven't you called it a day?"

"I've been chasing a missing mentalist."

"Danilov?"

"His wife called. He didn't come home and she was worried."

"Have you found him?"

"On our golf course. Tenth fairway near the green."

WITH only two wrong turns in the half-light of night, I finally found myself on the right fairway. Three shadows clustered near the green. As I neared, I noticed a fourth figure, this one lying on the ground at the feet of the others. Soon faces came into view—Miss P, and Harry and Mavis of sex-swing fame. Danilov lay on his back, motionless, as naked as the dancers at The Palomino and covered from head to toe in whipped cream.

"We found him passed out cold," Mavis said, awe in her voice, as I approached.

Not to be outdone by his wife, Harry added, "We came out here for some fresh-air nookie and tripped over the guy."

Was there some special aphrodisiac in the water in Oklahoma? If there was, I was going to have some of it trucked in, bottled, and sold at the bar. On second thought . . . perhaps that was not a good idea. I had enough problems as it was. I'd just keep it for myself . . . now that I was apparently single again.

"Too much information, Harry," I said. "I'm very visual."

Mavis giggled, as if she was thrilled a naughty movie featuring them might be running through my head.

"Mr. Danilov," I said. At his name, the figure on the ground began mumbling. I knelt beside him and was instantly sorry.

"Be careful," Miss P added a wee bit too late. "He's been sick."

"Thanks," I groused as I felt the damp soak my knee. "Danilov! Come on." I slapped his face gently. "What happened?"

His eyes flickered open. Looking around wildly,

he started, then calmed when he noticed me. "Where am I?" he croaked.

"On the golf course. What do you remember?"

"Wine. Magic Ring. Dinner. Call." He shivered. "Girl."

"Anything else?"

"No."

"Call Security," I said to Miss P. "Tell them somebody rolled Mr. Danilov and left him on the golf course." I motioned to Mavis and Harry. "Can the two of you help me get Mr. Danilov over to that bench? Miss P, find something to cover him with."

As we bent down to grab him, he grabbed my shirt with one creamed hand. The cleaners were *so* going to love me.

Something hanging from his neck caught the weak light. An Eden medallion. Crazy Carl's was safe in my pocket. Flash still had hers. Or the police did. This was another.

"Where did you get this?"

"She died," he whispered, chilling me to the bone.

"Who? Who died?"

"Long time ago. He killed her."

"Who killed her?"

"The Devil. And you're next."

"WHERE the hell is your mother?" The Big Boss's voice shouted out of my cell phone, which I had been fool enough to answer. "It's almost one in the morning and she's still not home." Even though I held the thing away from my ear, I had no trouble hearing him over the noise in the casino.

One in the morning? Really? I glanced at the time on my phone. Time had gotten away—it had taken longer than I thought to see Mr. Danilov properly cared for. Of course, I hadn't hurried. Then, with courage in short supply, I had once again taken refuge on my stool in Delilah's.

"I left her hours ago in the Burger Palais," I said, trying and failing to keep my voice light. "The evening had deteriorated. Mother said she would entertain Mrs. Kowalski while Mr. Kowalski cooled his jets in the holding cell and I cleaned the blood off the heir apparent."

I heard my father huffing into the phone as he digested that. "You have no idea where she is?"

"None," I said, my thoughts racing. Mona on the loose in Vegas? Anything was possible.

"Just find her," he shouted.

"Please?" I said, but the line was dead.

Well, that was fun.

I slid off my stool, actually grateful for a mission. Two chronologically mature women—the jury was still out on Mona's emotional maturity—on the prowl in Vegas. Where would they go? After making a quick tour of Pandora's Box and Babel, our club and lounge respectively, I felt fairly certain our two had gone over the fence.

Maybe Jean-Charles would know—he was probably one of the last ones to see them.

WITH only one table still occupied and the Burger Palais closing down for the evening, Jean-Charles sat at the bar nursing a glass of wine. He stared at a photograph in front of him, which he pocketed when he saw me. Reaching behind the counter for another glass, he filled it from the bottle in front of him, as I slid onto the stool next to his.

"This is not quite as good as the Bordeaux we had the other night, but it's passable for the price," he said as he raised his glass, holding it to the light.

I did the whole wine thing, then took a sip. "Nice. Fairly mature. Woody. Hints of fruit, but not too sweet. I like it."

He rewarded me with a weak smile.

"You look like you've got a case of the sads. Are you okay?" Instinctively I reached up and touched his face gently—there it was again, that feeling when our skin touched—then, realizing what I was doing, I pulled my hand back. "Sorry."

Grabbing my hand, he pressed my fingers back to the side of his face, closing his eyes for a moment—an intimate, unguarded gesture. "You have a nice touch and a warm heart, Lucky O'Toole."

"And look how far it's gotten me," I quipped, trying to recover from the powerful effect the man had on me. What was it with me lately?

"Does your mood have anything to do with the photo you were looking at?" I asked. I knew it was none of my business, but . . . "I don't like seeing you unhappy."

His eyes met mine and for a moment it seemed he wanted to say something, but then he shook his head and gave me a shrug.

"Will that person in the photo be joining you here?" Okay, that question was for me.

"Soon." His face brightened at the thought.

Terrific. As usual, my luck was running cold. With a sinking heart, I wondered what kind of woman had stolen the Frenchman's heart.

"That was quite a group you assembled tonight," Jean-Charles said, eyeing me as he twirled the glass stem between two fingers. "Is that man your lover?"

"Was." Only a Frenchman would use the term "lover." I closed my mind to the memories as I fought back a tear. Life without Teddie . . . Would I miss him more as a lover or as a friend? The fact that I didn't have an answer spoke volumes. "He wants to be a rock star," I said, leveling my voice.

"Will he be?"

"I have no doubt—he's brilliant."

"And what do you want?" The Frenchman eyed me with those robin's-egg eyes—they'd gone all deep blue and sexy.

What did I want? What did it matter? Life with Teddie had been a short course in the reality that what I wanted bore no relation to what I got.

"Right now, I want to find my mother. Were you here when she left?"

"*Oui*. She and the other lady stayed for dinner— your Mother is, how do you say it? A handful?"

"She appreciates handsome men."

He rolled his eyes and whistled. "And her daughter? Does she appreciate men?" Jean-Charles eyed me over the top of his glass.

I thought this was banter, but he looked serious. "Let's put it this way, the apple didn't fall far from the tree."

"What kind of answer is this?" His brow knitted in confusion. "What do apples have to do with men?"

"It's an expression. Look it up." Of course apples and men made Eden spring to mind, but I closed my thoughts to sins and Devils . . . I couldn't deal with any more tonight. "Do you have any idea where those two might have gone?"

"I overheard them saying something about a Greek garden."

"Greek garden?" I thought for a bit, then it hit me. With a sinking feeling I knew exactly where they had gone. I polished off the last of my wine and pushed myself off the stool. "I've got to go. Thanks for the wine. And again, I'm sorry for . . . well, for everything."

"A most entertaining evening, nothing to apologize for. Where are you going? It is late."

"Maybe too late. I'm off to rescue the male strippers at the Olympic Garden."

• • •

IN Vegas, male stripping is a contact sport.

I'm not talking about Chippendales or Thunder
Down Under, I'm talking real, in-your-face strippers. Gorgeous young men, buffed to the max and
attired only in a sack over their privates, ready to
do your bidding—within reason . . . and the law,
of course. You can touch, you can paw, you can
kiss, you can have a public lap dance or a private
one. You can sit next to the stage and risk being
called up to participate in a very graphic imitation of the sex act—forwards or backwards, or
whatever—imagination is the only limitation here.
If you watch a dance, you are expected to stuff
dollar bills into the sack, while the men preen for
you.

Mona's definition of Heaven.

One of the venerable strip clubs in Las Vegas,
the Olympic Garden sat at the north end of re-
spectability on the Strip. The first floor was a
garden-variety (even in my diminished state I could
still appreciate a pun, no matter how far I had to
reach for it) strip club. Groups of men and couples
watching thin, enhanced young women making
love to a pole, somewhat in time to the music—
almost benign if you knew what lurked upstairs,
in the women-only den of iniquity.

Plunking down a ten-spot at the door—locals
get in for a reduced rate—I shouldered through the
crowd, heading for the stairs. A lone female attracts
a lot of attention on the second floor—especially a

lone six-foot-tall female. The near-naked men clustered around me like moths to a flame.

I was in no mood to play. "Another time, fellas." One guy reached out to caress me. I grabbed his hand. "Don't mess with me. Not tonight. I said no, I mean it."

"You mean I can't touch you?" The young man, about my height, with chiseled muscles, flawless skin, and long black hair gazed at me with wounded doe eyes.

"No, you may not," I said.

"Then how about this?" He grabbed my hand and pressed it to the taut flesh of one of his butt cheeks. "You like? I dance for you." He rocked his hips provocatively.

My eyes went slitty. Amazingly, he got the message.

As I pushed past him into the room, he had a puzzled expression on his face—as if no one had ever turned him down, and he didn't quite understand.

With low ceilings painted black and dim lights, the room was cramped and crowded. On a raised L-shaped stage in the center of the room, a man dressed in a Marine uniform gyrated to a thumping beat, peeling his clothes off a piece at a time, to the delight of the crowd.

Women whistled and catcalled, pounding their open palms on the stage. Others rushed from their seats in booths along the walls, dollar bills held high, shouldering in for a chance to stuff the dancer's sack. The Marine gladly accommodated each, holding his little sack away from his skin, an opening just large enough to elicit giggles from the blushing girls as they stuffed the bills inside and pretended not to angle for a glimpse of his jewels.

A clothed young man with limp blond hair, a pockmarked face, a concave chest, and bored eyes stopped in front of me. He shifted his tray so he could take notes on a pad of paper. "Can I get you a drink," he shouted over the music.

I shook my head as I scanned the crowd.

He looked bored. "It's the rules: If you stay here, you have to order a cocktail."

Resisting the obvious pun as beneath me, I said, "Gin and tonic, no tonic."

As he filtered into the crowd, I felt a hand on my arm. Turning, I found myself staring into the frightened, tired eyes of my mother.

"I'm so glad you're here," she shouted in my ear. "I need your help."

"Why didn't you call me? The Big Boss took a chunk out of my ass and I've been chasing all over looking for you."

"I knew you'd be angry." At least she had a grasp on the obvious.

"Where's Kitty?"

Mother bit her lip as she nodded toward the stage. "I can't get her to come down."

Kitty, in all her glory, sat in a chair on the stage as the now near-naked Marine danced around her.

How I missed her before, I don't know . . . all right, I knew, but I'm not admitting to anything.

The Marine threw a leg over Kitty, then fell into the splits on the floor, putting his privates on display, along with his flexibility. If I tried that, I would need surgical repair. Jumping to his feet, he stuck his bum in Kitty's face—she seemed to be delighted—then he turned and straddled her, humping her chest. Rubbing her hands over his exposed skin . . . all of it . . . she laughed until she cried as cameras flashed and women cheered.

"You need to go get her," Mother said in my ear.

"Not me," I said as I cast about for a different solution. "I've shouldered enough humiliation the last couple of days to last a lifetime."

Mother squeezed my arm in a rare show of sympathy and affection. Today was sure one for the highs and the lows. "What do we do?" she asked.

I grabbed one of the other dancers who trolled the crowd. "I'll spot you a Franklin if you go get that woman off the stage and bring her here. We need to take her home."

In two loping strides he was on the stage. Scooping Kitty from the chair, he carried her down the steps, setting her on her feet in front of us. A large woman, apparently the mother of one of the brides having bachelorette parties at the Garden tonight, seized Kitty's vacated chair, clapping her hands in delight as the Marine danced around and over her.

I handed my knight with the tiny shield the

promised hundred, and grabbed one of Kitty's arms. Mother held the other as we escorted her down the stairs and outside.

"That was fun," Kitty slurred. "What nice boys."

The cabdriver was less than thrilled when he got a good whiff of Kitty—she was a hurl waiting to happen. I didn't blame him, but since he was my only choice, I was not going to cater to his delicate sensibilities.

I stuffed the two women in the back, then took the seat next to the driver. "First the Presidio to drop off the one you're worried about—I'll have to see her inside while you wait. Then we'll hit the Babylon."

"If she throws up back there, it's your funeral."

"Buddy, if you want to kill me, you're going to have to get in line."

I delivered Kitty to Teddie, then escorted Mother back to the Babylon. For some reason, I wanted to deliver her personally to The Big Boss. Maybe I wanted the comfort of family, the nearness of folks who loved me in spite of myself. Tonight, considering the hour and everyone's deteriorated moods, comfort was probably out. Family would be enough.

Dead on her feet, Mother clung to my arm as we rode up in the elevator.

"Mom, I know you were trying to help, and I appreciate that, I really do. But you need to take care of yourself. The Big Boss would be devastated if anything happened to you or your child. So would I."

She rested her head on my shoulder. I rested my head on hers as I stared at our reflection. The two musketeers, we'd always said, proud the two of us could do what Mr. Dumas thought would take three. Of course, the original Three Musketeers *were* men. . . .

"I never asked you how you feel about a sibling," Mona said in a tired, small voice. "I don't know why I didn't. I guess I take you and your even keel for granted."

Apparently Mona was feeling sorry for me—her sympathy eroding the little control I had left. "I'm thrilled, actually . . . for all of us," I said, taking a deep breath, praying the tears wouldn't come. Not now. Not yet.

The doors opened to frame The Big Boss, worry and fear etched in every line of his face. His eyes flashed anger and gratitude as he took his future bride's arm. "Mona, where have you been?"

She shot me a worried look as she transferred to The Big Boss's arm.

"She was entertaining my guest. I'm responsible, and I'm sorry," I said, more than willing to take one for the team. "Get her to bed. Tomorrow is soon enough for explanations."

I prayed he'd listen to reason—Mother looked the worse for wear—and the intervening hours would give us musketeers time to get our stories straight.

For a moment I thought he'd argue, but then he gave me a curt nod and turned away without inviting me in.

So much for family.

TEDDIE waited in my wingback chair by the window, his belongings in boxes by the couch, his mother nowhere to be seen . . . his suitcase by the door. He rose when I walked in. Black and blue and swollen, he looked . . . miserable. That made two of us.

"Thank you for rescuing Mother," he said with a self-conscious shrug. "And me."

"It's what I do." The awkwardness between us rooted me to the spot—too far to reach out and touch him, but too close to avoid the pain. "I see you've packed up."

"I think I got everything. If you give me a minute, I'll run the boxes upstairs, then I'll get out of your way—I'm sure you're tired."

"No more than you. Where are you going?"

"To the airport. I moved up my departure time. A plane is coming from LA. It should be here shortly."

I wondered if he could hear my heart shattering. "I see. Do you have a ride?"

"I thought I'd catch a cab."

"Not from here—not at this hour," I said. "I'll take you."

"You sure? You don't have to."

In two strides I bridged the gap between us.

With one hand I touched his cheek. "Yeah. Yeah, I do."

THE streets were as dark and empty as the silence between us when I drove Teddie to the Executive Terminal. Pulling up to the front door, I killed the engine and went to help him with his luggage. Not a word passed between us as we walked through the empty terminal to the waiting jet, its lights flashing, its door open, inviting. How I would love to climb aboard . . .

At the bottom of the steps, Teddie handed his bag to the pilot and turned to face me. "I'm really sorry I hurt you. I didn't mean to. It gets lonely on the road."

"I know. Dreams change, life moves in unexpected directions." Being careful of his split lip, I leaned in and gave him a tender kiss, lingering, savoring . . . making a memory. When our lips parted, I gave him my best smile, which wasn't very good. "Be safe, my love. Enjoy the ride. You are going to be brilliant."

I turned and walked away.

I didn't look back.

ALONE with the wreckage of my dreams, I swallowed my tears as I motored away. Unable to face the taunting echoes at home, I headed for the Two-fifteen and the west side of town. Dawn would paint the valley soon. And I knew the perfect place to greet the new day.

Home to wild burros and an occasional wild mustang, Red Rock Conservation Area had been my refuge for as long as I'd called Vegas home. At this hour, the park was closed, but I had a special rock, east of the entrance, off of Calico Basin Road, that provided the perfect vantage point from which to survey the whole of my city. Facing east, it would be the first to catch the light, to absorb the warmth and promise of a new start, a fresh beginning. Perfect.

Wrapping myself in the blanket I kept in the car for these sorts of emergencies, I scaled the angled face by memory and feel, then wedged myself in against the rock. The beacon of light shining toward Heaven from the point of the Luxor pyramid had been doused for the evening. In the cool, crisp air, the other lights of the Strip sparkled like strings of multicolored Christmas lights, beckoning, inviting all to the party. A party where, for a brief moment in time, the banalities of life fell away and, surrounded by the magic of Vegas, we could all be who we wanted to be. This was my town. My life was right here, and I was smart enough to know it.

And there's this thing about Vegas anyway. Those who have lived here might escape for a bit, but we always come back. The town and its attitudes crawl into your gut and you can't get rid of them. Most of us never even try.

Leaning my head back against the rock, I shut

my eyes, surrendering, but the tears wouldn't come. Maybe the time for tears had passed—one could only hope. More tears had been shed in the last twenty-four hours than in the last ten years of my life. I was hoping that would keep me for a while.

I didn't hear the crunch of tires on gravel, or see the headlights, until the car turned into the parking lot below me. The sleek, long outline of a limo. Who would be coming up here at this hour? And in a limo? I felt my brows crease into a frown. I did not want to share my rock or my misery with anyone.

The back door opened, and in the light I saw who wanted a piece of my rock. The Big Boss.

I wasn't sure if his presence was a good thing or a bad thing.

He reached inside the car and grabbed what looked to be a bottle and glassware. Waving them at me, he started in my direction. Paolo, our seemingly ever-present limo driver, lit his way with a flashlight—the thin beam swallowed by the vastness of the desert—then retreated to the relative safety of the car.

Unfazed and unwinded, The Big Boss arrived in front of me. "Care to share your blanket with an old man?"

"It's a free world," I said, wary of his unannounced intentions. "I can't stop you from sharing my rock. But if you've come to take another bite out of my ass, you can kiss the blanket good-bye. I have neither the patience nor the goodwill to take any more today."

"If you're in need of an attitude adjustment," The Big Boss said, as he plopped himself down next to me, "I'm your man." With a practiced motion he popped the cork on the bottle of bubbly, which sounded like a shot in the darkness, and poured us each a flute.

I didn't need to see the label on the bottle—one sip and I knew it was the good stuff. "They always say a girl should beware a man bearing gifts."

"Probably good advice," my father agreed. "However, I came to say I'm sorry."

"For what?" I took another sip from my flute, savoring the tickles of the bubbles. I didn't know how anyone could be angry while drinking champagne—it was such a happy, giggly beverage. Even though I was still a long way from those two emotions, I felt my mood lift, my outlook brighten.

"I want to apologize for my cowardice." The moonlight shaded my father's profile, the square set to his jaw, the tension around his mouth.

"I've never known you to be scared of anything or anyone."

"If you never know fear, you're a fool," my father said, pausing to stare across the desert toward his kingdom before continuing. "I've been afraid a great many times, but terrified only once."

"Of what?"

"A tall, thin slip of a fifteen-year-old girl with a

chip on her shoulder as big as the Hoover Dam, and a determination to prove herself as relentless as the summer sun."

"You were afraid of me?" I took another slug of champagne. This had been the weirdest day.

"Your mother sent you to me. Our relationship, yours and mine, was tenuous to begin with, remember?" The Big Boss found one of my hands in the darkness. He squeezed, and didn't let go.

"I had a bit of an authority issue, as I recall."

"A bit." He laughed at the memory. "But now that I had you, I couldn't face losing you again."

"I wasn't going anywhere."

"Maybe not. But what if I had told you that you were my daughter? What then?"

"I would've been angry. . . ."

"And fifteen," he added.

"I see your point; not the most rational age, but that doesn't excuse—"

"I know. That's why I want to say I'm sorry. I screwed up. I could've sent presents and cards—all the things a little girl wanted."

"Including a pony?"

He laughed. "That would have been your mother's call. I've been a real ass. Can you forgive me?"

"Of course." I let him loop an arm around my shoulders and pull me tight. "I just needed to have my say. I needed to be heard."

"That you were, loud and clear." He took the empty flute out of my hand, set it on the stone beside him, and pulled the blanket tight around me.

"And I needed to know why." I put my head on his shoulder.

"Do you have your answers?"

I could hear the deep rumble of his voice in his chest. "I understand why you did what you did. And I know you did the best you could given the circumstances."

Love. What a messy emotion—whether between a man and a woman or a parent and a child—not to mention absolutely terrifying. None of us gets it perfect, we just hope the emotion itself is strong enough to hold us together.

"So how do we tell them?" I asked.

He went still. "Tell who what?"

"How do we tell everyone that you are my father?"

"Are you sure?" I could feel the effort he needed to keep his voice level, emotionless.

"I thought I desperately wanted to keep life the same, no changes. But I realized if I do that, while I might succeed at limiting the downside, I'm limiting the upside as well. This is my life, in all its tortured machinations, and it's a grand adventure. I don't know how this next phase will play out, but I do know—if the past is any harbinger of the future—it'll be one hell of a ride. I guess what I'm trying to say is, it's time to be me."

"Why don't you tell your friends as you see fit, then we'll both handle the board and the public?" my father offered.

"You're going to have a time with the Gaming

Commission—our relationship should have been disclosed years ago."

For a moment, my father stared out over the bright lights of our city. "I haven't quite figured out how to massage that one, but I'll think of something."

I took a deep, steadying breath—I'd been doing a lot of that lately. "Sounds good. I'll hit my friends, then maybe an announcement over the internal communications closed-circuit. After that maybe a memo to the board—I don't know how any of this will affect them. Then I'll turn Flash loose, and you and I will brace for the storm."

We both fell silent. I know I was contemplating the future and the maelstrom ahead. I'm sure he was doing the same.

"How did you find me?" I asked, when I grew weary of worrying where my life was headed.

"Your mother told me about your day. After you left, she came clean about hers as well, and she insisted we find you. When you wouldn't answer your phone, I had Forrest look for you. He couldn't find you either."

"So you thought of this place," I said.

"Hmmm."

"Do you remember when you brought me here the first time?" I asked.

"Not the specifics. But I remember you were so upset."

"The minor movie star out by the pool . . ." I hinted.

My father chuckled. "Oh yeah. You got the best of him as I recall."

"Damn straight."

"Teddie will be back," my father said, poking me with the point of the blade when I least expected it. I guess that's what fathers are for.

"Maybe. Maybe not."

"He's in love with you and he's scared."

"Maybe. Maybe not."

"What are you going to do about it?" The Big Boss asked.

"Live well."

Chapter

TWELVE

♡

The sun peeked over the horizon, bathing the ridges in pinks and oranges as I backed out of the parking lot and followed The Big Boss's limo out to Charleston, turning toward town. Feeling more myself, but in desperate need of a shower, new clothes, and a new start, I headed for the office—the shower was small but functional, and I kept several outfits hanging in the closet for emergencies. I didn't want to ruin the new day by going home, with memories of what I had lost lingering there.

SHOWERED and scrubbed, spit-and-polished, I started to feel like my old self again—the old self who was okay with dining alone, sleeping alone. The old self who understood Teddie had to figure things out for himself. The old self who wasn't going to wait around on the off chance he might come crawling back.

An hour later, the papers on my desk dealt with and now residing in Miss P's in basket, I heard the office door open.

Miss P's head appeared around the doorframe. "What are you doing here? Where's Teddie?"

"Recent history to the contrary, I work here. And he's gone." I motioned to a chair across from me. "Come. Sit. I have something to tell you."

Her head disappeared and I heard her talking in a low voice.

"If Jeremy is here, he needs to hear this, too."

They both trooped in and took their positions, Miss P in the chair, Jeremy, one cheek propped on the arm, his hand resting lightly on his love's shoulder. They both stared at me, serious expressions on their faces, as if I was going to announce the end of life as we know it.

"This is not a bad thing. It's a good thing." I placed both hands, palms down, on the desk.

"You and Teddie are getting married," Jeremey

piped up, skewering my heart. He let out an "oof"
when Miss P's elbow hit him in the ribs.

"No. He's gone." Not wanting to talk about it,
I waved away the questions I saw on their faces. I
had no idea how to do this, so I did what The Big
Boss had always told me to do: I started at the
beginning. "Do you guys remember last summer,
when The Big Boss had heart surgery?"

They both nodded, clearly confused.

"He thought he might die, so he told me a secret, something he had kept to himself for years,"
I continued. "A secret he didn't want to die without explaining."

"Is he in trouble?" Jeremy asked, then another
"oof" as Miss P poked him again, this time shooting him a dirty look.

"Of course not." I tried to frown, but I don't
think I managed it. Then I paused. Knowing full
well you can cut off a dog's tail, but you can't sew
it back on, I steadied myself. Well, in for a penny . . .
"I'm his daughter," I said, hurling myself off the
cliff.

Stunned, they blinked at me. "Wow," Jeremy
said. "You're like Vegas royalty."

I deflated—that was the reaction I feared. "No,
I'm the same Lucky I was two minutes ago."

"Jeremy, why don't you leave us alone?" Miss P
asked.

"Righto." He rose to go. "I've obviously bug-
gered this to hell. I'll just shove off."

"Let me tell Dane, okay?" I asked him before he left.

When he turned those golden eyes my direction, I knew he saw right through me.

"Sure."

Miss P waited until she heard the outer door close. "You've had an interesting couple of days," she said. "Are you all right?"

"I'll let you know when I figure out which side is right side up." I moved to stand in front of the window overlooking the lobby. The day appeared normal enough, but it felt all out of kilter. "The Big Boss's bombshell doesn't change anything except other people's perceptions," I said, trying to convince not only Miss P, but myself as well.

"Another hurdle for you. You're no longer just a hotel executive—now you're fodder for the gossip mill. People are going to treat you differently. Can you handle that?"

"I don't see that I have any choice. Besides, it seems like a small price to pay to get a family in return."

"You've always had both The Big Boss and Mona."

"Mona's pregnant." I turned to look at Miss P. "That's between you and me until they make a formal announcement."

"I'm glad I'm sitting down," Miss P said, sounding out of breath. "Instant family! So, tell me about Teddie."

Unable to handle the sympathy I saw in my friend's eyes, I turned back to my window. "He left. He wants to be a rock star."

"Is he coming back?"

"He didn't mention it."

"If you want, I think I can add some perspective here," my friend announced.

"Really?" I returned to my chair and gazed at her across the desk. "Perspective is in real short supply right now, so any you can offer would be appreciated."

"I know about being a rock star, about the lure of the road, the intoxicating rush of performing in front of huge crowds." Her eyes glazed over as she retreated into the past. Then, reality returning, they snapped to mine. "If you ever breathe a word of what I'm about to tell you, they will never find your body in the desert."

"Scout's honor," I said, totally intrigued as I crossed my chest.

"Back in the seventies, I used to be a Deadhead," she said, sitting there, knees pressed together, perfectly coiffed and made-up, in her prim vintage Escada suit, sensible Ferragamos, and decorated with enough gold to buy a VW minivan. "For a couple of years, a friend and I followed the Grateful Dead around the country. We got to know some of the band members fairly well."

"You slept with Jerry Garcia?" I couldn't keep the awe out of my voice.

"I will neither confirm nor deny." She primly

pecked at a piece of lint on her skirt. "However, I can say, I got close enough to understand that traveling, performing, the adulation of the crowd . . ."

"And the young groupies," I added, and was rewarded with a blush.

"Yes, that too, I suspect," she allowed. "All of it is like a drug, stronger than any pharmaceutical you can imagine. The performers become so addicted, they can't quit."

"Hence the Rolling Stones still touring in their sixties," I said, personally appalled by the fact. I'd rather remember Mick Jagger as Jumpin' Jack Flash. "You think Teddie is succumbing to the addiction?"

"Why else would he leave?"

I could think of a reason: I wasn't enough to hold him. But I didn't say it—I didn't want to hear the words, to acknowledge the truth . . . or to have it confirmed. "A groupie addiction? Do they have a Betty Ford Clinic for that?"

"He'll have to realize what he's lost." She reached across the desk and squeezed my hand.

"Pretty heady stuff, I suspect. Awful hard to compete with that," I said. "Please tell me you drove a VW van with flower stickers and sold tie-dyed shirts to get by while chasing the Dead."

"Of course, that was part of the whole adventure. I still have some of the shirts, if you'd like one."

"Totally!" I leaned back in my chair as I looked at my friend with new respect. "Who would've suspected the rebel lurking in the Iowa farm girl? Of course, the whole cougar thing is a bit of a giveaway. Speaking of which, have you told your boy toy you'll be fifty on Friday?"

"I'm looking for some courage," she sighed.

"You and me both."

HUNGER gnawed for my attention as I headed toward Neb's to grab a bite—I couldn't remember my last solid meal. The headache growing into a thumper behind my right eye reminded me of all the liquid meals I'd consumed—a bad sign.

As I walked, I dialed Flash. "Hungry?" I asked when she answered.

"Stupid question. When and where?"

"Are you mobile?"

"Not a pretty sight, but still able to heed the siren call of food."

"Great. Neb's. Now." I was glad to hear Flash was on her feet but I wasn't surprised—I'd never found anything able to keep her flat on her back . . . other than a handsome, willing male of the species.

"See you in ten."

As I repocketed my phone, I was comforted by the whole Morse code, girlfriend-speak thing. Without me saying so, Flash had understood the message—I needed her.

Friends are like family, but better in a way— they chose to be in my life. And as I grew older, I realized their importance increased dramatically.

Men came and went, some staying longer than others, some saying they love you then leaving, but good friends are for life.

JUNIOR Arbogast called to me from across the casino. "Hey, I've been looking for you," he said, as he puffed to a stop in front of me. "I'm sorry it's taken me so long, but Bart Griffin proved to be more elusive than I thought. Apparently he's getting the Air Force's attention."

"Really? Why? Has he stuck a toe across the perimeter?"

"No, he said the base had gone on elevated security. And, no," he said, anticipating my question. "He didn't say why."

"Probably has something to do with the article in the *R-J*." I pursed my lips as my thoughts raced. Flash was making waves. What else was new? "Will he talk to me?"

"Tomorrow night. The Little A' Le' Inn. Ten o'clock?"

"Perfect. Thanks. Will you be there?"

"I'll make the introductions."

SEATED across from Flash, her face an interesting rainbow of colors, my anger seethed. I would find who was responsible. And they would pay.

Staring at my friend, I took a few moments to stuff the rage way down deep. Finally, with a tenuous control, my stomach full, my headache on the run, I reached for some of that elusive courage.

"I've got a story I want you to break this afternoon, but first I need your help."

"Cool." Flash pushed aside her plate, giving me her full attention.

"I've got a few more names we need background info on. Strictly bit players, I have a feeling, but I'm grasping for connections."

"Who?" Flash reached to pull back her plate, but then thought better of it.

"Mr. Mortimer, the head of the Magic Ring, and Bart Griffin."

"The talk show guy?"

"Yeah. I'd like to know if they have any connections to Area 51, the Air Force, Dimitri . . . you get the drift."

"Got it." Flash pulled a pencil from her bra and made a few notes. "Man, the whole city has gone ga-ga over this mystery—my bosses are clamoring for any little tidbit. I'm assuming anything I come up with, I can use?"

"Don't see why not." Sometimes I asked Flash to sit on a story for a bit, but I didn't think this would be that kind of story, although why I thought that was a bit of a mystery—especially in light of the beating she had taken . . . because of me.

Her pencil poised, she waited.

"You be careful, okay. I can't handle anything more happening to you because of me."

"I'm the one who put myself in the line of fire." She squeezed my hand. "It's what I do. You know that."

"Just the same."

"I'll be careful."

I took a deep breath. "Okay, now for my little tale. Recently, I was made aware of my father's identity."

Flash's eyes widened, but she said nothing.

I laid the whole The-Big-Boss-is-my-father thing on her.

"For real?" she said with awe in her voice, when I'd finished my little spiel. "He confirms?"

"He's the one who told me, but I expect you'll want to talk to him yourself. Have Miss P call him—he'll see you."

"Imagine. All these years I've been coming to the hotels to see you and I had no idea I was playing in your castle."

"They're not my castles."

"I'm kidding," Flash said as she immediately sobered. "Look, I can tell you're worried, but this doesn't change anything. Well, not between you and me, at least. Your life is about to get a bit more complicated, but as far as you and me go, we're totally cool." She shook her head. "Dane's going to find this pretty interesting, though."

"Why would he care?" I asked, working to keep my voice nonchalant. "I thought you two were together."

"Us? Honey, we're like water and oil. I tried to get him interested, but I'm just not his type. You, however, are right up his alley. Have you seen the way he looks at you?"

"He doesn't look at me any differently."

"Girlfriend, if you think that, you haven't been paying attention." Flash rose to go. "Thanks for the grits. I'm off to wrangle a good quote out of The Big Boss. But I'm telling you, if Teddie wasn't in the picture, Dane would be all over you like fleas on a farm dog."

"Teddie's history."

That stopped her. She slowly sank back down in her chair. "You want to talk about it?"

"No, but thanks."

She reached across and gripped my arm. "I'm always here if you need me."

Like I said, friends . . .

OF all the people I felt I needed to tell in person, I'd saved Dane for last. I don't know why I felt that I needed to give it to him in person. But, Flash was right, there was something between him and me—I just didn't know what. Or what I wanted it to be—not that I had much choice—it would be what it would be, that much I had learned from Teddie.

I dialed Dane's number, then paused before I hit the send button. Taking a deep breath, wanting this to be over with, I completed the call. Dane answered on the first ring—we agreed to meet at The Garden Bar.

For some reason I was nervous as I waited for him. Standing at the bar, I positioned myself so I could watch him as he strolled out of the hotel and across the rope bridge toward me. Long and lean, oozing masculinity, the light glinting off his wavy hair, which he wore a trifle long, a smile creasing the planes of his face when he saw me—he did make my heart beat faster—no need to deny that now.

"Hey," he said, as he stopped in front of me. His word was warm, but his manner reserved. "What do you need?"

"Kiss me."

"What?" Shock registered in his face.

"You mentioned the other night, when you said good-bye in my apartment, that you wondered what it would be like. Well, me too. And I don't want to wonder anymore."

"What will Ted say?" Dane asked, his face closing down.

"Nothing. He's history."

"I see." He stepped close. Wrapping one arm around my waist, he pulled me against him.

I could feel every inch of him, the heat . . . a warmth spreading from his body through mine.

"There's only one first kiss," he said as he brushed his fingers across my lips.

My breath caught in my throat when he gently kissed first one eye, then the other, as his hand slipped behind my head. His breath warm on my cheek. His nearness intoxicating.

Then his lips found mine. His kiss was gentle at first, then deeper, more demanding, as his hand fisted in my hair and my body molded itself to his.

We both were breathing hard when he pulled

back, his face a few inches from mine, my body still stretched the length of him. His eyes, dark and deep, held mine.

"Wow," was all I could manage to say as I tried to catch my breath and slow my heart before it leapt into my throat.

A grin lifted the corner of his mouth. "As first kisses go, I'd have to say that was pretty incredible." His voice was hoarse with emotion.

"Okay," I said, taking another one of those deep breaths. "Here's the deal."

"There's a deal?" He gave me a sardonic grin, but still held me tight.

"Not like you think. I have something to tell you, then I want you to kiss me again. Will you do that?"

"Is that a trick question?"

"You may not want to after what I have to tell you. Would you have a problem if I told you The Big Boss is my father?" I waited for realization to register on his face, then said, "Now, kiss me again."

He captured my lips with his. This time, the reaction was immediate, visceral, like an explosion somewhere deep inside. When I found the strength, I pulled back. "Any different?"

"Still mind-blowing." He put both of his arms around my waist, and leaned back. "Lucky, I'm not interested in your pedigree. Who sired you doesn't amount to a hill of beans and it doesn't change who you are. It's you I'm attracted to."

"I'm damaged goods, on the rebound, and

thinking of swearing off men for a while. I don't want a relationship right now, and I can't make any promises."

"If catching you on the bounce is the way I get my foot in the door, I'll take it. And I understand, no promises."

"Friends?" I asked. I *so* did not want to lose another friend by falling in love.

"A good place to start." He gently stroked my face. "How about a date, like normal people—maybe dinner and a show?"

"How about a trip out to Rachel and the Little A' Le' Inn tomorrow night?"

"Where?"

"North of Area 51 on the Extraterrestrial Highway. I need to track down a radio guy who's gone commando."

I couldn't shake the feel of Dane, his touch, the look in his eyes after he kissed me, as I charged into the day. What a stupid thing to do. Why had I done it? Erratic behavior on the rebound bounce—that must be it. Temporary insanity. I let my guard down for a moment, and I get a case of the stupids. I need a keeper.

Distracted and practically dysfunctional after a night without sleep, I was minimally effective as I dealt with a few minor issues: a couple who wanted to arrange a marriage in the Temple of Love, a man who wanted to ensure that his room would be filled with roses when he arrived this afternoon

with his wife for their thirtieth anniversary, and
Harry and Mavis, who had questions beyond my
areas of expertise—I sent them back to Smokin'
Joe's Sex Emporium.

I wanted to be like them when I grew up.

A quick nap on my office couch did little to replen-
ish my depleted stores. And now I was on my way
to face an irate ex-showgirl who wanted a pound
of my flesh—I must be punishing myself.

GiGi Vascheron, former star of the Calliope
Burlesque Cabaret, spent her days as a tenured
professor of medieval history at UNLV, leading the
unwilling through the tortured past. Having never
taken a history course while at UNLV, I didn't
know exactly what medieval history entailed, although I sincerely hoped GiGi hadn't developed
an expertise in torture.

Like everything else about Las Vegas, the university was much like any other university, but
wound a few turns tighter. Here, strippers by night
fought their way through English by day. Valets
and bartenders, bouncers and dancers, hookers
and dealers worked their way toward an academic
education one class at a time alongside an average
full-time student body—business school, medical
school, law school . . . all were possible. In addition, UNLV boasted one of the world's top hotel
and restaurant management schools, which made
sense. I was a proud alum and an occasional ad-
junct professor—to my everlasting wonderment.

GiGi's office was on the third floor of Wright Hall, one of the newer additions to a not-so-old campus.

Amazingly, I managed to find her cubbyhole without too much trouble. Through her open door, I watched GiGi as she regaled a group of young men leaning expectantly toward her as if drawn by an invisible force. The former showgirl looked accustomed to the adulation—not indifferent to it, but not overawed either. Tall and stick-thin, she wore her height with an aplomb I'd never completely developed. With a long cascade of auburn hair, peaches-and-cream skin, and bright, intelligent blue eyes, GiGi commanded attention. Her face was pinched with interest, her eyes dark and serious as she listened to one of her young students.

Lurking outside her doorway transported me back to my stint at the university. Hanging outside professors' offices waiting for an audience, I'd always felt like the condemned coming to plead for clemency—I guess that spoke volumes about my college experience.

In short order, the young gentlemen left and GiGi strode through the door after them. Extending her hand to me she said with a smile reflected in her eyes, "Lucky, so sorry to keep you waiting. Come in." She stepped aside and motioned me into her lair. "Can I offer you tea or anything?"

"If you're having some, great. If not, please don't bother." I took one of the chairs recently vacated by her young squires.

GiGi, her back to me, busied herself with tea preparation. "I need a little pick-me-up this time of day," she said. "When I was dancing, I couldn't get through the afternoon without serious caffeine. Juggling two jobs meant sleep was as rare as knights in shining armor."

"I guess you and I have dated from the same kennel club," I empathized, eliciting a grin. "I know I have no right to ask, especially given my responsibility for the demise of your show, but I've come to ask for help."

GiGi set a mug of steaming tea in front of me, then took the chair next to mine, cupping her own mug with both hands. "No hard feelings. I've bounced around this town long enough—I know the ropes. What can I do for you?"

I followed her lead and kept my face passive although I wanted to grin appreciatively at her apparently unintentional pun. "Have you been following the story about Dimitri?"

"How weird is it that his body disappeared like that? Do you have any idea what happened?"

"I've got a lot of questions but very few answers."

"What do you need from me?"

"I saw Dr. Zewicki talking to you. Do you know him well?"

"We've kicked around a bit. I met him when he was based here with the Air Force a few years ago."

"Was he up at Nellis?"

"No, Papoose Lake."

"Isn't that the place where that former employee claimed the Air Force was reverse engineering a flying saucer with the help of an alien who loved to eat strawberry ice cream?"

"That's the place." GiGi grinned at me. "You have to admit, the men in this town are a bit off-center."

Again, that wasn't the adjective I would've reached for. "Is Papoose Lake part of Area 51?"

"Not technically. They say both are connected underground, but I couldn't tell you if that's true or not. Dr. Zewicki never talks about it."

"Is he still based there?"

"No. His program was disbanded."

"Why?"

"Something bad happened. I don't know exactly what, but I got the impression someone died."

ROMEO, Las Vegas's finest detective, caught me as I pushed through the front doors of the Babylon. "Do you have a minute?" he asked. Rumpled, his lack of sleep echoing in his bloodshot eyes, he looked like he could use a hug.

I resisted—hugs were so unprofessional . . . but sometimes as necessary as the blood coursing through our veins. My resolve dissolved, I wrapped him in a bear hug, embarrassing us both. "Sorry, you looked like you needed that."

"You're probably right. And, for the record, I didn't mind."

Steering him toward Delilah's, I said, "I've got a couple of additional pieces to the puzzle, although I'm really not even sure if it's the same puzzle. Nothing about this thing is adding up."

"Tell me about it."

The bar was filling up, but I managed to snag a small table in the corner next to a larger one inhabited by men who looked like they had been there since yesterday. Romeo and I ordered Cokes—sugar for him, virtue for me.

"You go first," the young detective said. "I'm so wacked, I don't know whether I'm coming or going."

I filled him in on Dr. Zewicki and his tie-in to Papoose Lake—which I was willing to assume equated to Area 51—and the rumors of a death.

"Great," Romeo groused, which was so unlike him. "Assuming your sources are good, we've got an old case and a bunch of nutcases at Area 51. Someone is leading us down a blind alley. I can't see how any of this ties in to the case we're actually interested in. The missing magician? Remember him?"

Sarcasm. I must be rubbing off on him. "I'm working on a connection, but so far my luck is running cold." Which seemed to be a recurring theme, but I didn't want to whine. "Anything on Molly Rain?"

"Nothing unusual."

That would be unusual in and of itself where this case was concerned, but I didn't say so.

"She's kicked around town for a while now. Normal stuff—a few Cirque shows until she hurt her shoulder, then she took up pushing pasties, dressing nudes."

"For the record, nudes don't wear pasties. But they have dressers . . . I've always wondered about that."

"You would."

"Okay, that's the second bite you've taken. You want to tell me about it?"

"How do you handle the kinds of hours you and I put in and have a life, too?"

"Brandy?"

He nodded, a grin finally lifting a corner of his mouth. "The girl will be the death of me."

"Romeo, I wish I could help you find balance, but I still haven't learned how to juggle all the knives and not end up cut to the quick."

THIS last time, with Teddie, had sliced me up pretty good. Lost in thought, I pushed through the office door and tripped over my mother. Her long legs stretched in front of her, she sat in one of the chairs against the window, while clinging to my father's arm.

"Who sent you two to the principal's office?"

"Your *father* is taking me to get a marriage license," Mona announced, as she glanced at Miss P behind her desk. "We want you as a witness."

Miss P gave me a wink.

"You'll come, won't you?" my father asked me.

"Sort of a family outing before the proverbial you-know-what hits the fan."

Glee written on their faces, nervous energy pulsing through them, a hint of mischief in my father's eyes—the two of them were living proof that grown-ups are nothing more than teenagers with money.

Holding the door open, I said, "Let's go. The sooner we hit the trail, the larger our head start when Flash's bombshell hits the evening paper."

Instead of leading us to the front where the limo waited, The Big Boss steered us toward the garage.

"Are we taking Marilyn?" I asked. My father named all of his automobiles. Marilyn, a stylish twenty-year-old Bentley ragtop, fire-engine red with natural leather seats, and enough cool and sass to make even the most hardened teenager take notice, was his favorite.

"Only the best for my ladies," my father announced as he held the door open, first for me as I climbed in the back, then for his future wife, who took her proper place beside him. She even scooched over and put a hand on his knee when he slid behind the wheel—like two kids out for some serious lip-lock time at the drive-in.

Lounging in the back of the Bentley, my parents happier than I'd ever seen them, the cool early evening air running its fingers through my hair, I had a hard time finding fault with the moment—even with Teddie gone and the book closed on that chapter. That's one of the miracles of life, if you keep moving forward, even though one path may be blocked, another beckons.

With life in front of me, I drank in all the possibilities.

MARRIAGE is big business in Vegas, so the politicos streamlined the process, while getting their piece of the pie for county coffers, of course. First stop—the Clark County Marriage License Bureau. In most cities in the world, obtaining a marriage license is like trying to maneuver through the DMV while the disinterested clerks count the seconds until the government pension kicks in. Not so in Vegas. Here the marriage bureau is open until midnight every day during the week and all weekend long. In my sleep-deprived state all the days had run together, so I wasn't sure what day it was, but it didn't matter—at this hour we were golden.

The Big Boss had timed it right—no one waited in the plastic chairs bolted to the floor, we didn't have to take a number, or come back later. Instead, hand in hand, my parents strolled to an open window and the bored clerk manning it. I trailed behind and wished I had brought a camera when the clerk looked up.

Having Albert Rothstein appear in person at any Las Vegas municipal facility was on par with the president of the United States showing up for a company picnic. I leaned against a post as my parents took the two chairs and the clerk tried to find her voice. Somehow she managed to compose herself. Everything went swimmingly until she asked Mona her age.

"May I lie?" Mona asked the clerk, who seemed dumbfounded at the question.

The Big Boss settled back in his chair, a grin splitting his face. Mona versus an entrenched bureaucracy . . . I'd give even odds.

"No, I don't think you can lie," the clerk offered hesitatingly.

"But, if you don't know my real birthday, how can you tell if I'm lying?" Mona looked down her nose at the poor young woman.

"Ma'am," the clerk started, then ground to halt when she ran up against Mona's frown.

Taking pity on the woman, and not wanting to spend the rest of the dinner hour abusing a government employee—although there were days that held appeal—I waded in. "Mother, what does your passport list as your birthday?"

Apparently unwilling to speak the date aloud, Mother thrust the document at me. I took a gander, then understood why such a lie would never pass her lips—she'd be struck by lightning on the spot. And she was perilously close to making her previous maternity a physical impossibility—not to mention turning The Big Boss into a cradle robber.

I pulled Mother aside. "You've apparently been lying about your age to the government for years," I whispered, as I waved her passport under her nose. "Why the sudden attack of conscience?"

"I don't care if they take away my passport," she said, twisting her hands and looking at me with huge, frightened eyes. "But I don't want them to tell me I can't marry your father."

I gave her a big hug. "I doubt that will happen. Use the birth date on your passport—the government thrives on consistency."

"Are you sure?"

"Pretty sure. Whether you are lying or not will be a matter between you and Saint Peter," I added.

As expected, Mona gave me a wicked look—I doubt she held any expectation of discussing her merits at the pearly gates. In my book, not that God would ever take a gander, Mona had earned her spot in Heaven years ago when I stopped counting all the girls she had taken in, cleaned up, educated, and sent off to be senators and congressmen, lawyers and doctors, wives and mothers.

Mother again took her seat across from the clerk. "Just use the birth date on my passport. That will work, won't it?"

After a glance at The Big Boss, the clerk nodded.

All questions answered to the satisfaction of Big Brother, all blanks filled in, my parents signed on the dotted line, and The Big Boss forked over the fee.

As we filed out I said to the clerk, "They're doing this so I'll no longer be an illegitimate child. Sorta like trying to stuff the cat back in the bag, don't you think?"

Mother giggled and grabbed my arm. "Would you quit?"

"What? I like having been born in sin, under mysterious circumstances—it gives me a certain panache."

"Honey, you are like a bright light, a shooting star, a brilliant diamond," my father added. "You don't need any panache from us."

"A bit of an exaggeration." I looped my free arm through one of his. "But I'll take it. Thank you."

"Albert?" Mona stopped, jerking us all to a stop. "I thought you said Lucky needed to be a witness?"

My father shot me a wink. "I lied. I wanted her here and I knew you would also."

She squeezed his arm and kissed his cheek. "You think of everything."

Mona had no idea. And I might be wrong, but . . . I could feel it in my bones—for once, my father had taken my advice.

AFTER we had retaken our positions in the car, my suspicions were confirmed when The Big Boss said, "Let's take a swing through town."

"Oh." Mother shifted and put a hand on his arm. "Can we get a steak at Hugo's? We haven't been there in ages."

"Perhaps."

"I think we need to celebrate, don't you, Lucky?" The air carried her words back to me.

"Absolutely!" I had to shout to force my reply the other way.

"See that, Albert? It's two against one."

"But I'm the one holding all the cards," The Big Boss said as he motored Marilyn into the drive-through wedding chapel and wheeled to a stop.

He turned to Mother. Taking both her hands in his, he said, "Marry me, Mona. Marry me now."

I crossed fingers and toes, praying the woman would find some sense.

"Here?" she asked, her voice quiet—no fight in it. "In the drive-through?"

"I'm still that scrapper you fell in love with a hundred years ago—I came up the hard way, we both have—I'm a drive-through kind of guy."

Mother glanced at me. I gave her an encouraging nod.

"Mona," my father continued, "I've waited half a lifetime to be able to introduce you as my wife. I can't wait a moment longer. Please don't make me try."

I choked up—if Mona could resist that, her heart was stone.

"Oh, Albert." Mona dabbed at tears, trying not to smear her makeup. "Of course I'll marry you, here, now . . . anywhere."

"Lucky, will you be our witness?" my father asked.

"And our best person?" my mother added.

"I can't think of anything I'd like better."

My father eased the big car forward to the

window. A gray-headed man who looked half sober peeked his head out as he hastily tied his bow tie. His efforts at shaving had been lackluster—gray stubble dotted his face like patches of dandelions marring a smooth-mown lawn. In contrast, his thinning hair was carefully parted and slicked down. "You youngsters going to tie the knot today?" he said, giving my parents the once-over.

"About thirty years too late, but yes," my father said.

"How do you want it? Straight up? That means simple, no music or nothing. That'll set you back a hundred bucks. Short and sweet, we'll have you outta here and off to the honeymoon lickety-split. Know what I mean?" He leered at my mother. "If you want more, like music or Elvis or something, that's extra. Normally I charge twenty bucks for the wife to witness."

"That won't be necessary, we brought our own," The Big Boss said, fighting a grin.

"I see." The man eyed me down his long nose. "You know these people well enough to swear they're sober?"

I wanted to say I knew them better than "the wife" did, but instead I nodded, not trusting myself to speak. Sober, I could vouch for, but if he asked me to swear as to their soundness of mind, that was another thing altogether.

The man returned his rheumy gaze to my father. "So what's it going to be?"

"Straight up will be sufficient."

"But I'd like a hamburger and some fries with that," I added.

My mother stifled a giggle as the man glared at me. "We get that a lot," he said, then, extending his hand, he snapped his fingers at my father. "You got a license?"

I'd be willing to bet there wasn't a human alive who had snapped at my father.

The man scanned the paper when my father handed it over. "Albert Rothstein. Do you know you got a name like that bigwig casino dude?" He eyed my father. "You sorta look like him, too."

"Yeah, I get that a lot," my father deadpanned.

Mona had tears of silent laughter running down her face. I'd be willing to bet she was on the verge of peeing.

"Could we get on with it?" my father asked, remaining amazingly calm.

"Sure. Sure." The man pulled out a dog-eared piece of paper and started reading.

My father took my mother's hand.

And, with a song in my heart, I bore witness as Las Vegas royalty got hitched at the drive-through.

AFTER a very bored photographer took a few pictures, we headed for home.

"That picture taker is going to have a cow when he realizes how much those snaps are going to fetch. I bet *People* will pay six figures," I said, breaking the silence.

Mona looked at me wide-eyed. "Really?"

My father nodded. "Welcome to the fishbowl."

"How do you handle it?" Mona asked.

Before my father could answer, I said, "Don't do anything you wouldn't want to see in full color on the front page of the *R-J*. That means no more excursions to Olympic Garden."

"I understand," Mona said with sincerity.

Yes, but understanding and complying are two very different things, I thought, but today was too much fun to get into the nitty-gritty of life in the spotlight. "So." I clapped my hands. "How are we going to celebrate?"

"How about a family party?" The Big Boss suggested.

"Two hours, grand ballroom?"

"Can you pull it off?"

"Please," I huffed. "You're talking to the master. Besides, I have two assistants."

"What are you two talking about?" Mother asked.

"You'll see."

Chapter

THIRTEEN

*E*ven though Miss P, Brandy, and I were the best in the business, two hours pushed us to the max. As I walked through the ballroom, pride filling my chest, I thought we had pulled it off. Tables dotted the Grand Ballroom, each with purple tablecloths and vases of white flowers. Fully stocked bars were ready for business in each corner of the room. A DJ played dance music to appeal to those of all ages. The Big Boss and Mona formed a small receiving line at the door as employees started arriving.

Out of breath but riding a true love high, my colleagues and I put our heads together.

"Have you made sure that *all* the employees, including those working in the Bazaar shops, have been invited?" I asked.

"Brandy hit the retail and dining establishments, I worked the grapevine and the closed-circuit," Miss P confirmed. "The Casino Managers are rotating staff, as are the restaurants and housekeeping. Everyone else will drop by when it fits."

"Thanks," I said to my friends. "I owe you two a spa weekend on me. This was above and beyond."

"We're family." Miss P squeezed my arm. Then to Brandy, she said, "Come. Let's congratulate the happy couple."

They wandered off, leaving me alone. Leaning against the wall, I watched my folks. My father shook each employee's hand, from the lowliest to the Head of Operations, calling each one by name. Taking to her new role, my mother greeted every-one with a warm smile and a hug. Maybe she'd get the hang of life in the fishbowl, maybe not, but I knew one thing for certain: it would be an inter-esting ride.

Mrs. Olefson lingered in the receiving line await-ing a chance to talk to my father. I wondered how she had heard about the party.

"She was having a glass of wine with me," Jean-Charles said as if he'd read my mind. He joined me against the wall. "When your assistant informed us of the party for Mr. Rothstein and your mother, Mrs. Olefson insisted on being my date so that she could tell your boss what a won-derful asset you are to the hotel. She's quite a fan of yours."

"Leave it to the little old ladies to snag the hand-some men. I'm going to have to keep my eye on her." Turning, I looked into his baby blues. "Have you seen the evening news?" I asked him.

"No, I've been trying to locate satisfactory truf-fles. My supplier inexcusably ran out. Not to men-tion, his crabmeat was old—entirely unsatisfactory. How do you have old crabmeat this close to San

Francisco?" He took a breath, letting it out slowly. "Why?"

"No reason."

"The music should not be wasted. May I have this dance?" Jean-Charles extended his hand.

When I put my hand in his, for some reason it took my breath and hit my heart. I let him lead me to the dance floor and fold me into his arms—we fit like two halves. Life was trying to tell me something, but I didn't know what. It was bad enough I had hooked up with a guy who didn't love me after all, now I was falling for a guy who already had lost his heart to another? Could I pick them or what? Or maybe that was the point. If I picked someone I couldn't have, then what had I risked? For a smart woman, I could be really stupid. And now I had the hots for a co-worker . . . a new low.

Too tired to fight it any longer, I put my head on his shoulder and followed his lead.

Lost in the rhythm, the feel of him, the joy of being held in his arms, I let myself drift. The Frenchman was taken, but for this moment, as we moved as one in time to the melody and Michael Bublé sang about dreams that might come true, I could imagine . . .

We danced until the DJ stopped to take a break. How long had it been? Half an hour? An hour? Time had stopped.

"I must get back," Jean-Charles said, with a hint of reluctance, his arm still encircling my waist, his hand holding mine next to his heart, his face close to mine. "The restaurant is busy tonight and the staff is still learning."

"Thank you for the dance . . . dances," I said, but I didn't pull away.

"I would like to ask you a question." Jean-Charles's eyes turned serious. "Would you do me the honor of having lunch with me tomorrow? I work at night and it's hard for me to get away, otherwise I would take you to dinner . . . if you would be so kind as to accept. We work together, you and I, so we must know each other better."

I was feeling pretty good until that last part—this would be business. Nonetheless, it would be an enjoyable meal in the presence of the handsome Frenchman. So, being true to my new motto to live well, I said, "I can think of nothing I would like more."

His face breaking into a grin, he looked delighted—if he was faking, his act was worthy of an Oscar. "I will come by your office at one; is that all right?"

"Perfect."

As I watched him walk away I so hoped he wasn't playing me—I just didn't have it in me anymore.

AS the party wound down and I began dreading facing my empty apartment, I ran through the list of alternate sleeping arrangements. None of them ideal, and at a loss, I reluctantly bid my parents adieu and headed for home.

Miss P caught up with me in the lobby. "Lucky. Wait. I have a few messages."

Shrugging into her coat, with Jeremy helping, she stopped in front of me. "Norm Clarke wants a few minutes of your time. *People* magazine is holding the presses so they can include you in a feature article about the new *über*-wealthy. One of the gaming mags wants to do a feature on you. There are others, but you get the drift."

"Tell Norm I'd be glad to talk to him. Go through the list and pick out the ones I owe favors to, then we'll formulate a battle plan. As far as I can tell, my personal balance sheet hasn't changed. Tell *People* to kiss off—politely, of course."

"Of course."

"All of this can wait until the morning. You two run off and play."

Holding her elbow protectively, Jeremy steered Miss P toward the garage elevators. Pulling on my own sweater, I caught Dane heading in my direction.

"If you're thinking about going out the front, I'd reconsider," he said as he arrived in front of me, looking all hurried and disheveled . . . in a sexy sort of way. "There's a pack of newshounds out there as hungry as bears after a long winter. And about as mean, I suspect. The news of your parents' nuptials, on top of your paternity, has them worked up into a feeding frenzy. So far, Security is keeping them back, but I wouldn't be surprised if they call Metro for reinforcements."

"What would you suggest?" I asked, simply because I wanted to see his eyes go dark and his brows crease in concentration as he worked through the problem.

"As I see it, you have two choices: Make a run for it out the back or hole up here."

"The hotel is full and I doubt my parents would appreciate a bunkmate, so we're left with making a break. You up for it?"

As expected, he segued into his "male protection" mode. Men are so simple—hardwired to prehistoric, a damsel in apparent distress was all it took to flip the switch.

"You wait by the door on the fourth level of the parking garage. I'll get the car. When you see me . . ."

"I'll run for it."

He left me lurking by the door to the garage as he bolted into the darkness. From my vantage point my range of vision was limited, but so far, it looked like smooth sailing.

True to his word, Dane eased his borrowed Aston Martin near the door. I jumped through the passenger door he had thrown open for me. So far, we remained undetected.

I didn't bother to hide my face when we eased through a throng assembled at the exit to the garage—it wasn't like they didn't know where I lived. This wasn't Hollywood and no one published a map, but somehow word got around.

Dane paused on the street before turning up the

drive to the Presidio. A small group assembled by the front door.

"Willing to brave it?" he asked. "If not, you're always welcome to bunk at my place."

I started to speak, but he cut me off. "I have a guest room."

"That's a nice offer, but I can't."

"I promise I'll leave you in peace. You can trust me."

"I know," I said as I covered his hand with mine. "It's me I'm not so sure about. I want to apologize for throwing myself at you this afternoon—that was very bad form. I'm licking a few open wounds right now, and my behavior seems to be a bit erratic—my confidence has taken a hit."

"Teddie is one dumb SOB."

"You're kind to say so, and I appreciate your assessment, but I have to look inside myself to find my footing. I've linked my self-worth, at least where love is concerned, to other people's perceptions for far too long."

"Gotcha." Dane put the car back into gear. "Are we still on for a night of UFO viewing tomorrow?"

"It'll be the highlight of my day."

Well, that and lunch.

AFTER a brief verbal tussle, Dane conceded defeat and let me out at the curb to handle the gossip hounds by myself. Forrest lurked just inside the door, so if I needed him, he wasn't far away. The group circled me like a pack of coyotes—I wondered which one would rip out my Achilles tendon so the others could feed.

"Ms. O'Toole. Or should I say, Rothstein?" A young blond barracuda I'd done battle with before stuck her mike in my face. "How does it feel to be the bastard child of one of the last hardliners?"

Her bite missed the mark, and I whirled on her. "First rule of interviewing, try to get your subject on your side. I've been a child born out of wedlock my whole life, so why should it feel any different? Second, before you make insinuations in this town, I'd be darn sure you know what you're talking about. Lastly, my parents got married today—it was a wonderful day—but it changes nothing in my life . . . not my name, not my job, not my future."

"Technically, that may be true," a young man in the crowd said. "However, are you aware that you are listed as the owner of the Athena? And that an application for a gaming license in your name has been filed with the commission?"

"There is some mistake. I already have a gaming license."

The young man thrust some papers at me. My heart raced as I scanned them.

Dated three months ago. Title to the Athena registered in my name. An application for modification of my gaming license . . . with a signature that purported to be mine. It looked like mine . . . but I didn't remember signing it.

What was The Big Boss up to?

· · ·

AFTER the cacophony of questions downstairs, at least the apartment was quiet . . . and empty. But not nearly as bad as I thought it would be. The cleaning crew had been in and fumigated—the aroma of Pine-Sol was a dead giveaway.

After rooting for my phone, I tossed my Birkin on the kitchen counter. One glance told me all I needed to know: no calls. As my last act of defiance for the evening, I powered the damn thing off then slid it back toward my purse. Tomorrow was always the best day for dealing with bad stuff. Yes, I am a model procrastinator, and darn proud of it.

Newton greeted me with a "How the fuckin' hell are you?" This was new.

"Bad bird." I stuffed a crescent of browned apple through the bars of his cage.

"Asshole!" he announced, then grabbed the morsel and a chunk of my finger.

"Damn!" I stuffed the offending digit in my mouth to curb the blood as I eyed my feathered friend and wondered if he would fly away if I opened his cage on the balcony. I'd lost a lover in a similar manner—although I'd thrown open his cage at the airport—but I bet it'd work on a bird.

Deciding I'd lost enough friends for one day, I covered his cage and retreated to lick my wounds. My bedroom looked the same, felt the same, yet everything was different. Teddie wouldn't be home. He wouldn't call. We wouldn't make love. . . .

And somehow, that was okay. If he didn't want to be here, why would I want him?

The memories, the yearning, the hollowness in my chest, all had faded to a gray shade of hurt, whisper-thin, and I wondered if I had ever really loved him at all.

Then I noticed Teddie's sax still leaning in the corner.

My heart tripped.

His favorite instrument, well, his favorite musical instrument—he never would have forgotten it.

So why did he leave it behind?

MY hot bath did nothing but make me hot. Struggling with too many questions and emotions, I flipped the brain switch to neutral and willed it to quiet as I snuggled into goose down and Egyptian cotton. Yet, the wheels still whirred. I tried mediation . . . forty-five seconds later (yes, I watched the clock) I abandoned that idea as futile—staring at nothing, doing nothing, thinking nothing was so not me. I'd tried yoga once and giggled myself silly until the leader threw me out. I failed yoga. What did that mean?

"Christ!" I threw off the covers, climbed into a pair of sweats and a tee shirt, and retreated to the couch and the History Channel. After two programs on Sherman's March to the Sea, my eyes grew heavy. I could handle my life and the curves in the road. I could even handle the kooks and the crazies, but I had a real bad feeling about The Big Boss—he was maneuvering me.

A noise startled me out of a dream about angels and devils and eternal damnation. Listening, I didn't move. Someone was in my apartment . . . again. This was getting tiresome.

I watched as a figure, clad in black, moved through the great room toward my bedroom, apparently expecting me to be asleep in my bed. This was clearly no friend—my friends knew my nocturnal quirks better that.

With my gun in my nightstand, I resorted to a knife from the kitchen instead. Less than ideal, but it was all I had.

My pulse pounded—anger overriding good sense. The smart thing to do would be to leave . . . but I was never one to run from a fight. And I wanted answers.

One step, then a pause to listen, then another step, I maneuvered myself within striking distance behind the figure lingering in the doorway to my bedroom. I crouched, knife at the ready. "Stop right there."

The figure whirled and I stepped in, throwing my elbow at his head.

Bone connected with bone.

The figure dropped like a stone.

With the knife in one hand, I turned the inert body over.

Molly Rain.

No weapons.

After trading the knife for my Glock, I flicked on a light, then rested one cheek on the arm of the couch and waited for her to come to.

A few minutes, no more, and she started to stir. Groaning, she writhed on the floor. Then her eyes snapped open. "Lucky?"

"Why are you here?" I demanded. "And why the hell all the subterfuge?"

"You can put the gun down," Molly said, her voice shaking. "I'm not here to hurt you."

"I've got six inches and more than twenty pounds on you, and you're not exactly in a threatening position."

"Good point." She pushed herself to her elbow. "What hit me?"

"I did."

"Where'd you learn that?" Propped on one hand, she rubbed her temple where my elbow had left a red mark. "You pack quite a wallop."

"Growing up in a whorehouse had its advantages." I motioned with the gun. "It helps that I've been hardwired to the pissed-off position since your boss pulled his disappearing act. Trust me, you don't want to mess with me. Start talking."

Molly pushed herself to a seated position, then crawled over to the couch and pulled herself up. She settled back into the cushions with a groan, and closed her eyes, leaning her head back. "I need to know where Carl is."

"Carl who?" Putting a safe distance between us, I moved to lean against the wall, just out of reach.

"Crazy Carl Colson." She captured me with those startlingly blue eyes.

My heart sank. Poor Carl. Didn't he have enough demons haunting his dreams? Now he had to be stalked by real-life ones? "I don't know anybody by that name." I kept my voice as level as I could, but I probably wasn't very convincing.

"Yes, you do." Molly jumped to her feet, surprising me. "I can read it in your face."

So much for lying. "Huh-uh." I brandished the gun at her. "Sit."

She reluctantly did as I ordered. "I'm your friend," she said, trying a different tack.

"My friends come in through the front door."

Narrowing her eyes, she weighed her words. "You know Carl. He told me you were kind to him. You bring him blankets."

"Why would this Carl person tell you that?"

"He's my father."

"Really?" I paused to think. Carl had a daughter? This was the first I'd heard of it, not that I would have any reason to know. "If you guys are so tight, then why don't you know where he is?"

"When he gets scared, he runs for the storm drains—that much I do know. But he never would tell me exactly where. He didn't want me trying to find him when the Others were looking for him."

"Who are the Others? Is that why you broke into Danilov's apartment?"

Surprise flashed across her face, as if she wasn't expecting the question, then her composure returned. "I didn't break in—someone beat me to it."

"Who?"

"I don't know." If she was lying she was a darn sight better at it than me. "Carl told me Danilov had some papers having to do with the Others."

When Molly ran a hand through her hair and turned those turquoise eyes on me again, I saw real pain there . . . and something else, something that stirred a memory. What was it? This time, when Molly pushed to her feet, I let her pace. "Weird things are going on," she continued. "I've got a gut feeling my father is in danger. I really need to find him. Please help me."

"Oh man!" I let the gun drop to my side as I rolled my eyes. "You're the Ferengi!"

When I heard her sharp intake of breath, I knew I'd hit the nail on the head.

"That's why you didn't come immediately when I shouted for you after Dimitri received that threatening note. Come to think of it, when you did show you seemed flustered and out of breath." The more I thought about it, the more I knew I was right.

Molly paused as if weighing her options. "How'd you know?"

"I don't know too many people with almost turquoise eyes. They are a dead giveaway. Why don't I make us some coffee and you can tell me what's going on?" Still wary of her, I kept the gun in my hand, but I no longer threatened her with it. She and I were both looking for information.

Molly's eyes darted to the balcony door and for a moment I thought she would make a break for it, then she seemed to resolve some inner conflict and followed me into the kitchen. Pushing my purse out of the way, she boosted herself up to sit on the counter.

I set the gun within my reach, and out of hers, and busied myself with coffee. With the routine ingrained so it was almost a reflex, I quickly had the pot perking.

"I'll tell you what I know," Molly began. "Dimitri asked me to deliver the hat and the rabbit with the message."

"Why?"

"Publicity. His career, such as it was, was going down the crapper. He thought if he stirred things up, got some attention, maybe he could parlay that into his next gig."

I handed her a cup of coffee and tried to catch her eyes. That didn't sound like the Dimitri I thought I knew. But then, I'd been wrong before. "I hope you take it black. The milk has gone blinky." Along with half the people in this town, I thought, but I didn't say that. "Did you help him plan it from the beginning?"

"No. He had it all figured out. My job was to set the plan in motion and make it look real."

"You did a bang-up job." I took a sip of my java.

Closing my eyes I reveled in the caffeine hit—my body practically sighing in relief. If I didn't cut back on all the various forms of high-test I'd been relying on to get through the day, I was in for a huge comeuppance. "Things didn't work out quite as he'd planned, did they?"

Molly shook her head as she stared into her coffee mug. "I don't know what could've gone wrong—he'd been working on the trick for months."

A little earthly intervention, most likely, of the nonmagical, murderous variety, I thought, but didn't say. It seemed reasonable, but the proof was more than a bit thin . . . in fact, it probably vanished with Dimitri. Having been taught to hold my cards very close to the vest, I didn't air my suspicions. For all I knew, the sweet young thing in front of me could be in up to her eyeballs, though I couldn't imagine why. But she had already proven adept at breaking and entering, so who knew what her complete skill set included.

"So, is he dead or not?" I asked.

"I honestly don't know, but I have a real bad feeling." She looked up at me with those alarmingly blue eyes. "I mean, why would anyone take the body?"

Why indeed? Taking the first step toward reining in my stimulant addiction, I poured my coffee down the drain. "Here's what I'll do," I said. "I won't tell you where Carl holes up—"

"You *have* to!" Molly jumped off the counter, spilling coffee, her anger flaring.

I grabbed the gun. That settled her down. "I don't trust you," I said. "You're not coming clean with me on the whole Danilov thing. But for Carl's sake, I'll get a message to him. That's the best I can do."

Molly stared at me, a murderous look in her eye. "You have to hurry. The Devil is getting closer."

"Christ, I'm so sick of the friggin' Devil." I took her cup and stepped to the sink.

That was the opening Molly was looking for—she made her break. Caught by surprise, I was two steps too slow. Running, she hit the balcony doors, banging them against the stops as she burst through. Grabbing her rope with one hand, she threw herself over the balcony, and disappeared into the darkness.

Bending over the railing, I peered into the inky blackness, and pulled on the rope. Her weight on the other end, I wasn't strong enough to reel her in.

"Damn!"

Racing inside, the seconds turned into a minute or two as I searched for my phone. I couldn't find it. Christ!

With shaking hands, I rooted in my nightstand for my backup—one of the old yellow and black Nextels, bulky but it would do—if it still worked. Pressing the power button, I was glad to see lights and bars. I dialed the desk downstairs.

It rang and rang, but no one answered.

"Double-damn!"

I glanced at the time—almost five. Forrest didn't start his shift until six. Molly had timed it perfectly.

Glaring at the balcony doors as I sank into the couch and dialed Romeo, I made a mental note to get all the locks changed and dead bolts installed, posthaste. While I liked visitors, I preferred they arrive in the normal manner—much better for my blood pressure.

For once I was glad to see the eastern sky brightening—I'd actually gotten a fair amount of sleep. After five rings, my call to the young detective rolled to voice mail. I tried again. This time he answered after the second ring.

"Sorry, I was in the shower."

"Our aerialist just paid me another visit, and idiot that I am, I turned my back on her. She went over the balcony on a rope—she's long gone by now."

"Wow, you're thirty floors up."

"Amazingly enough, I know that."

"Are *we* in a good mood," Romeo said, laughing. "Sorry, it's early and I'm slow on the uptake— you're the first person to ream the day through my earhole. What did she want?"

"Sorry. My smile disappeared a few days ago." This time I came clean about Carl Colson.

"Do you think Mr. Colson is in danger?" Romeo asked when I'd finished.

"We have to assume he is."

"Do you want me to send a couple of uniforms to warn him?"

"That would scare him to death. Not to mention it might be dangerous for your men—I get the impression some of the people living in the storm drains wouldn't welcome the police."

"Point taken. Are you going to warn him, then?"

"Not personally," I said. "I seem to be attracting all kinds of attention. And I can't shake the feeling someone is keeping tabs on me. But I'll get word to him."

"You need me to watch your back?"

"No, thanks."

"What then?"

"Find Molly Rain."

AFTER a hot shower, I spent some time picking out my uniform for the day. What did one wear to lunch with a very urbane Frenchman? One could never go wrong with Chanel—I chose a fitted suit in an understated shade of dove gray, a sexy hot-pink lace cami that bordered on the indecent, and a pair of hot-pink Loubous with a lower heel . . . Jean-Charles was tall, but not that tall. I accessorized with my square-cut diamond earrings and nothing else.

Since understated seemed to be my mood today, I carried it over to my makeup and hair—subtly highlighting my eyes and cheekbones and letting my hair fall softly, brushing my shoulders and tickling my eyes. With one last look in the mirror, I checked the results. A confident hotel executive stared back—a perfect mask for the confused woman inside. How I wished the inner me would match the outer.

Despite turning my place upside down, I couldn't find my regular phone. Where I'd left it was anybody's guess. I tried calling my number, but no luck—oh it rang all right, just not within hearing distance. So, I called the phone company and had them roll my normal number to the one on this phone and launched into the day. The phone would turn up—it always did.

Needing some fresh air and perspective, I chose to walk to work. The day had brightened into one of those picture-perfect, bluebird days that remind us of why we live in Las Vegas: cool air, warm sun, and birds soaring on the early thermals. I took my time as I walked, trying to absorb some of the peace. But knowing that Carl had become the lightning rod for this devilish business, I found it hard to do. Well, that and the fact that I kept looking over my shoulder—I knew someone was there, I just couldn't see them.

I hated it when people came to Vegas to muddy up the magic.

Half oblivious to my surroundings, with the Babylon looming in front of me, I jumped at the loud shrill of my phone. Who would be calling me at this hour?

Teddie.

Staring at the phone, racked with indecision, I waffled through two rings, then finally punched the button rolling the call to voice mail.

Strolling up the drive to the front of the hotel, I didn't worry about the stray rabid journalist lurking about. In Vegas, news had a half-life of about an hour. Deciding a turn through the casino would do me good, I bypassed the stairs.

Early in the day the casino looked a bit bedraggled, as if everyone had gone to bed after the party, leaving the cleanup for later. Even dark and virtually empty, the big room still held whispers of the previous night's fun and frivolity. Contemporary music with a driving beat had given way to the languid ballads of Frank Sinatra and Etta James, which was always fine by me; I'm a sucker for a good love song.

Cruising through the rear of the casino, I bounded up the grand double-helix staircase to the Mezzanine, where huge windows let the light compete with the dungeon atmosphere of the gaming rooms.

At a tea table flanked by two Queen Anne chairs, Mrs. Olefson was taking her morning meal of coffee and scones—she in one chair, Milo in the other. The dog looked bored, perking one ear only when his mistress reached for a crumb. Carefully coiffed, attired in St. John, and properly accessorized, the diminutive lady appeared ready for an audience with the Pope or perhaps a chance encounter with the Queen.

"Mrs. Olefson, how are you this morning?"

"Fine, dear. How are you?"

"Limping along."

"What a nice party your boss had last night—so sweet of him to let me stay." With a snap of her fingers, she cleared Milo from the chair. "Sit with me for a minute, would you?"

"I'd be delighted." Mrs. Olefson apparently hadn't read the morning paper. I took Milo's place and, to his credit, he didn't seem bothered by it.

Mrs. Olefson pushed the coffee pot toward me and gestured to an empty cup. My resolutions being short-lived, and having a clinically low level of self-discipline, I helped myself. This health-kick thing was off to a rough start.

When I had settled back in the big chair, Mrs. Olefson said, "I have a problem I hope you might help me with."

"Fire away. Problems are my specialty."

"I've been thinking." She refreshed her coffee then glanced at me. "I really like it here. The rooms are lovely, the staff is so friendly—some of the ladies from Housekeeping even come by to check on me. And your French chef plies me with wine." She gave me a wink. "I keep telling him he is courting the wrong lady."

"I'm under the impression he already has one of his own," I said.

"Really, he's never mentioned anyone." For a moment Mrs. Olefson's face clouded, but then she brightened. "No matter if he does, she couldn't be as wonderful as you."

"You're very kind."

"Last night, I told your boss how special you are. Maybe he'll give you a raise." The little match-maker/promoter gave me a self-satisfied smile.

"Perhaps. Thank you." I set my coffee cup on the table, feeling virtuous that I had limited myself to just one cup. "Now, what did you need my help with?"

"Oh yes." She set down her cup and sat up straight. Taking a deep breath, she gave a nod, as if to herself, then said, "Would it be possible for me to move into the hotel?"

"You want to live here?" I didn't know what I was expecting, but that wasn't it.

"Yes. I can pay for it."

"That was not a concern of mine," I reassured her. "Could you let me talk to my . . . boss? I doubt we'll be able to keep you in the Sodom and Go-morrah Suite, but if you're willing to take some-thing smaller, I think we may be able to work something out. I can't promise, but I feel confi-dent."

"A simple room with no view would be suffi-cient."

Her question had caught me off guard, but the more I thought about it, the more I liked the idea of having her around. God knew we all could use a den mother. Made of sturdy Midwestern stock, I had no doubt she would be up to the task. "How long were you thinking of staying?"

"Could we leave it open-ended?" She looked at me with wide eyes. She wanted to be with friends—that much was clear.

"I'll see what I can do."

MISS P breezed into my office. "I'm starting to worry about you. This is the third time this week you've beaten me to work."

"Yeah, well, early bird and all of that, you know. I made notes on your list of journalists who want a bit of my time. Could you arrange all of that? I'd prefer to do it by phone, as you know." At her nod, I handed her the last of the paperwork. "We must kill a tree a day just in this office alone. Can you get Brandy to look into how we can handle some of this stuff electronically?"

Miss P raised an eyebrow. "And drag you kicking and screaming into the twenty-first century?"

"I want information before I commit. As we all know, change is inconsistent with my personality." I motioned to a chair. "Is Jeremy with you?"

"He stopped to talk to Jerry, but he should be here any minute."

"Great, I've got something I hope he can help me with."

Miss P shrugged out of her coat—a trick while balancing the papers I'd handed her, but she managed. "I take it you want coffee?" she asked.

"No, thanks. I've had enough."

That stopped her. "Okay, what's up? This is not the Lucky I know."

"Would you quit it?" Unwilling to let her read me, I avoided her eyes, pretending instead to be absorbed by my cockroach paperweight, moving it a few inches to the left, then back again. "I know it's not spring, but I feel the need to clean house," I offered as an explanation.

"Out with the old, in with the new?"

Her words hit closer to the mark than even I realized.

Jeremy saved me from having to elaborate, or invent an excuse not to. "G'Day."

I don't think I'd ever get tired of hearing him say that. If I was Miss P, I'd just have him talk to me each evening, so I could sit back and listen— which was probably a male fantasy anyway, so not too difficult to pull off.

"Take a seat, both of you." I motioned to the chairs opposite my desk. "I need some help."

AFTER I gave Jeremy his marching orders, he left and Miss P and I put our heads together, checking average room vacancy, revenue per room, and all the other variables we could think of that went into profit.

"You're committing a room to a nongambler, so no gaming revenue there," Miss P said after over an hour of throwing around numbers. "That's the only revenue stream you're going to have to compensate for."

"I can almost cover the average amount each guest keeps in play—she'll eat three meals a day either room service or in one of our restaurants. And we're assured of room rental for every night of the term—one hundred percent occupancy for that room."

"Do you think it's enough to sell The Big Boss?"

"He's basking in nuptial bliss; he'd buy a Rolex off a street vendor."

Chapter

FOURTEEN

♡

The outer door swung open as my assistant and I were congratulating ourselves.

"Anyone here?" It was the unmistakable voice of Chef Bouclet.

"In here," I called, ignoring Miss P as she waggled her eyebrows. I glanced at the clock—eleven-thirty. My heart sank—I so hoped he wasn't here to cancel.

Jean-Charles filled my doorway, taking away not only my breath, but my spoken-for assistant's as well. Tall and trim, wearing those darn Italian slacks that left just enough to the imagination to sidetrack rational thought (today's color was an interesting medium brown with just a hint of bronze to give it life), a soft sweet-butter colored shirt, a slim-cut tweed blazer in browns and greens with a hint of golden yellow, a green scarf tied around his neck (which on anyone else would look doofy, but on him it was perfect), he greeted me with a smile that sparkled in his eyes. He even looked a little bit nervous.

My luck had clearly turned.

His eyes never leaving mine, he reached for my hands as I moved to greet him. "You are stunning," he whispered as he kissed each cheek.

"So are you." Whatever game he was playing, my defeat was close at hand. I was toast—and I didn't care. I just wanted him to look at me like he was doing now . . . for a long time.

"I know I am early." He glanced at the clock. "Perhaps too early, but I couldn't wait any longer to see you. Are you able to leave now? I have something to show you . . . and something I want to tell you . . . before we have lunch."

There went the fantasy, splattering like a water balloon dropped from the top floor. I guessed I would hear all about the girlfriend before the morning segued into afternoon—the one whose picture he kept close to his heart. So why did he want to see me? Did he want me to be a second-stringer? That would be crushing.

"I think I can break away." I handed Miss P my phone. "You have the helm. I'm taking some personal time. Would you please be so kind as to remove any personal messages from my voice mail—I don't want to hear them."

"I never took you to be an SUV kind of guy," I said, as I watched Jean-Charles maneuver his black Mercedes ML 550 through traffic. He had nice hands, artists' hands, with long, thin fingers that belied their strength . . . and most likely the softness of their touch.

My stomach clenched—some things were just not meant to be.

His brow creased in concentration, he chewed on his lip as he drove. "I'm not a comfortable driver—I've spent my adulthood in large cities where owning a vehicle was an impediment—so I thought a larger car might be wise."

"Good thinking. Americans have transformed the art of driving into a duel to the death."

"That works in my favor—Europeans have a long history of duels." Jean-Charles relaxed as he exited the parkway. "I've been practicing. Can you tell?"

"You've only terrified me twice, so far," I deadpanned, then shot him a grin in response to his stricken glance.

"You like to joke?" he asked without the smile I was looking for.

"I've been told it's a defense mechanism."

He pursed his lips, but said nothing.

"Where are we going?" I asked, as we dove into a residential neighborhood in Summerlin.

"It's a surprise." Bypassing the guard shack protecting the entrance to a gated community—one of the most coveted addresses in Vegas and home to retired athletes and politicians, scions of the local and national business communities—Jean-Charles took the lane marked "residents." The gate opened.

Truly at a loss, I decided to sit back and let things unfold.

He parked the car in the driveway of a large Mediterranean-style two-story and killed the engine.

"What are we doing here?" I asked.

"This is my home. We finished only yesterday moving my things in—I've not even spent a night here." His nervousness palpable, he finally looked at me. "I wanted you to be the first to see it." He must have sensed my hesitancy. "Please?"

I don't know why I even try to anticipate what life has in store for me—I'm always wrong. A simple business lunch . . . right! And when I had no fight left.

Needing time to adjust, I waited while he came around to open my door. Taking his proffered hand, I was again surprised by my reaction—not sizzle and burn this time, but something else, something solid and sure . . . something new, and old, as if I'd known him forever.

Damn.

After leading me to the front, he fumbled with the keys for a moment, then moved aside as he pushed open the door.

As I knew it would be, the home was breath-taking. An eclectic assemblage of antiques and modern pieces, all in different styles from different eras, the home was the perfect jumble of contrasting tastes and contradictions that blended into sheer perfection—a true reflection of its owner.

"Oh, Jean-Charles! This is amazing!"

With the pride of ownership, he led me from room to room—the upper floor held five bedrooms *en suite*, all encircling a game room that could easily accommodate a pool table, foosball, and a beanbag pit for watching the enormous flat screen. The main floor had a great room and dining room combination, all with French doors opening to the pool area. An office and a library opened off the main area. A gourmet kitchen with a casual eating area and a family room with a fireplace and wet bar comprised one wing off the main room. The other wing held the master suite—a comfortable space with a fireplace, seating area, bed large enough for a family of four, and a bathroom and closet to rival mine.

When we finished the tour, he led me back to the family room off the kitchen. He motioned for me to sit on the sofa, while he lit the fire. Instead of sitting next to me, he remained standing, propping an elbow on the mantle and a foot on the hearth.

"I have something to tell you." His face drained of color.

"Look," I said. "Does this have something to

do with the photo you carry in your pocket? With the person who will be meeting you here, to come live with you in this beautiful home?"

His hand drifted to his breast pocket as he nodded. *"Oui."* His eyes were a deep, serious blue.

"Then let me make this easy on you," I said, with a surprisingly heavy heart. Why did his touch have to make me feel so good? "You have a girlfriend, maybe even a wife, and you want to let me know so I don't misinterpret this ease developing between us. Not necessary. I know the score."

With a soft smile, he pulled the well-handled photo from his pocket. Moving to sit beside me, he showed it to me. "This is Christophe. He is five years old." Jean-Charles's eyes met mine. "He is my son."

I stared at the visage—a mop of golden brown hair, dimples, blue eyes that rivaled his father's, and a smile to melt your heart.

"He's adorable. Where is he?"

"In France, for a visit with my parents. They are watching him while I get things settled. I want to build a life for us here, where young boys can still run and play. We have been in Manhattan for the last three years—there is no room there to be a child."

"I see."

"When he is not here, it is like a hole in my heart." Jean-Charles took a look at the photo then repocketed it. "This is the longest we have been apart. He is amazing—the most curious little boy.

Right now he loves animals—he's fascinated with all of them—especially the babies. My mother probably had something to do with that."

"What do your parents do?"

"They own an inn in Provence. My father is the chef. My mother tells him what to do, and he pretends not to like it."

From the look on his face I could tell he missed them. "Do you have any siblings?"

"A twin sister, Gisele. Her daughter, Chantal, is bringing Christophe to me. They will be here in a few weeks, but it seems like an eternity."

"And Christophe's mother? Where is she?"

His face sobered as he swallowed hard. "She died."

I grabbed his hand. "I'm so sorry."

"I've never told anybody this—I've never been able to speak of it. I'm not sure I can." He took a deep, composing breath—I knew the drill. "With Christophe . . . something happened, an artery tore deep inside her. They couldn't stop the bleeding."

I pressed a hand to my mouth.

"I held her . . ." He buried his face in his hands for a moment. When he looked up, his eyes were dry, but filled with painful memories. "She gave me a beautiful son. He is my life."

"What a horrible thing," I said, at a loss. "Christophe, he is a lucky boy, to have a father like you."

"Perhaps not the best father—for a long time I was angry." Jean-Charles reached for my hand, holding it in both of his. "Now I let people think

I am a silly man, vain and demanding—a prima donna."

"Why?"

"I don't want to let anyone close." Pain flashed across his face. "The pain of losing someone you love . . ."

"I understand."

"I've always been able to push away everyone. But with you . . . I tried, but I simply cannot. Our dinners together, they have brought me so much joy. I even like our war of words over the plans for the restaurant—you know my business almost as well as I do. I wait always for the chance to see you again. Last night, I came looking for you— the party was a good excuse."

"You don't need an excuse."

"But you are hurting, *non*?"

"Still smarting a bit, but I'll live."

"You may not want another man in your life?"

Completely in the dark, and afraid to hope for a dream, I took a deep breath. "I can be silly at times, but not so stupid that I would push away a good thing just because the timing is awkward."

"Perhaps you did not love him as much as you thought?" Jean-Charles phrased it as a question, but I heard it as a statement.

"Perhaps. I let him go."

"Yes," Jean-Charles said. "With love, you fight for it."

I didn't tell him that Teddie didn't fight for it either—maybe he knew that. "I'd like to know that kind of love," I said, amazing myself with my candor. What was it about this Frenchman and his effect on me? And what was he trying to tell me? And why was my heart beating so fast?

"I have known love only once," Jean-Charles said. "When I met you, you made me remember what it was like. When I touch you . . ."

"I know."

The worry left his face. "I thought you felt it, too, but I didn't know." My hand still in his, he covered it with his free hand. "Will you have me in your life, this man who is not so perfect, who can be demanding and a perfectionist, who has a beautiful son, and who will try so hard to keep that smile on your face and put one on your heart?"

"You are in my life. We are partners. Remember?"

"That is not what I mean." He sighed in frustration. "No, that is what I mean . . ."

My heart sank.

"But only part. I know it is unwise to mix business and the heart, but I cannot help how my heart feels. You like me, *non*? You feel what is between us?"

"Yes. On both counts." I broke eye contact and turned my gaze through the French doors. A beautiful day, sunlight streamed through the branches of the trees shading part of the pool. A breeze tickled the water, fracturing the light into a million sparkles. "Jean-Charles, combining work and pleasure is like lending money to friends—something you should never do because you will end up with neither."

He gave me a slight shrug. "My mother, she is like you—she is the heart. My father—I've been told I am much like him—he creates food to feed the soul. Together, they make one."

When he put it that way, it didn't sound stupid at all.

"I'm not sure I can handle a relationship now, especially one that would require such a delicate balance," I said, looking at my hand in his and avoiding his eyes.

With one finger under my chin, he tilted my face until I had to meet his gaze.

"This thing between a man and a woman is like a fine Bordeaux—first, it should be allowed to breathe, to reach its fullness. Then it should be savored slowly, at the peak of perfection." Turning my hand in his, he pressed my palm to his lips. "I will not rush you. When you are ready."

When was the last time *those* words passed the lips of a red-blooded male? Whenever it was, I bet the earth had yet to cool.

"We will argue," I warned.

"Most surely." A gentle smile lifted the corners of his mouth. "Then we will reconcile."

"Mmmm." He made that sound as succulent as a perfectly flakey, golden croissant dripping with butter. And if he kept looking at me the way he was right now, I'd be ready to . . . reconcile . . . any minute.

"Will you let me kiss you?"

For some reason, the word *no* eluded me.

Tracing the line of my jaw, he then cupped my chin, lifting my lips to his. Tenderly he captured my lips—light, sweet, stealing my breath. Then he deepened the kiss—darker, more insistent, lighting a fire, a need . . . a recognition.

Damn.

TRUE to his word, Jean-Charles kissed me, nothing more. But in his kiss I glimpsed life's goodness, life's possibilities. It was, perhaps, the best kiss ever.

What was it with me? Was I genetically predisposed to find relationships that were like gliders—soaring, riding waves of superheated air—then spiraling down to a controlled crash, an abrupt landing, devastation? Or was I simply a glutton for punishment? Who knew? What I *did* know was that I needed to tread very carefully with the handsome Frenchman or I could find my ass in a crack.

Still tingling from the kiss, I watched as Jean-Charles opened a very fine Bordeaux, then poured us each a glass.

"To new beginnings," he said as he raised his glass.

We toasted his new life and, I guess, a new chapter of my own. We talked of hotels, in France and in Vegas, of families, of dreams . . . of life.

Now the bottle was empty and I relaxed into the curve of his arm as we both sat on the couch, admiring the fire, and enjoying the comfort of each other. "Are you hungry?" Jean-Charles asked.

"Not particularly. Why?"

"I had planned to take you to lunch, remember?"

"This is better." His hand on my thigh, I traced his fingers. I still couldn't believe I was here—that this was happening. "Although, a few crackers with cheese to soak up some of the wine would probably be a good idea. We both have to work—and I know my boss would like for me to arrive sober."

"I have just the thing." Jean-Charles disengaged. "Wait right here."

After a few minutes of banging in the kitchen, he reappeared. Spreading a red and white checkered tablecloth on the floor, he then set down a plate of various cheeses, a basket of crackers, and some red grapes. "Voilà."

"Perfect." I joined him in an impromptu picnic.

After we had our fill, I said, "What? No dessert?"

"You wound me." Jean-Charles reached to touch my lips. His eyes turned the deepest blue. A smile lifted one corner of his mouth. "I am French. We are experts at dessert."

Chapter

FIFTEEN

♡

"Well, you look like your planets have shifted," Miss P announced when I wandered into the office, riding my little cloud of *joie de vivre*. "That must've been quite a lunch," she scolded. "Of course, when you dine with a scrumptious chef, what would you expect? However, dinner is underway and Dane has been calling here every fifteen minutes asking when you two are heading to Rachel."

"Oh?" I squinted at her, trying to bring the world back into focus. "I forgot."

"Are you going to tell me about it?" she asked.

I shook my head, still not that aware of my surroundings. "No. I don't think so." I wandered into my office and dove into my closet, looking for the pair of blue jeans I'd stuffed in my bag this morning.

Miss P followed me. "I've never seen you look like this."

"I've never been like this."

"This one's different, isn't he?"

"Ah-ha!" I said, as my hands closed around the jeans I was looking for. Then, jeans in hand, I rose and turned to look at my friend, life returning to focus. "Everything is different."

Stepping into the bathroom, I changed uniforms—if things went well, tonight would be a jeans and Nikes kind of night. With a grin, I shrugged into the tie-dyed tee shirt Miss P had brought me—it fit like a second skin. I glanced at my reflection—a Deadhead in training—I liked it.

"*Different* looks good on you." Miss P lounged in the doorway.

"It feels good." I gave my hair a flip and wiped under my eyes, but the dark lurking there had nothing to do with smeared mascara. "But don't go making any giant leaps—I'm a complete disaster when it comes to personal relationships, and I will not let that compromise my job. Work is the one thing that holds me together."

"Chef Tastycakes has gotten under your skin," she said, smirking. "I can see it in your eyes—heck, it's written all over your face. I know the signs." Miss P made the whole thing sound like some sort of an affliction, a dreaded disease. "Welcome to the club."

"A club, is it?" I grabbed my bag and stepped around her into my office. "Well, I'd really like to stick around, maybe have you show me the secret handshake or something, but adventure awaits."

"That reminds me," Miss P announced as she followed me. "I almost forgot—your parents want you to stop by for a minute, if you can. They're sitting at the bar at the Burger Palais."

I couldn't hide my grin as I said, "Delighted. Could you let them know? Then call Dane, ask him to meet me out front in an hour. Do I have the Ferrari?"

She nodded.

"You're going home soon?" I asked.

"Brandy's pulling the graveyard." She held up her hand as I started to object. "Jerry's holding her hand."

I gave my fearless assistant a hug, then launched myself into the evening. As I bounded down the stairs to the lobby I whistled "La Vie en Rose."

JERRY caught me racing through the lobby. "I was just coming to find you."

"What's up?"

"You know how you asked me to keep tabs on those folks and report anything unusual?"

"A tall task, I know."

"I feel real bad about not catching the mentalist guy, Danilov, getting rolled last night. He went out to the golf course—I didn't think that was a big deal—people do it all the time."

"Jer, we do the best we can."

"Well, it bothered me, so I started looking for links."

"I guess you came up with something or you wouldn't be here." Jerry loved to string me along when he had something good. It usually irritated me, but for some reason, tonight I seemed impervious to irritation.

"I don't know what it means."

I frowned at him—okay, only partially impervious to irritation. "Jer!"

"Okay, Danilov left the magician's dinner early. He went to meet this woman—short, stocky, wavy black hair. She was giving him the what-for. When she left he was pretty shaken."

"And that's when he went out to the golf course?" I asked, not really following.

"Yeah." Jerry's eyes narrowed. "But here's the weird part: Later I saw the same chick bending that astronaut's ear. When she handed him some amulet on a chain or something, I thought the guy was going to freak."

"What did he do?"

"I can't describe it—it was like he was a different person, inhabited by aliens or something."

So Molly Rain could come and go, not only from my apartment but from the hotel as well, and the police couldn't get a line on her? Romeo and I needed to have a chat.

"Do you know what's going on?" Jerry asked.

"Haven't a clue. Keep me posted if you see the woman again, okay?" Molly was clearly working through the list of known associates of her alleged father—she seemed desperate to find him. I wondered why.

"You got it."

"Oh, hey," I called after him as he walked away.

"How'd you handle Teddie's father the other night?"

"*That* was Teddie's old man?"

I shrugged.

"He was such an ass I kept him until he was stone-cold sober, which took a while. He filed a complaint before he and the Missus headed back where they came from, but it was worth it."

"What complaint?" I asked, grinning. The look on his face told me my message was received; Mr. Kowalski's missive would disappear.

MY parents had saved a stool for me at the bar, which was perfect—with a large mirror behind, I could watch Jean-Charles's reflection as he worked in the kitchen. Straddling the stool after I had given both of them a kiss, I ordered a soda and lime.

"You can't be my daughter," my father said. "Wearing jeans on the job and drinking fizzy water."

"This is the new me—although the jeans are only because I'm going to Rachel to look for UFOs and talk to a radio show host who's gone commando."

Both my parents stared at me.

"Don't ask," I said, waving away their questions. "So how's married life treating you?"

They both grinned—my father squeezed his wife's hand. Question answered.

"So what did you want to see me about?" I asked.

"No reason, really," my father said. "We just wanted to see you."

A lie. They were worried about me. I pressed my hand to his face. "I'm fine, really."

I caught the reflection of Chef Bouclet in midtirade as he ordered his staff around. He was the leader, and everyone else had to follow—and quickly—he'd told me. His reputation depended upon it. I took his word for it—although shouting made me nervous.

If my father and mother noticed my interest in the chef, they didn't say so.

"I have something I need to talk to you about, Father," I said, then smiled as his eyes widened at the term of endearment—we hadn't talked about it, but Father felt right—he didn't seem to be a "Dad" kind of guy. "Three things, actually. First, do you remember meeting Mrs. Olefson yesterday?"

"The little lady from Saginaw? She's quite a fan of yours."

"She wants to live in the hotel."

His eyes found mine. "What do you think?"

"I've worked the numbers." I pulled out the folded scrap of paper on which Miss P and I had jotted our notes and pushed it toward him. "I'd like to do it. She's very lonely. No family to go home to."

The Big Boss didn't look at the paper. "Then do it. As my daughter has often told me, sometimes there are things you can't quantify—they are simply the right things to do."

"Right," I nodded, momentarily taken aback—apparently there was an epidemic of "different" going around. "Okay, next thing. I want to sell my place. I'd like to live in the small apartment next to yours until I find a home that suits me."

"Fine." My father kept his expression passive, his voice modulated.

"Honey, are you sure?" my mother asked, leaning across my father.

"Yeah," I said. "It's not because of Teddie and all of that. I just don't fit there anymore—the place is like someplace you rent while trying to figure out who you are and what you want."

"Do you know what you want?" my father asked.

I glanced at the reflection in the mirror, then back to him. "Getting there."

"What's the third thing?" he asked.

"When were you going to tell me about the Athena?"

Surprise registered on his face and he immediately shifted to defense mode. "Don't get mad. I'm not trying to maneuver you—I know how much you hate that." He relaxed at my grin. "The truth is, I need you—I can't do all of this by myself anymore. You've run several of my properties. You've managed every department at least once—

this business is in your blood and you know what you're doing."

"I can't sit in an office all day talking to accountants and bankers," I objected. "And going over profit and loss statements. My strength is handling people—it's where my heart is."

"I'll deal with the bean counters," my father said. "I'm smart enough to know you're the grease that makes all of this work—the glue, if you will. I couldn't afford to keep you squirreled away in an office. You've already been intimately involved in the redesign. Remember your idea for a service-centric boutique hotel—one that is very hands-on in the finest European tradition—the one you've been harping at me for years about? Here's your chance, you've earned it."

For once, I was completely at a loss.

I didn't know whether to shake his hand as a colleague or throw my arms around his neck as a daughter.

Jean-Charles rescued me. "Sir," he said as he extended his hand to my father, then faced mother. "Mrs. Rothstein. I am honored."

My mother beamed.

Then he turned to me, indecision in his eyes.

My whole world had changed today. I no longer knew what rules defined it . . . and I didn't much care. Standing, I faced him. This was his restaurant, his staff, his guests—he could choose a greeting he felt comfortable with.

Running his hands down my arms, he caught

my hands. He pulled them around behind his back and leaned in for a long, lingering, delicious kiss. He stepped back, his eyes still closed.

When he opened them, my heart tumbled.

"*Bonsoir*," he whispered.

"Mmmm, you too."

A few of the patrons and most of the staff whistled appreciatively. We both turned to the amused glances of my parents.

My father leveled a stern gaze at Jean-Charles. "You will be good to my daughter?"

Watching my chef's face, I tensed, waiting for a reaction.

He kissed me again. "I promise."

"When did you find out he's my father?"

"Your relationship was obvious the first time I saw him look at you—it was the look a father saves for his daughter."

"It doesn't bother you?"

"Lucky, it is not him I wish to make love with."

"Well," my father blustered. "I can't tell you how relieved I am to hear that!"

This time it was my turn to capture Jean-Charles's lips with mine. Mother was right—he was truly delish. As I reveled in the feel of him, the taste of him, I wondered what Christophe would think of his father's recent choices.

And how the heck would I handle intimacy with a co-worker—championship-level stupidity for someone as inept as me?

And why did my resolve to go slow, to keep

work and play separate, vanish like fog under the heat of the sun when the handsome French chef looked at me? Clearly my brain had abdicated the throne and another body part was running the show—first my libido, now perhaps my heart— sort of like the inmates running the asylum. I was *so* screwed.

Death and destruction, or bliss? Once a gambler . . .

Time would tell, I guess. One hurdle at a time

"I've got to go," I announced, reluctantly. "I leave you in good hands," I said to my parents. I turned back to Jean-Charles. Tracing the line of his jaw, I said, "I'll see you tomorrow. I'll think of you in your new home tonight. Enjoy it. You are starting a new adventure. And I'm here to tell you, life in Las Vegas is magical."

DANE waited by the Ferrari.

I tossed the keys to him. "Want to drive?"

"Serious?" His eyes widened and I thought he might drool as he stared at the car.

"I feel like living dangerously," I said as I waited for him to open the passenger door, then I slipped inside.

Overcome with car lust, he didn't even have a witty innuendo to offer in reply as he settled himself behind the wheel. Instead, he ran his hands over the leather, touching each control briefly.

"Are you familiar with Ferraris?" I asked.

He shook his head, still unable to verbalize any

thought whatsoever—assuming he still had any.
Men and fast cars . . .

"They're very simple, really." I gave him the
short course in clutchless transmissions, paddle
shifters, and almost five hundred horsepower, then
settled back for the ride.

Even though the night had turned cold, I insisted on opening the roof and setting the heat on
high.

Dane didn't seem to mind. With quick reflexes
and a natural feel for a machine that probably had
served him well as a pilot, he threw the car around
the curves, accelerating smoothly through the apex,
his confidence growing.

I tightened my seat belt and enjoyed the speed-
rush. Staring up at the night sky as the lights of
Vegas retreated, I marveled at the multitude of
stars in the Milky Way and how small and insignificant I was—just a speck of cosmic dust. Even
still, my life was important—worth fighting for.

Dane took the Ninety-three exit off the Fifteen
heading toward Ely, then settled the car down at
an even hundred miles an hour. The open two-
lane wound up a long valley, following a spring-
fed creek that the locals had dammed at various
points, corralling precious water into several small
lakes.

"I can't put my finger on it, but there's something different about you," Dane said, both hands
on the wheel, eyes on the road.

"Maybe, for once, I'm getting comfortable in my own skin."

"We all get to the point where we chuck the BS and concentrate on what matters."

"When did that epiphany hit you?" I turned on the radio and was delighted to find Luis Miguel still in the CD player. I set the volume low, for background music—a clear night, a good friend, and an adventure needed a soundtrack.

"I guess I grew up on my first tour in the Persian Gulf War. It's amazing how getting shot at on a regular basis reduces life to its most elemental."

Immediately I felt guilty for all my juvenile vicissitudes. "So how come no girl back home?"

"I guess I've never found where I fit, never found home."

Kicking off my tennis shoes, I put my stocking feet on the dash—probably a cardinal sin in Ferrariland. "I always knew where I fit, just not exactly how."

"Getting any closer to figuring it out?" Dane downshifted nicely through a tight turn, then accelerated out of it.

"Some of the pieces are falling into place."

WE passed the rest of the ride up to Alamo with me regaling Dane with tales of the weird and wonderful UFO lore surrounding Vegas, Area 51, and Rachel—our destination.

"For as long as I can remember, the desert

around Vegas has attracted all kinds of reports of UFOs. I don't know whether it's the Air Force and the flight testing they do out of Area 51 on all their experimental aircraft, or what."

"I'm pretty much a skeptic," Dane admitted. "But as a military pilot, I heard some of the rumors. Didn't the Air Force have some program to look into all the reports?"

"Project Blue Book. However I don't think they were really trying to prove the existence of UFOs as much as they were trying to cover up any embarrassing sightings by their own people."

"Which did nothing but pique interest and fuel the 'cover-up conspiracy' theory which had its birth with the Roswell incident," Dane said. He knew more than he was letting on.

"I'm not much of an expert," I told him, "but we've had a couple of UFO crashes, one near Ely and one out toward Mesquite—neither of which has been satisfactorily explained. And the Air Force shut up at least one of their pilots who claimed to have been followed by UFOs—they passed him off as a head case. Which is how all the debunking continues—the powers that be point fingers and shout that anyone who has seen something weird is a nutcase."

"Do you believe that?" Dane glanced at me.

"No. The military is covering up something— whether it's the existence of their Black programs and experimental flying machines or extraterrestrials popping in for a visit, I don't know. And it doesn't much matter at this point. Vegas and Rachel get a lot of mileage out of the whole thing."

"So you're willing to throw logic out the window for the bottom line?"

"That bottom line makes my paycheck possible. And since when did logic have anything to do with Vegas? Vegas is like Brigadoon—a magical city that appears when the sun sets and the lights come on, where anything can happen."

"Even aliens?"

"Can you think of a place on this planet where they would feel more comfortable?"

NORTH of Alamo, we hit the turnoff for the Extraterrestrial Highway, heading west again, into the desert, away from the vegetation and life along the creek.

A tiny hamlet on the north side of the Area 51 Federal Reservation, Rachel was the kind of town that kept records such as: 1974 population: 3 women, 2 teenagers, 2 children, and 62 men. Which, if you think about it, makes you wonder—3 women and 62 men? Normally those odds might sound appealing, but in light of recent experience, I didn't think the women had as much fun as one might think.

The town began as a mining town in the 1970s and would probably end as the mecca for UFO hunters and alien spookologists. Most of the industry in the region (one mine and a futile potato farm) had long since pulled up stakes, leaving only two alfalfa farms hanging on the ragged edge of economic viability. The kids were all bused to Alamo for school—fifty miles away. Heck, the poor folks of Rachel didn't even get a stop sign until the 1990s, not that they needed one. Now, most folks simply ignored it.

The epicenter of Rachel is a conglomeration of buildings known as the Little A' Le' Inn. I stopped there once in May—I was the only living, breathing human from horizon to horizon except for the proprietress, who had her nose stuck in a novel as she sat behind the bar. I asked her when her busy season was. She announced, "This is it!"

So you can imagine my surprise this evening when Dane eased the Ferrari into the potholed parking lot and we couldn't find an empty space.

People spilled out of the bar and the tented addition. They sat on rocks and bumpers of cars. They gathered around a time capsule embedded in concrete by the crew of the movie *Independence Day*, which had been filmed in the area. They touched the "alien spaceship" that hung from a tow truck parked next to the road.

Finally, we gave up searching, parked the Ferrari on the frontage road, and hiked in.

I stopped two men coming out of the Inn who looked weird enough to know Junior Arbogast. "You guys seen Junior?"

"At the bar," one of them announced, letting the door slam shut as I reached it.

They didn't use their manners, so I didn't use

mine. However, Dane, being a graduate of the Texas School of Chivalry and Kind Acts, used his, opening the door for me. Stepping through, I stepped back in time. Wood floors creaked under the weight of the mass of humanity stuffed inside the rectangular room. Computer renderings of UFOs and aliens were tacked to the white walls. Along the left wall, in between the single-hole, single-sex restrooms, hung a panoramic picture of Area 51 taken when it was still possible to climb a nearby peak named Whitesides Mountain and look down into the installation. Glass cases, bookshelves, and racks of tee shirts occupied part of the front wall and all of the rear—everything in the joint was for sale. A bar stretched the length of the wall to the right—red vinyl upholstered stools supported patrons guzzling beer and small clear bottles of Alien vodka. Music from the 1970s whined from the jukebox, and smoke, mingling with the smell of a hot-fat fryer, hung like a cloud.

Tonight three bartenders and two waitresses worked the crowd that occupied all the tables inside, as well as four or five picnic tables outside under the tent.

As promised, Junior nursed a longneck at the far end of the bar. Both of his elbows on the counter, he held the bottle with two fingers and lifted it to his lips in a casual, practiced manner, taking a pull. Being from West Virginia, this was probably an innate skill.

Dane and I worked our way through the crush

of bodies—I made a beeline for Junior while Dane angled toward the bar and tried to get a bartender's attention.

At a tap on my shoulder, I turned to face Harry and Mavis. The crowd pressed around us forcing me too close to Harry for comfort.

"What are you two doing here?" I asked, raising my voice to be heard.

"You know any aliens interested in a threesome?" Harry asked.

"Seriously?"

"Ha! Gotcha!" A huge grin split his face. "Me and Mavis come out here every year. It's a real hoot. Earlier we caught that astronaut dude and bent his ear a bit about all this alien stuff."

"Dr. Zewicki?"

"That's the one," Mavis said. "He was distracted and a bit rude if you ask me, but where else are simple folks from Muskogee going to brush up against a celebrity like him?"

"Are you two going to the séance later?"

"Wouldn't miss it," Harry announced. "You'd be surprised at the strange stuff that happens during that thing."

I disengaged from Harry and Mavis, eventually working my way close enough to Junior for me to tap him on the shoulder. I motioned toward the door. With Junior following me, I caught Dane's attention and pointed outside.

"Quite a crowd," I said when I'd filled my lungs with fresh air.

"There's always a crush when the UFO guys are in town. They put on presentations up here before taking everyone away from town for viewing."

"Presentations?"

"On the latest UFO theories, mainly. Dr. Jenkins is regaling everyone with UFO shit as we speak. The crowd really laps that stuff up. But it's sorta funny though."

"What's funny?" I asked.

"They scheduled Jenkins and his BS right after I did a talk on hoax busting—sort of canceling us both out."

"Did many of the believers come to hear you?"

"You'd be surprised." Junior took another long pull on his beer. "The true believers want the hoaxsters outed. And are there a ton of them—from crop circles to video and photos of UFOs—the advent of PCs and Photoshop was a boon to my business. You'd be surprised at the lengths people go to get attention."

"Probably not. I live in Vegas, remember?"

Junior rewarded me with a grin. "Good point."

"Other than the séance later, is anybody else putting on a show tonight?"

"I've seen Danilov around. I don't think he's on the schedule, but who knows. With this group, anything is possible."

He had no idea. "Speaking of which, have you been able to find out anything on Danilov and Area 51?" I asked.

"I shook down a few guys who used to work

there—not the most reliable sources, but they were the best I could do. Whatever that program was, the government has a real tight lid on it." Junior stepped away from the crowd, out of earshot, motioning us to follow. "Word has it your buddy Danilov was into some weird mental stuff—mind reading, posthypnotic suggestions, you know the drill."

At least that was some kind of support for the mentalist's version of life in Eden.

"There was this guy, Carl—nobody knew his last name. He was the star of the program—apparently his abilities were off the charts. My guys said everything went okay for a while, but then weird stuff started happening, the participants became unstable. Everything fell apart when one of them died."

"Do you know who and how?"

"A woman." His bottle empty, Junior looked around for a can. When he couldn't find one, he stuck the bottle in the waistband of his jeans. "I don't have a name. The official version is she killed herself."

"But your friends don't believe the official version?"

"Nobody did, but what were they going to do? Take on the whole government?"

Tilting at windmills—my stock-in-trade.

"That's the best I could do," Junior said. "I hope I helped."

"Another piece to the puzzle." I scanned the

crowd milling around in the darkness. "I've never seen so many people up here."

"This is a pretty big crowd, even for this event," Junior allowed. "Bart Griffin has everyone worked up."

"Do you know Mr. Griffin well?"

"I've known him a long time, but can't say as I know him well. He keeps pretty much to himself."

Dane joined us with fresh refreshments, beers for him and Junior, a Diet Coke for me.

"What got him interested in the paranormal stuff?" I asked. "Was he Air Force?"

"Test pilot back in the day. Now he loves to stick it to them."

"He had a falling-out with the Zoomies?" Dane asked.

"I'll say." Junior leaned in closer and lowered his voice. "Nobody's supposed to know this—he was ushered out of the service, an administrative discharge. You still want to talk to him?"

"That's why we're here," I said. "You know where he is?"

"He wants us to meet him at the black mailbox at ten." Junior tossed his empty in a can and took a pull on the fresh one.

"Black mailbox?" I popped the top on my Diet Coke and drained it. Even at night, in late fall, the desert was as dry as ashes after a fire.

"Nineteen miles east of here, back the way you came. They've seen some really good UFO shit out there. Want to follow me?"

· · ·

"**WHAT'S** the significance of an administrative discharge?" I asked Dane once we were back in the car and following Junior back up the lonely highway.

"They can be given for a lot of things, but mainly for psychological reasons."

"You mean he went nuts?"

"Not necessarily. The Air Force simply considered him unfit for duty."

"From test pilot to head case. Big fall."

"In the Air Force, it would be huge."

Midway between mile markers twenty-nine and thirty, Junior eased his rental to the shoulder. Cars clustered in the desert near the hardtop, surrounding a white mailbox. Making sure the car was clear of the road and not stuck on the soft sand, Dane killed the engine.

Junior poked his head in through the top. "Nice ride."

"Perk of the job," I said.

"I'm gonna have to get me a job like yours," the West Virginian remarked as he pulled the crotch of his jeans and waggled a leg, shaking the boys down. "Bart's over here."

"I thought you said we were meeting him at a black mailbox?" I said as he helped me out of the car.

"It used to be black, then they had to replace it. Even though the new one is white, the old name stuck."

We followed Junior to a camouflaged Jeep Wrangler, open topped, with huge sand tires and antennas mounted to the roll bar. A man, his face hidden in shadow, sat in the driver's seat, the tip of his cigar glowing red in the darkness.

"Bart, this is the lady from the casino."

"Lucky O'Toole," I said and stuck out my hand.

The man in the jeep said "Bart Griffin" as he took my hand and gave it a good shake. "I understand you are a friend of Mr. Fortunoff's?"

"An acquaintance. He worked for me."

I leaned against the jeep and gazed up into the darkness. "Anything cool flying tonight?"

"Not yet, the night is young. If the Air Force is going to break out anything unusual, they wait until the last employees leave after eleven."

"What can you tell me about the notes? First 'pray be quick,' then 'pray tell.' What was the last one?"

"Answer tell."

"Right. Do you know what they mean?" I asked the radioman.

"Haven't a clue. Dimitri asked me to read them three nights in a row if anything happened to him."

"Did you know him well?"

"Well enough."

"How'd you two meet?"

"We went way back. Can't really remember the first time we met."

That was helpful. Why did I get the impression

this guy was hiding something? "How was the request made?" I asked.

"Got a letter, postmarked from Henderson, mailed two weeks ago."

"Handwritten or typed?"

"Typed."

"Return address?"

"Nope." He sucked on his cigar, the tip glowing a bright red.

"How did Dimitri ask you to do this for him?"

"Same way—typed letter."

"Did he sign it?"

"Yup."

"You got the letters?" I asked.

"Sure." Mr. Griffin rooted in a computer case resting on the passenger seat. Extracting a few sheets of plain white typing paper, he handed them to me.

Grasping them by the corners, between two fingers, I asked, "May I keep these?"

"Don't see why not."

"Is that all you got?" I tucked the papers between my sweater and my shirt, careful not to handle them any more than necessary.

"Sorry," Bart said without enthusiasm.

I gave it one last shot. "You got any theories about all of this?"

"Knowing Dimitri, it all started with Houdini."

UNDER the glowing orb of an almost full moon, the crowd assembled around the Little A' Le' Inn pulsed with energy by the time Dane and I joined them. As if cowed by the symphony provided by the creatures of the night—the howls of coyotes, the whisper of bats gliding by, the croak of a frog, the trills of grasshoppers—people talked in hushed voices.

At the stroke of eleven, Dr. Zewicki strode to the stage, taking the single chair. The crowd fell silent, expectant. Footlights supplemented the moonlight, washing the stage in a soulful shroud of half-light. Shining from down below, they shadowed Zoom-Zoom's features, giving him an altered, sinister look.

All the world's a stage. . . .

Glancing around me, I didn't recognize anyone. Not that I thought I would—despite the moonlight, I couldn't see very far.

Dr. Zewicki's deep voice boomed, making me jump. "I will have to ask all of you, no matter what happens in the next hour, please do not attempt to interfere. Remain quiet and calm as I summon the spirits."

This whole thing was creeping me out. Despite my buoyant cynicism, I reached for Dane's hand, clutching it. His touch was warm, reassuring . . . solid.

Hands on his knees, Zewicki settled back in the chair and closed his eyes. Not a sound emanated from the crowd. Minutes ticked by, ratcheting the crowd to a fevered pitch until it was like a boiler ready to blow its rivets.

Without warning, Zoom-Zoom bolted upright, his eyes wide. "I'm sensing a spirit. Walter, his name is Walter Rogers."

"My husband," shouted a female from the rear of the crowd.

"Walter died from a gunshot. Violence." Dr. Zewicki closed his eyes. "Night. Fear. Anger."

"Yes, yes!" the woman cried. "He was a SWAT team member. He died in a drug raid."

The show went on as Zoom-Zoom provided details—supposed messages from Walter—causing the woman to sob by the end. Then Dr. Zewicki repeated the performance several times with other crowd members—each of them plants for the performance, I felt sure, although I had no proof.

My eyes were growing heavy and my patience thin when Zewicki said, "There is one other presence here, a recently departed colleague."

Zoom-Zoom shut his eyes for a moment, milking the crowd.

"Dimitri Fortunoff is here."

What game was he playing?

"Mr. Fortunoff, can you name your killer?" someone shouted.

The crowd drew a collective breath and held it, waiting, hoping.

Finally, Dr. Zewicki shook his head. "He cannot."

The crowd deflated.

"But, Mr. Fortunoff has a message for us. He

says in honor of the Great Houdini, he shall return."

LIKE the gawkers at the scene of a bloody accident after the ambulance has left, the crowd filtered away, talking in excited voices. Dimitri's disappearance had captured the city and these folks knew they'd just been given another piece of the puzzle. Even I was smart enough to know everything was pointing toward Halloween—the anniversary of Houdini's death. But just what kind of stunt this was, I hadn't a clue.

"Want another beer?" Junior asked Dane and me.

"Not me," I said.

"I'll take one," Dane answered. "If it's okay with you," he said, turning to me.

"Sure, but let's hit the trail in half an hour or so. It's getting late and, since it'll take us an hour and a half to get back, it's even later in Vegas."

"Meet you at the car in thirty minutes." Dane and Junior headed toward the bar.

Alone, shrouded in darkness, I felt the pull of the desert. Drifting out of the light, away from the noise, I lost myself in memories. As a child, I'd often sought solitude in the Mojave—my refuge. Surrounded by the power of nature, bolstered by the resiliency of life, I found perspective.

Tonight an unfamiliar sense of peace accompanied me as I gazed at the Milky Way and dragged my toes through the sand. For the first time in probably forever, I was at peace with my life. If I had known how cathartic unburdening myself would be, I would have done it years ago. Of course, with life, everything was a timing issue. Now was the time. I had been ready.

A smile tickled my lips as I thought of Jean-Charles. Was he a timing issue as well? I was ready, so he appeared? How was I going to handle him? And Dane? How did he fit in my life? I couldn't shake the feeling that I was standing high in the air on the edge of a glass overlook—like the one they have at the West Rim of the Grand Canyon—fighting that insane urge to leap off.

A hand grabbed my elbow.

I felt a sharp object pressed to the small of my back. Adrenaline pumped. My heart pounded.

"Don't turn around," a voice, low, menacing, muffled . . . unfamiliar . . . growled in my ear. "Walk."

The sting of the knife pricking flesh.

The man pushed me deeper into the desert.

Hidden under the cover of darkness, he pulled me to a stop. "Don't," he hissed as I tried to turn. "Stay away from Carl. Consider this your last warning."

A blinding pain to my head.

My world went dark.

Chapter

SIXTEEN

♡

"Lucky?"

Voices. Pain.

Like a swimmer caught in a riptide grasping at rope, I clung to the voices . . . to the ache. Real and visceral, they pulled me to the safety of consciousness. Pushing myself to my knees, I paused, waiting for the world to stop spinning. My temple throbbed. Tentatively touching it, I felt a goose egg and the warm ooze of blood. Spitting sand, I gathered my strength.

"Over here," I shouted, then crumpled at the slash of pain, my hands grasping my head. It felt as if someone had split my skull with a meat cleaver.

Dane fell to his knees beside me, his hand on my back, his face angled to see mine. "What the hell happened?"

Junior skidded in beside him. "Christ almighty! You're bleeding."

"Someone delivered a message," I muttered.

"Who?" Dane said, as he circled my waist and helped me to my feet. "Steady."

Leaning into him, I gripped his arm. "I don't know who. I never got a look at him."

"Can you remember anything about him?" Junior asked, as he held on to my other arm.

"I didn't recognize his voice."

"So you don't think it was anyone you know?"

"The guy was trying to disguise his voice, and he said very little."

"So he might have been worried you'd be able identify him?" Dane said.

"That's the logical conclusion."

The men walked me back to the Little A' Le' Inn and eased me down onto a bench in front of one of the outdoor picnic tables. "Could one of you find me some aspirin or something? My head is splitting."

Junior went in search of much-needed drugs.

Gently, Dane probed my temple. "Heck of a bump, and you're going to have a thumper for a while. You should go to the hospital, you know. Stuff like this can cause internal bleeding that can be a real problem."

As I popped four extrastrength aspirin and chased them with a slug of water, I knew he was right.

Damn. How I hated hospitals.

WITH the doctor's blessing, I finally headed for home. A second dose of aspirin kept the headache tolerable. Fury made me feel like my old self again.

Four bells sounded as Dane eased the Ferrari to a stop in front of the Presidio.

"Give the car to the valet at the hotel, they

know what to do," I said, as I undid my seat belt and opened my door.

"Sure thing."

"Thanks for driving me up and back." Pausing, I touched his face, then brushed my lips over his. "Weird night, but I'm glad I got to share it with you."

"Likewise. As first dates go, it was unusual. You sure you're okay?"

"Absolutely."

"I'd feel better if you let me stay. Head injuries are tricky things."

"Thanks, but I'll be fine. And you staying would not be a good idea. Remember, no promises," I said, as I climbed out of the car.

"Understood. I'm a big boy. Quit worrying about me."

"I always worry." Before I shut the door, I said, "I lost one friend by rushing to the next level. I'm not about to do it again."

"Gotcha."

I wished he'd stop saying that.

PLACING my hands in two Baggies, I spread the notes Bart Griffin had given me on my kitchen counter, looking at them closely in the light. To my untrained eye, the printing looked the same. Dimitri's signature could've been computer generated, but Romeo and his techs would tell me for sure. Pulling off one Baggie, I used the covered hand to stuff the papers inside the plastic bag.

With the papers carefully secured, I reached for my phone. The old Nextel felt odd in my hand.

Jeremy answered on the first ring. "How's it going in the land of heat and running water?" he asked.

"I take it you won't be calling a nice corner in the storm drain system 'home' anytime soon?"

"They have rodents down here so large they'd take a saddle. I'm charging you double for this."

"I'll gladly pay it. How's Carl? Has he let you talk to him?"

"He's still as wary as a dingo, and about as mean, but he's starting to warm up. He brought me a hot dog a little while ago."

"Where have you holed up?" I tried to picture what it would be like in the drains after midnight.

"Right now, I've moved closer to the entrance—I don't get reception when I'm in deeper. When we're done, I'll move back inside. Most of the time I stay close to the cutoff for Carl's place so I can see anybody coming."

"The ante has been upped," I said, then filled him in on the séance and Zewicki's weird pronouncement. "Watch your back. I don't know who's coming for Carl or when, but no doubt someone will."

"Righto."

"Have you seen any activity?"

"No, people pretty much leave Carl alone."

"Let me know when Carl starts talking to you,

okay?" With Carl, gaining his trust was key—and it took time.

"Righto."

"Jeremy, you are armed, aren't you?"

"Lucky, I've handled so much worse than this. You don't want to know."

He was right. I didn't.

AS I punched the end button, terminating the call, I noticed the blinking light indicating a message waited. Having been out of cell coverage since I'd left the Fifteen heading up toward Alamo, I wasn't surprised. I dialed my voice mail and was rewarded with a mellifluous French accent and the warm tones of a voice that had wedged itself in my heart.

"I owe you a lunch. Tomorrow at one? If you can't make it, let me know. I will count the hours. Be safe. Sweet dreams."

I replayed the message five or six times, then permanently saved it.

SUN streamed through the window. Morning. Hadn't I just slipped between the sheets? Rolling over I pried my eyes open—yup, morning. And by the looks of it, it was no longer early. The display on my phone said nine-thirty. Wow. What had happened to the nightmares? My temple no longer throbbed and, from the feel of it, the bump was much smaller. Like the sting after a slap, the hint of a headache teased me. A reminder, a warning, that didn't have the desired effect. If they wanted a fight, they were going to get it.

Ignoring the siren call of caffeine, I hit the shower. Choosing the black lace lingerie today, I picked a nice pair of Dana Buchman pants in light brown, a dark brown V-neck cashmere sweater—the V so deep the lace peeked through—a pair of canvas Chanel flats, cascades of David Yurman gold, and my diamonds.

Affixing one diamond to my ear as I strode through the bedroom on my way to greet the day, I caught Teddie's sax out of the corner of my eye. Picking it up I put my lips where his had been and blew—managing a fingernails-on-chalkboard squeak.

Suddenly, I felt so sad. When he had held me, how had he seen only an interesting roll in the hay and I'd seen something more? We had sacrificed our friendship for a few months of hot sex—not a good trade at all.

Deep inside, I guess I had known the end from the beginning.

I wanted to be in love. I wanted someone to call my own. I wanted hot sex.

Teddie had been a choice.

I had a feeling Jean-Charles might be an inevitability.

SAX in hand, I hit the up button on the elevator. When it opened I inserted the special keycard and rode up one level. Stepping into Teddie's great room, I wasn't assaulted by memories, but I felt them lingering in the corners. His baby grand sat still and silent, awaiting the deft touch of its owner. The rooms were quiet, empty, with no life . . . no magic.

I laid the sax on Teddie's couch, placing the keycard next to it.

After one last glance around, I whispered, "Good-bye, Teddie, my love."

When the elevator doors closed behind me, my heart was free.

MISS P had beaten me to work on her birthday—it was not a proud moment.

"Happy Birthday," I said to her as I staggered through the office door.

"What happened to you?" she asked, her eyes wide as she took in the bump on my head, which was now turning a nice shade of purple.

"Hit my head. Nothing serious."

She stared at me. Unwilling to meet her gaze, I looked over her shoulder.

"Really," I implored. "I'd forgotten how dark the desert could be." Still unable to look her in the eye—she knew I was lying, I wasn't about to give her proof—I let my nose lead me to the coffee pot.

Pummeled by the emotional punches I'd absorbed recently, my efficiency was suffering and my mind wandered. I needed a vacation. Or even a weekend. Or a cup of coffee . . . simple problems, simple solutions. After deciding now was not the time to let my energy flag, I poured myself a cup of the witch's brew.

My body sighed in anticipation. I chose not to be bothered by that. Is being addicted to a legal stimulant any better than being addicted to an illicit one . . . besides avoiding possible jail time? After guzzling half the mug, I refilled it before even stepping away from the pot. Too tired to play my own silly game, I assured myself, if it was legal it was fine, and quit thinking about it.

Apparently Miss P decided to let me and my little white lie off the hook as she joined me in trying to get up to speed on a day that was already spinning—which was like trying to jump onto a spinning carousel and find a handhold before it threw you off. As I fielded phone calls, made a few of my own, and signed my name too many times to count, I couldn't shake the feeling that my life was like a giant game of Whack-A-Mole.

"Teddie has left two voice messages. He needs to talk to you. He says it's important. He wants you to call—no matter the time."

"Well that's good, since I have no idea where he actually is." I snapped the pencil I had been writing with clean in two. I tossed the two ends into the trash. "What could he possibly tell me that's so important? He wants me to send him more underwear? Christ. He left. He needs to leave me alone."

Miss P looked at me a moment. "Still some lingering feelings?"

"Of course. We had some good times together. I thought I was in love."

"Weren't you?" she asked quietly.

"I was in love with the idea of being in love."

"I see."

She was baiting me, that much was clear, but I was in no mood for games. "He taught me to open my heart. Will you accept that? And I'm grateful to him for it. . . . I think. Bloody painful as it is, I guess it's better than refusing to feel, but I'm not a complete convert yet." I refilled my coffee from the pot in the kitchenette. "Can we please do some work?"

ONCE again under way, the morning raced by. Jeremy checked in to tell me that he was going home for some shut-eye—a friend of his was pulling the next shift—and that Carl was starting to warm up to him—thanks in part to the Krispy Kremes Miss P had dropped by at my request. And then Jerry called, reporting on the people I had asked him to keep track of. Those who had gone to Rachel for the UFO viewing had returned—except Jenkins. Jerry and his security team hadn't been able to locate him—a fact I passed on to Romeo when he came to fetch the notes Bart Griffin had given me the night before.

When The Big Boss knocked on my inner office

door, which in a fit of wishful thinking I had pulled closed so I could work unmolested—I was poring over the preparations for the Houdini Séance. With Dimitri's whereabouts still unknown, I had to assume I was short one Masked Houdini.

"Am I interrupting?" The Big Boss asked just to be polite.

I waved him in as I shouted to Miss P, "Call Marik Kovalenko, ask him if I can stop by in an hour."

"Will do," she shouted in reply.

After he shut the door, my father took one of the chairs across the desk from me. Stepping around the desk, I propped one cheek on the corner so I faced him. From the serious look on his face, I knew he came on business, so I waited for him to get down to it.

"Do you have time to meet with the architects?" he said, in a transparent effort to beat around the bush. "They want to go over your last changes to the restaurant space at the Athena."

"When?"

"Five o'clock. It shouldn't take more than a couple of hours unless you're particularly difficult." My father shot me a grin.

Where the architects were concerned, difficult was my middle name.

"Where?"

"Maybe the meeting will go more smoothly if we stake out a corner of Delilah's and ply them with liquor?"

"You got it," I said, liking his thinking. The architects were almost as uptight as bankers and tax lawyers. "However, I don't think you came all the way down here to ask me to join you in a meeting."

"Your mother wanted me to come talk to you. She's worried. This thing with Chef Bouclet . . . so quick on the heels of the Teddie implosion. Now you want to sell your place . . . I told her you know what you're doing, but she insisted."

"Putting you directly in the line of fire," I teased. Running my fingers through my hair, I took a moment, trying to figure out how to explain the unexplainable. "All of this has been building for a while. Jean-Charles and I have been working together for the last six weeks or more on a daily basis, certainly time to get to know each other. The attraction has been there all along, but with Teddie in the picture, I wouldn't do anything. Teddie's been pulling away for some time—I just didn't want to see it."

"Understandable."

"And don't think I'm diving in without checking the depth of the water. I'm fully aware of all of the pitfalls of dating someone I work with—the volatile Frenchman being an exceptional case of judgment gone awry. I just can't seem to resist the train wreck I see coming."

"A family trait," my father admitted.

Why did everything in life come with a hitch?

. . .

MIRACLE worker that she was, Miss P had wrangled an almost immediate audience with the great Marik Kovalenko. Maybe he had the answer to the whole weird phrases Dimitri asked Bart Griffin to publicize each night. After all, if anyone knew Houdini's secrets it was Marik.

He waited by the rear door, arms crossed, leaning against the doorjamb, soaking up the late morning sun, when I pulled up. Dark, brooding, and dangerous, at least with the light on his face I could be fairly sure he wasn't a vampire.

"I'd be willing to sleep with you to get to drive that car," he said, as I unfolded myself from the Ferrari.

"How could a girl refuse?" I said with a grin.

"Do you want to come inside?"

"After your opening salvo, I'm not sure I can trust myself," I said with a smile as I slipped past him. "But I'll risk it, if you will."

When we were once again settled on the couch upstairs and I had his attention, I said, "I went to visit Bart Griffin last night. He said all of this Dimitri stuff began with Houdini. Early in his career Houdini and his wife did a mind-reading act. You told me that the whole act hinged on code words for numbers, then changing the numbers into letters of the alphabet. What code did they use?"

Clasping his hands and looping them around one knee, Marik leaned back. "They had their own code. For a long time they kept it a secret, even after they had quit the act—Harry wanted it that way. Before he died, he whispered a special word to his wife. He promised to try to make contact from the Great Beyond using the code only the two of them knew to spell the word."

"That way she would be sure it was him," I said, musing out loud.

"Right."

"He died on Halloween and his wife held séances on the anniversary of his death for ten years hoping he would make contact."

"But he didn't."

"No, and his wife finally said ten years was long enough to wait for any man."

"My kind of gal," I said. "What about their code?"

"Harry's wife finally let it be known." Marik dropped his knee and rose to his feet. "I have it around here somewhere. Give me a minute?"

I nodded and he disappeared through a doorway next to the bar—presumably leading to his office.

A few minutes later, he returned, a piece of paper in his hand. "What were the words Bart Griffin has been reading on the air?" he asked as he again sat beside me. "They were actually phrases, right?"

"Yes, the first one was 'pray be quick.'"

He scanned the paper, making notes.

"What are you doing?" I asked.

"Harry and Bess, his wife, had ten words—one

for each number, one through ten." He extended the paper to me and I scanned it quickly.

"So the real question is whether our words appear in the Houdini's list?"

"Right." We put our heads together as we looked at the list.

"'Pray' is the first word," Marik said. "So let's assume it corresponds to the number one."

"Why wouldn't it?"

"The code was not only words translating to numbers, then numbers to letters—it was also in the way the words were spoken. If the words were spoken with no pauses in between, in a normal conversational cadence, then corresponding letters would run together forming a word. But if there was a pause between, then the numbers stood on their own."

"I don't understand."

"Okay," Marik said as he moved closer and we both bent over the list. "Say you wanted to spell the word *dad*. That would be the fourth letter, the first letter, then the fourth letter again. Look at the list. Spell it using the words in the code."

"Now. Pray. Now." I matched the numbers corresponding to the letters, four, then one, then four, to the words on the Houdini's list.

"Good, now spell *mom*."

With only ten words and M being the thirteenth letter, I was stumped.

"See," Marik explained. "That's where the Houdinis would use a pause between the words indicating they should stand alone. So for the thir-teenth letter they would have used the word for *one*—pray. Then waited a beat and used the word for *three*—say."

"Clever," I said, warming to the puzzle. "Since we don't know the pauses in Bart Griffin's broad-cast, let's just play with it and see if it spells any-thing."

"Okay." Marik bent his head over the words. "First was 'pray be quick.' That's one and ten in the Houdini code."

"So it's either an *A* and a *J* or it's eleven and a *K*."

"Not necessarily. 'Be quick' is also a phrase in their code, the only phrase, I might add, and it could mean zero."

"That would put us back at ten . . . so a *J*. Why don't we go with that and see where it gets us?"

"Give me the next one," Marik said.

"'Pray. Tell.'"

He made a quick calculation. "That would be fifteen."

"The last was 'Answer. Tell.'"

Head bent, he looked over his notes for a few seconds. "Twenty-five," he muttered under his breath as he calculated. "All the words are here."

"What does it spell?" I asked, unable to wait any longer.

"Joy."

"Joy?"

He nodded.

"What the heck does that mean? And how can anyone find joy in all this mess?"

"I don't know," the magician said. "Let me think about it."

"You think, but time is getting short." I took a deep breath. "I have a favor to ask."

"Okay."

"Will you conduct the Houdini Séance tomorrow night? I know it's asking a lot," I said, racing on, trying to get my pleading in before he shut me down. "But with Dimitri out of pocket, I have no idea if I have a magician or not. And someone such as yourself would make the whole thing really spectacular. I can afford to pay you—probably not anywhere near what you're used to getting." I stopped and looked at him. "Please?"

"Tomorrow night?"

"You can do anything you want. One of your old illusions, an escape, whatever . . . just don't die on me."

He shot me a grin. "I'll try not to—I haven't died in a trick yet."

"So you'll do it?" I pretended to act calm, as if I was not teetering on the edge of desperation—I don't think I pulled it off. Not that I could have—lately I'd been an open book.

"Yes. I'll do it," Marik said. The idea obviously intrigued him. I had no idea why.

Dumbfounded, I could only stare at him for a moment. "Really?" I asked when comprehension dawned. "No 'unreasonable demand'? No 'I have her over the barrel so I'll take everything I can?' No 'here is my chance at a pound of flesh?'"

"Will you accept the possibility that I want to do an old friend a favor?"

No way in hell, I thought, but nodded benignly.

An old friend a favor? My ass. That was way too easy. After holding a grudge all this time? Why did I get the feeling lately that almost everyone except me had an agenda? What could Marik be angling for?

"Thanks," I said, fresh out of clever. "I'll clear you with Security—you can have access to the Arena and the stage anytime you want."

"I better get started." He gave my knee a pat. "Don't worry. I'll dream up something spectacular."

Somehow, that didn't give me a warm fuzzy.

I made it back just in time to freshen up before Jean-Charles filled my doorway. "Do you have a lot of time or a little?" he asked as he reached for me, circling my waist.

I glanced at Miss P, who lurked behind him. At her grin I said, "As much time as you want."

"They would send out search parties if we took that much time." He kissed me long and sweet.

Looping my arms around his neck, I wound my fingers in his hair where it curled over his collar, and reveled in his kiss. I could *so* get used to this.

Pulling back, he started to say something, then thought better of it, and kissed me again. This time deeper, taking my breath away and sending pulses of heat racing through me until I swore my knees would buckle.

Heat and desire . . . and something more. The Fates were rubbing my nose in it—they didn't have to, I was paying attention. This one was special . . . I got it.

"What did you have in mind?" I asked, surprising myself that I actually mustered enough wind to give the words voice.

"Marché Bacchus. Do you know the place?" he asked, his lips playing against mine.

"Hmmm. Sounds divine. I have to be back by four, though."

A "local's" restaurant far from the tourist areas, Marché Bacchus had started as a wine store and small café hidden in a residential development in Summerlin, overlooking a small man-made lake. Its reputation grew, along with the sophistication of its kitchen. After a recent expansion, the restaurant now attracted Vegas powerbrokers and hotel restaurateurs who flocked to partake of its casual and unique ambience and its simple, yet elegant menu. And it was just the sort of place a five-star chef would love to kick back in.

The owner greeted Jean-Charles with a mixture of the warmth one would have for an old friend and the respect one would have for royalty. He seated us at a two-top next to the lake, in front of an open outdoor fireplace. If Hollywood had ordered up a "romantic setting" they couldn't have done any better.

As we sat, and the waiter shook out my napkin and laid it across my lap, my phone rang.

Teddie. Again.

This time I didn't waffle—I punched the button rolling the call to voice mail, then turned the phone off. Miss P could handle any emergencies while I was busy having a life.

I glanced with disinterest at the menu the waiter handed me—who could think about food when there was an interesting Frenchman so close?

"What do you want?" Jean-Charles asked when the waiter departed, leaving us alone.

"Why don't you order for me?" I laid the menu down on the table.

"Choosing food is like buying shoes—the style is subjective, but the fit is critical. I am not sure what you like."

I like handsome Frenchmen who look at me as if I am beautiful and who treat me as if I am special, but since I already had one—and I doubted he was on the menu anyway—I said, "No rodents. No bugs—and, for the record, chocolate covering does nothing to enhance their palatability. No slimy things that crawl on the ground—escargot sound exotic, but a snail is still a snail. Have you seen what happens when you put salt on them?"

Amused, Jean-Charles nodded. "It is too bad you feel that way about escargots—they are brilliant here. Is that all?"

"Let me think. I'm not particularly gastronomically adventurous. No weird glands—that includes sweetbreads *and* Rocky Mountain oysters. Squid, but no ink. I'm not keen on intestines—but I can pretend when it comes to hot dogs. Other than that, I'm pretty good."

The waiter reappeared with a bottle of red wine, which he presented to Jean-Charles, who nodded, then let the waiter do the uncorking.

"Oh, and I'm not that thrilled about coconut milk in anything other than a piña colada," I concluded.

"Should I write this down?" Jean-Charles eyed me over the top of his menu. Even though the menu hid his mouth, I could see his smile in his baby blues.

"Wouldn't hurt, especially if you plan on making a habit out of taking me to dine."

"I'm rethinking that," Jean-Charles teased as he took my hand. "You didn't tell me you were so demanding,"

"You didn't ask."

"Anything else I should know?"

"Not that I'm willing to admit."

He ordered for both of us . . . in French. The waiter didn't seem fazed; either he spoke the language or our meal was going to be an adventure.

With all the formalities out of the way, Jean-Charles poured me a glass of wine. "I know it's a school day, but a nice meal without a fine wine is like sex without love—momentarily pleasurable, but ultimately unsatisfying. Try it. I think you'll be pleased."

Since I agreed with his take on casual sex, I had no doubt I'd like the wine as well. "Very good," I said after a whiff and a sip. "So how was your first night in your new home?"

"I didn't sleep there."

"Why not?"

"You were not there. Christophe was not there." Jean-Charles patted his chest. "Without the heart, it is only a house . . . it is not a home."

He was preaching to the choir.

Still holding my hand, he absentmindedly traced the lines on my palm. How could something so simple be so sensual?

"Lucky, I have something to say." He looked unsure as he glanced at me.

"Okay." I tried to keep my heart from sinking, but failed. "You want to back off?"

Surprise flashed in his eyes. "Of course not."

"What then?"

He took a deep breath. "I want you in my bed," he continued. "I want to hold you all night. I want . . ."

The waiter cleared his throat as he delivered our soup—French onion—how could it have been anything else? "Sorry, sir," he said. His cheeks colored when his eyes met mine.

Jean-Charles gave me a wink as he moved the

cheese crouton aside and took a tentative sip of the steaming broth. Nodding at the waiter, he said, "Brilliant, as usual. My compliments."

"You were saying," I prompted after the waiter beat a hasty retreat. Taking a sip of soup, I almost groaned in delight—authentically French, it was not the over-cheesed, over-salted, over-beef brothed concoction Americans had come to expect. Would a groan be bad form? Who knew? Maybe, to a chef, a groan might be like a belch in Japan—the highest form of compliment. I had some learning to do—how could I stay in the game if I didn't know the rules? Jean-Charles would have to enlighten me . . . but later. I was pretty engrossed in his current topic.

Still holding my hand, Jean-Charles continued, "I want to give you pleasure, to fall asleep with you in my arms."

"If you keep this up, we won't make it to the main course."

"You see my problem, then," Jean-Charles said with a self-deprecating grin.

Swirling the wine in my glass and pretending to be fascinated with it, I took a few moments to think. What was best to do? Even though I was ready to jump in—he had me in a lather already—I knew that wasn't the right approach. There were so many concerns, so many considerations—having a relationship with this man was going to be like negotiating peace between Palestine and Israel—the unexpected was waiting to bite me on the butt.

"Perhaps it will be best if we keep it slow," I finally said. "We have to adjust to this new aspect of our working relationship. And then there is Christophe. I feel certain you don't want to force your hand there. Wouldn't it be better for him to meet me, hopefully like me, then spring our relationship—whatever it is—on him?"

"But I want . . ."

"I know." I squeezed his hand, delighting in his touch. "Believe me, you and I are on the same page. But let's get our sea legs first, okay? Then, when Christophe gets home, we'll see where we are."

"I cannot deny you are wise, even if I don't want to accept your words. I am sometimes impulsive."

At least we have one thing in common.

"Are you nervous at meeting my son?" Jean-Charles inquired with insight rarely encountered in the male of the species.

"Of course," I admitted. "I'm nervous about all of this."

He waved away my comment. "But you like children?"

"A world without children is a world without wonder and magic. I'm a big believer in magic."

"You will like Christophe. I am sure of it."

"Tell me about him." We both dove into our soup before it got cold.

As Jean-Charles told me stories of his son, I watched his emotions parade across his face—pride and delight . . . unwavering love. While he talked, I searched for something, anything, about him I didn't like. I was still searching when dessert arrived.

AS I strolled through the lobby, basking in the afterglow of a delectable lunch—Tarte Provençale followed by cheese and fruit, then finished off by the most delectable Chocolate *Pots de Crème*—I realized that, in the last few days, work had taken a backseat to life. So this was how normal people felt all the time! I could get used to this! Of course, I was wise enough to note that most people didn't have three-hour lunches with wine and a Frenchman—but then, most people didn't work twenty-hour days either, so I refused to feel guilty.

After the most delicious kiss, Jean-Charles headed to work at the Burger Palais and I headed to my battle with the architects. All things considered, I liked his option far better than mine. I was getting a whole lot of the what-do-you-know-you're-just-the-boss's-daughter routine from the elder of the two designers—it was time to cut the guy off at the knees, but I didn't want to lose my smile.

So, I started thinking about Dimitri's riddle . . . *joy*. What did it mean? How the heck could anybody find joy in all this mess? Pushing open the stairwell door, heading toward my office, a stray thought stopped me dead.

Could *joy* be a *who* rather than a *what*?

Chapter

SEVENTEEN

*F*lash answered on the first ring.

"Girlfriend," she said, "you cut a wide swath. Teddie takes a dive and you turn right around and start *parlez-vous*ing with a certain hunkalicious Frenchman. Dane's got a serious case of the down-in-the-mouths, and I've still got my line out trolling for a story. I want to be you."

The Dane comment hurt but I didn't know what to do about it—I'd been clear about no promises. "Don't be hasty—I'm on my way to disembowel an architect."

"You get to have all the fun."

"In all your research into Dimitri Fortunoff, Danilov, and Area 51 have you found any mention of a woman named Joy?"

"No."

"If you do, I'll throw some of the fun your way."

"I'll play," Flash said. As if she could've turned me down! "Joy who?"

"What, you think I'm going to make this easy?"

. . .

MISS P still manned her desk when I pushed through the door. "Don't you need to go home and get ready for dinner? As I understand it, The Beautiful Jeremy Whitlock is taking you out for a five-star evening."

"Jeremy can't make it," she stated flatly. She didn't sound upset, but with her, it was hard to tell—unlike her boss, she didn't wear her heart on her sleeve.

"How come?"

"He's working," she said, raising an eyebrow.

"I know that, but I thought he was going to call one of his guys to be Carl's sentry for the night." I refused to feel like a heel—Jeremy and I had this all worked out.

"He decided Carl was ready to open up to him and changing the guard right now would set him back." Miss P finally smiled at me. "Look, this is important. I have birthdays every year. Besides, it doesn't matter when we celebrate as long as everyone is there."

"Even though we have planned it for Saturday, I'm not sure we'll be able to pull it off, all things considered. When this Dimitri thing blows over, we'll pick a time, okay?"

"Speaking of which, Romeo is on his way up. He didn't sound good."

THE young detective didn't look good, either.

Dark circles under his eyes, his hair as disheveled as his clothes, a frown instead of his normal grin, Romeo stopped in front of me. "We found Jenkins."

"Where?"

"Wandering in the desert. The guy was dehydrated, hallucinating. It was lucky he stumbled over the boundary for Area 51, tripping all their sensors, or we may never have found him . . . alive anyway."

I sank down into a chair against the window as I stared at him. "What?"

Romeo parked his butt on a corner of Miss P's desk. Miss P stared at both of us, her eyes as big as saucers.

"The Feds turned him over to Lincoln County. Flight for Life took him to Sunrise Hospital." Romeo ran a hand over his eyes, as he leaned his head back for a moment and took a deep breath. "He's going to make it, but he still wasn't making a whole lot of sense when I saw him."

"How did he end up wandering around by himself in the desert?" I asked.

"He was in pretty rough shape—whether somebody assaulted him or he'd fallen—he couldn't remember. The only thing he kept repeating over and over was 'Carl is the key.' Do you think he was talking about the Carl you know?"

"Makes sense." My mind whirled. Everybody seemed to think Carl was the key. The key to what?

"It'd be nice to know if Carl was anywhere near Rachel last night," Romeo mused.

"Finally!" I threw up my hands. "A question to

which I can actually provide an answer. Jeremy Whitlock has been watching him around the clock." I glanced at the clock—Jeremy was due to check in within the hour. "He can give us Carl's whereabouts for the last twenty-four hours. And he should be warned that someone has upped the ante."

"Don't worry," Miss P said. "Jeremy can handle whatever comes his way."

"Yes, but it's easier to do when you know it's coming." I turned to Romeo. "I know I'm shooting for the stars here, but do you know if Jenkins figures in our crazy little Dimitri drama? And if so, would you have perhaps an inkling as to how?"

"I ran Jenkins just like you asked," Romeo said, his voice flat as if he was running through a recitation of statistics. "He has the whole pedigree you'd expect and enough letters after his name to use up most of the alphabet. His job history didn't put him anywhere near the others."

I leaned my head back against the window and sighed. I don't know why I was disappointed that Romeo hadn't made a connection—it's not like any of the facts we knew already added up. Eventually though, something was going to have to connect. "So you didn't find anything," I stated with finality.

"Well, not in the regular check, but since everyone seemed to have some military connection, I ran his name through that filter." Romeo gave me a lopsided grin as he milked the moment.

"And?" I tried to frown as I looked up at him, but it was hard to pull off when I felt the flush of hope rise in my chest.

"He's getting retirement pay from the Air Force."

"You didn't say he was in the Air Force."

Romeo leaned forward, his hands on his knees. "According to his records, he wasn't."

The ticking of the clock on the wall and my heartbeat were the only sounds puncturing the silence as I processed this new tidbit. "Somebody erased part of his background," I announced, half-rhetorically.

"It would seem so," Romeo agreed.

"That begs the questions: Who? and why?" I glanced at Romeo. "You wouldn't happen to know his pay-grade, would you?"

Romeo's eyes sparked, as if I'd asked the right question, made the right connection. So he was the teacher now? "His retirement pay is at two-star flag rank."

"A high-ranking muckety-muck. Interesting." Hands together, elbows on my knees, I steepled my fingers. "How did you get looped in on his disappearance and eventual recovery?"

"This morning, after you told me Jenkins didn't come back from Rachel with the others, I made a few inquiries. He wasn't registered at that motel. . . ."

"The Little A' Le' Inn?" I prompted.

"That's the one," Romeo said. "I've got a friend

in the Lincoln County sheriff's office—we went to the academy together. Even though technically Dr. Jenkins wasn't a missing person, I put the bug in the guy's ear. I had a feeling. I can't explain it."

"Like hearing voices?"

"Yeah." The kid gave me a very tired rendition of a sheepish grin. "I didn't want to say it like that. I figured you might think I've got a big hole in my screen door."

I *had* been half-teasing. But this whole thing was screwy—a lot of people believed in all this mind-bending hocus-pocus, and where there's smoke . . .

Heck, it even had me looking over my shoulder, swearing someone was lurking in the shadows. Both Danilov and Crazy Carl talked of voices and being connected. Molly seemed to weave in and out like mist through the forest. Zoom-Zoom swore he could connect with our dearly departed. Bart Griffin had an ax to grind with the Air Force, and Dr. Jenkins had a slick mind-reading trick. Everyone had a screw loose . . . including me, but none of it provided any insight into my missing magician.

"I'm about ready to ask Dr. Zewicki if he could conjure up a dead woman, presumably named Joy—although I'm still guessing at this point—and talk to her. I bet she could clear this whole thing up," I announced, only half-joking.

"Couldn't hurt. Some departments are actually using psychics to solve crimes," Romeo added, sounding as close to the end of his rope as I was.

"Zewicki was the last guy Jenkins remembers talking to before his death march into the desert. When you see the astronaut, let me know—we're looking for him as well, but he hasn't turned up."

"I can't prove it, but I have a feeling psychics are part of our crime . . . not part of the solution." Discouragement nipped at my heels. "If someone actually knocked Jenkins over the head, maybe looking at the tapes of folks returning on the buses last night might tell you something."

"I'm game. I've turned over every rock I can think of."

USING my master keycard, I let Romeo and myself into Security. We paused as the door closed behind us, letting our eyes adjust to the dim light.

"Wow," Romeo exclaimed. "You guys don't miss a trick. Where don't you have cameras?" His eyes traversed the banks of monitors covering the far wall, each rotating through feeds from every corner of the property.

"None in the bathrooms or the guestrooms, but that's about it. Everywhere else is covered. When you have tens of millions of dollars flowing through the hotel in any given day, it pays to be vigilant."

"And what are those guys doing?" Romeo pointed to a separate bank of monitors on the side wall.

"They're the gaming experts watching both dealers and players for any signs of mischief." Most of the guys watching the feeds had done time for scamming the casinos. They'd paid their debt to society and now we used their expertise to catch the amateurs.

"I'm glad you called when you did," Jerry said, as he joined Romeo and me. "I pulled the tape just in time, before it went back into the hopper to be used again."

"You know Detective Romeo?"

Both men nodded as they shook hands.

"Romeo, bring Jerry up to speed. I know we have tapes of who got on and off that bus to Rachel last night. Maybe one of them looks the worse for wear. At least it'll give some idea of who went up there from the hotel."

Romeo started to say something, but I silenced him with a raised hand. "I know folks could've gone up there on their own, but at least it's a start."

THOUGHTS whirling, I left the two of them to review the tapes. They didn't need me. And I was needed at a showdown with the architects. I prayed my father was loosening them up.

Glancing at my watch—still twelve minutes left to plot the overthrow of Rome. Hoping Jeremy had come out of his hole a bit early, I dialed his number.

The call rolled to voice mail.

"Damn."

I tried it again. This time someone answered, but the static was too thick. My phone dropped the call. Worries niggled at the edges of my confidence—I knew Jeremy was okay, I just knew it. But what if they'd surprised him? Overwhelmed him?

Pacing in front of Delilah's, I was on the verge of chucking the architects and racing off to warn Jeremy myself, no matter who was following me, when my phone rang. I glanced at the number and my pulse slowed.

"Jeremy?"

"Still living and breathing," came the Aussie-tinted reply.

"That is not funny." I filled him in on Jenkins's interesting night in the desert. "It looks like Carl is the eye of the storm. Has he told you anything yet?"

"We've become pretty good mates. I asked him about a daughter. He swears he doesn't have one, but I can't tell whether he's blowing smoke trying to protect her, or whether he's telling the truth. When he mumbles about family, it's a sister, not a daughter."

"That's the thing about Carl—it all gets muddled up. I'm not sure he even knows what he knows." *What had happened to him?* "Has anyone come looking for him?"

"Not a soul."

"And I trust you would know if he had left and gone, say, out to Rachel?"

"The guy is afraid to get too close to the light. Something has him spooked pretty bad."

Him and me both.

And I didn't like it one bit.

NOW I was in the perfect mood to deal with the architects. I bounded up the stairs into Delilah's. Sean caught my eye and pointed to the bottle of Wild Turkey then raised two fingers. I shook my head—my days of double bourbons were over. My father and the two designers were already seated at a table in the corner, their beverages of choice in hand, the plans spread out on the small table in front of them. The three men rose as I joined them. That would probably be the last nicety for the next two hours.

"Gentlemen," I started in. "I have reviewed your plans and they are simply unacceptable. You seem either unwilling or unable to listen to my concept and reduce it to lines on paper that can be effectively costed-out and that the contractors can follow. Sit back, relax, and listen. You get one more shot at it, then I'll find someone else."

The elder architect spluttered and fumed. Turning to The Big Boss, he said, "Al, we've done business for a long time. I'm sure you find our plans acceptable."

My father's face closed down, his voice cut like a knife when he said, "Ken, you seem incapable of getting the point here. Lucky may be my daughter, but she is the best hotel man I know. Not to mention, she owns the project you are bidding on, so why you keep trying to crawl up my ass is beyond me."

That pretty much killed any opposition.

The younger architect smirked—I bet he didn't like being little more than a step-and-fetch puppy. Wondering what he had to offer, I ignored the Neanderthal and gauged my conversation to the youngster.

As I started in, my father leaned back in his chair, a smile on his face.

"**YOU'VE** got the bit in your teeth. It's fun to see you run with it," my father said to me as we watched the architects walk across the casino, on their way to the garage. "That was a pretty gutsy move, pissing Ken off. His firm is the best in the business."

"He's no good to me if he won't listen—if I don't have his respect. Besides, he's a dinosaur; he didn't understand what I'm trying to do. The younger guy got it though. I'd like to see what he comes up with."

"Your concept is solid, your conclusions sound. They'll get their act together."

"It doesn't really matter—there are more fish in that barrel."

"I do have one question, though." My father freshened my glass of wine, which was unnecessary, as I hadn't touched it. "You were willing to listen to all their recommendations except for the one killing the wood oven in the new restaurant. How come you dug in your heels on that one?"

"Jean-Charles and I have gone over everything. He was adamant about the oven. I'd priced it at fifty thousand by the time we made OSHA happy, so when the architects came in at thirty-five thousand, I was in the money."

"Would you have caved if you had not been?"

"No. I promised my chef, and I keep my promises."

"Yes, you do."

"I learned it from you."

"Let me ask you one other thing." My father gave me a grin. "What did you have to give Jean-Charles to make him give up the fresco? I thought he was committed to that."

"I told him I would find an acceptable replacement."

"He let you get away with that?"

I smiled, remembering. "Yeah. We'll have our battles, but we'll work together just fine."

"So were *you* his reward for playing so nicely?" My father pricked me with his verbal knife, but the blood would be mine.

"No, your Van Gogh."

That wiped the grin off his face.

Then he burst out laughing. "That Frenchman is in for one hell of a ride. God help him."

AFTER my father left, Miss P joined me in the bar.

"I'm really sorry about ruining your birthday

dinner," I said. Even though the choice was Jeremy's, I still felt like a heel—despite my best efforts.

"No worries. As I said, it's not the 'when' that matters. Have you called Teddie?"

I flagged down a cocktail waitress and ordered a bottle of Dom Pérignon. "Not yet. Haven't had the time."

"Or the courage?"

"It's not that." Avoiding my friend's eyes, I looked instead over her shoulder and pretended to be fascinated with the waitress as she wiggled her way back to bar. "Okay, maybe a little of that. He actually did me a huge favor, cutting me loose. But it's weird, even though I don't want him, I want him to want me. Does that make any sense?"

"Sure. You want to be the dump-*er*, not the dump-*ee*."

"I knew I could count on you to spare my feelings."

We settled back in comfortable camaraderie as the waitress popped the cork—to applause from the patrons in the bar—and poured a flute of bubbly for each of us.

Raising mine in toast, I said, "To a good friend." I paused, making sure I had her attention before I continued, "and the new Head of Customer Relations at the Babylon."

Miss P's glass was halfway to her lips when my words registered and her eyes widened. "What?"

"A promotion and a rather hefty raise. You deserve it." I took a sip of champagne—a celebration of life.

"I don't want a promotion—I want to work with you."

"We're not breaking up the team, just reordering responsibilities. With an expanded role at the Athena, my title will be Vice President of Customer Relations. We will still office together—your department now will be my responsibility in the corporate hierarchy—but I will be more hands-off. You and Brandy have been handling the daily stuff for a while now. And doing a bang-up job, I might add. Come on." I held my glass out.

With a grin, and dawning understanding, she clinked hers to mine. "Can I call you Veep?"

"Not if you want to keep all your body parts."

"Will you keep your office?"

"No. It belongs to the Head of Customer Relations." She started to object, but I held up my hand. "However, if it's acceptable to you, I would like to expand our little corner of the universe. If we incorporate the empty office space behind ours, we could still fit me in. What do you think?"

"All of this isn't because you're feeling guilty about my birthday, is it?"

"Can you think of any other reason?" I said, trying to keep from smiling. It was hopeless. My face split into a grin. "Congratulations."

"What about Brandy?" Miss P asked.

"That's a decision for the Head of Customer Relations."

"Is there money in the budget to give her a raise as well?"

"Her six-month review is coming up. That might be a perfect time to hammer out the details of her employment going forward."

With delight coloring the apples of her cheeks, and her flute clutched tightly in her hand, Miss P leaned back in her club chair. "Wow."

The look on her face warmed my heart—sometimes life served up a bowl of cherries.

While Miss P processed the ramifications of the last few minutes, I let my eyes wander over the casino. Friday night before Halloween, the place was packed. I couldn't see an empty slot machine, a space at a table . . . nothing. And it made me proud. The Babylon had been a huge leap of faith, a gamble of immense proportions, and we had pulled it off. The thing that intrigued me, the genesis of my concept for the Athena/Cielo, was the makeup of our gamblers here at the Babylon. Not all of them stayed with us—our rooms were the priciest on the Strip—but they came to gamble with us because the Babylon was a classy, fun place to spend the evening.

The amount of money in play is the only accurate measure of a casino's success. The room rates and occupancy levels are nice, but not a major contributor to the bottom line. So, I could have a luxury property, but I needed to focus on luring everyone to the casino—which would be an even taller task given that Cielo would be at the wrong end of the Strip.

Well, you know what they say about nothing ventured. . . .

EACH of us was consumed by our own thoughts, so neither one of us noticed Romeo until he pulled out a chair and joined us.

"May I," he asked, after he had plopped into the seat.

"What did you and Jerry find?"

"Pretty much what you expected—Dr. Zewicki, Dr. Jenkins, and Danilov each went out on the bus—all of them gave presentations along with your buddy from West Virginia."

"Junior Arbogast," I said, leaning forward.

"They all went out on the bus, but Danilov is the only one who returned with the group."

"We know what happened to Jenkins. What about Zewicki?"

"We've been looking for him, can't find him."

"And Molly Rain?"

"I thought I saw someone from the back who could've been her, but nothing concrete."

"And Mr. Mortimer?"

"Didn't see him. But as you know, anyone could've gotten there by car."

I turned to Miss P, but before I could speak, she put down her glass. "I'm on it."

"Where's she going?" Romeo asked, as he watched her retreat.

"To call car rental companies. It's a long shot. She'll let me know if she finds anything."

"Man, you guys are almost as good as Metro."

"Almost?" I rolled my eyes. "Please!"

MISS P would only be irritated if I tried to help her—she had a system and woe to anyone who got in the way. So I sat with Romeo in the bar, not sure where to go or what to do. Even with the open bottle of bubbly cooling in the ice bucket next to me, I had stopped at one glass. Congratulating myself on my self-discipline, with thoughts tumbling, I again scanned the crowd, looking for problems—an old, ingrained habit.

I let the wheels spin freely. So we had a magician—presumably still alive, although no one knew for sure—and his elaborately staged exit. And we had an assistant in on the plan, who could climb walls like Spider-Man and appear and disappear as if by transporter on Captain Kirk's orders. She claimed to be Crazy Carl's daughter, but Carl either couldn't or wouldn't confirm. And then there was our whole cast of characters, each of whom had some connection either to the others or to Eden.

"I'd beat more bushes if I had any idea where to look for them," I remarked to no one in particular.

Romeo grabbed Miss P's abandoned glass,

wiped the rim with a napkin, then poured himself a shot of bubbly. If he saw my raised eyebrow, he ignored it.

"We have clean glasses, you know," I said. "This is a high-class joint."

"Not necessary," he said, as he settled back in his chair. "Besides, the alcohol kills the germs."

"A derivation of the five-second rule." I nodded sagely as I refilled my glass, trying not to be ashamed of my lack of willpower. "I'm all in favor."

"Do you think the folks watching can hear what we're saying?" Romeo asked, as he glanced up at the cameras embedded in the ceiling.

"Big Brother is watching."

The young detective pulled a pen from his inner coat pocket and scribbled on a paper napkin, then folded it and pushed it to me.

Raising one eyebrow, I took the note and read. 'The window at the Danielses' was cut from the inside.'

I opened my mouth to speak, but Romeo jumped in. "I'm not supposed to know. It's all hush-hush at the department. So, this is on the Q-T, right?"

"Absolutely," I said, trying to process the information. "What does it mean, besides the obvious?"

"They wanted us to think someone broke in. But why?"

"FUCK you, bitch!" Newton greeted me the next morning as I pushed through the door of my office, walking straight into Miss P's glare. Instead of going home last night, I had taken a small employee room in the back of the hotel. Home just wasn't home anymore.

"What's the bird doing here?" I asked. In strange surroundings, my night had been fitful. My morning wasn't looking much better.

"Your father," my assistant growled.

"My father?"

"He said you'd probably need some clothes."

I narrowed my eyes at her. She looked normal . . . well, as normal as she ever did. Hooking my thumb over my shoulder, I said, "I'm just going to go out that door and walk back in again, then maybe all of this will make sense."

Miss P sighed as if it took everything she had to muster the patience to talk to someone as moronic as me. "I assume you know he sent a crew to move all of your personal items out of your apartment and into the one next to his?"

"No, I didn't know." I lowered myself into the chair across from her. We might as well stencil my name on the back of the thing—I'd been residing there pretty often lately. "Maybe you'd better start at the beginning."

"While I was calling the car companies last night, he came around looking for you. I told him I had last seen you at the bar. When he couldn't find you there, apparently he called Jerry."

"And when Security couldn't find me, he assumed I'd trotted off with a divine Frenchman or something along those lines?"

"Right."

"It would have been so easy for someone to call me," I said, adding a much-needed dollop of logic to this whole illogical conversation.

"He thought you were . . . busy."

"If I had been . . . busy . . . I wouldn't have answered the phone."

"Precisely!" Miss P announced, as if she'd won the debate. "So why waste time calling in the first place?"

At a loss for words, I could only stare. That's the thing about circular conversations, I was never quite sure how I got roped in, I couldn't find an exit, and winning was never an option. Okay, that's three things instead of one, but who's going to quibble?

I resisted saying the obvious—that I wasn't busy. My engine was clearly revving at a far lower RPM than everyone else's this morning—I had yet to get up to speed and was in danger of being lapped down the backstretch.

"That's when your father decided you would need a change of clothing this morning."

"I'm really glad my private life is such public knowledge."

Finally, Miss P grinned.

"How did we get from a change of clothing to the bird in the office and all of my stuff upstairs?" I raised a hand, stopping her comment. "That was rhetorical. I know my father—the if-a-little-is-good-then-more-must-be-better guy."

"You got it. Overboard as usual. But his heart's in the right place . . . except for the friggin' bird."

Newton glared at her and said, "Asshole."

She looked at me wide-eyed.

"Creepy, isn't it?" I responded, knowing what she was thinking. "If I didn't know better, I'd swear he understood every word."

The door swung open admitting Brandy, fearless assistant number two, looking scrubbed, refreshed, professional, and ready to meet the day.

The bird let out an earsplitting wolf whistle.

"There is no justice in the world," I announced, when my ears stopped ringing. "I'm his provider and I get 'Fuck you, bitch.' Little miss beauty queen sashays in here and she gets an appreciative whistle."

Brandy walked over to the cage. "What a cute bird. Whose is it?"

Newton preened for her.

"Yours," I teased . . . sort of. "I'm going upstairs to look for my lost youth."

THE door was open, the crew just finishing up, when I arrived at my new, temporary home. A smaller version of The Big Boss's suite, with warm wood floors, faux-painted walls in a rich shade of orange, lush Persian carpets, comfortable furniture, and a wall of windows framing a dramatic view of the Strip, it would be a nice home while I discovered where I really lived.

Nodding to the workmen as they hung my art

on the walls, I wandered, picking up knick-knacks.
I couldn't shake the feeling that maybe I really
was running away, from the memories, the disap-
pointments . . . myself.

Somehow, I needed to close the chapter with
Teddie. Even though I denied it, I had loved him . . .
part of me still did. When he left, he took a little
of my heart. Maybe that's how life works—the
people you love add to your life, but take a part of
you in return.

I sank onto the couch in front of the windows
and buried my face in my hands. Vaguely aware
the hammering had stopped, I jumped at the hand
on my shoulder. Looking up into the eyes of my
father, I moved over and offered him part of my
perch.

"Few men are worth your tears, honey. The
ones who are won't make you cry." He put his
arm around me, pulling me to his shoulder.

"I'm not crying. Just trying to catch up." I closed
my eyes and tried to relax.

"Your last forty-eight hours have been doozies."

"Tell me about it." And, thankfully, he didn't
know the half of it—aftershocks of my recent
French earthquakes still rolled through me. "Thanks
for all of this, by the way."

"A bit overboard. Your mother bent my ear
about it. Told me I was meddling."

"Expediting, I would say. And saving me a ton
of hassle. Thank you."

"Everything okay?" he asked, his way of probing. Unlike his daughter, my father was an expert at beating around the bush.

"Perfect."

"I thought it would be."

I let him hold me a moment longer—there was nothing quite like a father's shoulder.

AFTER a quick shower, I managed to locate my underwear drawer and a fresh pair of stockings. Today seemed like a red lace day . . . and a sexy, feminine, girly-girl Dolce and Gabbana day as well. I added a pair of Christian Louboutin shoes because, somehow, French seemed *perfectement*.

THE bird eyed me when I returned to the office, but with Brandy sitting at her desk near his cage, he remained strangely quiet.

"Brandy, a minute, please?" I asked, as I sailed through the outer office, into mine.

"Everything's on go for tonight," she said crisply. "All the bands showed up—the roadies are setting up as we speak. Banquet services, Security, we'll have our final meeting at two this afternoon. Do you want to be there?"

"You handle it."

The girl maintained a calm exterior . . . professional . . . in control, but her huge grin betrayed her.

"Where are we on Mrs. Olefson?" I had asked Brandy to find a nice room for our permanent guest—the new addition to our Babylon family.

"She's booked the suite through the weekend. Monday we are moving her to a nice room in the west tower with a Strip and mountain view."

"Has she seen the room?"

Brandy crinkled her brows as if trying to figure out how to tell her boss that was a stupid question.

I bit back my grin.

"Of course. She's delighted and wants to schedule tea with you and, I quote, 'your Frenchman' next week."

"Remind me on Monday. I can't plan anything now—this weekend is going to be a real killer."

Chapter
EIGHTEEN

♡

*L*unch came and went before I knew it. Buried in a sea of paper and phone calls, I didn't come up for air until well past three. Needing a break, I decided to check on Marik and his preparations for tonight. Brandy's desk was empty—she was off at her meeting. I left Miss P holding down the fort, and Newton muttering sweet expletives in her ear.

My phone rang just as the door closed behind

me. Irritated, and more than a little bit sick of fielding phone calls, I pressed it to my ear.

"Hey," Teddie said, his voice quiet, unsure. "I can't believe you answered."

My heart skipped a beat, then settled back into its steady rhythm. I didn't tell him that I wouldn't have answered had I been smart enough to look at the caller ID. Curiously, the sound of his voice wasn't the punch to the solar plexus I'd expected, although it did leave me with a hollow feeling somewhere near my heart. "Hello, Teddie. What do you need?" I tried, but I couldn't keep the ice out of my tone.

"Just to hear your voice."

Stopping, I looked out over the crowded lobby below. The guy was working me like a yo-yo, stringing me along like a twisted version of walk-the-dog. "I don't know how to talk to you right now. And I'm not sure I want to."

"I know." Distance echoed between us, both real and imagined. "We really screwed this up, didn't we?"

"We?"

"Okay, me. I really screwed this up. I never should have slept with you in the first place."

That was going back further in time than I expected.

"I had you in my life," he continued. "Now I've lost you. I know sharing our lives won't work—we don't want the same thing. But can we go back?"

"This was what I warned you about in the

beginning." I squeezed my eyes tight against the pain, then refocused. "I don't know how to be your friend anymore, Teddie."

"Can't we figure it out?"

I gripped the phone, his mother's words echoing in my memory. "No, Teddie. Keeping a connection between us makes it impossible to move on. I'm sorry."

After a long silence, he said, "You can't mean that."

"Good-bye, Teddie," I said.

"No, wait," he said, before I could disconnect. "I have one other thing I think you should know."

"What?"

"I just got the weirdest phone call. A gal from the truck pool at the Babylon called me. She wanted to know if you had taken the van off-road. Apparently there was some damage."

A chill chased up my spine. "What did you tell her?"

"I told her there was no way it was us—we didn't take it any farther than Trop and Decatur."

My heart sank. "Damn."

"I take it that wasn't the right thing to do?"

"It's okay," I said, trying to slow my heart and marshal my thoughts. "How would you know what was going on?"

"I thought it would be okay to talk to the gal. After all, she called from your phone."

AT least I knew I hadn't lost my phone.

Flash fell into step as I strode across the lobby. "I'm starved," she said. "Want to buy me breakfast?"

"Can't. I'm chasing my tail."

"I've always found it more fun to allow others to chase that part of my anatomy."

"You would."

"Are you going to tell me where you were last night?" Flash asked with a grin. "I looked for you all over."

"So are you here merely to ask about my sex life?"

"Inquiring minds want to know." Her face turned serious. "Actually I wanted to bring you up to speed on the various blind alleys I've been running down. Or up? Which is it?"

Her bad news took my black mood down a notch . . . all the way to abysmal. "Don't worry about ruining my day."

"That good, huh?" Matching me stride for stride as I shouldered through the lobby on my way to the office. "You were right, Dimitri had a wife. She died a couple of years ago . . . suicide, they said. But her name wasn't Joy."

"And to think you got my hopes up with the suicide angle." A man who was clearly eavesdropping shot me a worried look. I pulled Flash out of earshot. "No Joy connected to anybody else?"

"I checked everybody's relatives, known friends,

lovers, distant cousins—everybody—and came up with nada."

"Did Dimitri's wife have any siblings?"

"Her obit mentioned a brother named Carl and some various lesser and sundry relatives, a stepfather, nothing interesting."

"Carl Colson?" So he did have a sister! Maybe he wasn't so crazy after all.

Flash's head swiveled my direction, her eyes shooting daggers. "Yeah. Are you holding out on me?"

"Of course not. I'm psychic."

"And I'm Mother Teresa."

I wondered if psychic abilities ran in families. Carl was off the charts; I'd be willing to bet my last dollar his sister was also. "You sure her name wasn't Joy?"

"No. It was a weird name, I'd never heard it before."

"Just for grins, why don't you let me in on the secret?"

"You don't need to get huffy."

"Bodies are piling up while you jerk my chain."

"Alaia, okay? Her name was Alaia."

I stopped in my tracks, jerking her to a stop as well. "Say again."

"Alaia."

I clapped my hands and shouted, "Bingo!"

Heads turned. I didn't care.

"What?"

"We have our Joy! You're brilliant." If I hadn't been standing in the middle of the lobby masquerading as a hotel executive, I would've done a happy dance.

"You're not making sense," Flash groused. "Don't tell me the voices are talking to you, too?"

"Alaia, a derivation of the Spanish word *alegría*, meaning . . ."

"Joy."

"Close enough," I said, my spirits soaring.

"You sure?" Flash asked.

"Of course I'm sure. The word means happiness, jubilation, etc. Alaia is actually a Basque name, I think."

"How the heck do you know these things?"

"Speaking Spanish is part of my job description. And as for the name, remember that internship I did at the Ritz in Madrid? I worked with a girl named Alaia."

"What does all this mean?"

"It means we're going to catch that bastard."

Flash's eyes widened when I pulled my phone out of my pocket. "Are you going back to the age of the dinosaur? That technological relic belongs in the Smithsonian."

"My other one walked off. This is a spare." I punched Romeo's speed-dial. Nothing. Damn. His number was in my old phone. "Would you go to my office and ask Miss P to call me with Romeo's number?" I asked Flash. "I want to check on the preparations for tonight's magic show. Won't take me a minute. I'll meet you at the office."

"You got it."

AT the main entrance to the Arena the phone rang. "What's his number?" I asked.

"What?" Jerry's voice came back.

"Sorry, I thought you were Miss P. What's up?"

"We found Zewicki. Housekeeping pulled him out of a laundry bin on the tenth floor. Bound and gagged, he was mad as a hooker on vice night. He said Danilov jumped him."

"How long ago?"

"Ten minutes, no more."

"Is Danilov still on the property?"

"Negative. We didn't catch up with him in time. I'm sorry."

"Damn."

"But I do know where he went."

"One of these days, Jer. One of these days . . ."

"Your buddy, Danilov, caught a cab. The doorman heard him ask to be taken to Trop and Decatur."

PACING, I dialed Jeremy. *Come on. Come on. Answer the phone!* The call rolled to voice mail. "Damn!" I muttered—apparently "damn" was my new favorite word. I tried twice more to reach him even though I knew it was futile—he was buried in the bowels of Vegas.

Thoughts racing, I resisted running after Danilov.

A minute to think. It was all there right in front of me. . . .

A missing magician whose wife died. Her name was Joy—in Basque. Her brother was Carl Colson, who was in this secret mind-bending program at Area 51. Bart Griffin had an ax to grind with the Air Force. Zoom-Zoom and Danilov both had connections to the same program. If Jenkins's mind-reading trick wasn't a trick at all . . . I'd be willing to bet my last dollar he was the "expert" called in to play God. Play God, deal with the Devil.

Assuming psychic abilities clustered genetically, I could assume Joy was the girl who died in the program. Who everyone thought was murdered. But the death had been swept under the carpet.

And the murderer walked.

Damn!

LIKE a banshee after a wicked soul, I flew through the Arena oblivious to my surroundings. Grabbing a surprised Marik by the arm, I growled in his ear, "Come with me."

He jerked his arm away. "I'm busy," he snapped.

"It's important." The murderous look I gave him did the trick.

"Where are we going?"

"To spring a trap."

THROWING myself headfirst into the cab at the head of the queue, with Marik close behind, I barked out our destination, then said, "There's a hundred in it for you if you make this bucket of bolts fly."

A gamer, the cabbie joined the chase.

Gripping the handle, with feet braced, I fought to dial my phone with my free hand. "Call Romeo. Tell him to meet us in the storm drain, Trop and Decatur, fifty feet in, take a right, follow the shouting," I barked to Miss P when she answered. "He should bring backup."

Taking the right turn onto Trop faster than I thought physics allowed, the cabbie punched it on the straightaway. My phone flew out of my hand as I grabbed for anything solid. Any attempt to retrieve it would risk serious bodily harm, so I didn't try. It wouldn't matter anyway.

"Are you going to tell me what this is about?" Marik asked.

"Let me tell you what I know. You can fill in the details." I gave him a glare. "I've been wracking my brain trying to figure out what happened to Dimitri, who was responsible. I was looking for one person, maybe two, but the more I dug, the more connections I made. Then it hit me—all of you guys are in this up to your eyeballs. Both you and Dimitri are Ukranian, and you called him Dimchka—a term of endearment used mainly for relatives or family. Which is it?"

His face a mask, Marik looked at me for a moment, then he gave a slight, resigned shrug. "Cousin."

"All of you—Zewicki, Bart Griffin, Danilov—are trying to catch a murderer and it just might get Carl killed." Along with Jeremy, but I didn't say that aloud—saying it made it real. "Dimitri added the needed publicity—casting a wide net to reel in a murderer, and his disappearance had the added benefit of allowing him to work behind the scenes while the rest of you acted out this little farce on a very public stage."

Marik didn't deny it. "Go on."

"The whole Danilov robbery threw me off for a while," I continued, gaining momentum. "Very clever. You knew Metro wouldn't give a simple robbery much attention. So you staged it, setting the trap."

"When did you figure it out?"

"When I got the Joy connection." As the cab screeched to a stop at the familiar corner, I pulled a couple of bills from my pocket after retrieving my phone. "Thanks! Keep the change."

Marik and I ran for the entrance to the drains.

AT the dark opening, I put a hand on Marik's chest, pushing him behind me. "Follow and be quiet."

With no flashlight, the darkness was virtually impenetrable, snuffing out the tiny cone of light from the entrance like a blanket over a flame. My hand on the wall, I felt my way, trying to follow the memory of my previous visit. The back of my sweater fisted in his hand, Marik followed closely, silently.

Jeremy's post was empty. I shut my mind to the possibilities.

Carl's growl echoed through darkness. "You're one of them." He sounded angry, scared, coiled like a lion lured by the scent of blood and ready to pounce.

"One of whom?" Jeremy's Aussie accent tripped my heart.

Stopping at the corner, I flattened against the wall, then eased my head around.

In the flickering light—remnants of a fire—I could see Jeremy. He stood, not ten feet from me, his arm around Danilov's neck. If he was aware of my presence, he didn't show it.

Danilov hung like a ragdoll in Jeremy's arms, a trickle of blood oozing from a cut on his temple.

Carl, his feet braced, his eyes wild, held his rifle leveled at Jeremy's heart.

Taking a deep breath, I stepped into the room.

Marik stayed hidden in the shadows behind me.

"Carl, put the rifle down," I said, as I eased toward him, my empty hands outstretched.

He swung the rifle toward me, then recognition dawned. "Lucky?"

"It's over now, Carl. Give me the rifle."

"No!" Carl shook his head, an exaggerated motion like a wild animal driven mad by the unrelenting bites of insects. "The Devil has come. He must be killed." Pain and madness flashed across his face. "He killed her . . . sister."

Pressing the heel of one hand to his temple, he squeezed his eyes shut. "Voices . . . anger." Carl let the muzzle of the gun drift down.

"It's okay, Carl. We'll get the Devil." I sensed Marik easing out of the shadows as I walked toward Carl, keeping his attention. I brushed shoulders with Jeremy, who hadn't taken his eyes off Carl.

"Careful," he whispered. "He's having a bad day."

Quick as a snake, Danilov grabbed my arm, his fingers sinking into my flesh. "The Devil . . ."

"No!" Carl shouted.

I saw him raise the gun.

Throwing myself at Jeremy, I pushed with every ounce of strength I had. "Carl, no!"

The report of the gun hammered my ears. A sharp sting across my shoulder. Thrown backwards, I fell. My hand flew to my shoulder as I shouted again, "Carl, no!" A warm trickle of blood oozed between my fingers, as I rolled then pulled my feet underneath me. "He's not the Devil. There is another."

Carl lowered the gun.

A flash of black, Marik darted around me. He grabbed the gun, easing it from Carl's fingers. "It's over, Carl. Everything's okay."

Carl's shoulders sagged as he let Marik have the rifle.

Danilov moved.

"Stay down," I barked at him. Slowly I stood. Glancing at Jeremy, my heart froze.

A red splash of blood soaked his shirt.

"No!" I dropped to my knees beside him.

He groaned and his eyes fluttered open when I yanked the tail of his shirt from his pants and lifted the thin fabric.

An angry red gouge sliced his side. Oozing blood, it looked painful as hell, but not life-threatening. My world stopped spinning and I could breathe again.

Tearing his shirt, I wadded the cloth and pressed it over the wound.

He grimaced, then grinned. "It would've been a lot worse if you hadn't gotten a severe case of heroics. Stupid of you."

"What can I say? Adrenaline always short-circuits that whole common sense thing."

He squeezed my shoulder. "Thanks."

"No worries. If I'd let anything happen to you, Miss P would make my life miserable. As it is, she's going to have her pound of flesh when she gets a gander at you."

Brushing the hair out of my yes, I straightened and looked around. The rifle lay in a puddle where Carl had stood. "Marik?"

No answer.

We were alone. Terrific.

The three stooges had disappeared.

HIS arm around my shoulders, Jeremy and I had made it halfway back to the entrance when we heard the sound of running feet. Outlined against the light streaming in through the opening to the storm drain, figures hurried toward us.

"Lucky?" Romeo shouted, his voice filled with worry, echoing in the small space.

"Here."

The young detective appeared in front of me. "Let me help you." He shouldered Jeremy, who appeared to be walking a bit easier now, having made his peace with the pain. Romeo's men closed in around us.

"Take us to the Babylon, would you?" I asked the young detective. "We need to hurry. I'll fill you in on the way."

"THIS is not my day," I muttered, as we approached the Babylon and I caught sight of the traffic jam. The circus had started.

Romeo, silent as he digested my story, now shot me a grin. He beeped his siren and flashed his lights as he barked orders into his bullhorn. As the crowd parted he asked, "So give me the bottom line. Who are we looking for in all this mess?"

"I can't be certain, but I'd say the Devil has two X chromosomes."

His eyes widened as he shot a startled glance my way. "Molly Rain?"

"Call it a strong hunch, but she was looking for evidence concerning the murder in Danilov's apartment. I have a feeling Dimitri or one of the others told her about the papers in Danilov's safe, then she panicked when the staged burglary occurred, as they hoped she would."

"Papers? Danilov told us only some cheap jewelry had been taken."

"Didn't you sort of wonder why anyone would keep the cheap stuff in the safe?" I asked the young Columbo.

"They could've had significance in the whole hypnotism thing—the talismans."

"I thought of that, too. But when Molly broke into my apartment and mentioned something about papers being stolen . . . well, it didn't have significance at the time, but later, when I started thinking they all might be in on something . . ."

"She had to suspect she was being baited," Romeo said, putting a few puzzle pieces in their proper places.

"Probably, but she couldn't risk any evidence being out in the open—even though the odds of the Air Force cooperating with any investigation were minuscule. But now with the whole world watching, they forced the Air Force's hand. I know things have changed with more openness under the Freedom of Information Act, but not enough time has passed for info about all of this to be disseminated yet—if it would ever be."

"So this whole thing was a trap?"

"Revenge, one of the most primal motives."

"So which one of them set the trap?" Romeo asked, as he inched the squad car to the curb in front of the hotel.

"They all did."

"Danilov, Zewicki, Mortimer?" he asked, his eyes showing his disbelief.

"I don't know about Mortimer, yet, but Danilov, Zewicki, Crazy Carl, Bart Griffin, Marik Kovalenko, and Jenkins . . . especially Jenkins . . . were all in it up to their collective asses."

"Cool. Like *Mission Impossible.*"

"Not cool," I growled, as I let the rage inside me bubble to the surface. "Those clowns have turned a killer loose in my hotel on Halloween." I cast my arm toward the teeming lobby and the lines of costumed revelers waiting to get inside.

"Shit," Romeo, The Master of Understatement, announced.

IGNORING his pain, Jeremy matched Romeo and me stride for stride as we maneuvered through the throng packing the lobby. All shapes and sizes of people in varying degrees of inebriation slowed our progress considerably. Dressed in various stages of undress, some even dispensing with clothing altogether—their costumes painted on bare skin—the early partiers' infectious revelry did nothing to improve my mood. Even the excited voices echoing off the marble walls couldn't conjure the hint of a smile. Apparently I was immune to fun . . . a new low.

"Jerry," I barked into my push-to-talk. "We got major problems."

"I'm all ears," came his reply.

I gave it to him short and sweet, as I dodged a couple, their skin painted in tiger stripes, tails attached to their ample backsides. Harry and Mavis. I should have known. "Excuse me," I said as I eased around them.

"Hey, there," Harry said. He looked like a greeter at a nudist camp on party night.

Afraid of the letting my gaze drift lower, I kept my eyes on his and concentrated on keeping them there.

"Looks like you need a costume," Mavis said, eyeing me. "We have some leftover paint, if you want it."

"They won't let you in dressed like that," Harry added.

"Thanks, I'll take my chances," I said as I eased by.

"Who was that," Jerry asked in my ear.

"Sex-swing couple." I launched again into the crowd, Romeo and Jeremy on my heels. "Use every resource you have. Let me know when you locate any one of the players in this little game of cat and mouse, okay?"

"Wilco. Where will you be?"

"Backstage looking for a magician. He's given me the slip once already. And if it's one thing I hate, it's vanishing magicians."

AFTER I flashed my badge, the security guard waved us through the main entrance to the Arena, the

Babylon's venue for prizefights, rock concerts, hockey games and, tonight, a Houdini séance—assuming Marik Kovalenko was a handshake kind of guy.

A circular cavern, the arena held twenty thousand when packed to capacity. The entrances were all on the upper levels, with rows of seats periodically separated by flights of stairs cascading down to the main stage on the floor. Like a net waiting to fall and hold us all hostage, a latticework of catwalks festooned with lights was suspended above the seating areas. A rectangular object, cloaked in a dark cloth, hung from one of the catwalks, cables angling down, connecting it to the stage—presumably a prop for tonight's show. A few klieg lights focused on the stage—a single bare platform in the center of the arena floor—bathing it in stark light. Away from the stage, the light faded quickly, leaving the rest of the Arena shrouded in shadow punctuated by dim lights showing the stairs and the exits—like the trail of emergency lights in an airplane after an accident.

Racing down one set of stairs, the two men still dogging my heels, I quickly scanned the vast space. Once again, I keyed my walkie-talkie. "Jerry, we need a sweep of the Arena before we let anyone in here."

"My guys are on their way."

I arrived at the stage out of breath and out of patience.

"Let's split up," Jeremy suggested as he stopped at my shoulder. Bending over, he clutched his side. The red stain had grown.

"Jerry," I wheezed into my Nextel. "We need the doc on the stage in the Arena." Jeremy straightened, his eyes locked on mine, his mouth set in a firm line as he shook his head. "And bring two of your guys to hold our patient down," I continued. My stare never wavered from Jeremy's as I said to him, "You're in no shape to take down a killer. You could put all of us in danger." Not that we weren't already, but I hoped he ignored that little fact.

"She's right," Dane said, as he appeared at Jeremy's shoulder.

I hadn't noticed him following us. "Where'd you come from?"

"When it comes to trouble, I'm like a bloodhound given a scent. What can I say, it's a knack," he said, as he clamped a hand on Jeremy's shoulder. "I'll take care of him."

Jeremy, his face ashen, pain etching creases around his mouth and darkening his golden eyes, didn't put up a fight. Instead, he sagged into the nearest seat. One less worry.

If my hunch was right and Molly Rain was our killer, where would she be . . . and who would she be after? Danilov had said Carl was the key. And he'd said they were all connected. Therefore, if the woman who had been murdered was indeed Joy, Dimitri's wife and Carl's sister, and assuming off-the-chart psychic abilities ran in families, then Carl could indeed hold the key to his sister's murder.

A bit of a stretch for us skeptics, but for believers . . .

And, last time I saw him, Carl was with Marik.

Clutching at straws, I grabbed for the only one I had. "Romeo, come with me." I started for the tunnel leading to the dressing rooms and backstage areas. Turning to Dane, I said, "I'm looking for Marik Kovalenko. Do you know him?" At his nod, I continued, "If you see him, I don't care if you have to shoot him, but don't let him get away."

"Yes, ma'am."

"And watch your backside if Molly Rain sticks her head in here. Despite her mild-mannered exterior, apparently she's capable of murder."

"Gotcha."

Romeo and I took off at a run.

IN stark contrast to the Arena seating area, backstage was a sea of activity. Costumed bodies darted like heat-seeking missiles, their sequined costumes sparkled like fireworks on the Fourth of July. I felt as if I'd been dropped into the middle of a circus. Right in front of my eyes, an elephant docilely munched hay, as if this chaos was business as usual, which for him it probably was.

I snagged a scantily clad performer by the arm. He turned heavily made-up eyes to me as I said, "Marik?"

Giving me the once-over, the man nodded toward a screened area off to the side. "Over there. But be careful, before a show his bite is worse than his bark."

As Romeo and I pushed through the bodies, I could feel the excitement—adrenaline shimmered off the performers, intoxicating, exhilarating. Teddie's drug of choice.

I hadn't stood a chance.

Being a head taller than almost everyone around me, I scanned over the crowd. Finally, I caught a glimpse of Marik, his face closed into a scowl, as he barked at a young woman I remembered seeing at his warehouse.

Like a bullet from a rifle, I launched myself toward him, performers scattering in my wake. He didn't notice me until I arrived in front of him.

"Your ass is mine," I snarled. "How dare you bring all of this to my hotel?"

Marik dragged me behind the screen, out of sight and earshot. He glared at Romeo, who followed, but said nothing to the detective. I chose not to waste time and the drop of good humor I had left on trivialities such as introductions.

"Would you calm down?" Marik hissed. "It's all under control."

"Under control?" Despite my best efforts, my voice held a tinge of panic. I grabbed the magician's arm in a vise-like grip. He winced, which made me feel better. "Carl is on the verge of a meltdown. And, thanks to you and your little band of killer catchers, he may cross to the dark side and never come back."

Guilt flashed across Marik's features, probably saving him from a slow and painful death when all of this was over.

"How could you?" My control tenuous, I vibrated with anger.

"He's more stable than you think," Marik said.

Whether he was trying to convince me or himself was anybody's guess, but now was not the time to argue. "Where is he?"

"Safe." I started to argue but Marik put a finger to his lips.

He had a point. In the Babyon, even the walls had ears. "You had Molly Rain pegged from the beginning, didn't you?"

Marik's eyes widened in surprise as he nodded. "Yeah, but we got shut down by the brass."

"Nobody was willing to risk a Black program over one casualty," I said, suddenly sure.

Anger flashed in his dark eyes. "The whole thing was—how do you say it?"

"Swept under the rug?" Romeo suggested.

"Right. It was like Joy had never existed. She simply vanished." Gently, he eased his arm from my grasp, then rubbed the spot where I had squeezed.

"And Dimitri, our vanishing magician? He's been watching me, hasn't he?"

"We had it all planned until you showed up asking Carl questions. None of us had any idea you knew him."

"I could have led the killer to your bait, so you kept an eye on me," I explained, not needing Marik's confirmation. "So how do we find Molly?"

"Look no further," purred a female voice. A voice I knew.

Molly Rain.

The three of us whirled and found ourselves staring into the business end of a silenced Glock.

The baited trap had sprung, but not quite as Marik and Company had planned. If they had just bothered to ask, I could've told them that was almost always the case. But there was a better chance of snow in July than anyone listening to me, even though I could teach the course in Things That Can Go Wrong.

Molly, her hands holding the weapon steady at the center of Marik's chest, calmly glared at us. Clearly in control and enjoying it, she gave a smile that froze my heart. "Give me Carl, Marik. And the papers."

The magician took a step toward her. Lowering the muzzle, calmly, she squeezed the trigger.

A popping sound, and Marik staggered back, clutching his thigh.

"I wouldn't," Molly said, as she again raised the gun to point at his chest.

I eased toward Marik, but he shook his head. Moving his hand, he straightened. The bullet had grazed his leg, nothing more. A tic worked in his jaw. Murder lurked in his eyes.

"I won't be so generous next time," Molly said

as she took dead aim at his heart. "Give me Carl. Now."

"I'm the only one here who knows where he is," Marik said, his voice saber-sharp.

"Have it your way." Molly swung the gun to my heart. "Tell me or I kill your friend."

Before I could react, Romeo shouted, "No!" as he lunged for Molly.

Taken by surprise, she whirled but was a fraction of a second too late.

The bullet caught Romeo in the shoulder, spinning him around. He fell at her feet.

Marik and I dove for Molly.

Quick as a cat, the woman swung the handgun at Marik's head.

Metal connected with tissue. I cringed at the meaty thunk. Grabbing for her, my hands closed around cloth as she fell back, twisting away from me. Staggering, I tried to follow. Too quick, she pulled out of my grasp. Backing away, the gun pointed at me, she disappeared through the curtain.

I keyed my Nextel as I dropped to my knees at Romeo's side. When he blinked at me, I started shouting. "Security, officer down staging area of the Arena. Call paramedics and Metro. Shooter is female, five foot four, dark, curly hair, blue eyes, armed and dangerous."

"Get her," Romeo groaned. "I'm okay."

Launching to my feet, I bolted. Pushing through the curtain, I shouted, "Did anyone notice a young woman?" I gave a brief description.

One young man pointed toward the tunnel leading to the Arena. "That way."

One mistake was all I needed, and Molly Rain had just made it.

POUNDING through the tunnel, I skidded to a stop next to the stage. Scanning the Arena, I let my eyes adjust to the relative darkness. Pairs of security personnel had fanned out across the vast space, sweeping it in grids.

Where are you, Molly? I know you're here.

Forcing my pulse to slow, my breathing back under control, I focused on a section at a time, spending a few seconds on each, trying to catch movement. Half of the Arena scanned, and on the verge of panicking, I saw her.

Crouching low behind the top tier of seats, she had meticulously worked her way around the Arena. I saw her pausing to peer over the seat back in front of her. Twenty-five feet and she would make her escape.

Putting my two pinkies in the corners of my mouth, I let loose an ear-piercing whistle. Security whirled. And, as I'd banked on, Molly stopped in her tracks, ducking down.

I pointed to the nearest pair of guards and motioned to close the distance. They pulled their guns and moved immediately, following my hand signals. A couple of pros. Thank God.

My momentary satisfaction evaporated.

Hurdling seats, Molly bounded toward the Arena floor.

Crouching, one guard squeezed off a couple of rounds.

Without pausing, and not taking time to aim, Molly shot back, peppering the Arena.

The rapport of rapid-fire hit me like bullets to the chest.

Molly kept going. Metallic clicks sounded. Out of ammo, she threw away the gun. Then with one hand, she grabbed a rope hanging from the lighting grid high above. Hand-over-hand, she pulled herself higher and higher.

Darkness swallowed her.

"Damn!"

Without conscious thought, I kicked off my shoes. Running, I leapt on the ladder bolted to the wall near me. Rung by rung, I climbed as fast as I dared, shutting my eyes to the growing distance between me and the ground. Fury drove me. Time slowed.

At the top, on hands and knees, I felt the vibration of someone running. Hands on the side rails, taking a deep breath, I forced myself to my feet. Following the hollow ring of footfalls, I ran.

The thin metal grid shook violently with each stride.

God, let this thing hold.

Aware of Security and police streaming into the Arena below, I shouted into my walkie-talkie,

"Don't let anyone up here. This thing wasn't designed to hold much weight. Just secure all the ways down." I repocketed the device without waiting for a reply.

Scanning ahead, I again looked for movement, something passing in front of a light . . . anything. Twenty strides, nothing. Then I saw it. A shadow. Not more than fifty feet. Bolting out of the darkness, heading in my direction. Then stopping.

For a fraction of a second, Molly's eyes met mine. Then she turned and ran. One hand on the rail, she threw herself around a ninety-degree turn. Stumbling briefly, she regained balance and darted. I ran after her.

Following her shadowed outline, I paused only to make the sharp corner around a turn. Then another. The catwalk shook as I pounded after Molly. I tried not to think about it.

Even though she had a head start, I could sense I was closing the distance between us.

I slipped around a turn, recovered, then ran after her. Fifteen feet. Ten feet.

Suddenly, Molly skidded to a stop and whirled. Before I could react, she threw an elbow at my head. Bracing, I ducked to the side. Her elbow glanced off my jaw. Momentum jackknifed me over the waist-high rail. My stomach lurched. Hands grabbed for the rail. Too late.

My body slipped into space.

Chapter

NINETEEN

♡

*O*ne last lunge.

My hand brushed metal. My fingers grasped the narrow tubing. Pain forced a cry as my shoulder took my weight. How I held on, I'll never know.

Summoning more strength than I knew I had, I twisted until my other hand closed around the railing. Like aftershocks, the tremors of Molly running reverberated through the metal and down my arms.

Pulling, I tried to get a foot onto the catwalk. Strength failing, my arms shaking, I tried again. This time my foot found purchase. Using my legs, I pulled myself back to safety.

Head down, adrenaline overriding fear, anger fueling my muscles, I found my footing and ran. The vibrations grew louder, more pronounced, as I bolted through the darkness. After finding all the exits guarded, Molly must've turned back.

Trying to quiet my ragged breathing, I stopped and listened. Yes, she headed this way.

Glancing over her shoulder, Molly didn't see me until she was within no more than five or six strides. Skidding to a stop, her eyes wide, with fear or madness I couldn't tell, she whirled. I ran after her. Closing the distance, I bided my time. Fifteen feet. Her breath coming in tortured gasps. Ten feet.

I leapt. Reaching.

Nothing but air.

I landed with a thud. My breath left me in a whoosh.

Seeing stars and gasping for air I rolled over in time to see Molly standing on top of the rectangular box suspended from cables. With a glance at me, and a self-satisfied grin lifting the corner of her mouth, she jumped, caught a ledge, then pulled herself through a trapdoor in the ceiling.

Still fighting for my wind, I looked at the full length and breadth of me. No friggin' way would this body fit through that hole.

Damn!

"Help me out here, Jer," I gasped into my push-to-talk. Glancing down toward the floor, I said, "I'm over the orchestra section on the main entrance side, midway. She just disappeared through a trapdoor in the ceiling. I need to know where it goes and where she turns up."

"You got it."

SOMEHOW, I had made it off the catwalk, reclaimed my shoes, and hit the main entrance to the Arena without killing myself—or taking any hostages—when Jerry's voice came over the radio. "Lucky, your gal disappeared through an access port for the air-conditioning system."

"Great. How far can she go?"

"Only ground floor. We've got the cameras positioned. When she reappears, my people will be all over it."

BY the time I fought my way to the casino, now filled with overflow revelers waiting to gain entrance to the Bondage Ball, I realized finding Molly Rain was going to be as difficult as finding the one burnt-out bulb that shorted out a whole tree of lights. Not only was the hotel as full as a Hong Kong ferry, almost everyone was in costume, their faces masked.

After getting an update on Jeremy, Marik, and Romeo—all had refused to go to the hospital and were treated and released by the paramedics—I wandered the ground floor of the hotel, waiting, hoping for Molly to reappear.

The festive atmosphere and several hundred near-naked people did little to improve my mood. Usually I enjoyed the creativity people showed in fashioning a costume out of two scraps of cloth, elastic, a piece or two of fake fur, spray paint, and various colors of plastic wrap, but not tonight. However, a bodybuilder painted red, with horns on his head, a forked tail, his privates nestled in a red banana bag, did turn my head.

As luck would have it, Dane caught me mid-ogle.

Instantly my hormones hit high alert—an involuntary reaction—and one I immediately squelched. Right now I had way more trouble than I could handle. And one thing I knew for certain about Dane: The man was trouble with a capital T. Or maybe it was Temptation with a capital T? Who knew? Either way, my life was messy enough as it was.

"Enjoying the show?" he asked, his lips close to my ear, his breath warm on my cheek.

"Parts," I replied, as I watched the devil's perfect backside until the crowd swallowed it and its owner.

"We seem to have a lot of devils tonight." Dane had followed my gaze and was now treating me to a delicious, wry grin.

"Aren't we lucky?" Sometimes even I can't resist.

"Molly hasn't reappeared?" Dane grasped my elbow and gently steered me toward the lobby.

I eased my arm from his clutches. I really didn't like being maneuvered, no matter how subtly. "Not yet." I resisted the urge to check with Jerry one more time. "But she can't live in there forever. And when she shows . . ." I left the sentence hanging, the implication clear. However, truth be told, I had no idea what would happen when she left her hiding place, but my bravado sounded good, so I went with it.

Dane was wise to my shtick, but he let me get away with it anyway. I liked that about him.

He checked his watch. "The Houdini Séance ought to be gearing up here in a minute. Are you going?"

"I've got ringside seats." I reversed course and headed back toward the Arena. "Care to join me?"

"I thought you'd never ask."

This time when he took my elbow, I went willingly.

IN the Arena the seats were filling rapidly, eerie music wafted from the loudspeakers, and a curtain now formed a backdrop to the previously exposed stage. Like mortar between bricks, excitement filled the empty spaces, joining each of us as spectators to the spectacle to come. That was the magic of the theatre: the anticipation, the expectation of a remarkable show, of entertainment, of delight. And it was particularly true of magic shows. I'd seen more magic than any human should, but I was still enraptured and amazed. And, if things played out as I thought they might, tonight would be perhaps even more memorable . . . if I really was lucky.

Dane and I followed the other patrons as they filed down a set of stairs, tickets clutched tightly, looking for their seats. Instead of a ticket, my employee badge got us past the ticket-takers, but not without curious stares. I guess I did look a bit worse for the wear. Hastily, I ran my fingers through my hair, trying to get the knots out. Rubbing under my eyes, and pinching my cheeks, I knew it wouldn't help, but the familiar routine helped calm my nerves.

My clothes were filthy—I didn't even bother brushing them down. My shirt was torn and stained with a dab of dried blood where the bullet that took a chunk out of Jeremy had grazed my shoulder. My shoes were now the color of the water in the storm drains, stained with God knew what. I closed my mind to the revolting possibilities.

Who knew, when I chose my outfit today, brown would prove to be the perfect choice?

I clapped a hand over my mouth, swallowing the absurd giggle threatening to escape.

Dane shot me a worried glance as, shoulder to shoulder, we took the stairs two at a time.

"I'm held together with masking tape and baling twine, but I'll get through it," I assured him, hoping my words carried the conviction I didn't feel.

A shiver chased down my spine as I glanced at the catwalk high above. I'd come so close. I could still taste the bile in my throat. Today had definitely been a hazardous duty day.

And it wasn't over.

Reaching the floor, we joined the security personnel who formed a cordon around the stage. Shading my eyes against the bright lights and looking back up into the audience, I could just make out the security folks dotting the Arena—Jerry must have called in everyone on the staff, bless him.

A killer was not going to kill again. Not in my hotel. Not if I had any say in it.

In addition to covering all the bases, Jerry had Mr. Mortimer under lock and key, which was good. But it bothered me that Security had not been able to locate Dr. Zewicki, Danilov, Crazy Carl, or Dr. Jenkins. Bart Griffin was on the air—at least he had been a little while ago—but that was little comfort, he could be transmitting from anywhere, or he could have recorded the show earlier.

As I scanned, hoping to find a familiar face or two, I was overcome with the feeling I was standing at the harmonic convergence, the epicenter, of something really bad. And I'd always wanted to be in the center of the action. What *had* I been thinking?

The lights dimmed and, with the exception of a few whistles and catcalls, the crowd quieted.

When the lights came back up, I turned my attention to the stage and realized, if the threat came from the audience, from the darkness beyond the lights, we were screwed. "Dane," I whispered, leaning into him.

He bent his head down to mine, but said nothing.

"What do you think about heading up higher?"

His eyes lifted to the catwalk overhead. "Vantage point might be better." With that, he melted into the darkness.

The crowd cheered as Marik, transformed in a

clean black pirate's shirt and tight pants, appeared, limping only a little. Without a word, he launched into his disappearing pachyderm routine. It wasn't really appropriate for a séance, but I guessed it was the best he had ready, and I didn't think the well-oiled crowd would mind. From the cheers and the *ooohs* and *ahhhs*, it seemed I was right.

My attention half on the crowd, the people I could see anyway, and half on the stage, I let my mind freewheel, hoping something would hit me, something wrong, something out of place. It was an old trick from my days wandering the casino floor looking for trouble.

After Marik completed the whole elephant routine to raucous applause, he cleared the stage, preparing for the séance. The lights dimmed. After a few moments of shadowed figures scurrying on the stage, the lights once again brightened, revealing nine candelabras, each holding a large, round candle, and ringing a large oval table in the center of the stage. A steaming cauldron sat in the center of the table—which I thought was a bit of overkill, but what did I know? A young woman dressed in a long black robe lit the candles one by one.

The stage now aglow in candlelight, the young woman disappeared and six cloaked figures filed onto the stage, hoods shrouding their faces. One stepped forward and lifted his hood, letting it fall down his back.

Marik.

"The lights are nine," the magician said. "Three times three."

The crowd was so quiet I almost believed they had disappeared.

"We are six, two times three," Marik intoned, as he motioned for the others to reveal themselves and take their places at the table.

I closed my eyes and dropped my head. I could identify each of the five helpers—Zewicki, Danilov, Jenkins, Griffin . . . and Carl, under a sheen of sweat, a wildness to his eyes. Talk about hiding in plain sight. Why didn't they just paint a target on the guy?

I felt like radioing Romeo, who I knew was nearby, to come arrest the lot of them. But for what? I'd be damned, but I couldn't think of a law they'd broken . . . yet.

Crossing fingers and toes, I prayed the fools had an ace up their sleeve.

With a gesture, Marik silenced the murmurings of the crowd. "Tonight, on the anniversary of the great Harry Houdini's death, we will try to summon his spirit," Marik said, raising his arms as if beseeching the complicity of the gods . . . or Houdini. Marik had a wild look about him, his dark eyes intense, his face unsmiling, his hair loose, falling in a dark cascade over his shoulders, accentuating his feral features.

"What about Dimitri Fortunoff?" shouted a voice from the audience.

"Yeah, he's supposed to return tonight," another voice joined in.

One hand to his chest, the other arm hanging at his side, Marik bowed to the crowd. "You ask much from this humble servant. But, perhaps, the spirits will be willing."

That shut everyone up. You could hear a pin drop. Heck, even I was riveted, caught up in whatever was going to happen, as unable to alter its course as I was to change the path of a tornado.

Standing over his seated accomplices, Marik took his place at the head of the table. Raising his arms, he gestured and the rectangular object tethered high above us began to descend toward the stage. All eyes watched its slow decent. Halfway down, the black shroud over it was pulled away, revealing a large, bronze casket.

I jumped at Romeo's voice in my ear. "That's Houdini's casket. It was his last escape."

"Before or after he died?" I asked, only half kidding.

Romeo snorted as he appeared at my side but didn't say anything. Apparently, he thought I was being cute. That's me, too cute for words.

"This one I know is a replica," Romeo whispered. "Houdini was buried in the real one."

"Convenient."

When the casket reached the stage, Marik positioned it on a stand in front of the table. Opening it, he released latches on the outside, dropping the sides. All of us could see the bronze box was empty.

Then he relatched the sides and motioned for Carl to stand and move forward.

Apparently Carl had been at rehearsal, as he shed his cloak and climbed inside the casket box.

Tempting fate in my book, but nobody asked me.

Marik secured the lid then, letting his arms drop to his sides, his head fall forward, he motioned for his tablemates to join hands. When they had complied, he said, "Our beloved Harry Houdini, we bring you gifts from life into death. Commune with us, Harry Houdini, and move among us."

Another cloaked figure appeared on the stage and moved behind Marik. If he was surprised he didn't show it.

Even though I was close enough to see the magician sweat, I moved to get a better angle on the newest addition. Shorter than Marik, hooded and cloaked, it had to be Molly. When Marik flipped off his mike, I was sure of it.

I saw the glint of metal in Molly's hand. A knife.

"Lift that thing back up to the catwalk," she hissed. "I want Carl and I mean to have him."

At that moment, a rapping noise sounded. Three knocks. They sounded like they came from the casket.

For a moment, Molly's attention shifted.

Marik seized the opportunity. Knocking her knife aside, he grabbed her wrist. From her weak-kneed response, I could tell he was hurting her.

The knife clattered to the stage. Two security personnel jumped onstage, grabbed her, and whisked her away.

It was all over that fast. And I think it took the crowd by surprise. They rustled like a herd of cows unsure of the coyotes in the darkness, not knowing whether to run or stay, so they remained rooted where they were.

The knocking sounded again.

Marik, his composure firmly in place, turned back to the audience.

No one moved. And, if they were like me, they weren't breathing either. I turned to comment to Romeo, but he had disappeared.

Marik walked around the casket, then, standing next to it, opened it with a flourish. Reaching in he grabbed a hand, helping the cloaked figure inside to stand.

The figure turned toward the audience. Slowly he raised both hands to the hood obscuring his face. Then, with one motion, he threw the hood back, revealing himself.

Dimitri Fortunoff.

For a moment time stopped.

Then the crowd roared and pandemonium reigned.

"HECK of a show," was all I could think of to say, words having left me, by the time I managed to reach Marik backstage. Surrounded by his little band of merry men, he was grinning like a fool. A champagne cork popped. Someone thrust a plastic cup into my hand and splashed bubbly into it.

I looked into the sad eyes, but smiling face, of Dimitri Fortunoff.

"It's over." He held up his glass in toast.

I mushed my cup to his. "You guys played one heck of a risky game. Carl—"

"Knew what he was doing," Dimitri interrupted. "At least he seemed to until he lost it."

"I'll take your word for it. But then Danilov broke. That must've been a surprise."

"When we told him you knew where Carl was, he was worried you would inadvertently lead Molly to him before we were ready."

"Then he led her there himself," I finished. "But don't be too hard on him. He had a good reason."

I'd said too much, but thankfully Dimitri didn't push me further. "And you followed. Thank you, by the way. Carl and Danilov owe you, big time. I'd never seen anything shake Marik until I saw him after the altercation. He had no idea Carl would try to shoot Danilov. And he was in no position to stop him. If it helps, the whole thing didn't go down quite as we planned."

"Nothing ever does," I said, as Teddie flashed into my semi-fried brain. Then Jean-Charles. And The Big Boss. "I'm the poster child for the unexpected."

"Keeps life interesting." Dimitri drained his glass,

then, holding the bottle by the neck, poured himself another. He held up the bottle and raised an eyebrow.

I declined with a shake of the head. "You were the one following me, weren't you?"

"Guilty. We needed to cut you off if you headed back to the storm drains."

"Understood. I guess I should say thanks for watching my back, but since all of this is your fault in the first place, my gratitude would be misplaced."

"It was the least I could do."

I started to agree with him, then decided to drop it. After all, no one had been permanently perforated, so sins could be forgiven. Besides, I really like it when the bad guy gets what's coming to him . . . or her, as the case may be. Somehow, when that happens, it makes the world seem a little bit better.

"I have a feeling Danilov and Carl have more of a history than you know," I said, slightly altering the course of the conversation. "It sounds like some crazy stuff went on in Eden."

"Carl and Joy took the worst of it. They were the most talented." Dimitri pushed aside his sadness with visible effort. "Then Jenkins got to Molly. She couldn't handle it. We didn't see the signs until she flipped."

That answered the last question. "Jenkins, he was playing outside the rules, wasn't he?"

"Yeah. He let loose Satan incarnate and they

shut down his program and ushered him silently, without fanfare, out of the military."

"And covered up not only his participation in Eden, but Molly's as well."

"Sweeping the dirt under the rug." Dimitri raised his eyes to mine. "If it's any consolation, we didn't leave Molly to prey on the public. We had been promised she was getting psychiatric care. Imagine our shock when she showed up in Vegas."

"You hired her to keep her close?"

"She didn't know me. I was Joy's husband, but I had nothing to do with Eden."

The magician was right, that did make me feel better about all of them. "That leaves Jenkins, who was shamed, no longer the luminary, the shining star."

"He landed on his feet, but it wasn't the same."

"And hopefully he'd learned a good lesson," I said.

"What was that?"

"Just because you can, doesn't mean you should."

"I think we all learned that the hard way," Dimitri said, as he refilled his own glass and turned his sad eyes to me. "Catching the killer was retribution for him, I think. Maybe for all of us."

I let that comment go. What was there to say? I suspected he was right—a chance at closure, at moving on . . . at saying good-bye.

"Marik told me how clever you were seeing through our charade," Dimitri said after a bit. "But how'd you come to the conclusion it was Molly we were after?"

Rethinking my need for alcohol, I stuck out my glass and watched the magician fill it before I began. "For starters, I could tie everyone to Eden or to one another in some way."

"Except Molly and Mortimer," Dimitri explained for me.

"Yes, except for them." As I took a sip of champagne, the others joined us, all of them looking very pleased with themselves. Since no one had been hurt and justice had been done, I started to share their good spirit. Of course, the bubbly wasn't hurting. "Then Bart Griffin's message got me thinking. If you guys were trying to actually deliver a message, then the recipient had to know a lot about Houdini."

"But that didn't necessarily leave out Mortimer," Zoom-Zoom added.

"No, even though he claimed he didn't know what the code words meant, he could have been lying," I agreed. "But Molly showed her hand twice. First, I started to suspect her when she broke into my apartment the second time. Why she went to all the trouble to scale the building and leave again by the same route when, with her talents, she could have used the fire escape, a much easier route."

"Why did she do that, do you think?" Marik asked as he joined us.

"Dimitri was watching the front of the building. The fire escape is plainly visible from there.

On the other hand, my balcony is on the side of the building, somewhat out of sight."

"And what was her second mistake?" Danilov shouldered in next to Marik.

I still wasn't sure I trusted the man, and what he did in Eden was probably criminal, but the others apparently held him in high esteem, so I answered. "My phone."

I turned and locked eyes with Zoom-Zoom, who lurked behind the others. He took a step back.

"Your phone?" Danilov said.

I nodded. "Tell me, who knew where Carl was? All of you?" I held my gaze with Dr. Zewicki.

"Only Dimitri, Danilov, and myself," Marik said. "We thought the fewer who knew, the safer."

"Well, somebody had to tell Molly that not only did I know where Carl was, but that Teddie did also."

"Who would do that?" Marik asked.

"Her accomplice."

"What?" Marik, Danilov, Jenkins, and Griffin said in unison—the latter two coming in late to the discussion.

"Isn't that right, Dr. Zewicki?" I advanced on him.

He cowered back, but Marik grabbed his arm.

"You were sniffing around the van pool when Teddie and I brought back the van. Later, when you heard from the rest of the gang that I had been to see Carl, you put two and two together. You knew I wouldn't tell where I had gone, but you thought if you could get your hands on my phone, then you could dupe Teddie into telling you."

"You're nuts!" the astronaut said as I advanced on him.

"You were the last person seen with Jenkins before he found himself wandering lost in the desert. You also had a tight relationship with Molly, one I witnessed myself."

"But, I tried to stop Danilov from leading Molly to Carl! I ended up bound and gagged in the laundry for my efforts," Zoom-Zoom implored, his voice cracking.

"No, Danilov discovered your duplicity, immobilized you, and rushed to warn Carl," I said, as I searched the group that had gathered around for the face of the mentalist. "Isn't that right, Mr. Danilov?"

"I can't prove anything," Danilov responded, as he pushed to the front of the throng. "I acted on a hunch, that's all."

"You both are nuts!" The astronaut looked imploringly around the group. "Surely you don't believe her, do you?"

Stony silence greeted him.

"You can't believe her!" Zewicki's voice rose. He glared at me. "You can't prove any of this."

"Not a damned thing," I admitted. "Maybe Miss Rain will roll on you, maybe she won't, but I do know one thing: With this group, paybacks are hell."

I found Carl in a corner, out of sight, and apparently out of mind. Seated on the floor, hugging his knees to his chest, he glanced up at me as I lowered myself to sit beside him. "She's gone," he said simply, as if I would understand.

"I know." Putting my arm around him, I pulled him tight. "Are you going to be okay?"

He nodded once, his mouth set in a determined line. "I could hear her, you know . . . my sister. She talked to me, even after . . ." He swallowed hard. His eyes held tears, but no madness. "She kept me company, just like when we were kids. It was like she'd never left, never died."

Figuring Carl only needed someone to listen, I stayed quiet.

"But now, I don't hear her anymore. I know she's gone. She thanked me, said good-bye, and told me she'd be waiting, but not to waste the life I had left." He sat up straight and wiped his eyes. "I'm not sure how to do that by myself."

"But you're not by yourself. None of us are. And, truth be told, none of us know how to muddle through by ourselves." I made a sweeping gesture, taking in the whole of the backstage, encompassing Marik, Danilov, Bart Griffin, and Jenkins, who stood just out of earshot watching us. "That's the magic of friends: We're all here for each other."

THE night was late, I was tired, and I needed a hug, *une étreinte*, if you will. And I knew just the place to get one.

The Bondage Ball had grown in intensity, the overflow filling every nook and cranny of the hotel's public places. Staggered by the crowd's intensity, I paused at the entrance to the casino unable to muster the courage to dive in. A band played on a stage in the far corner. By the time the music reached me, the decibel level had fallen just below terminal levels. For the revelers dancing near the stage, the amount of alcohol necessary to withstand the pain boggled the mind.

A woman in full S and M regalia (such as it is) and carrying a whip in one hand and holding a leash in the other, sashayed by. The leash was attached to the metal spiked collar around her escort's neck. Clad only in a black leather thong and the collar, he looked happy. I couldn't get my mind around that, not that I really wanted to. Sometimes life is too real. This was one of those times.

Flash found me there, mouth agape, weighing my options. "Girlfriend, the party looks awesome. What's keeping you on the sidelines?"

"Good sense and self-preservation," I said, as I gave my friend the once-over. "Besides, I left my whips and chains at home, silly me."

"What *were* you thinking?" Dressed as Little Bo Peep in a dirndl with cinched waist, a gathered neckline that perfectly framed her ample chest, and just enough length to put her legs and nothing else on display—if she didn't bend over—Flash looked ready to join the fray. With her hair in two loose braids, her pink stilettos on her feet, her lips painted a come-hither red, she would fire many a male fantasy tonight, of that I was certain. Amazingly, her bruises had faded until I had to look for them, finding only the barest shadow under her makeup.

"Did you get your story?" I hooked my arm through hers, I don't know why. I guess I just felt like it.

"Written and filed, thanks to you." She patted my hand on her arm. "Another headline in the *R-J*. I owe you."

"I'd say we're square—we both took lumps for the team this time around. Are you going to join the festivities?"

She snagged a flute of champagne from a passing waiter. "I never thought I'd say this, but I'm just not in the mood."

"Me neither," I sighed, shouldering an unexpected weight of sadness—melancholy was so not my thing. Maybe Teddie had hit me harder than I thought.

She cast troubled eyes up at me. "Do you think we're getting old?"

"Us?" I rolled my eyes. "Never."

"Wise, then?"

"Wisdom would be good," I said. "If the Fates are going to give us wrinkles, there sure as heck had better be a quid pro quo."

"Amen to that."

"I'm thinking a hamburger might be just what the doctor ordered." I shot Flash a grin.

She waggled her eyebrows at me. "Count me in."

JEAN-CHARLES held the door for his last patrons as my little party arrived. On the way, Flash and I had corralled Miss P and The Beautiful Jeremy Whitlock, who, with his lady love at his side, seemed to be recovering nicely.

"Is the kitchen still open?" I asked.

"For you, always." Jean-Charles grabbed my hand and pulled me to him. He wrapped an arm around my waist, holding my body to his. He was really good at that. When he lowered his lips to mine, his kiss held all the fire, all the passion, all the promise I hoped for. The ball of warmth exploding in my core was an added benefit. I wondered just how long I'd be able to resist. Just how long a cool head would prevail. Just how long I'd wait before I screwed up my life once again. Right now, the smart money was on "not very long at all." Of course, right now my defenses *were* down. . . .

My friends had eased around us into the restaurant by the time we came up for air.

"You French," I teased, as I put an unsteady hand in my chef's chest, pushing him to a safer distance. Breathing was impossible when he was this close. "You always want dessert first."

"But, of course!" His face clouded as he took his first good look at me. "What has happened to you? You are all right, *non*?"

"But, of course!" I teased, forcing a jaunty smile. "I'll explain later. Right now you have guests."

With my hand clutched firmly in his, he pulled me inside the restaurant, closing and locking the door behind us. We joined the others who were now seated around the table in the kitchen.

Jean-Charles whispered to me, "Will you get some glasses and a couple of bottles of wine from the bar?"

As I moved to do as he asked, he clapped his hands for attention. "Welcome, my friends. The kitchen is open. What is your pleasure?"

Boy, he'd better not ask *me* that question!

A few minutes spent rummaging behind the bar while excited voices and easy laughter wafted from the kitchen and I'd managed to find two bottles of nice Bordeaux, enough appropriate glasses, and my smile. As I walked across the restaurant, arms laden, I caught sight of Dane, his nose pressed against the window, his arm raised to rap on the glass.

Seeing me, he stepped back, waiting.

After depositing my armful on the nearest table, I unlocked the door for him and held it wide. "Come on in. The party's in the kitchen."

"When Romeo finishes, I think he and Brandy might join us as well," Dane said as he stepped inside, then grabbed a bottle and some glasses off the table.

"I doubt he'll be too long," I said, picking up what was left to carry. "Molly Rain fired a loaded weapon, injuring a police officer. Any way you look at it, that's a felony and a hefty one at that."

"And she'll still do time on the other murder?" Dane asked.

"Doubtful," I said, not liking it one bit. "They didn't have any proof, only supposition. So they lured her into committing another felony, one she'd do time for. I guess they'll have to be satisfied with that. I guess we all will."

"Do you really think the astronaut helped her?"

"I don't know," I said as I took a deep breath, then let it out slowly. I didn't like thinking about the seedier sides of human nature.

"Why would he?" Dane pushed.

"She had the talent, he had the platform?" I offered. "I don't know. Who knows why people do what they do?" I turned to join friends, to partake of the comfort they offered.

"What about the others?" Dane's hand on my arm stopped me.

"They got what they wanted and I can't think of any law they broke." I stopped just outside of earshot of the others in the kitchen. "They didn't think she'd shoot Romeo, but they put too many innocents in the crossfire. It was a dangerous game they played. And, although I understand it, that doesn't make it any easier to swallow. All that being said, they got what they wanted and remained in the clear. Sort of divine justice."

Dane's smile lit the emerald in his eyes. "You and me are reading from the same hymnal."

EVERYONE greeted our newcomer, Miss P patting the chair next to her—smart woman. There were worse ways to spend a few hours than bracketed by two of the most tempting of the male species. Of course, in Vegas, that often was just the start to an interesting evening . . . or so I've been told.

I busied myself with glasses and wine. After serving those seated at the table, I grabbed a glass for myself and one for Jean-Charles, who was monitoring food preparation in front of the stove. "Are you sure you don't mind doing this? You've already had a long day," I asked him as I watched his practiced movements, his studied nonchalance, his attention to detail.

"Apparently not as long as yours."

"Can we not talk about that now? I'll tell you if you wish, but most questions you have will be answered in the morning paper."

He raised his eyebrows, but instead of asking more questions, he raised his glass. "To the future."

I clinked my glass with his.

Behind me, Jeremy cleared his throat. "I have a toast also."

We gave him our attention.

"To my beautiful lady on the day after her fiftieth birthday. No matter the years, you will always be the light of my life."

That elicited *awww*s from the women as we toasted the two of them. She had found the courage to face life, to face the truth no matter the cost.

When I looked at her, her eyes caught mine and I could tell she knew what I was thinking. We raised our glasses to each other.

"Now, it's my turn," I said. "To the same beautiful lady, who happens to be the Babylon's new Head of Customer Relations."

Excited voices chattered away as I turned back to my chef and the meal he was preparing, which now smelled divine. "May I help?"

"Are you good with a spatula?"

"Tossing burgers ought to be well within my limitations." I took the utensil from him and, smart enough to know I was to do as I was told, I awaited further orders.

"What will you do now? Aren't *you* the Head of Customer Relations?" He pointed to a patty. "That one. Flip it now."

Under the pressure of his scrutiny, I complied . . . perfectly. I just love it when that happens. "You're looking at the new Vice President of Customer Relations. A nominal change, I can assure you. It means only that I will keep doing what I've been doing, but will add the responsibilites of Cielo to my laundry list of to-dos."

"So you will be close to me?"

"You'll get tired of seeing my face," I said only half in jest. We would fight, of that I was certain. But would we ever . . . reconcile? Time would tell.

A smile on his face, he turned back to the stove. "That one." He pointed to another burger.

Getting the hang of it, I flipped more confidently this time. Jean-Charles rewarded me with a brush of his lips across mine.

"Remind me why I never much cared for food preparation?" I whispered.

My phone rang, startling me. Who would call me at this hour? Grabbing it from my pocket with one hand, I looked at the number.

Teddie.

My heart skipped a beat. Slowly, I terminated the call.

My smile must've faded as Jean-Charles asked, "Who is that?"

"Nobody."

THE BEAT GOES ON. . . .